Y0-BRQ-768

DISCARD

WEST GEORGIA REGIONAL LIBRARY SYSTEM

# THE WORKS

OF

# JULES VERNE,

TRANSLATED BY

EDWARD ROTH.

---

## OFF ON A COMET!

APPROACHING JUPITER.

# OFF ON A COMET!

A

## JOURNEY THROUGH PLANETARY SPACE

*(A SEQUEL TO "TO THE SUN?")*

FROM THE FRENCH OF

## JULES VERNE

BY

### EDWARD ROTH

𝕎𝕚𝕥𝕙 𝕋𝕙𝕚𝕣𝕥𝕪-𝕤𝕚𝕩 𝕱𝕦𝕝𝕝-𝕡𝕒𝕘𝕖 𝕆𝕣𝕚𝕘𝕚𝕟𝕒𝕝 𝕴𝕝𝕝𝕦𝕤𝕥𝕣𝕒𝕥𝕚𝕠𝕟𝕤.

ÆONIAN PRESS

MATTITUCK

Republished 1976

*Library of Congress Cataloging in Publication Data*

Verne, Jules, 1828-1905.
  Off on a comet!

  Translation of pt. 2 of Hector Servadac.
  Reprint of the 1878 ed. published by Claxton,
Remsen & Haffelfinger, Philadelphia.
  I.  Title.
PZ3.V594Of15     [PQ2469]   843'.8   76-25454
ISBN 0-88411-902-5

AEONIAN PRESS, INC.
Box 1200
Mattituck, New York 11952

*Manufactured in the United States of America*

# CONTENTS.

208484

WEST GEORGIA REGIONAL LIBRARY SYSTEM

# LIST OF ILLUSTRATIONS.

## LIST OF ILLUSTRATIONS.

# THE WORKS

OF

# JULES VERNE,

TRANSLATED BY

EDWARD ROTH.

---

# OFF ON A COMET!

# OFF ON A COMET!

## CHAPTER I.

### THE THIRTY—SIXTH GALLIAN.

"GALLIA'S my comet — *mine!*"

What was the meaning of these strange words? In vain had the Captain and Procopius asked themselves this question every spare moment of the homeward trip. In vain had the Count endeavored to sound it on their return. Fully as perplexed as the others, he had at last to give it up as a problem requiring much further development before its solution was possible.

For surely, thought he, these words could not mean that the enormous block on which they were all at present flying through space was a chip of the Earth struck off by a comet! The idea was too absurd for serious consideration. Struck off by a comet — what comet? Before the 31st of December in the previous year no comet likely to perform such an astonishing

feat had ever been seen or heard of. And what did
the gasping astronomer mean by *Gallia?* A comet
of that name, or the detached block now reeling wildly
through the solar world? Did he mean anything at
all by such an incomprehensible expression? Might
not this as well as all his previous revelations be
nothing more than the mere vapid outpourings of a
scientific monomaniac's uncontrollable imagination?

The astronomer, however, did not certainly look
like a monomaniac. He was without any doubt the
author of three remarkable documents whose careful
calculations had been so strongly confirmed by observations and so fully borne out by actual facts. It
was he alone who had flung leather cases and tin
boxes into the sea; and it was certainly he who had
lately despatched the messenger bird to the only in-
habited spot on the asteroid. Measuring Gallia's
progressive distance from the sun, and calculating her
tangential velocity were intellectual feats that could
hardly be expected from a mere monomaniac. Did
not their correctness prove beyond all doubt that he
was in possession of clear and precise knowledge regarding the exact nature of her elements?

Whatever, therefore, he might mean by his strange
words, he certainly knew enough about Gallia to make
our friends desirous of knowing more. He had un-

questionably calculated the nature of her orbit, and
in all probability could readily tell whether it was a
hyperbola, a parabola, or an ellipse. In other words,
it was most likely that he could easily answer the all-
important questions: Was Gallia's return to Earth possible? If so, when might such a return be expected?

The reader, however, must by no means suppose that
the Captain, the Count, and Procopius were so completely absorbed in asking themselves these questions
as to be forgetful of their first duties towards their
unconscious guest. Quite the contrary. Their very
first care was to do everything in their power to restore him with the least possible delay from a trance
which looked so like death as to be exceedingly alarming. The best prescriptions in Procopius's pharma-
copœia and the best drugs in the *Dobryna's* pharmacy
were put into instant and most careful requisition.
But for a long time the most devoted attention and
the most unremitting care remained without satisfactory result. The body lay still as a corpse and almost
as cold. It was kneaded, and rubbed, and manipu-
lated, and pulled, and turned over, and pounded by
the Captain and Procopius until they were almost
breathless; but all in vain. The Count administered
cordials and other stimulants of the most wonderfully
revivifying effects; but still in vain. The three friends

desisted at last, and looked at each other in despair and uncertain what to turn to next.

"Keep on, gentlemen!" whispered Ben. "He's not dead yet! I know the Savants! They're a tough lot! A cat is no harder to kill than an astronomer. Or if you are tired, let me and Negrete take a turn at him."

The Captain and Procopius yielding their places, the relays went to work with such a will and vigorous determination that the Count had to interfere occasionally, and remind Ben Zouf that rubbing a man's exhausted body to restore suspended animation did not necessarily mean flaying him alive.

"No danger of that, Count Timascheff!" exclaimed Ben, quickly. "It's our hands that will be the first to suffer. Negrete's are catching fire already! The astronomer's bones are iron, his muscles steel, his skin parchment and as rough as an old file! But — Good! I feel his heart beating! Rub, Negrete! Rub him well! There's lots of mischief yet in the little man! Rub, Negrete! Bring a pot of water here, somebody, to keep our hands cool!"

Then he would begin again furiously rubbing the dry bones backwards and forwards, as if brightening up a rusty sword for inspection parade, keeping time with the well-known soldier's catch:

" To polish the blade of my sabre true,
O tripoli give to me ! "

Making some allowance for Ben's love of exaggeration, he had really given a pretty good description of the astronomer's body. Stripped of furs and all its other envelopes, it could not be more than five feet three inches long ; the frame was as thin as a skeleton — but not altogether from starvation — those hard muscles had never been covered with much adipose tissue. But the skin was decidedly healthy looking, and at last a faint tinge began to show a gradual renewal of the circulation. Cries of satisfaction were reëchoed by the surrounding crowd ; but a new stimulus had now intensified the Captain's curiosity. With the features of the unconscious astronomer, to his utter amazement, he felt himself to be perfectly familiar ! But where had he seen those well-remembered lantern jaws that had never borne a greater crop than eight or ten hairs at the utmost ? Where had he often gazed at that polished skull, so smooth, so round, so bare, as to always remind him of the big end of an ostrich's egg ? Where had he admired that nose so long, so bony, and so peculiarly bridled up at the nostrils ? Above all, where had he seen that terrible pair of spectacles which he now held in his hand, of the well-known kind that we always conceive to be inseparable from the wearer's existence, forming

2 * B

as it does an indivisible part and parcel of his individuality?

But while the Captain is puzzling his brain in the difficult endeavor to attribute to their real owner the familiar features of the unconscious form lying before him, we take advantage of the opportunity to inform the gracious reader that the astronomer was no more and no less than his old teacher, Palmyrin Rosette, the famous Professor of Mathematics, in the Lyceum Charlemagne.

After a few years in the Lyceum, young Servadac had gone to Saint Cyr, and from that time to the present, a period of sixteen or seventeen years, teacher and pupil had never laid eyes on each other.

At school, as we already know, Servadac had never distinguished himself for profound application to study. On the contrary, for a while at least, he was generally acknowledged to be the laziest of students and the most reckless of the scapegraces. What scores of tricks, for instance, did himself and the rest of the band of young urchins equally hair-brained and fond of fun, play on this selfsame luckless Professor, Palmyrin Rosette!

Who slipped a few grains of salt into the distilled water of the laboratory, thereby causing reactions of the strangest and most unexpected nature? Who half emp-

THE PROFESSOR.

tied the bulb of the barometer and then half frightened the Professor out of his wits by pointing to the depressed state of the glass? Who cunningly heated the thermometer with a match, suddenly driving the mercury up to 150° on a winter's day? Who put flies between the lenses of the telescopes and thereby led the astronomers to believe they had discovered immense monsters crawling over the moon? Who often succeeded in so completely destroying the isolation of the electric machine that, after a quarter of an hour's brisk action, the exhausted Professor gave up in disgust all hope of getting a single spark out of the conductor? Who bored an invisible hole in the cylinder of the air-pump, through which the air always entered as fast as the poor Professor pumped it out? Who, while the Professor was intently watching the success of a reaction, gave the signal for all the pupils either to slip noiselessly under their desks or steal quietly out of the hall, so that, when he was once more ready to resume, he suddenly found himself without an audience? Who else but young Servadac, or one of the "noble band" acting under his able instructions!

Of these and other fooleries of the kind, in the case of most Professors, the young scamps would soon get sick and tired. But in the case of Professor Rosette it was far otherwise. His comical explosions of anger,

ever varied, ever new, afforded inexhaustible amusement. His fuming, frothing, and eloquent denunciations of the culprits, always produced the richest fun.
He could never keep his temper, even by way of a
change. He could never learn from experience. Every
day some new trick on the part of the boys. Every day
some new and original outburst on the part of the
teacher. His class had a delightful time. Every one
liked to be a member of it, though at examinations it
was invariably ranked the lowest and least satisfactory
in the Lyceum. In fact, with most of the boys it was
simply a year lost, as they had to go over the same
course again under a private teacher.

After a few years' unsuccessful experience as an in-
structor of youth, the Professor withdrew from the
Lyceum altogether, and devoted himself wholly to
astronomical studies. He wished to enter the Observatory, but his well-known peppery, cross-grained
disposition closed its doors against him. Possessed,
however, of a certain income that placed him above
want, he turned astronomer on his own account, and
soon commenced attacking right and left, with some
ability too, every modern system and theory of astronomy without exception. He did not even confine himself to criticism. He was a most indefatigable
workman. To his observations the scientific world is

indebted for the discovery of *Palmyra, Rosetta,* and *Lutetia* among the Minor Planets, and also for the calculation of the elements of the little comet marked 325 on the Catalogue. Wholly engrossed in these absorbing studies, he had withdrawn himself so completely from society and the world at large that it is by no means surprising that he and the Captain had never met again, nor that Servadac had failed to recognize in the frail piece of humanity lying before him his old teacher Palmyrin Rosette.

In the meantime Ben had been rubbing away as vigorously as ever and was ably assisted by Negrete. The Count and Procopius would now and then whisper in each other's ears their impressions of the whole scene.

"That little man," said the Count, "is a bunch of nerves; a regular Ruhmkorff coil."

"Yes," answered Procopius; "he is a perfect human gymnotus. If we were in the dark we should see Ben Zouf's fingers blazing with electricity."

The friction, the kneading, the pounding and the pressing continued to give the most encouraging results.

"Now turn him over a little on his side," said the Captain, "till he is nearly on his face; then turn him on his back again. Keep on doing this for fifteen or twenty turns."

The direction was implicitly obeyed, and its good effects were soon seen. The body by its own weight gently compressed the chest; and the chest, expanding by its elasticity, soon filled itself with air. The closed lips began to quiver. A faint sigh could be heard. Then a second — a third — a fourth. The eyes half opened, closed, then opened wide and looked around, but evidently quite unconscious of the place or the circumstances. The lips separated; the mouth pronounced a few words, but in so low a tone that the listeners could not catch their import. The right hand began to twitch a little. It lifted itself, and touched the forehead hastily as if in search of something missing. Instantly the features contracted, the eyebrows frowned, the face flushed as if a fit of anger had brought back life, and a shrill, impatient voice exclaimed:

"My spectacles! Where are my spectacles?"

The Captain instantly handed them to Ben Zouf, who had taken them off to facilitate the shampooing operations. They were carefully readjusted on that eagle beak, their natural resting-place. Then a new sigh, indicative of much satisfaction, was heard; and the lips opened to give vent to the expression "Brum! brum!" half cough, half exclamation.

Nobody watched all these proceedings with greater

"FIVE HUNDRED LINES TO-MORROW!"

interest or delight than the Captain. He stooped eagerly over the astronomer's flushing face, the better to catch every change of that familiar but long-forgotten countenance. He was carefully scanning each feature in its turn when, all at once, the eyes opened and shot an angry glance at him so suddenly that he involuntarily started back. At the same time a snappish voice in the well-known accents of old was heard exclaiming:

"Pupil Servadac, five hundred lines for to-morrow!"

It was an instantaneous revelation to the Captain.

"Professor Rosette!" he exclaimed in profound surprise. "My old teacher here before me in flesh and blood!"

"Very little of the flesh and less of the blood," murmured Ben, gently renewing his operations, for the eyes again closed, the hand dropped, and for awhile very little breathing could be heard.

"Don't be alarmed, Governor," said Ben, confidently. "He's only asleep again. No fear of a little man of his build suddenly dropping off. They are all nerve. There is no dying in them. I've seen scores of them, Governor; drier than even our subject here and much further gone too; but they all came back!"

"How much further gone, Ben Zouf?" asked Procopius, innocently, not aware of Ben's love of fun. " From what did they come back ? "

" All the way from Egypt, Lieutenant," answered Ben, with a wink at Negrete. " Wrapped up in nice clothes, too, and lying comfortably in a beautiful painted box."

" You mean mummies, don't you ? " asked Procopius, somewhat haughtily.

" Exactly, Lieutenant. Mummies, the very image of our little astronomer ! "

" Ben Zouf ! " said the Captain, thinking it high time to interfere ; " you have done good work with your hands ; don't spoil it all with your foolish tongue ! Help me to carry my old teacher to a warm corner where he can sleep all night without danger of further disturbance. He is probably out of all danger now."

Instead of waiting patiently for their guest's complete recovery, the Captain, the Count and Procopius spent most of that night in arguing and conjecturing, in erecting hypotheses more or less plausible, and then demolishing them at a blow.

What *did* he mean exactly by Gallia ? they asked each other again and again. Did the calculations regarding distance and velocity refer to the comet Gallia or to the new spheroid that bore them through space ? Was the name *Gallians*, lately usurped by the Captain and his friends, a mere misnomer? In other words, were they, according to Procopius's theory, living on the surface of a block blown off the Earth into space by some mighty explosion, or, as the astronomer's words seemed to hint, were they flying through space on a comet's back on which some incomprehensible and mysterious event had suddenly placed them?

"My friends," said the Captain at last by way of closing the discussion, "let us conclude again for the hundredth time that all our present disputations are simply useless. But my old Professor is here now, and, if we can only manage to keep him in good-humor, he will tell us everything to-morrow. But, by the by, I must tell you a little of what I remember him to be in my boyish days."

He entered into pretty full details of his picture and probably he exaggerated a little, but the outline was correct, and his summing up was just. The Professor was a difficult character to get along with. Whatever were your relations with him, you were always on the strain. He was an original in every sense of the word, absolutely incorrigible, obstinate as a mule, with a hot temper that he never thought of controlling. But with this his faults ceased. He was a magnificent mathematician. Arago had considered him one of the best in Europe. With all his temper and selfishness, he

3

was a highly honorable man and as simple as a child. "Humor him a little," said the Captain, in conclusion, "overlook his puerile eccentricities, and you can do what you please with him. Bend a little to the storm; it will soon pass away, and nobody will be the worse for it."

"My dear Captain," said the Count smiling, "nothing will give us greater pleasure than to try to keep on good terms with your old Professor. Why should we not? In all probability he is the only human being in existence capable of answering to our satisfaction certain questions regarding which we are naturally exceedingly curious."

"You are right there, Count," said the Captain. "If he cannot solve our problems, nobody else can."

"Except the author of those calculations and notices that we have received on several occasions," observed the Count quietly.

"But who can be the author of these notices if it is not my old Professor?" asked the Captain.

"Some other astronomer perhaps, cast away on some other islet of our spheroid," answered the Count.

"That hypothesis of yours can't hold, Father," said Procopius with a smile. "It was in these notices that we first saw the name Gallia, and Gallia was the first word uttered by the Captain's old Professor."

But the Count, though not pretending to maintain a contrary opinion, was not yet quite convinced.

" Let us take a look over his notes and calculations," said he.

A look was enough. The same hand that penned the documents, wrote the calculations, the notes, and the figures. Even the peculiar handwriting on the door was easily recognizable. The papers were mostly detached sheets scrawled all over with geometrical diagrams. Of these, three were repeated the oftenest : *hyperbolas,* open curves whose two arms are infinite and continually getting further apart ; *parabolas,* also open curves whose arms, though not diverging so rapidly as in the case of the hyperbola, still keep widening out forever ; and finally *ellipses,* whose curves are always closed, no matter how great the prolongation of the axis.

These three curves, as Procopius observed, are precisely the three curves described by comets in their orbits, which must therefore be either hyperbolic, parabolic, or elliptical. If either hyperbolic or parabolic, the comets describing them are once seen from the Earth and are never seen again. They go wandering off forever into the regions of infinite space. But a comet describing an elliptical orbit reappears periodically and often with a regularity that is exceedingly wonderful.

The papers showed that the astronomer had been studying cometary elements, but from the nature of the curves themselves nothing could be predicated. All astronomers undertaking such calculations start with the supposition that the comet under examination describes a parabola.

"In fact," concluded Procopius, "the only result afforded by an inspection of these papers is this: our astronomer, while at Formentera, has been studying very thoroughly the elements of a new comet whose name has not yet appeared in the Catalogue."

"Did he commence his calculations before or after the first of January?" asked the Captain.

"A very important question," said Procopius; "but I am sorry to say I cannot answer it."

"Wait a little, Captain," said the Count, "and you can propound your question to the astronomer himself."

"I can't wait!" exclaimed the Captain, walking up and down impatiently. "I would give a month of my life for every hour that he has still to sleep."

"You would probably make a bad bargain," said Procopius.

"What!" asked the Captain, "to know what doom fate has in store for our asteroid —"

"I don't wish to disenchant any of your illusions, Captain," continued Procopius; "but whatever your old Professor may know about Gallia, it does not follow that he knows anything at all about the fragment of Earth that is our present abode. What connection exists between the sudden appearance of a comet and the sudden projection of a portion of the Earth into space?"

"Connection!" cried the Captain. "Certainly there is a connection. There is no doubt in my mind on the subject any longer. The whole thing is as clear as day!"

"What whole thing is as clear as day, Captain?" asked the Count quietly, and looking rather puzzled.

"That the Earth was struck by a comet in the first place," cried the Captain; "and, in the second, that the shock struck off the very portion of the Earth on which we are now flying through space!"

The Count and Procopius looked at each other for awhile without uttering a word.

The Captain's conclusion had forced itself on him with irresistible power. An encounter between the Earth and a comet, though extremely improbable, was by no means physically impossible. Viewed in fact by the light of subsequent events, something like a shock of this kind must really have taken place. It was an exceedingly plausible explanation of most puzzling phenomena; it was to all appearance the real key of the riddle, furnishing a potential cause for most extraordinary events.

3 *

"You may be right, Captain," said Procopius after some reflection. "That such a shock could have taken place does not exceed the limits of possibility, and it certainly could have struck off quite a considerable block from the surface of the Earth. If this be the case, the enormous disc that we caught a glimpse of on the night of the catastrophe must have been the comet itself, deviating a little in all probability from its normal orbit, but moving with too much velocity to be detained by the Earth's attraction."

"Ye — es," said the Captain slowly, "that may account for the presence of the enormous disc I saw that night on the Sheliff."

"Here then is our newest and latest hypothesis," said the Count, "and I certainly acknowledge that it looks very plausible. Indeed it is by long odds the most plausible of all so far. It harmonizes our own observations completely with those of the astronomer. It is to the comet that suddenly whipped us off the Earth that he gave the name of Gallia."

"Very probably, Count."

"Still, Captain, I must say one thing about your theory is decidedly puzzling. In fact, the more I think over it the less I can explain it."

"What is that, Count?"

"I can't see why our astronomer should give himself

more concern regarding the fate of an insignificant comet than that of the earth-block on which he himself was flying with inconceivable speed into the boundless realms of space!"

"Oh· Count," replied the Captain quickly, "you don't know what odd fishes these scientific men are! And the oddest, the queerest, the most fantastic of them all is my old Professor himself!"

"Besides," observed Procopius, "the calculation of the Gallian elements may have been made before the shock. The Professor probably had an opportunity of seeing it as it approached."

"Well observed, Procopius," said the Count. "Now let us formulate the Captain's hypothesis, as well as I understand it. First: A comet came in contact with the Earth on the night of December 31 to January 1; Second: The shock struck off an enormous fragment of the terrestrial globe, which fragment ever since that period has been gravitating in the regions of planetary space. Am I right, Captain?"

"You are perfectly right, Count."

"We may now retire to rest, brother members of the Gallian Academy of Sciences," said Procopius smiling, "with the consoling assurance that if we have not yet reached the entire truth, we cannot be very far from it."

Thus ended the memorable day of April 19.

# CHAPTER II.

## THE MYSTERY REVEALED.

THE interest in the lately arrived stranger seemed to be confined pretty much to the Gallian leaders, the rest of the little colony taking the arrival and everything connected with it coolly enough. The Spaniards naturally indifferent, and the Russians, blindly confident in their master, gave themselves very little trouble in investigating causes and effects. Their philosophy was very simple. Was Gallia ever to return to Earth? If so, so much the better. If not, what was the use of grieving? Accordingly, the astronomer once comfortably deposited in his place of rest, the remainder of the day was devoted to its ordinary duties by these matter-of-fact philosophers, and during the night that followed not a wink of sleep was lost, not a moment's repose was disturbed by uneasy thoughts.

Of Ben Zouf, however, it must be said that he did not close his eyes once for five minutes during the night. Self-appointed nurse and apparently highly rel· ishing his task, he never left for an instant the bedside of the unconscious patient. He had bound himself to set the astronomer once more "on his pins," as he said, and he would consider his honor compromised by the least sign of neglect towards the sufferer. How he coddled him, and humored him, and petted him! How sternly he counted the drops of the strengthening cordial! How uncompromisingly he insisted on their being taken at the proper intervals! How carefully he counted the sighs and treasured up the words emitted now and then from these pale and quivering lips!

These words, it must be admitted, were neither many nor various. They were almost completely limited to the single expression *Gallia!* repeated in every tone of the scale from the lowest basso-profundo mutter of uneasiness to the shrillest scream of anger. Was the astronomer dreaming that somebody was trying to steal his comet? Or was he contesting its discovery? Or was he trying to invalidate every claim advanced towards priority of observation? These questions Ben answered in the affirmative.

"My little astronomer," he muttered to himself, "is one of those fighting characters who even in their sleep are not satisfied without a tussle."

But this was almost the only conclusion that Ben could arrive at. Listen as he might, he could never catch a syllable worth reporting to the Captain. Be-

C

sides, as the night advanced, the astronomer's sleep grew sounder and sounder, his pulse firmer and firmer, his breathing more and more regular. In fact, towards morning he was snoring away in a style that showed his lungs to have been nearly, if not fully, restored to their normal vast capacity as an inflatory apparatus.

In fact, the noise he made was so great just as the sun was rising that Ben Zouf hesitated awhile before going to the great door that closed the end of the principal gallery, at which he imagined he heard somebody knocking.

"Snore away, my brave little astronomer!" he exclaimed. "Such strains are not the most melodious in the world, but to me I must say that just now they are very delightful music. They show that you are becoming yourself once more, and therefore able to answer the questions the Governor is so much puz—*Sacré nom d'un Kabyle!* there's that knocking again! Who on earth can be there at such an hour!"

So saying, he hurried impatiently towards the great door that served not so much to keep out troublesome visitors as to afford some protection against external cold.

"Who's there?" he asked in no amiable tone, interrupting another violent pounding.

"A FRIEND."

"A friend," answered a mealy-mouthed voice.

" What friend ? "

" Isaac."

" You, Shylock! What the mischief do *you* want here ? "

" I want you to open the gate, my good Signor Ben Zhouf."

"What for? Sell us your goods? We don't want them! Be off ! "

" Oh Signor Ben Zhouf, I want to speak a few words to the Governor-General. Only one or two little words, my good gentleman Signor Ben Zhouf! "

" His Excellency is asleep ! "

" I can wait till his Excellency awakes ! "

" Well, wait there as long as you please,·and be hanged ! " answered Ben hastily returning towards his patient, when he met the Captain coming out of his room.

" What's all this noise, Ben Zouf?"

" Nothing worth mentioning, Governor."

" I thought I heard distant thunder! "

" It was only the astronomer snoring, Governor ! "

" But I certainly heard pounding ! "

" It 's only Dutch Isaac knocking at the gate."

" What does he want?"

" To speak a few words with you, Governor."

"Admit him at once, Ben Zouf! I must know what brings him here."

"No need of letting him in to know that, Governor. His own interest, to be sure!"

"Open the door, and hold your tongue!"

The instant the bolt was drawn, Isaac, poorly protected against the cold, in spite of an extra gabardine or two, rushed in hastily, and began saluting the Captain with the usual cringing bows and the usual titles of honor.

"What do you want, Isaac?" asked the Captain quickly as he directed his steps towards Central Hall, whither he was closely followed by his shuffling visitor.

"Oh! Signor Governor, has not your Excellency heard something lately?"

"You come here after news, do you?"

"I can't contradict your Excellency, Signor Governor. And I know your kindness will not refuse telling a poor man —"

"I tell you nothing, Isaac, because I know nothing myself!"

"But, Signor Governor, the strange gentleman that your Excellency brought here yesterday —"

"You are aware of his arrival then?"

"I am, Signor Governor. A few days ago I could see the ice-yacht start northwards on a very important expedition. Yesterday I saw it return safe and sound, which filled my soul with real delight, s' help me Father Abraham! But besides the Governor-General and the Russian Captain, there was another gentleman too landed here with a great deal of care and ceremony."

" Well?"

" Governor-General, please your Excellency, I should like to have a few minutes' conversation with that strange gentleman."

" Are you acquainted with him?"

" Oh, no, your Excellency. But I should like to ask him a few questions. He is probably come from —"

" From where?"

" From the northern shores of the Mediterranean, your Excellency. He must therefore be able to give me —"

" Give you what?"

" A little news from Europe, please your Excellency, Governor-General," said Isaac, as he watched the Captain with a cunning but keen and penetrating glance.

The Captain could hardly help admiring this magnificent development of astounding obstinacy. Three months and a half's residence on Gallia had apparently produced no effect whatever on this most pig-headed of disbelievers. To take his body from the Earth was an easy matter; but to take his thoughts off seemed an

4

utter impossibility. The most extraordinary phenomena were utterly lost on him as evidence. The shortening of the days and nights, the change in the direction of the sun's course, the diminution of gravity, the total disappearance of humanity in general — all this had not weighed as much as a feather against his stubborn misconception. He was still on the Earth! The water around him was the Mediterranean! A part of Africa may have been destroyed by an earthquake, but Europe, a few hundred miles to the north, was still to the good! Its inhabitants were still there, and, if he could only get there now, he would soon be once more buying and selling and turning an honest penny, as he had often done before! By making double profit in the harbors of Europe the *Hansa* could easily indemnify herself for her losses on the African shore! It was his firm belief in such a state of things that had brought him fishing for news to Nina Hive so early in the morning.

Any further attempt to undeceive him being evidently useless, the Captain's only reply to Isaac's questions was to shrug his shoulders, shake his head, and turn impatiently away.

The Jew had therefore no resource left but to turn to Ben, who, having found his patient all right, again presented himself upon the scene.

"Oh Signor Ben Zhouf," he exclaimed, directing a

keen eye towards Ben, "I'm not wrong then! A strange gentleman did arrive yesterday?"

"Yes, he arrived yesterday."

"Alive?"

"I hope so — at least very few corpses have such a healthy old pair of lungs!"

"From what part of Europe did the gentleman arrive, Signor Ben Zhouf?"

"From the Balearic Islands," answered Ben, curious to see what Isaac was aiming at.

"The Balearic Islands!" cried the Jew, his cunning eyes glistening with pleasure. "What a lovely spot for trade! Many a good bargain I struck there! The people there know my *Hansa* well!"

"They know her better than they like her, I'm willing to take my oath!"

"These islands can't be more than fifty or sixty miles from the Spanish coast. Very likely the worthy gentleman can tell us something about Europe!"

"Oh! he's the boy that can tell you something delightful about Europe, old skinflint!" said Ben, trying to lead him on. "Something to raise the cockles off your heart, Pharaoh, if you've got such an article!"

"He can, Signor Ben Zhouf? Sure?"

"As sure as you love money better than your salvation, you wicked old miser!"

"I don t love it so much, Signor Ben Zhouf—though I'm a very poor man, s' help me Father Abraham!— that I would not mind — no — I would not much mind giving two or three good silver reals for a few minutes' conversation with the worthy gentleman."

"Now you know you're not telling the truth, Shylock! Not much mind! You know in your heart you would very much mind! Every real would be like having a finger-nail pulled off!"

"Ah, Signor Ben Zhouf, you be one very funny gentleman! Well, I might mind very much — but s' help me .Father Abraham! I'd give them all the same. On one condition though — I should speak with him immediately."

"You can't speak with him immediately, Pygmalion! He's fast asleep now and must not be disturbed."

"Signor Ben Zhouf!" said Isaac eagerly, lowering his tone almost to a whisper, "if you would be so kind as to wake him up, I should not mind —"

"Isaac!" cried the Captain suddenly and in the sternest tones, "if you attempt to disturb the stranger before his own good time, I shall have you clapped in irons on the spot!"

"Oh! Signor Governor-General," cried Isaac, rather startled but still in a whining and persistent voice, "I shall await his and your Excellency's good pleasure on the subject, whatever it may be. But it is only natural that I should desire to know —"

"And know you shall!" replied the Captain. "I even want you to hear with your own ears the very first news from Europe that the stranger has to communicate."

"I must be around myself at the time, too!" said Ben to Isaac. "I don't want to miss the lovely phiz you'll put on when you hear — but, by the beard of Mahomet! there's the old boy awake at last and nobody to wait on him! Coming, sir! Here you are, sir!" and he ran towards the chamber with all speed.

"Joseph! Joseph!!" the astronomer's voice was heard calling in a high key and angry accents. "Where is the infernal scoundrel? He's never at hand when I want him! Joseph!!!"

At this unusual noise the Count and Procopius came hastily rushing out of their rooms, and all hurried in a body towards the astronomer's chamber, Isaac a little ahead.

They found him sitting up quite sturdily in bed, strong and stirring, though only half awake and still crying lustily for Joseph.

"Joseph! you infamous villain, bring me my door directly!"

"Certainly, sir; there's your door, sir!" cried Ben

4*

Zouf, hastily arranging the old door covered with diagrams within easy reach at the foot of the bed. "Anything else, sir?"

The astronomer, fixing his eyes keenly on Ben, asked with an angry frown:

"Are you Joseph?"

"I'm Joseph or any one else you please, at your very good service, sir," replied Ben with a ready bow and the cheerfulest of smiles.

"Well then, Joseph or any one else I please, bring me my coffee, and be alive about it!"

"Your coffee, sir? Yes, sir, immediately!" cried Ben, running back to the kitchen.

The Captain now approaching and offering assistance, the astronomer looked at him quietly.

"My dear Master," asked the Captain, "don't you remember your old pupil at the Charlemagne?"

"Yes, yes, Servadac," replied the astronomer. "I remember you well — too well, in fact. I hope you have got more sense than you had sixteen years ago."

"I think I am a little improved since those days, my dear Master," replied the Captain with a merry twinkle in his eye. "Do you remember the rhymes you wrote about me, and which unfortunately reached my father's ear?"

"Rhymes!" grumbled the astronomer. "I don't remember anything about such fooleries!"

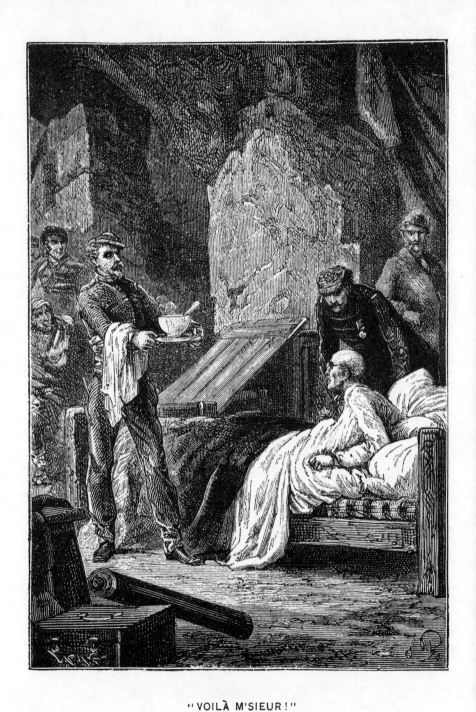

"VOILÀ M'SIEUR!"

" I remember them well, my dear Master," cried the Captain, " and shall never forget them. Here they are :

> With tongue that ever goes click-clack,
> Who shows of sense the greatest lack ?
> Who is the worst of all the pack
> Of lazy, idle, scheming black-
> Guards that keep me on the rack ?
> It is that scapegrace Servadac !
>
> Who best deserves to have his back
> Favored with many a swinging whack ?
> Who ——"

" Crazy as ever ! " interrupted the astronomer, impatiently. "Another confirmation of the old proverb :

> Silly in school,
> Always a fool !

But where's that coffee ? Without coffee no clear brain ! And I want my brain to be clearer than ever to-day ! "

"*Voilà, M'sieur!*" cried Ben, rushing in with an enormous cup of coffee steaming hot.

The coffee disposed of, the astronomer got up, and having washed and dressed with some help from the Captain, soon felt himself quite strong and comfortable. Then leaving the room, he entered Central Hall, looked around with a vacant glance, as if trying to collect his thoughts, and finally took a seat in the most comfortable arm-chair he could find.

Then in a voice which, in spite of a rather scowling and crusty look, was cheerful enough to recall the *All right's*, the *Va bene's* and the *Nil desperandum's* of the messages, he opened the proceedings.

"Well, Messieurs, what do you think of Gallia?"

But before even the impatient Captain could utter a syllable in reply, Isaac rushed forward and, throwing himself on his knees before the astronomer, cried out:

"Oh, my good gentleman, tell me the truth for the love of heaven! I'm a poor man, s' help me Father Abraham! but I should like to know the truth!"

At the sight of the strange, weird-looking figure kneeling before him, the astronomer contracted his brows with the frown of offended dignity and cried out in angry tones:

"What's that? Take that away!"

"That's no account whatever!" cried Ben, seizing Isaac by the collar; "but nevertheless that has to keep its distance."

Ben, however, found it much easier to collar Isaac than to remove him from the astronomer's presence. The old Jew struggled so forcibly and cried out so persistently that Ben hardly knew what to do.

" Only one little word, Signor Ben Zhouf," repeated Isaac, piteously. "Let me say one little word to the good strange gentleman ! "

"Let Isaac ask his question, Ben Zouf," said the Captain ; "perhaps the Professor won't object to answer it."

Ben retiring, Isaac was free.

"Oh! my good, gracious, kind gentleman ! " he exclaimed, clasping the Professor's feet in his earnestness, "I ask it of you in the name of the holy Fathers Abraham, Isaac and Jacob! Tell me something about Europe ! "

The Professor started up, stiff and straight as an arrow.

"About Europe ! " he exclaimed. "This man wants to know something about Europe ! ! "

"Yes, yes, I do ! " gasped Isaac, with extended arms and body bent forward.

"Why do you want to know something about Europe ? "

"Because I want to return there ! "

"He wants to return to Europe ! ! — What day of the month is it, Servadac ? "

"The twentieth of April," replied the Captain, promptly.

"Well then, sir, on this twentieth of April," replied

the Professor, with gleaming eye and triumphant voice, "Europe is precisely one hundred and twenty-three millions of miles behind us!"

"Oh Holy Abraham!" cried the Jew, falling on the floor as if struck with apoplexy. The sudden blow was more than his miserable form could bear, exhausted as he was with hunger, cold, and intense excitement.

"What!" continued the Professor, surveying his audience with the contemptuous glance that the Captain remembered so well. "Are you all here as great ignoramuses as this jackass?"

"Not quite, my dear Master," said the Captain, signalling to Ben what was to be done; "a few minutes, however, will be enough to tell you all we know."

As soon as Ben had picked up Isaac's helpless body, deposited it carefully on a sofa and administered a few restoratives with satisfactory effect, the Captain began a hasty but comprehensive narrative, summarizing every event that had taken place from the 31st of December to the present time. How Ben and he had found themselves left alone on the island; how the *Dobryna* had started on a voyage of exploration; how she had discovered no trace of the old Earth except a few points at Tunis, Gibraltar and Sardinia; how at three different times anonymous messages had fallen into their hands; and, finally, how the Isle of Gourbi had to be abandoned for Terre Chaude, their present volcanic habitation.

The Professor heard the whole story, though with decided symptoms of impatience. At the conclusion, he asked the assembly hastily:

"Messieurs, where do you think you are at the present moment?"

"On a new asteroid gravitating through interplanetary space," answered the Captain.

"And this new asteroid, in your opinion, is —"

"An enormous fragment torn from the Earth."

"Torn! Ah! Torn indeed! A torn fragment of the Earth! And by whom or by what torn?"

"By an encounter with a comet to which you have given the name of Gallia, my dear Master," replied the Captain.

"Not bad, Messieurs, upon my word, not at all bad!" said the Professor, straightening himself up. "But I can tell you it is something better than that!"

"Better than that!" exclaimed Procopius greatly surprised.

"Better than that!" echoed the Captain and the Count.

"Yes!" continued the Professor in ringing tones.

"True indeed it is that the Earth was struck by a comet, on the night of the 31st of December and 1st of January, at two hours, forty-seven minutes, and thirty-five and six-tenths seconds after midnight. But the comet only grazed her for a moment, and instantly departed, carrying off the few morsels of the Earth that you discovered on your exploring trip."

"What ! ! " cried the Captain, the Count, and Procopius in a breath.

"Yes!" continued the Professor in tones resounding with exuberant triumph; "and you are all now riding on *that very comet*, on GALLIA, on MY GALLIA ! "

# CHAPTER III.

## THE LAST WORD ON COMETS.

"YOUR Gallia!" cried Procopius, the coolest of the party and therefore the first to speak.

"Yes, my Gallia!" answered the Professor proudly. "You look astonished, sir, at the idea of a comet being mine! Pray do you know, sir, what a comet is?"

"I should think so, Professor," answered Procopius quietly, much amused at the idea of being treated like a school-boy.

"You should think so! I know you should think so! Everybody should think so," laughed the little man scornfully. "There is no end to self-deception! Come, sir. Let us hear your definition of a comet!"

"A comet," replied Procopius without hesitation, "is a heavenly body consisting of a central point called the *nucleus*, of a nebular envelope called the *coma*, and of a trail long and luminous called the *tail*."

"Mathematically correct!" cried the Professor with another mocking laugh. "Your definition of a comet, sir, is faultless in every respect — except that your

heavenly body may have neither *nucleus, coma,* or *tail,*
and yet be a comet after all!

"Your definition, sir," continued the terrible Professor, "might do very well for a lecturer on astronomy
in a school for young ladies or before an audience of
such numskulls as young Servadac here was likely to
become, but it will not stand the test of science!
Modern astronomy is somewhat more exacting in its
definitions. They are simpler, clearer and more precise. Listen to Arago's definition of a comet : ' Comets,'
he says, ' are heavenly bodies endowed with a peculiar
motion of their own. They describe curves so exceedingly elongated as to be sometimes invisible from
the Earth.' This is definition enough. With the first
condition fulfilled, a comet cannot be confounded with
a star; with the second, it cannot be mistaken for a
planet. So, being neither a planet, a star, nor yet a
meteor, our heavenly body must of necessity be a
comet."

Loud applause, started by the Captain, greeted this
learned burst, nobody clapping hands more warmly, or
with greater good-will, than the undiscomfited Procopius
himself. Here was an opportunity to fish for the information that his friends were all dying to hear, and the
Lieutenant was not the man to let such a chance slip
through his fingers.

A LECTURE ON COMETS.

"Professor," said he in tones of the deepest respect, "I thank you most sincerely for the valuable information you have just imparted. But will you not kindly let us have a little more? Neither my companions nor myself have studied as much regarding Comets as we should have done. But just now we are so situated as to make every item of knowledge on such a subject profoundly interesting. We feel that we are in the presence of the man of all men most capable of gratifying our natural curiosity. Would it be too much to ask you for a short summary of the present state of human knowledge with regard to Comets?"

"Once start the Professor talking," thought Procopius to himself, "and who knows where he may bring up? In all probability before he gets through he will tell us what kind of an orbit Gallia is following, when we are to return to Earth, or if we are to return at all!"

The Captain and the Count, instantly divining the idea, seconded it most warmly.

"Professor," said the Count, "we have books enough in the library, but, for what we want to know, books are dumb."

"You'll find me such a good listener, my dear Master," said the Captain, "as to make you almost forget that I was the worst pupil you ever had at the Charlemagne."

The Professor was visibly pleased. Did he suspect a
trick? Did he determine that those who sought to fool
him should be caught in their own trap? His eyes certainly flashed bright beneath his spectacles; he gave a
dry significant cough or two ; and for an instant a roguish
smile played around his lips.

"Messieurs," said he, stirring a glass of sugared water
that Ben had just laid beside him, "if you are really and
truly willing to listen for some time to what must prove
exceedingly dry to ordinary and uncultured ears, I shall
be most happy to oblige you to the best of my power.
I am always willing to talk about Comets. They are
and for a long time have been my especial study. Of all
the heavenly bodies they are my especial favorites. When
a boy I often prayed to be carried off on one, but without ever dreaming that Heaven would one day grant my
prayer. I think you are most fortunate in having the
opportunity of hearing me saying my say on the subject,
for what I don't know about Comets — and I say it in
all humility — is really not worth knowing."

Deep and respectful applause greeted this introduction,
and every one took a seat, even the Spaniards and the
Russian sailors, and tried to make himself as comfortable
as he could while listening to the Professor's lecture on
Comets.

The Professor took a few sips of the sugared water,

adjusted his spectacles, and launched out boldly into the heart of his subject.

"Messieurs," said he, "without further preface I will take it for granted that you require the latest and most reliable information on each of the following heads :

" 1. WHAT IS THE NUMBER OF COMETS IN SPACE?

" 2. WHAT ARE PERIODICAL COMETS, AND WHAT ARE NON-PERIODICAL COMETS?

" 3. WHAT ARE THE CHANCES OF A COMET'S COMING INTO COLLISION WITH THE EARTH, OR WITH ANY OTHER PLANET?

" 4. WHAT WOULD BE THE CONSEQUENCES OF SUCH A COLLISION?

"Let us take these questions in order, and give them the best answers we can.

"*What is the number of Comets in space?* Kepler said that Comets are as numerous in the heavens as fishes are in the sea. Arago, founding an argument on the number of Comets actually observed whose perihelion point is within Mercury's orbit, calculates that the solar space within Neptune's orbit, is furrowed by more than seventeen millions and a half of Comets. Lambert, however, asserts that there are more than five hundred million Comets within the orbit of Saturn alone, and other calculations have actually swelled them to seventy-four quad-

5 *

rillions. But with these terrible numbers I must neither distract nor weary you.

"The truth is: nobody knows the number of these streaming orbs; nobody has ever counted them; nobody ever will count them. That they are extremely numerous is, however, beyond all question. To amplify Kepler's comparison, it may be said with perfect truth that a fisherman standing on the sun's surface, holding a rod long enough, could fling his line in no direction without hooking plenty of Comets.

"But that is not all that can be said on this point. There are Comets running a vagabond race over the face of the universe that are never influenced by solar attractions. There are even Comets so disorderly, so inconstant, so unruly that they capriciously quit one centre of attraction to attach themselves just as capriciously to another. They change their systems apparently at the merest random, some showing themselves for a short time where they had never been seen before, others disappearing just as suddenly and never showing themselves again.

"But to keep to our own Comets, that is, to those really belonging to the solar system and which appear and disappear with some kind of regularity — have these, you will ask, such a fixed, inalterable orbit as would effectually prevent all possibility of collision with each other or with the Earth? Well, they have nothing of the kind. Their orbits are never safe from external influences. Ellipses now, by and by they may become parabolas, even hyperbolas. Even if there were no other disturbing influence, Jupiter alone would be enough to cause infinite disorder. He is *par excellence* the great muddler. He is always in some Comet's way, sure to throw it out of kelter the moment some wretched astronomer has succeeded in calculating its elements after months of patient observation.

"What we know then of the present state of the cometary world may be given in a word or two: Their numbers are beyond all calculation, and their movements beyond all law.

"Now comes the consideration of the second question: *What are periodical and non-periodical Comets?*

"Throwing a hasty backward glance over the records of astronomy, we find that, of the five or six hundred Comets that have been at different times the object of serious observations, no more than forty have had their revolutionary periods even guessed at. These forty may be divided into Comets Periodical and Comets Non-periodical. Those of the first class make their reappearance after intervals of time longer or shorter, but still pretty regular in their occurrence. Those of the second withdraw from the sun to immeasurable dis-

tances and never return at all. Of the latter we cannot
say much, so that the most of this portion of my discourse will be devoted to the consideration of the
Comets Periodical.

"These are subdivided into two classes: The *short
period Comets;* and the *long period Comets.* We shall
take each in its turn.

"The chief *short period Comets* are ten in number,
and their movements have been calculated with extreme
precision.  They are 1 HALLEY'S; 2 ENCKE'S; 3 GAM-
BART'S or BIELA'S; 4 FAYE'S; 5 BRÖRSEN'S; 6 VICO'S;
7 D'ARREST'S; 8 TUTTLE'S; 9 WINNECKE'S; and 10
TEMPEL'S.

"A few words regarding the history of each of these
may throw some light on that of others. We shall find
one of them in particular conducting itself in such a
way as to strangely remind us of our own — I mean —
of *my* Gallia's doings.

"*Halley's Comet,* so called in honor of the illustrious
English astronomer who made it his especial study in
1682, and even predicted its return after a period of
seventy-six years, is the oldest Comet known.  It is sup-
posed to have been the Comet that announced the death
of Cæsar, and since that event to have appeared again
at several famous epochs, such as the destruction of
Rome by Alaric, the siege of Paris by the Normans,

HALLEY'S COMET IN 1835.

the victory at Hastings, the destruction of the Latin kingdom of Jerusalem, the suppression of the Templars, the invasion of Tamerlane, the capture of Constantinople, the beginning of the great Religious Troubles, the assassination of Henri Quatre, the founding of Philadelphia, etc., all occurring at pretty regular intervals of seventy-six years or a little more or less. The variation of the exact interval is accounted for by the disturbing influence exerted on the Comet by the neighborhood of Jupiter or Saturn, which may cause a retardation sometimes amounting to as much as six hundred and eighteen days. Its reappearance in 1835 had been so closely predicted that a difference of only three days existed between the time calculated and that of its actual return. It will come again in 1912 to amuse our grandchildren. It resembles Gallia in two respects: first, it has a retrograde motion around the sun, that is in a direction from east to west, the contrary to that of the planets; secondly, its perihelion distance from the sun is nearly that of Venus, or about sixty-seven millions of miles. Its aphelion distance is, however, considerably greater than that of the planet Neptune. Halley's is the only short period Comet visible to the naked eye.

"*Encke's Comet* is so called not from its having been discovered by Professor Encke of Berlin — its real discoverer was Pons of Marseilles — but he calculated its elements so correctly and its retrospective and prospective periods so faithfully, that astronomers could not bear to call it by any other name. Encke's Comet has the shortest period of all known Comets, its reappearance being due every 1200 days. Since its first known period it has never missed its time once; that it will be always so punctual remains to be seen. Its orbit lies within that of Jupiter, but certainly the period of its revolution seems to be gradually shortening. To what this acceleration is due, no one thus far is able to say. Some attribute it to the presence of an ethereal medium; others to planetary disturbance; others again to the repulsion of solar heat. But whatever may be the cause, the fact seems to be incontestable; and the inevitable consequence must be the absorption of the Comet into the incandescent mass of the sun at an epoch not very difficult to calculate. When it appears again in January, 1875, it will be the subject of very careful observation.

"*Gambart's* or *Biela's Comet* is in some respects very remarkable. It was discovered in 1826 by Major Biela, an Austrian amateur astronomer, stationed at Josephstadt, a little town in Bohemia. Ten days afterwards it was discovered by Gambart, director of the observatory at Marseilles. Both astronomers immediately set to work calculating its elements, and Gambart soon discovered its identity with a comet that had been already observed in 1805 and 1772. His calculation that its revolution around the sun was effected in about 6¾ years enabled him also to predict that it should appear again on October 29, 1832. More than that, its path should cross a particular point of the Earth's ecliptic, at which if the Earth itself should be at the same time, a collision was inevitable! Universal consternation everywhere, most of all at Paris. Few of you were born at that time, Messieurs, but I remember it well. In vain did Arago, my honored master, show that the Earth could not possibly reach the dangerous point until a month later. People would not be convinced. The dreaded October 29 came and passed. No collision occurred. It was all exactly as Arago had calculated. But no matter for that! In that terrible cholera year people were ready to credit anything! Many would not believe themselves out of danger until the 31st of December, 1832, was past and gone forever.

"The return of Gambart's Comet in 1839 was anxiously watched, but it was too close to the sun to be visible. In 1845–46 it appeared again, but presenting the curious aspect of a comet breaking up; it was actually splitting into two nebulosities. In 1852, when the two portions appeared once more, they were at a considerably greater distance apart.

In 1859 both portions were confidently looked for, but Gambart's Comet was never seen again! It never will be seen again. It is dissipated forever. The catastrophe so much dreaded in 1832 has actually taken place. But it was attended with no danger. Last November, when our friends the Terrestrians found themselves admiring the celestial fireworks of countless midnight meteors, they little suspected that the Earth was tunnelling a path through the scattered shreds of Gambart's Comet.

"*Faye's Comet,* the fourth on our list, was discovered in 1843 by Hervé Faye, a young astronomer attached to the Observatory of Paris. He also calculated its parabolic and elliptic elements, and showed that, as its course from perihelion to perihelion lasted about seven years and a half, its return might be expected in 1851. Professor Challis, of Cambridge University, England, found it at its perihelion on the second of April, 1851, only one day later than the day predicted, thus verifying the accuracy of the calculations made by Faye himself and also by Goldschmidt and Le Verrier. Its orbit is the least eccentric of all cometary orbits known, its perihelion nearly coinciding with that of Mars and its aphelion not much exceeding that of Jupiter. It has appeared regularly in 1858, in 1865, and also in 1873.

"*Brörsen's Comet*, discovered by Brörsen of Kiel, Denmark, in 1846, has a direct movement, and its period of about 5½ years is well established by its punctual reappearance three times out of the five times expected. Probably its too great proximity to the sun prevented its being seen on the other two occasions. Its aphelion, like that of Faye's, is a little more distant than Jupiter, but its perihelion is much nearer to the sun, being within Venus's orbit.

"*Vico's Comet* was discovered at Rome in 1844 by the Jesuit Father Di Vico, Director of the Observatory. The astronomers soon ascertained its period to be about 5½ years and its motion direct. But whether it has returned at times unfavorable for observation, or, disturbed by some planet, it has wandered away into the infinities of space, certain it is that Vico's Comet has never been seen since.

"*D'Arrest's Comet*, discovered in 1851 at Leipsic, was calculated to have a period of about 6⅔ years. It has made its reappearance several times, but the elements calculated for it latterly are very different from those of 1851, owing to considerable perturbations caused by other planets, Jupiter particularly, which it approaches very closely. Its period is at present 100 days longer than at the time of its first discovery.

"*Tuttle's Comet*, discovered at Cambridge, United

6

States, in 1871, was soon found to present a great similarity of elements to those of a Comet observed in 1790. Further labors established the identity of the two Comets. Its returns in 1803, 1817, 1830, and 1844, were not observed, but its next return in 1885 will in all probability be strictly up to time, its inclination being so considerable as to place it altogether beyond the disturbing influences of Jupiter and Saturn, though its aphelion is more distant than theirs. Its period is 13⅔ years, and its motion direct.

"*Winnecke's Comet,* discovered at Bonn in 1858, was proved almost beyond all doubt by Clausen's calculations to be identical with a Comet discovered in 1819 by Pons at Marseilles. Its motion is direct, and its period about 5¾ years. It should return again to the Earth early next year, but at that time Gallia will be still too far away to notice it.

"*Tempel's·Comet,* discovered at Marseilles in 1867, had its periodicity established the same year. Its time is about 5⅔ years, but its return last year was delayed fully two months by its having approached Jupiter too closely. Its motion is direct.

"Not to detain you too long, Messieurs," continued the Professor quickly, and without looking around to see whether they were attentive or not, "we shall lose very little more time with the rest of the *Short Period Comets.*

Very little is really known about them, and I only mention them at all because this is their proper place.

"*Pons's Comet,* discovered at Marseilles in 1812, has a period of about seventy years.

"*Olbers's Comet,* discovered at Bremen in 1816, has a period of about seventy-four years.

"*Di Vico's Comet,* discovered at Rome in 1846, and a few days afterwards by Bond of Cambridge, United States, has a period of about seventy-three years.

"*Westphal's Comet,* discovered at Göttingen in 1852, has a period of about sixty years.

" *Stephan's Comet* was discovered at Marseilles in 1867, but the calculation of its elements is due to Searle of Cambridge, United States. Its period is thirty-three years, and its motion, like that of all the others, direct.

" Now we approach the second part of the second division of our subject, namely, those Comets whose periods, though sometimes predicted by astronomy, are of very long duration. I shall, however, mention only a few of the most remarkable.

" In 1264 a brilliant Comet appeared in the sky with a tail more than a hundred degrees long, and having, as Chinese observers describe it, a curvature like that of a sabre. It was visible all August and September, but it disappeared, it is said, on the second of October, the very night Pope Urban IV died. It returned probably in 1556, when it is said to have hastened the abdication of Charles V, but though due in 1860, it has not been since observed. A strange Comet, of unusual brilliancy indeed, suddenly appeared in June, 1861, but it was only amateur astronomers that called it *Charles V's Comet.*

"The great Comet of 1680, called *Newton's Comet,* had a tail longer than the distance from the sun to the earth. It furnished Newton with an opportunity for proving that Comets revolve around the sun in conic sections; but astronomers have by no means agreed as to the period of its orbit. Whiston, Newton's successor in Cambridge, calculated it to be 575 years, but Encke gave its revolution a period of no less than 88 centuries. If Encke is right — I give no opinion of my own — this is not the place for it — we must relinquish forever the idea so long entertained of considering Newton's Comet to be the Comet that was seen at Constantinople in 1105, that was seen in 575 close to the sun at noonday, that appeared at Rome in 43 B. C., after Cæsar's death, or finally the Comet so obscurely referred to by Homer in the fourth book of the Iliad.

"*Chéseaux's Comet,* the brightest that appeared in the eighteenth century, was first seen early in February, 1744. At that time it was brighter than Sirius; a week later it was equal to Jupiter; in the beginning of March it rivalled even Venus in splendor. By the eighth of

DONATI'S COMET.

March its tail had divided itself into a number of branches like a fan. The discoverer has left us a striking picture of the extraordinary appearance it presented in the eastern sky; about half an hour before sunrise.

" The celebrated *Comet of* 1811, discovered by Flaugergues of Nismes, created an extraordinary sensation by its size and brilliancy. It was visible during September and October, but, according to Argeländer's computation, it will not return for 3000 years.

" The great *Comet of* 1843 was one of the most brilliant of the present century. It suddenly showed itself near the sun, and in the United States, where it was first discovered, Clark of Portland recorded it as being as well defined as the moon. on a clear evening. In southern latitudes especially it presented a stupendous spectacle. In spite of its splendor, however, astronomers have not been able to agree in any one point regarding its elements except that its direction was retrograde. It moved with extreme rapidity and approached nearer to the sun than any other comet on record, its perihelion being hardly half a million miles distant.

"*Donati's Comet,* discovered at Florence in 1858, was also remarkable for its extraordinary splendor. Its tail grew every day brighter and wider; from its head, moreover, streams of light appeared to shoot back-

6 *                         E

wards, amounting to as many as seven in number. Its motion was retrograde, and its discoverer calculated its period to be about 1880 years. Faye and Roche estimated its matter to be about a seven-hundredth of the Earth's.

"The *Comet of* 1861 broke suddenly on the northern hemisphere out of the sunbeams fully six weeks later than it had been seen in the southern. Its tail was 120 degrees long, and in all probability the Earth passed through a portion of it on the 30th of June. This comet recalled Donati's somewhat by its bright shoots of light and the occasional peculiar curvature of its branching tail. The period of its revolution was calculated to be about 422 years.

" The next comets, Messieurs —"

The Professor suddenly interrupted himself, and glanced around with eyes flashing lightning through the spectacles. A sound — the most unwelcome of all sounds to speakers — the snore of a sleeper had burst upon his ear. Ben Zouf was the culprit.

Long before this Ben had made several ineffectual attempts to signify to the Captain that he could not stand the Professor's lecture any longer and that he wanted to leave the apartment. But the Captain, thoroughly interested, had impatiently signalled him to remain where he was and on no account to disturb the Professor by any noise or restlessness. Ben had at last appeared to resign himself to his fate, but, whether from real drowsiness or artful calculation, his eyes grew heavier and heavier, his head nodded and nodded till at last it lay motionless on his breast.

Then came the snore which had stopped the Professor in the middle of his lecture.

"Still at your old tricks, Servadac!" exclaimed the Professor, regarding his former pupil with a glance of burning rage; "well, all right! Class is over!" and he started to leave the room.

But the Count and Procopius were too quick for him. They blockaded his road, protested that his lecture was intensely interesting, that they could listen to it for hours yet, and that if he was not too tired, nothing would give them greater pleasure than to hear the rest of it.

The Professor had certainly been extremely mortified but, like most people of easily excited irritability, he could not retain his anger long. The earnest efforts of the Count and Procopius visibly softened him, and the sight of the Captain hastily seizing the half-conscious Ben by the collar and unceremoniously kicking him out of the room wonderfully contributed towards restoring his good-humor.

" My dear Master," said the Captain, hurrying back

and hardly able to speak from excitement and want
of breath, "how can I possibly excuse myself for allowing that unfortunate fellow of mine to interrupt
your most absorbing lecture by his beastly snoring?
It is all my own fault, I must acknowledge. I should
have known him better. But he understands nothing
about books, and really has not slept a wink for the
last twenty-four hours."

This the Count confirmed as an actual fact to his
own knowledge, but he did not think it necessary to
state that Ben had lost his rest by nursing the Professor.

"My dear Master," continued the Captain, "do not
punish us too severely for a fault which, though exceedingly unfortunate, was the result of mere inadvertency.
Nothing like it will ever happen again. Let us have
the rest of your lecture by all means! Never in all my
life have I found you in better vein!"

The Professor could not resist. To show, however,
that some grains of anger still continued to rankle in
his breast, he would not resume in the exact place where
he had broken off, but passed immediately to the third
part of his discourse.

"*What are the chances of a Comet's coming into collision with the Earth or any other planet?*

"Look at this door, Messieurs! Look at this sheet

of paper! What do you see? Comet orbits and planet orbits crossing each other and intermingled with each other in apparently the most hopeless confusion. But, I need hardly say, this confusion exists nowhere in space. The planes containing these orbits are all inclined more or less to the plane of the Earth's ecliptic. Not a single one of them coincides with another. There is plenty of room for all. Still, in spite of the superabundant room afforded by infinite space of three dimensions, comets are numerous enough to bring it within the range of possibility that one of them may sometime or other come into collision with the Earth.

"Leaving Gallia out of all consideration for the present, let us try to find a reply to the general question: In order that a Comet should strike the Earth, what conditions are absolutely necessary?

"At least three:

"1. The Comet must enter the plane of the Earth's ecliptic. 2. The Comet must cross the very point of the Earth's orbit where the Earth itself is moving. 3. The distance separating the centres of the two planets must be less than the sum of their radii.

"Otherwise no encounter can take place.

"Now, can these three conditions occur simultaneously? If they can, such a collision is possible. Laplace says: 'The probability of such an encounter, however

slight originally, may become very great at last by a
long series of accumulations in a long series of
centuries.' When Arago was asked this very question,
what was his reply? 'The doctrine of probabilities gives
us the means of finding an answer. By this calculation
we find the chances against the Earth's being struck
by the nucleus of an unknown Comet to be at least
281 millions to unity; that is, out of 281 millions of
chances against there is only one chance in favor of a
collision between the bodies.'

"He illustrated the nature of these chances by an
example: 'Granting,' said he, 'the possibility of an unknown comet coming in contact with the Earth and
thereby instantly annihilating the whole human race,
what risk does a human being run every day of losing
his life by such encounter? Exactly the same risk as he
would run of losing his life if there was in an urn only
one white ball among 281 million black balls, and if his
death was to be the consequence of the white ball being
drawn at the first offer.'

"The bare possibility, therefore, though an exceedingly slight one, of such a collision may be granted; or
at least, the impossibility of such an event cannot very
well be established.

"Has anything like this ever happened? Has the
Earth been ever struck by a comet?

"Arago says positively, 'No! The fact that the Earth still turns on an invariable axis is positive proof that she has never been struck by a comet. Terrestrial latitudes are constant. They have been so for ages. The axis is still what it has always been. The oblique collision of the Earth with a tolerably large comet would instantly disturb the axis of rotation. Instead of a spinning, the Earth would have a wobbling, motion. The terrestrial latitudes would undergo variations that show no sign of ever having existed. Their constancy therefore proves that the Earth has never yet been struck by a comet.'

" But the fact of the Earth's having been never yet struck by a comet, I need hardly remind you, is by no means a proof that it never will be, or that it never can be. Remember what we know already of Gambart's Comet in 1832. There is no doubt whatever that, had it come a month later, it would have struck the Earth. Remember also what I said about the destruction of that comet. Some years later, its remains actually enveloped the Earth, unknown to the Terrestrians, who called its particles the November meteors !

" Now comes our fourth question :

" *What would be the consequence of such a collision ?*

" The answer evidently depends on the nature of the comet; that is, whether its nucleus were solid or gaseous.

"The nuclei of some comets are nebulous to such a degree that stars even of the tenth magnitude have shown through them as through an exceedingly fine gauze. These comets are, of course, so subject to change of form as to be almost impossible of recognition afterwards. The same nebulous matter enters into the composition of their tails. These are, in fact, nothing but immense evaporations of the nucleus under the influence of solar heat. Of this there appears to be no doubt. The tail may be a thin white streak, or a long feathery broom, or a many-leaved fan, but it never commences to show itself until the comet comes within a distance of 70 or 80 millions of miles from the sun. When comets appear, as they sometimes do, altogether without a tail, it is because their matter is denser, solider, harder, and therefore better able to resist the evaporating influence of extreme solar temperature.

"In case of a meeting between the Earth and a Comet with a gaseous nucleus, there could be, properly speaking, no collision at all. According to Haye, a Comet's nebulosity would offer no more resistance to the Earth than that of a spider's web to a musket-ball. Unless the matter, therefore, of which the tail is composed be an unhealthy or an inflammable gas, there is absolutely nothing to be afraid of in case of a collision. But even supposing it to be an inflammable gas or an unhealthy vapor, what would be the result? Would it set the atmosphere on fire and instantly consume everything on the Earth's surface? Would its introduction into the terrestrial atmosphere be destructive to human life? I must acknowledge I have not yet found a good reason for positively affirming that either of these eventualities should be the result of an encounter. Whatever would be the consequence of a clash between two atmospheres of equal density, I do not see how anything very terrible could result from an attack made by cometary nebulosity. Babinet of Paris says that the terrestrial atmosphere, however rare in its uppermost regions, is absolute solidity in comparison with the haze surrounding a comet, and could easily resist all attempts at penetration. So extremely thin in fact is this vapor that Newton ventures to say : 'A gaseous comet, with a radius a thousand millions of miles in length, if submitted to the same degree of condensation as the earth, could be easily kept in a good-sized thimble.'

"An encounter then between the Earth and a nebulous comet need not therefore give rise to great alarm.

" But suppose a *solid comet* struck the Earth, what would be the result?

" To answer this question, we must first ask : are such things as solid comets known to exist? Evidently they

7

*must* exist if the gaseous matter is ever sufficiently condensed to become solid.  How is solidity proved?  Very
simply.  Any comet that hides even a star from the eye
of the spectator must be comparatively solid.

"Now 480 years before Christ, according to Herod-
otus, as Xerxes's army was leaving Sardis the sun suddenly withdrew his beams, though the sky was bright
and unclouded.  Dion Cassius, a writer remarkable for
the accuracy of his dates, speaks of another eclipse
which preceded by some days the death of Augustus.
According to the best astronomers, these two eclipses
could not have been caused by the interposition of the
moon.  They have therefore been attributed to the
passage of two comets across his disc.

"It must be acknowledged, of course, that such solitary instances are by no means strong enough to establish the existence of comets sufficiently large or
sufficiently solid to deprive the Earth for a while of
the solar light.  But more recent observations put the
question beyond a doubt.

"According to Fréret of Paris, the Comet of 479
was of such magnitude that it might have occasioned
the extraordinary eclipse of the sun which took place
at the time.  The great Comet of 1500 called *Asta* or
*Signor Astone,* could be seen equally well by day or
night for eight or ten days.  The Chéseaux Comet of

1744, already spoken of, was also bright enough to be seen during sunlight. In 1774, Messier of the Academy noticed that the light of a star was eclipsed by a small comet. In 1828, Encke's Comet was noticed at Geneva to completely occult a small star over whose face it passed. The great Comet of 1843 we have already alluded to as having been seen by the naked eye in full sunshine, by observers in Florence, at the Cape of Good Hope, in Mexico, and particularly at Portland, U. S., by Mr. Clarke, who compared its light to that of a pale moon. The first Comet of 1847 was quite visible in London though in the immediate neighborhood of the sun, and, finally, the fifth Comet of 1857 though side by side with a midnight moon.

"Solid nuclei, in fact, have not only been known to exist, but have even been measured. As may be expected, they are of different dimensions. The Comet of 1798 (Messier's) and the Comet of 1805 (Gambart's) had nuclei of about 25 miles in diameter. The great Comet of 1843 had a nucleus whose diameter was more than 5 thousand miles in length. If this comet had come in contact with the Earth, the advantage could hardly have been all on one side.

" On this subject I must, however, say that the nuclei of most comets are subject to extreme variation of dimensions. Take Donati's Comet of 1858 as an ex-

ample. Bond of Harvard calculated its diameter of
July 19 to be six thousand miles. But as the Comet
advanced towards the sun, its nucleus steadily diminished in volume till the 5th of October, when its diameter was only four hundred miles, that is, 15 times
less than first estimated.

"Even the nebulosities or envelopes have been measured, and have been found to vary from two thousand
miles to about a million and a quarter.

"To resume the last part of our discourse, it is
known that: 1. Comets exist without any nucleus at
all; 2. Comets exist whose nucleus is so vaporous as
to be almost perfectly transparent; and, 3. Comets
exist whose nuclei are more radiant than the planets,
perfectly opaque and probably quite solid.

"In case of a collision with comets of the first two
kinds very little danger need be apprehended. Lexell's
Comet of 1770 approached the Earth within a distance
less than a million and a half miles; yet the length of
the year 1770 did not vary by so much as a single second. Laplace says, on the contrary, that the Earth's
action retarded the revolution of the Comet by two
whole days.

"Now take a comet of the third class, whose mass is
dense and solid. Duséjour of Paris calculates that
even if a comet of the solid kind approached the

Earth twice nearer than the Moon ever does, even then the proximity would produce no greater effect than to make the terrestrial year sixteen or seventeen hours longer and to make the terrestrial ecliptic two degrees more oblique.

"But in case of a direct collision between the Earth and a solid comet of equal mass, what would be the consequence?

"Much would depend on the nature of the encounter. If the comet merely grazed the Earth, the Terrestrians might hardly notice the injury at all. They might indeed lose a few bits of surface, a little.water and some atmosphere, but, in other respects, they might hardly be even aware that anything unusual had occurred. This is really what my Gallia has done; and, in the absence of stronger evidence than any afforded so far, I anticipate considerable difficulty in convincing the Terrestrians hereafter that there was any collision at all.

"But if the encounter were direct in its nature, the testimony would be of a most convincing character — if there was anybody left to testify to. There is no doubt whatever but that the Earth's rotary velocity would be instantly arrested. Human beings, trees, houses, everything movable would be suddenly hurled forward into space with a speed of little less than 19

7 *

miles a second. The seas, suddenly shot from their
basins, would instantly overwhelm everything on land.
The central parts of the globe, still liquid, bursting
through the crust, would overflow the surface in every
direction. The axis suddenly changed, a new equator
would instantly take the place of the old. The revolutionary velocity being greatly retarded, the centrip-
etal and the centrifugal forces would no longer counter-
balance each other. Consequently, the Earth would
seek the sun in a line gradually becoming straighter
and straighter, and would at last reach him after a
fall of between sixty and seventy days.

"Even adopting as true Tyndall's theory that *heat
is only a mode of velocity*, the consequences would be
no less appalling. A simple calculation enables us to
estimate the amount of heat sure to be developed by
a collision between the Earth and anything strong
enough to stop her motion. Mayer and Helmholtz
have made the calculation, and find that the quantity
of heat generated by the colossal shock is sufficient
not only to melt the entire Earth but actually to
reduce it to a state of vapor. They have gone even
further in their calculations. The destruction of the
Earth would not be the only consequence of the collision. The Earth's fall on the sun would generate
an amount of heat on the solar surface equal to that

developed by the combustion of 5600 *worlds of solid Carbon.*

" A comet, however, capable of producing such an effect as this has never appeared yet, and in all probability never will.

" To conclude with a word or two this last part of our subject, I shall once more remind you, Messieurs, of Arago's calculation: For the Earth to be touched at all by a comet, the chances are 1 for and 281 millions against.

" As sometimes happens, the vast improbability has taken place; the Terrestrians have drawn the white ball this time in the shape of my Gallia!"

# CHAPTER IV.

## THE PROFESSOR'S STORY.

NEVER had Professor been favored by a more attentive or interested audience at the beginning of his
discourse. Even the Russians and the Spaniards, who
could not understand one word in fifty, had remained
listening for at least a quarter of an hour with a patience
truly admirable, and a curiosity deserving a better reward. But, long even before the Ben Zouf episode,
they had begun to slip away on tiptoe, one by one, the
accomplished lecturer, the keen-eyed observer of the
starry host probably never once noticing their exit.
But the Captain, the Count, and Procopius had manfully held out to the last. More. They had tried to
manifest all through an interest which they were in
reality very far from feeling. Very little of what the
Professor told them they had not known already.
Books they had read in abundance. Observations they
had made with care and precision. Speculations they
had cautiously and intelligently discussed. From nothing so far had they learned the truth — the important

truth most immediately concerning themselves. This they were burning to know, but this was precisely the very point on which the Professor had not chosen to throw the least particle of light. The amount of information contained in his lecture they certainly could not help admiring, delivered as it was in clear forcible language, without notes or preparation, and on the spur of the moment. But the only real attraction his lecture really possessed for them was the expectation that every moment the Professor would answer the all-absorbing question — would Gallia ever return to Earth again? Judge of their disappointment, therefore, when the Professor, suddenly stopping, sat down and looked around with the air of a man who has not only said a good deal, but who has really said all he wants to say.

They looked at each other for a while rather gloomily, and the Captain could hardly suppress an impatient exclamation. But a glance from the Count hinted that he should not spoil good prospects by over-zeal.

" The Professor is in great humor for talking to-day," whispered the Count, " and if we do not get out of him everything we want to know, it will probably be our own fault. He is a little exhausted just now and looks sleepy. Let us wait till he recovers."

After a light doze of a few minutes, the Professor suddenly raised his head and began looking round curiously,

F

as if in search of something. For the first time the slenderness of his audience seemed to break on him. His brows began to frown fearfully, and his voice soon sounded angrily as he exclaimed :

"Where are all the others?"

"They are just outside, my dear Master," said the Captain earnestly; "they withdrew a little for fear of incommoding you. Shall I bring them in?"

"Yes! Immediately!"

"All of them?" asked the Captain, dubious of the nature of the reception likely to await Ben Zouf.

"Yes! all! No exception!"

In a few minutes all the Gallians were once more assembled before the Professor, Pablo and Nina in front, but Ben Zouf, looking a little ashamed of himself, keeping as much as possible in the rear.

"Now then, Servadac," said the Professor, "introduce your company. I am ready."

"Professor Rosette," said the Captain, bringing forward the Count, "I have the honor to present my friend Count Timascheff."

"Delighted to see you, my dear Count," said the Professor most graciously. "I hope you have no trouble in making yourself at home here."

"None whatever, Professor," answered the Count. "It is not exactly of my own accord that I find myself

THE INTRODUCTION.

on your Gallia. Nevertheless, I sincerely thank you for your generous hospitality.''

"Now, my dear Master," continued the Captain, speaking rather hurriedly to prevent Rosette from noticing the Count's irony, "I must introduce my friend Lieutenant Procopius, commander of the steam yacht *Dobryna*, in which we have circumnavigated Gallia.''

"How! Circumnavigated!" exclaimed the Professor.

"Yes, my dear Master, completely circumnavigated. You shall hear all about it as soon as we get through the introduction. — My Orderly, Ben Zouf—"

"Aid-de-camp to the Governor-General!" hastily added Ben, suddenly growing quite bold upon seeing the Professor's vacant stare, totally void of all recognition.

Then were presented in rapid succession old Isaac, the Russians, the Spaniards, and, last of all, young Pablo and little Nina. They were all received most affably by the dignified Professor, who, for at least once in his life, did not improve the opportunity of scowling at children.

The only one of all presented who ventured to speak without being spoken to was Isaac, who could never keep his tongue still.

"Signor Professor," he asked abruptly, apparently

forgetting the unpleasant results of his last question, " Oh Signor Professor, when are we to get back ? "

" Who talks of getting back ? " asked the angry Professor, not deigning to look at his audacious questioner. " We 're hardly started yet ! "

" Now, my dear Master," said the Captain, the moment the ceremony of introduction was properly got through, " if it is not asking altogether too much after your very interesting lecture on Comets, we should be delighted to learn to what fortunate accident we are indebted for the unlooked-for presence among us of our illustrious guest."

The Professor needed little pressing. He was soon telling his story with a good deal of spirit and originality, but in such a jerky, rambling, incoherent, episodical style very different from that of his lecture, that, to spare the gracious reader's patience, we take the liberty of presenting it in a condensed form.

The French Government, desirous of verifying the measurements of the arc of the Meridian of Paris taken by Delambre and Méchain towards the close of the last century, appointed a scientific commission for the purpose, to which, much to his disgust, Professor Rosette had received no nomination. The real reason was probably his ugly temper, but the Professor attributed his exclusion altogether to jealousy and envy. Smarting under the disappointment and burning with revenge, he undertook a series of astronomical observations on his own account, fully determined on finding something done by somebody else to be quite wrong, and immediately letting all the world know it. He soon flattered himself that he had discovered a serious error in the measurements of the triangulations connecting Formentera with the Spanish coast, a work at which Arago and Biot had labored from 1805 to 1808 with great care and success.

Quitting Paris for the Balearics, he erected an observatory on the highest point of the lonely island of Formentera, where he lived for some time like a hermit, his only companion in this self-imposed exile being Joseph, his faithful serving-man. He had employed one of his old assistants to take charge of a lighted lamp on the summit of the rock Mongó, the highest point in the neighboring coast of Spain and easily visible in Formentera by means of a telescope. The Professor's scientific apparatus was by no means extensive. A few books, some mathematical instruments, provisions for two or three months constituted the whole stock, not forgetting a refracting telescope of great power, 10 inches diameter, made by Grubb of Dublin, and presented to him by his friend and admirer Lord Ross as a mark of singular affection and esteem. From this telescope he hardly ever separated himself day or night, especially night.

8.

The lovely Spanish climate would have made night-watching an enchanting pastime to even the least enthusiastic of observers, but night-watching had now become a passion with the Professor. From the moment the sun had set until he rose again the next morning, the Professor, his regular triangulation labors once over, would never leave the window, his eye glued to the telescope, as he eagerly sounded the infinite depths of the starry sky with the hope of lighting on some discovery that should make the world ring with his name and his jealous enemies die of vexation.

But his regular triangulation labors required the greatest patience and exactness. He knew the difficulty of his task. He knew that even to take the correct bearing of the fire-signal on the Spanish coast had cost his predecessors, Arago and Biot, a labor of no less than sixty-one days. He was satisfied therefore with his progress however slow, and was even beginning to calculate that another week would end his task, when all at once a thick mist of extraordinary intensity fell on the Spanish coast and by day as well as by night shut it completely out of view. This was the strangely persistent mist that was alluded to in the first part of our history in the following words: " Every one had tried to account for them, but the best meteorologists

NIGHT WATCHING WAS THE PROFESSOR'S PASSION.

acknowledged themselves vanquished. Even on the ocean the fogs had been so dense that the great mail-steamers were obliged to be continually blowing whistles and firing cannon for fear of a collision." *

Now by a very strange and in fact most unaccountable piece of good luck, it happened very often, even quite usually, that in the neighborhood of Formentera a wind would spring up suddenly and with sufficient violence to blow away this mist, or rather make holes in this vaporous envelope through which the heavens could be seen at night. This was a great and most unexpected treat to the Professor who, cut off by the mist from the Spanish coast and not knowing how to employ his time, had begun to think of returning to Paris. Unable to do anything else at the time, he commenced studying with great care the only visible portion of the heavens — that in the neighborhood of the constellation Gemini — expecting to make some discovery there which would make all the celestial maps wrong.

Gemini presents at most about a dozen stars visible to the naked eye, but to a telescope 12 inches in diameter it reveals between six and seven thousand. The Professor's telescope had not quite this unusual power, but, as already observed, it was one of great excellence and answered his purpose exceedingly well.

---

* " TO THE SUN ? " page 16.

It happened one night that, while ranging through the smaller stars of Gemini and registering them carefully on his chart, he all at once lit on a brilliant speck, of which, as he soon ascertained, no map contained any traces. It was no doubt, he thought, some star not recorded in the catalogue; and he began to examine it with some curiosity. But after a few nights' careful contemplation, seeing that this new heavenly body was very rapidly displacing itself among the other stars, the Professor asked himself what the unknown stranger could be. A new planet? Had he at last made the immortal discovery?

He now watched with redoubled attention. But the rapidity with which the new-comer displaced itself soon convinced him that it was no planet. It must be a Comet! In fact, its nucleus soon began to show itself; then its envelope; then its tail. It *was* a Comet, and approaching the sun with tremendous velocity!

It need hardly be said that all further thoughts of triangulations were instantly and completely abandoned. Every night regularly, fog or no fog, the assistant on Mongó mountain lit his signal-fire; but the Professor never looked in the direction of the Mongó mountain. His only objective point now and henceforth was the long-tailed meteor that blazed so brightly among the stars of Gemini. His sole thought now was to be not

only its first discoverer, but also the first calculator of
its elements, and thus acquire the prescriptive right to
be the first to give it a name.

When an astronomer sets about calculating a Comet's
elements, he begins by always taking for granted that its
orbit is a parabola, that is, one having an open curve.
Experience has shown this to be the best way to begin.
There is very little danger of its leading to a mistake,
and if a mistake is made it is soon corrected. Comets
are never seen until approaching their *perihelion* or
nearest point to the sun, which is one of the foci of their
orbit. In this portion of the orbit, whether it is an ellipse or a parabola, the difference in the curves is not
appreciable, both orbits having a common focus, and a parabola being nothing but an ellipse prolonged to infinity.

To determine a straight line two points are sufficient;
but to determine a circle at least three points of its arc
are required; three points are also sufficient to determine the elements of a Comet. Three points are enough
to enable us to trace its route from star to star, and thus
fix what is called its *ephemeris*.

But the bare three points did not satisfy the enthusiastic
Professor. Availing himself of every advantage afforded
by the rents in the mist that everywhere else obscured
the sky, he took ten points, twenty points, even as many
as thirty points, and thus ascertained with exceedingly

8 *

great accuracy the *elements* of the rapidly approaching Comet.

Now what are a Comet's *elements ?*

They are five in number; these once known, all the other quantities can be easily calculated.

First. The *inclination* of the plane of the Comet's orbit to the plane of the Earth's ecliptic. The greater this inclination, the less the danger of a collision, and *vice versa.*

Second. The *longitude of the ascending node*, that is, the point of the Earth's ecliptic through which the Comet would pass when proceeding from south to north. This longitude, otherwise called the Right Ascension, is marked by a figure from 0 to 360, counting from the vernal equinox, always the starting-point in astronomy.

Third. The *longitude of the perihelion*, that is, the exact point in her course around the sun at which the Comet begins to return. This gives us the direction of the major axis of the curve in its own plane.

These three points once ascertained, namely, the *inclination* of the two orbits, the *longitude of the ascending node*, and the *longitude of the perihelion*, the plane of the Comet's orbit in space is fixed.

Fourth. The *Perihelion distance* of the Comet, that is, the number of miles she is distant from the sun at her nearest point. This gives us the exact position of the major axis, and decides the form of the parabolic or elliptic curve, one focus being evidently the sun's centre.

Fifth. The *Direction* of the Comet's motion; that is, whether, like the Earth, it moves from west to east, or the contrary. If like the Earth's, its motion is called *direct;* if not, *retrograde.*

These five *elements* the Professor was not very long in ascertaining. He verified them again and again, subjecting his conclusions to the closest criticism. He soon found them to agree invariably with each new observation. Concluding, therefore, that his calculations were correct, he wrote out the Comet's *Ephemeris*, that is, a statement of the exact place which it should occupy among the heavenly bodies every day of the year, whether it was visible or not. Comparing this *ephemeris* with those of all other Comets previously discovered, he soon satisfied himself to his unbounded joy that he was the first discoverer of *Gallia*, the name he finally gave the new planet, after hesitating for some time between the rival claims of *Palmyra* and *Rosetta.*

Of the five *elements* thus ascertained, we shall call the reader's attention to the first, the fourth, and the fifth. First. What was the *inclination* of the Comet's orbit with the plane of the ecliptic? Answer — The Comet's orbit made *no angle* at all with the Earth's ecliptic. It *coincided* with it; therefore *a collision was quite possible.*

Fourth. What was the nature of its orbit? Answer — *Elliptic*, not *parabolic;* therefore the Comet might return to the Earth again.   Fifth. What was the direction of its motion?   Answer — *Retrograde,* not *direct;* this accounted for the sun's rising in the west and setting in the east.

None of the elements, however, possessed an interest for the Professor in comparison with the first.   A *collision possible!*   Let us look into this.   One night's calculation satisfied him that a collision between the Comet and the Earth was *not only possible, but absolutely certain!*   Was he paralyzed with terror?   Terror !   He was paralyzed with joy !   It was with an indescribable thrill of the wildest astronomic ecstasy that he ascertained the time of the inevitable collision to be on the morning of the first of January, a few hours after midnight !

Any other man would have run away in the greatest consternation.   He never dreamed of such a thing.   He remained manfully at his post.   He did not even publish a single word regarding his astounding discovery. The papers told him that the impenetrable mists still rendered all observation impossible in both hemispheres. No observatory had made the slightest announcement regarding the approaching danger.   He was himself in fact the only discoverer.   What could be gained by revealing the fact ?   If the mist cleared away, the astronomers would soon discover the stranger themselves ; if it did not, the astronomers would not believe a word he said. The rest of the human race would, of course, be instantly thrown into an agony of terror. But what good could that do? Not the slightest! His discovery, therefore, he kept to himself. No other human being had the slightest suspicion of the nearness of the impending blow. And when the catastrophe would take place, no other human being would have the slightest idea of the nature of the blow that struck them.

He knew very well, of course, that the shock should be a terrible one, the two colliding bodies moving with immense speed in opposite directions. He knew too that the point of the Earth first struck would be some point in Northern Africa, not very far from Formentera. But all this only whetted his curiosity. "I wish to be on the spot," he said, "when she comes! The Comet being solid, the crash must be a rouser!"

The collision took place, as we already know. The Professor, like the inmates of the gourbi, was struck senseless. As soon as he recovered he called aloud for Joseph, but no Joseph was to be seen. Nothing remained even of Formentera except a little islet, hardly spacious enough to hold the observatory.

Let the Professor himself conclude his story.

"Extremely singular modifications I found to have been produced in a few moments: displacement of the cardinal points, diminution of gravity, proximity of the horizon, etc. But I had no notion, as you had, Messieurs, that I was still on the Earth. No. The Earth I soon knew to be still gravitating in space as before, accompanied by the moon as before, and following exactly the same orbit as before. She had been merely grazed by Gallia, and had lost nothing but the few insignificant portions of her surface that you discovered. It had all passed off very well, much better indeed than anybody could have expected, and we Gallians in particular have very little to complain of. Instead of being still on the Earth, ground to powder under the Comet, here we are now perfectly happy, and enjoying the unspeakable advantage, never hitherto accorded to man, of a magnificent promenade through interplanetary space! Don't you agree with me, Messieurs?"

"Professor!" answered Ben Zouf, breaking the chill silence that pervaded the assembly at the conclusion of the strange narrative, "without meaning offence, I think your Comet knew very well what it was about when it struck the Earth. It picked out a soft spot!"

"Soft spot! soft spot!" cried the Professor, in tones shrill with anger, darting a lightning glance at Ben

THE PROFESSOR WAS STRUCK SENSELESS.

through his terrible spectacles. "What do you mean by a soft spot? Where could my Comet have met a hard spot?"

"At Montmartre!" answered Ben boldly. "Had your Comet tackled on to old Montmartre, she'd have met her match! Old Montmartre would have given her something she had not bargained for!"

"Montmartre!" exclaimed the Professor in accents of the supremest contempt. "A miserable molehill like Montmartre resist my Comet! Give my Comet a fair sweep at the Himalayas and she would cut them down as a mowing-machine cuts down grass!"

"Montmartre a molehill!" cried Ben, beginning to forget his manners in his exasperation. "I'd have you to know, Mr. Professor, that old Montmartre is big enough and strong enough to knock the breath out of a score of your flimsy Comets! You don't know what a dreadful fellow old Montmartre can be —"

"Hold your tongue, Ben Zouf!" interrupted the Captain, smiling a little in spite of himself at the ridiculous contest. "You must not contradict the Professor! I don't know what's got into you. My dear Master, please excuse him to-day. He hardly knows what he is saying. His head is a little turned on Montmartre. But he will be all right to-morrow!"

The Professor was soon pacified, the Count and

Procopius joining the Captain in his entreaties, but Ben returned to his seat growling and surly. At first he had taken a kind of liking to the Professor and was quite proud of having saved his life, but from this moment he conceived an inveterate hatred against the " comet-man," as he contemptuously called him, swearing he would never forgive him for having spoken so disrespectfully of his beloved Montmartre.

" Professor," said Procopius, who though an attentive listener was still in as much doubt as ever on two very essential points, " you have of course calculated the path of Gallia's orbit in space and the length of one of her revolutions? "

" I have, Lieutenant," answered the Professor. " I have calculated it twice; once before the collision and once after."

" Twice! " observed Procopius, assuming a look of extreme surprise. " Undertake a work of such difficulty twice ! "

" Certainly twice. The encounter had no effect on the Earth's orbit, but it might have considerably affected Gallia's."

" Gallia's orbit has then been much changed by the shock ? "

" Considerably changed. Observations taken posterior to the encounter and taken with extreme pre-

cision warrant me in making so positive an assertion."

" You know the elements of the new orbit then?"

" Oh yes," replied the Professor quietly.

" You know, for instance —"

" What I know is this. Gallia encountered the Earth
in her ascending node at 2 hours 47 minutes and 35
seconds after midnight on the morning of January the
first. On the tenth of the same month she cut the
orbit of Venus. She kept outside the orbit of Mercury.
On the fifteenth she passed her perihelion. On the
twentieth she recut the orbit of Venus. On the first
of February she cleared her descending node. On the
tenth she cut the orbit of Mars. On the tenth of March
she entered the zone of the Minor Planets, captured
Nerina for a satellite —"

" All this we know very well already, my dear Master," interrupted the Captain, " thanks to the very clear
and comprehensive bulletins we were so extremely fortunate as to light upon. Only they had neither name
nor address."

" What!" asked the Professor with a proud air of
undisputed superiority and conscious merit. " You did
not know they were mine? Whose else could they have
been? Who else threw them by hundreds into the
sea?"

9                          G

"Nobody else!" answered Count Timascheff, with great gravity. "It was unpardonable in us not to recognize them as yours at once!"

"But, Professor," persisted Procopius, who, not finding his questions answered, began to suspect that they were purposely avoided, "you have not yet told us —"

"Why the shock did us so little harm," interrupted the Captain, afraid lest the Count's cold irony and Procopius's importunity might irritate the peppery Professor. "How in the world did we get off so well?"

"Oh, that is easily explained," answered the Professor, "and not only that, but the little harm in general done to the Earth. Except the loss of a few square lines of territory she has suffered actually nothing. I am perfectly satisfied that neither her orbit nor her axis has been in the slightest degree modified. The velocities were simply too great and the resistances too slight. What shock, for instance, can a rifle-ball shot through a pane of glass, give the rest of the window? You can calculate the whole question easily yourselves. The Earth was moving at the time with a velocity of 19 miles a second. Gallia was moving in an opposite direction with a velocity about twice as great, or nearly 40 miles a second. Imagine a railroad train shooting along at the rate of nearly sixty miles a second, or at least 180 times quicker than a ball the moment it leaves the cannon's mouth. Determine the result yourselves. The Comet, whose nucleus is extremely hard, did what a bullet fired at a screen of thin paper would do. It skimmed the Earth so rapidly that it actually had not time to do any further damage."

"Yes," said the Captain, reflectively, "that must have been the way—"

"Of course it was the way," resumed the Professor, "and nothing else was the way, especially as the Earth's surface was grazed very obliquely. But if Gallia had attacked her point-blank, she would have penetrated her to what depth I do not know, but with what amount of disaster I can easily imagine. Yes!" with a malicious twinkle through the spectacles at Ben, "even Montmartre would have been butted into a hole fifteen thousand feet deep!"

"Stick to your Comet, Mr. Professor," said Ben, very angry but doing his best to keep his temper. "Don't distress yourself about old Montmartre! Stick to your Comet! It's a subject you know something about — perhaps!"

"Silence, Ben Zouf!" cried the Captain, desirous above all things of keeping the Professor in good-humor. He was in fact extremely desirous to get an answer to one or two questions which, like Procopius, he now began to suspect the Professor to be desirous of avoiding. His only hope was now that the Professor, by being kept in good-humor and encouraged to talk on every subject, might at last unwittingly let drop the information they were all so desirous to obtain.

But Isaac did not understand this roundabout way of getting at things. His stiff neck had at last bent a little. In spite of himself, he began to get a glimpse into the real state of the case. But the *how* or the *why* of the past possessed no interest for his practical, grasping mind. The *when* alone of the future troubled him. For the last hour he had been listening with ill-disguised impatience to what he growled at as mere gabble and twaddle. Now he thought his chance was come, and he made the most of it.

"Signor Professor!" he cried, springing suddenly forward, his voice trembling with anxiety, "shall we ever get back to Earth again? How long shall we have to wait?"

"You appear to be in a great hurry," was the only reply given by the crusty Professor.

"What Isaac asks of you so abruptly, Professor," said Procopius, "I should like to formulate a little more scientifically."

"Formulate, my good sir."

"Gallia's former orbit has been somewhat modified, you say?"

"Yes; incontestably."

"Is her new orbit still a hyperbola?"

"No!" answered the Professor.

"Is it a parabola?"

"No!"

"It is an ellipse then?"

"Yes: an ellipse."

"And its plane still coincides with the plane of the ecliptic?"

"Yes, still coincides."

"Gallia is then a periodical comet?"

"Yes, one of a short period, of a very short period, as her revolution around the sun, making every allowance for the disturbances that may be caused by Mars and Jupiter, will be accomplished in exactly two years."

"Then, Professor," pursued Procopius eagerly, "the chances seem to be that, two years after the encounter, Gallia will find herself in exactly the same spot where she had been before?"

All waited for the answer to this home thrust with breathless interest.

"Ye — s," replied the Professor, slowly and unwill-

9 *

ingly, "I should say that something like it is — very much — to — be — apprehended!"

"To be apprehended!" cried the audience with one voice.

"Certainly!" answered the Professor, stamping in his earnestness. "We are all very well off here. I tell you if it depended on me, Gallia would never approach the Earth again!"

# CHAPTER V.

## THE PROFESSOR QUITE AT HOME.

A FEW hours after the close of this remarkable interview the Captain, the Count, and Procopius were diligently comparing notes together. Of the absolute truth of the Professor's story no doubt was possible. It explained everything, not excepting the shallowness of the sea, the metallic dust of the bottom, the crystal formation of the coast.

"Yes!" said the Captain, "it completely clears up at last the enigma of the enormous disc I saw the first night after the cataclysm. It was the Earth itself that shone dimly behind the black clouds. It was the proximity of the Earth itself that raised to such an altitude the tide of the Gallian Sea that very night — the only instance we have ever had of a tide in Gallia. It was the Earth itself, accompanied by the moon, that Ben and I saw rising in the west on the evening of the thirteenth of January and which has been puzzling me so much ever since!"

"I cannot help agreeing with you, Captain," said

the Count. "Nothing can be clearer than the past, now that we look at it through the Professor's explanation. But how about the future? Is that clear too? The Comet's orbit may be elliptical, but does that prove that she will ever return to the Earth?"

"The Professor seems to think that she will," answered Procopius; "and I don't see why we should entertain the least doubt regarding the correctness of his calculations. So far, he has been perfectly correct, and he certainly is an extraordinary man."

"An additional reason why we should do everything to promote his comfort," said the Captain. "He is a most valuable acquisition to our little community, and in fact may be considered quite indispensable."

The next days were devoted to the task of providing the Professor with comfortable quarters. Fortunately he was one of those men who are not hard to be pleased in domestic arrangements and who find no trouble in accommodating themselves to everything. Let him only continue to do as he was doing, namely, passing days and nights in the skies, up among the stars, pursuing planets, riding on a comet's back, etc., and such questions as where he slept, what he ate or drank — only he should always have his coffee — he considered extremely insignificant.

In all probability he had hardly noticed the wonderful ingenuity and forethought that had turned the black jaws and womb of a volcano into a passable, even a pleasant, human abode. He even refused curtly and unceremoniously the use of the best chamber in spite of the Captain's and the Count's earnest entreaties that he should accept it. He had no desire to live in society. Give him, he said, some sort of an observatory, well situated both with regard to having a good view and being free from disturbance, where he could completely surrender himself to his astronomical observations, give him this, and he would trouble them for very little more.

It was in search of something of the kind that Servadac and Procopius started early next morning. Once more they were very fortunate. On the mountain side about a hundred feet above the main entrance, they soon discovered a niche or crevice, not very roomy indeed, but sufficiently capacious to hold an astronomer and his instruments quite comfortably. It had even space enough for a bed, a table, an armchair, a wardrobe, a bureau and several other indispensable articles of furniture, not forgetting of course the famous telescope, which a little ingenuity soon set so skilfully on its tripod as to admit of complete facility of handling. A little rill of lava, run over from the great fall, brought heat enough to render the general

temperature of this improvised observatory quite tolerable.

Here the Professor installed himself the very first
instant it was ready. Here he passed all his time,
rapidly swallowing the food brought to him at regular
intervals, sleeping little, observing during the night,
calculating during the day—in a word, living in a world
of his own, completely abstracted from the rest of the
little community. It was, probably, under the circumstances, the best possible arrangement for all. The
wisest treatment of an original of the Professor's
intractable nature is to give him completely his own
way.

The cold meanwhile had become pretty sharp, the
mercury standing no higher than 22 below zero, Fahr.,
or 54 degrees below freezing-point. And the mercurial
column was getting lower steadily. None of those os-
cillations of the thermometer so common in capricious
climates could be noticed here. The mercury sank
regularly every day, and it would continue to sink until
it should reach the lowest extremity of the colds of space.
Then, if the Professor's calculations were right, it would
begin to rise again, a sure proof that Gallia's journey
was once more becoming sunward.

Another phenomenon also contributed powerfully to
this total absence of oscillation on the part of the mercu-

OBSERVING DURING THE NIGHT.

rial column. Not a breath of wind disturbed the Gallian atmosphere. Not a particle of air suffered displacement. Everything, liquid or fluid, on Gallia's surface was frozen hard as a rock. No storms, therefore, of wind or rain, no electric disturbances of any kind. No cloud, mist, or vapor flecked the sky either at sunrise or sunset. None of those moist fogs or dry hazes, of such frequent occurrence in the Earth's circumpolar regions. The sky's serenity was of a purity invariable and unalterable, and whether pervaded, as in the daytime, by the solar rays, or, as in the night-time, by the effulgence of the stars, its temperature was constant, light or darkness leaving the mercurial column equally unaffected.

This extreme tranquillity of the atmosphere rendered the extreme cold comparatively easy to endure. It is well known, in fact, that excessive cold is by no means the direst foe that Arctic adventurers are called on to encounter. What dries up their lungs, after disordering them with such fatal effect, is not the fearful cold, but the sudden and violent winds, the cutting blasts, the smothering fogs, and the terrible snow storms. These are the polar navigator's deadly foes. But in calm weather, when the atmosphere is in a state of permanent tranquillity, whether he is a Parry wintering at Melville Island, a Kane on the 81st degree, a Hayes on the 82d, or a Hall approaching the 83d, if only well clad and well fed, he can easily brave cold the most intense. He has actually enjoyed it when the alcohol had fallen as low as 76 degrees below zero! Doctor Hayes says that this great depression of temperature, though at the least wind painful and dangerous, is hardly perceptible to the senses at periods of profound calm.

The little colony at Terre Chaude therefore found itself in very favorable conditions for enduring the colds of space without much inconvenience. Furs, prepared skins, and warm clothing of all kinds were in the greatest abundance. Food was good and plentifully supplied. Even out-door exercise could be enjoyed heartily, the extraordinary calm almost counteracting the extreme cold.

The Governor-General kept a close eye on the sanitary condition of his people. He made it his especial business to see that every individual among them, without exception, was well clad and well fed. Out-door amusements were not only prescribed, but rigorously insisted on. No one could exempt himself from the regular every-day programme. Even Pablo and Nina were not excepted. Not that these children had the least desire, however, to remain an instant longer within the mountain's dark cavities than they were obliged. Wrapped up and muffled until they looked like a pair of young Esquimaux, they were always the first on the skating-ground. Here their shout was the loudest, their laugh the merriest, their enjoyment the keenest. In fact, the joyous spirits of these innocent creatures, their graceful movements, their consideration for others, their never-ending playfulness and good-nature, acted on the rest like a charm, and contributed powerfully towards maintaining a state of cheerfulness among the little colony that under existing circumstances was of untold value.

It is hardly necessary to say that among the joyous group on the skating-ground Isaac's form was never visible. He kept himself altogether in the *Hansa*, apparently more gloomy and unsocial than ever. In short, a new light had broken on him. He doubted no longer. He felt he was on a Comet, millions and millions of miles away from the Earth, that dear spot so often the scene of many a profitable bargain.

Did his new situation affect him for the better? Did he reflect seriously and gratefully on the wonderful circumstances in which he now found himself? Did his heart soften towards the few human beings that the kind good God had left him for companions in the dreary land of death around him? Did he look on them no longer as fair game to be trapped and victims to be plundered, but as poor suffering fellow-creatures to be cherished and loved and made much of?

10

Alas! no such thought ever crossed his mind. He could not change for the better and be Dutch Isaac. His was a nature intensely and perhaps unalterably selfish. Instead of softening, he hardened; instead of thinking a little about others, he thought more than ever about himself; instead of contributing his share cheerfully towards the common good, he now busied himself exclusively in devising plans to make the most of the dreadful condition in which the Gallians were placed. It never seemed to occur to him that his own condition depended absolutely on the beck of the Captain. He never appeared to think of gratitude nor even of ordinary policy. He had unbounded confidence in Servadac's strict honor and integrity. Under the safeguard of a French officer, he felt himself perfectly secure as long as that officer could maintain his authority. But as to doing anything himself towards maintaining that authority, towards propitiating the Captain, towards gaining the good will of the colony by showing some active interest in its well being — such ideas he no more thought of than he did of turning preacher. His only thought was how to make the most of the situation, and here is how he reflected on his chances.

The Gallians should either return to the Earth, or they should not. If they missed returning and were to spend the rest of their days on the Comet, though gold would not be worth a great deal, it was clearly much better to have it than to be without it. But if they got back once more to *Terra Firma*, which, as the Professor asserted, would positively be the case, gold would be as valuable as ever. And here was a splendid opportunity to get plenty of it. In fact, if he only played his cards in a skilful manner, Isaac felt that, instead of losing by his two years' forced absence from the Earth, he had it in his power to be a considerable gainer. There was plenty of gold, both Russian and English, in Gallia. All he had to do to get it was, as he said, to play his cards well and never show his hand. By this he meant: First, to dispose of all his merchandise before the return to Earth, where it would be comparatively valueless; Second, to dispose of it only by degrees, a little at a time, none at any time unless when the demand, far in excess of the supply, should command a fair profit, that is, 2 or 3 hundred per cent. He giggled noiselessly as he rubbed his dirty hooky hands together. "I have them all under my thumb!" he muttered; "it will be my own fault if I do not keep them there!"

But we have taken up too much time already with the wicked old spider. Let us leave him spinning his cobwebs in the dark and lonely cabin of the *Hansa*, and return to the company of his contemplated victims and the more congenial atmosphere of the Nina Beehive.

On the twelfth of May, the Professor formally invited the Captain, the Count, and Procopius to his observatory. He wished them to examine a new document, but their visit was to last just one hour, not a moment longer. It is needless to say that the invitation was eagerly accepted. The Professor welcomed the party with one hand, while with the other he pointed at a sheet of paper spread out on the table.

They examined with great interest a diagram very carefully drawn, showing Gallia's elliptic orbit from the perihelion point nearest to the sun to its aphelion point between Jupiter and Saturn. This orbit was divided into twenty-four unequal parts, corresponding with the twenty-four months of the Gallian year. These curves represented the exact course of the monthly runs, which were further indicated by figures giving each amount in million leagues. The twelve first segments diminished gradually in length as they approached the aphelion point, thus strictly corresponding with Kepler's Third Law. This point once passed, the monthly runs should again increase in length according as Gallia approached the sun. During the month of April she had travelled 39 million leagues;

GALLIA'S ORBIT.

and on the first of May her total distance from the sun had bee¬ about 110 million leagues. Nothing could be clearer, more positive, more indisputable. If she continued to move with the same regularity that she had exhibited so far, nothing was more certain than that at the end of her two years' revolution, she would again meet the Earth at the identical point of her former collision. But what would be the consequences of this new encounter? Our three friends would like to know, but neither had the courage to ask the intractable Professor.

The Captain, however, began beating about the bush.

" My dear Master," said he, " I see by your diagram that during the present month of May Gallia is to travel only 30 million leagues, and that on the last day of the month she is to be only 139 million leagues from the sun. Is that quite certain ? "

"Nothing can be more certain ! " answered the Professor testily.

"And we have left behind us the zone of the minor planets ? "

" Can't you make use of your eyes? Don't you see where the Asteroid Zone is marked down ? "

" Oh, yes, I see ! Gallia then will — ah — will reach her aphelion point exactly one year after her perihelion ? "

" Exactly one year after."

10 *  H

"That is on the 15th of next January, is it not?"

"Of course on the 15th of Jan— Bah! What am I saying? Not at all on the 15th of January! Why do you say the 15th of January, Servadac?"

"Because, my dear Master, I always understood you to say that from the 15th of January to the 15th of January was exactly a year, of twelve months, nothing more, nothing less."

"A great deal less!" exclaimed the Professor.

"Less than twelve months!" cried the Captain.

"Yes, Servadac, a great deal less. Not less, I grant you, than twelve Earth months, but much less than twelve Gallia months.—What do you find so irresistibly comical in my observations, sir?" continued· the terrible Professor, suddenly turning on Procopius, on whose lips he had just detected a rising smile.

"I am only enjoying the idea, my dear Professor," replied Procopius quietly, "of your undertaking to re-form the Calendar."

"I undertake nothing, sir! Facts establish everything! Let us put ourselves in harmony with the resistless logic of incontestable facts!"

"Certainly, my dear Master!" said the Captain. "Nothing like logic! Let us follow it blindly — I mean manfully, wherever it chooses to take us!"

"I suppose, my dear sir," continued the Professor,

ignoring the Captain altogether, and evidently bent on demolishing Procopius, " that you admit that Gallia will return to her perihelion after a revolution two terrestrial years in length?"

" Well, yes, I admit it," answered Procopius.

" This revolution, constituting, as it does, the complete course of Gallia around the sun, must also constitute the Gallian year, must it not?"

"Yes, I admit that readily."

" This Gallian year, like every other year, should be divided into twelve months?"

"Y-e-s, if you like to so divide it, my dear Professor."

" How if I like? What has my liking or not liking got to do with it?"

Before Procopius could give an answer, the Captain, aiming above all things in keeping the Professor in good-humor, burst in rapidly:

" Of course it must be divided into twelve months, like every other year!"

" And of how many days must each of these months consist?" asked the Professor, once more directing his observations to the Captain.

" Of sixty days evidently," cried the Captain quickly, "since each day is in reality only half a day long!"

The Professor frowned.

"You are quite wrong, Servadac!" he cried as snappishly as an impatient teacher cries at a stupid pupil. "You don't mind what you are saying!"

"I'm on your side any way, my dear Master," said the Captain trying to smile.

The Professor tossed his head contemptuously.

"Volunteered help," he observed with considerable asperity, "unenlightened by reason or good sense, is oftener a clog than an aid. I want none of it!"

"Please explain the difficulty to us, my dear Professor," interposed the Count, an amused spectator of the whole scene. "We are all puzzled, myself as much as my friends."

"Puzzled!" exclaimed the Professor, giving his shoulders an impatient shrug. "Why puzzled? Nothing can be clearer! Come now, answer all! Must not every Gallian month comprise two Earth months?"

"Certainly!"

"Answer all! Why?"

"Because the Gallian year lasts two Earth years!"

"Answer all! How many Earth days in two Earth months?"

"Sixty Earth days!"

"Answer all! How many Gallian days are in sixty Earth days?"

" One hundred and twenty Gallian days ! "

" Correct ! Why so ? "

" Because our Gallian days are only twelve hours long ! "

" Now you see, don't you, of how many days each of our months must consist ? "

" Yes, clearly ! Each Gallian month must consist of one hundred and twenty Gallian days ! "

" I thought I could enable you to understand it at last ! " said the Professor with some complacency.

" We understand it all now perfectly, Professor," said the Count ; " but don't you think such a calendar likely to cause confusion — ? "

" Confusion ! " answered the Professor, " not at all ! Since the first of January the Gallian is the only calendar I reckon by."

" Your months then, dear Master," said the Captain rather gaily, " must contain one hundred and twenty days each ? "

" Exactly. Where is the harm in that ? "

" No harm whatever, unless perhaps that instead of being as we are at present in May you would put us only in March."

" Yes, Servadac ; yes, Messieurs, in March exactly. To-day is the 266th day of the Gallian year corresponding to the 133d of the terrestrial year. It is the 12th of Gallian March and in sixty Gallian days from now it will be —''

"The seventy-second of March!" interrupted the Captain. "Bravo, dear Professor! your calendar is admirable! I see it at a glance! Nothing like following up Logic to the bitter end!"

A flash through the spectacles showed that his pupil's irony had not escaped the Professor. At this moment, however, the clock fortunately struck nine.

"Time's up, Messieurs," said the Professor hastily, putting away his diagram. "Please to withdraw! I will send for you again when I shall have something new to communicate."

It was not until a month and three days afterwards, June 15th, that he sent for them again, and even then he dismissed them in five minutes, no more time being required for the news which he had to communicate. It was as follows: The present day was April the sixtieth, new calendar; in the latter half of March (the whole month of June) Gallia would have travelled no more than 27 million leagues; her distance from the sun would then be about 155 million leagues. The temperature was still steadily on the decrease; the atmosphere was as pure and calm as ever; in short, everything was in strict order and giving perfect satisfaction.

" *Tutto va bene!*" concluded the Professor, signalling his guests to depart, and talking several languages
at a time. "*Ol draï!* (this was his best offer at *all
right.*) *Parfait! Nil desperandum!*"

A week or two after this, the Captain, the Count,
Procopius and Ben Zouf were assembled in Central
Hall, reading, talking, discussing, employing every con-
trivance they could think of to make the morning pass
pleasantly, when suddenly who should burst into the
room but the Professor!

"Lieutenant!" he exclaimed, marching straight up
to Procopius, "I'm going to ask you a question.
Answer it without circumlocution or reserve of any
kind!"

"My dear Professor," replied Procopius, a little
stiffly, "I don't think I'm in the habit —"

"Yes! yes!" interrupted the Professor, impatiently.
"Don't waste time! I know all about that! Answer
my question, yes or no! Here it is! Have you circumnavigated Gallia along her equator or as nearly so as
possible?"

"Yes, Professor," answered Procopius, obeying a
wink from the Count..

"Very well, sir!" resumed the Professor in a tone to
remind you of a lawyer browbeating a stubborn witness,
"now, sir, did you or did you not, during this voyage

of circumnavigation, lay down the *Dobryna's* course on the chart?"

"Only approximately, Professor," was the reply, "that is to say, with no more aid than that afforded by the log and the compass. The altitude of the sun or stars I was unable to calculate."

"Very well, sir! Now what did you find to be the result of your calculations, such as they were?"

"That Gallia's circumference was about 2000 miles, which would give about 636 miles for her diameter."

"Y—e—s," said the Professor slowly as if talking to himself, "that would give a diameter about twelve times smaller than the Earth's."

He said no more for a few moments, and appeared to be lost in thought.

"Well!" he exclaimed suddenly, "in order to test and in fact complete my studies of Gallia, I must now have her surface, her volume, her mass, her density, and her gravity."

"As to her surface and volume, Professor," said Procopius, "nothing is easier than to calculate them, knowing her diameter as we do."

"Who said it was difficult to calculate them?" asked the Professor snappishly. "Such 'calculations' as that I could make before I left off wearing petticoats!"

"Oh!" cried Ben Zouf, hastily clapping his hand

"BE LIVELY, SERVADAC!"

on his mouth to suppress a noisy laugh. Since the fight about Montmartre he could not endure the Professor, and even the Captain's presence could now hardly keep him in order.

"Pupil Servadac, take your pen, sir!" continued the Professor, turning severely on the Captain. "Knowing the circumference of Gallia, what is her surface?"

"Certainly, dear Master," said the Captain, assuming the air of a diligent school-boy. "We have but to multiply the circumference by the diameter."

"Yes! yes! Don't be all the day about it! It should be done long ago! How much is it?"

"It is 2000 multiplied by 636," cried the Captain quickly, "or 1 million 272 thousand square miles!"

"Right, Servadac!" said the Professor. "Gallia's surface then, Messieurs, is about 160 times less than the Earth's."

"Poh!" muttered Ben, loud enough to be heard by those around him. "A tom-tit comet! I should be ashamed to discover it!"

"Now then, be lively, Servadac!" resumed the Professor. "What's Gallia's volume or bulk? Come, what's her volume?"

"Her volume — her volume," repeated the Captain slowly, trying by gaining time to collect his scattered thoughts.

11

"Certainly her volume! What! Servadac, do you forget how to calculate the volume of a sphere whose surface you already know? I'm ashamed of you!"

"I don't forget, my dear Master," said the poor Captain perspiring with eagerness, "I don't forget at all, but won't you give a fellow a little breathing time?"

"No, sir! Not a moment! No breathing time in simple mathematics!"

The Captain was half puzzled. The Professor was getting more and more excited. The bystanders had as much as they could do to keep from roaring. Even the cool Count had to cough and use his handkerchief.

"Come, come, Servadac!" continued the impatient Professor, "not done yet! What's the matter! The volume of a sphere —"

"Is equal to the surface," said the Captain, scratching his head, "multiplied by — by —"

"By one-third of the radius, sir!" cried the Professor, losing all patience. "By — the — third — of — the — radius! I shall have to tell you your name next, I suppose! Done yet?"

"Very nearly, dear Master! Let me see! The third of Gallia's radius is 106 and her surface is —"

"We know what her surface is! Will you be a year finding out her volume?"

"All right, dear Master! Hm — Hm —," cried the Captain, figuring like lightning.

"Well? How much is it?"

"134 millions 832 thousand cubic miles!" cried the Captain.

"Yes, that's Gallia's volume, gentlemen," said the Professor, looking around with an air of triumph. "My Comet, you see, is something to talk about!"

"Undoubtedly your Comet is a very respectable comet, Professor," observed Procopius, who wanted to say something, "even if she is at least 2000 times smaller than the Earth, whose volume in round numbers is about —"

"About 260 billions of cubic miles, sir! I know all that very well!" interrupted the Professor impatiently.

"And consequently she is at least 40 times smaller than the Moon, which is 50 times smaller than the Earth."

"I don't deny it, sir!" said the Professor angrily. "But may I take the liberty of asking what is the objective point of all these observations?"

"Simply this, Professor," said Procopius quietly. "Gallia, if seen at all, would appear to the inhabitants of the Earth no larger than a star of the seventh magnitude!"

"Holy name of a Bedouin!" exclaimed Ben, affecting contemptuous surprise; "is that the kind of a Comet we're on?"

"Hold your tongue, sir," cried the Professor, seriously irritated at this unseemly interruption.

"Call that a Comet!" cried Ben, the terrible avenger of Montmartre. "*I* call it a marble, a pea, a pin's head!"

"Hold your tongue at once, Ben Zouf, or quit the room!" cried the Captain, becoming quite angry and hastily approaching him.

"Such a Comet!" continued Ben laughing boisterously, while he cautiously backed away from the Captain; "a mustard-seed! a grain of sand! the little end of nothing! Ha! Ha! Ha! If I could not discover a better Comet than that I would shut up shop!" and for the next minute the vaulted caverns outside were heard ringing with his derisive cachinnations.

The Professor, though deeply irritated, would not compromise his dignity by appearing to notice the language of one whom he considered an underling. The storm would have probably fallen on Procopius had not that wily gentleman immediately taken the most energetic measures to ward it off. Opening his memorandum-book, apparently in a great hurry, he whipped out a loose sheet of paper and began contemplating it with the greatest apparent interest.

"Professor," said he with all possible seriousness, "I have just discovered that Gallia is no such small comet after all. Her diameter is at least 22 times greater than that of either the first comet of 1798, or of Gambart's, which appeared in 1805. It is nearly twice the size of the first comet of 1799, or of the only comet that appeared in 1807."

Though mollified a little in spite of himself, the Professor could not bear to show it.

"I have heard all this before, Lieutenant," he interrupted impatiently. "Tell me something I don't know! Perhaps *you* don't know that, when my Comet approached the sun, her tail was long enough to reach Mars!"

"I have no doubt, Professor, that your Comet is as large as any ten of the asteroids put together," said the Count, quietly putting in his oar.

"Large!" cried the Captain, rapidly dotting down and adding up some figures on a piece of paper. "I should say she is large! What is her superficial extent? More than 1¼ million square miles! That is considerably larger than the united areas of Italy, France, Spain, Austria, Germany, Denmark, Holland, Belgium, and the British Islands! What simpleton can call that a small Comet?"

"Well, Gallia's dimensions are not of the enormous order," said the Professor, visibly softening under the

11 *

insidious attacks of the conspirators; "but, take her all in all, and you will find her to be one of the most re- markable Comets that have ever shown themselves within the historic ages.   In fact, she is at present indissolubly connected forever with terrestrial history.   She is, there- fore, well worth our closest attention, Messieurs, and what I desire you to do now is to continue the study of her details.   They are intensely interesting.   We know already her diameter, her circumference, her surface, her volume.   That is certainly something, but it is not enough.   I desire you to obtain by direct measurement her mass and density, and thus learn what amount of gravity she exerts at her surface."

"Her mass and density!" exclaimed the Count, open- ing his eyes.   "That sounds like putting Gallia into the scales and weighing her!   Shall you not find such a task a rather difficult one, Professor?"

"Difficulties I meet with every day, but I conquer them!" said the Professor magnificently.

"They bend before you, my dear Master," cried the Captain enthusiastically, "like reeds before the blast!"

"For my part, however," said Procopius, "I see a difficulty in the task great enough to render it almost an impossibility.   We can't tell of what substance the kernel of Gallia is formed."

"You can't?" asked the Professor.

"No," said the Count. "We know nothing whatever about it. Until that is ascertained—"

"Poh!" interrupted the Professor slightingly. "The nature of Gallia's substance gives no complication whatever to the problem."

"When you set about it, my dear Master," said the Captain, "I hope you will not forget that we are most anxious to give you all the assistance that may be in our power."

"I can't commence it at once," said the Professor impatiently. "I have the month's observations and calculations still to go through. You can wait until that part of my work is done, can't you?"

"How, Professor!" answered Procopius. "We shall be most happy to wait as long as ever you please!"

"And even longer!" cried Ben's voice in jeering tones from the dark end of the Hall.

"Well then, Messieurs," cried the Professor, hastily picking up his papers and bouncing out of the room, "I'm leaving you now, and you must not expect to see me before the sixty-second of April!"

# CHAPTER VI.

## GALLIA'S ELEMENTS.

GALLIA, meantime, went on pursuing the even tenor of her elliptic orbit without trouble or interference from any quarter whatsoever. Her little moon Nerina stuck faithfully by her side, performing her little revolutions of half a month with the most admirable exactness. Everything, in short, was working with the utmost smoothness, and no obstacle, external or internal, so far seemed likely to disturb the general harmony until the end of the Gallian year.

But, in spite of all these flattering assurances, the Captain, the Count, and Procopius still felt anything but assured. Would Gallia surely return to the Earth? If so, how was the meeting to take place? Should not the second shock, in all probability, be attended with most disastrous consequences? Was there any possibility of avoiding or even of diminishing these consequences?

Though continually debated, these puzzling questions always remained unanswered. The Professor, the only one who could venture to approach them, still remained

shut up in his observatory, where not a single member
of the community, even the redoubtable Ben included,
would undertake to disturb him.

We must however say that, with the exception of
the three chiefs, no member of the community mani-
fested the slightest desire to disturb him with these
questions or with questions of any kind. The Russians
resembled the faithfullest of dogs in devotion to their
master and in forgetfulness of self. Wherever *he* was,
there *they* were perfectly satisfied to be. Nor did the
Spaniards' practical philosophy show any signs of wearing out. About what should *they* ask questions? Why
trouble themselves about returning to the Earth? Did
they ever have easier or better times there? What matter where Gallia was going? Supposing she *did* quit the
solar system and start off on a journey through other parts
of the starry universe, what difference would it make to
them? As long as they had enough to eat and drink,
heat enough to keep them warm, pure air enough to
keep them healthy, and, particularly, as long as they
had nearly every hour of the twelve so completely at
their disposal that they could dance, sing and castanet
to their heart's content, why should they be curious to
know if they were returning to Earth, or even to know
whither they were going at all?

But undoubtedly the happiest members of this model

I

colony were Pablo and Nina. School once over — and
the Captain by his brightness, his fun, and his natural
love of children made the school hours delightful —
what grand times they had playing "hide and seek"
in the galleries, climbing the rocks outside, skating over
the glassy sea, or fishing on the banks of the warm lake!

How could these innocent creatures ever think of
troubling themselves with dark surmises regarding the
future? What cause could they have for regretting the
past?

One day Pablo asked his little companion if her
parents were yet alive.

"No, Pablo," was her reply. "They died so long
ago that I can't remember them. How about yours?"

"Mine are dead too, Nina. What were you doing
in that island when the Governor found you?"

"Tending goats among the rocks, Pablo. What
had you to do down there? Tend goats too?"

"No. I was employed in a livery-stable. I had to
drive ten horses over the plain every morning to water
them."

"Hard work I should think."

"Yes, but I loved the horses, Nina."

"I loved my goats too, Pablo, and they loved me,
didn't they, Marzy?" and she looked lovingly at the
goat nestling at her feet.

NINA AND PABLO.

" Ma-ah ! " said Marzy.

After a few moments' pause, "It's much nicer here, Pablo," resumed the girl.

"No comparison, Nina."

"Besides goats and horses we have men to love, Pablo."

"I like them all, Nina, but that Dutch Isaac!"

"Oh Pablo! Poor old Isaac has no one to care for him! He is all the time by himself in that lonely ship!"

"I'm glad of it, Nina! I should hate to see his ugly old face around here. He always looks so cross, and he never stops mumbling to himself."

"Perhaps he is thinking, Pablo, of his poor little boys and girls that he has left behind him!"

"I should not like to be one of his little boys, Nina! I should run away at the very first chance!"

"I would not run off, Pablo! I would stay with him, and then he would have somebody to talk to."

"I should like to be the Governor's son, Nina."

"You *are* his son, Pablo. He calls you his little son and me his little daughter!"

"Then you and I are brother and sister, Nina!"

"Of course we are, Pablo. And the Count and the Lieutenant are our uncles!"

"And Negrete is our grandfather!"

"And Benni Zufo is our big brother!"

Here the children laughed heartily.

Then resuming a grave and steady air, Nina raised her forefinger towards her companion and said :

"They are all our dear friends, Pablo. We must do everything to please them and make them happy."

In fact these poor children were as happy as the day is long. Every one loved them. Even the animals knew them and recognized them with delight. What past memory of the hot plains of Andalusia could excite a regret in Pablo? Why should a recollection of the barren rocks of Sardinia start a tear in Nina? The new, in fact, not the old, seemed to be their world. They were the only real Gallians on the Comet.

On the sixty-second of April—July 31 old calendar— faithful to his promise, the Professor informed the Captain and his friends that he would meet them that morning in Central Hall. Already expecting that notice, they obeyed it with alacrity, promising themselves, among the other subjects on which they desired information, that they should soon learn something positive regarding the mysterious substance forming the material of Gallia.

"Messieurs," said the Professor, hastily entering, "I am glad you have answered my invitation so promptly. Now please take your seats and listen attentively while I read my regular report regarding the first half of the month of April."

(This was the month of July, according to the old calendar.)

"Gallia has made 51 millions of miles, and her present distance from the sun is about 420 millions of miles, about 4½ times greater than the distance of the Earth from the sun. Her present velocity, however, is almost equal to the Earth's, being little more than 50 millions of miles a terrestrial month.

"Now to the main point. To-day we have to complete our study of my Comet's elements. We shall first take her gravity.

"Now what is to be the standard of gravity? You all know that the Earth exerted a certain force on a certain substance at a certain distance, say a few yards, from her surface. A pound weight, for instance, was pulled down with a pound force. This unit was therefore the standard of terrestrial gravity. But you have all remarked that this standard would not do for Gallia. Here an Earth pound is *not* pulled down with an Earth pound force. You have all remarked how considerably your muscular strength has increased in consequence of this diminution of gravity. But the exact ratio of this diminution of gravity, the exact ratio of this increase of muscular power—none of you have calculated, none of you, I think, are able to calculate. This, therefore, is what we are now about to ascertain.

12

"We must premise by defining the meaning of the terms *mass* and *density*.

"What is the mass of a body? The mass is not its *volume* or *bulk*, but the collected quantity of its matter, and it is represented in figures by what is called its *weight*. A cork ball has a greater *volume*, but an iron ball, much smaller, has a greater *mass*. This explains the meaning of *density*. Mass is the weight of the whole body: *density* the weight of a *given part* of it. An iron ball may have a greater *mass* than a gold ball, but the gold ball has greater *density*.

"We have to find the answers to three questions:

"First. *What is the absolute gravity of Gallia?* that is, *How much does what on Earth we called a pound weigh on her surface?*

"Second. *What is the absolute quantity of Gallia's matter?* that is, *What is her mass, and consequently her weight?*

"Third. *What is the total quantity of matter contained in Gallia's volume or bulk?* that is, *What is her density?*

"These questions once answered, Messieurs, Gallia will have no more secrets for us. We shall undertake to solve them by the rigidest and simplest of all means — by actual and direct measurement. Remember the order of the questions. We shall, first, ascertain Gallia's *attraction;* second, her *weight.*"

Here Ben suddenly ran out of the Hall as if in a great hurry.

"Third and last, her *density.* Now, Messieurs, we shall begin by ascertaining how much an Earth pound weighs on Gallia's —"

"I can't find it, Professor!" cried Ben Zouf, suddenly rushing back into the Hall and looking very much distressed.

"What can't you find, sir?" exclaimed the Professor, furious at being interrupted.

"A pair of scales to weigh your Comet in, Professor!" answered Ben, looking as innocent as a baby. "Besides, Professor," he went on, with a sly wink at Negrete, "even if I could find one, I don't know how you could hook it up."

"Servadac," said the Professor with as much dignity as his hot temper allowed him to assume, "this man of yours is a bigger jackass than even *you* ever were when a boy. If you don't debestialize him a little, I shall have to bid you all good-by for another month."

The Captain's only reply was a rush at Ben. But his intention to seize him by the collar and give him a good kicking was this time frustrated by his Orderly's superior agility. After a *bootless* chase outside for a minute or two, the Captain came back to his place, flushed and breathless, and looking decidedly irritated.

The Professor was going on as if nothing had occurred.

" Messieurs, in consequence of Gallia's smaller mass, her attraction, I need hardly say, is less powerful, and consequently every object must weigh less on her surface than on the Earth's.  But what is the absolute difference of the two weights ?  That is what we must first find out.

" How shall we set about it ?—"

" I really don't know, my dear Master," answered the Captain readily, mistaking the Professor's rhetorical flourish for a direct question requiring an answer ; " an ordinary pair of scales would not do at all.  Each pan being equally influenced by Gallia's attraction, it would never aid us to find out the exact relation between an Earth pound and a Gallia pound."

" Very true," quickly observed the Count, repeating the Captain's blunder ; " the pound weight having lost as much of its own weight as the object you were going to weigh —"

" Messieurs ! Messieurs ! " interrupted the Professor, losing all patience at these uncalled-for remarks, " if you tell me all this for my particular instruction, you are simply wasting so much breath !  I know all that as well as you do !  Probably a great deal better !  Answer only when you are asked !  Until then listen attentively !

Don't say one word more until I get through this little problem in practical astronomy!''

Having restored complete silence by this burst, the Professor paused a little while to collect his thoughts, and then resumed:

" How shall we set about it? How shall we find the difference in the two weights? In one way, and one way only—by practical experiment. Have you such things as a spring-balance and a pound weight in your possession?''

This time the Professor's pause was a real one, made to elicit information and not to produce a rhetorical effect, but the Captain and the Count were so much afraid of making another blunder that they kept still as mice. The Professor tried to be more explicit.

"I ask you again have you no such thing as a spring-balance among your stores? Nothing else will do. A spring-balance shows the weight absolutely, not relatively. Attraction exerts no power on it whatever. If I suspend an Earth pound to a spring-balance, the needle will tell me its Gallian weight. This will therefore at once give us the exact difference between Gallia's attraction and the Earth's attraction. Therefore I repeat my question. Have you a spring-balance? Come! Don't all speak at once!''

It now began to dawn on the audience that the Pro-

12 *

fessor was asking a real question, but as nobody was quite certain on the point, nobody would open his mouth by way of reply. The Captain therefore looked at the Count, the Count at Procopius, Procopius at the Russians, the Russians at the Spaniards, the Spaniards at Pablo and Nina, and Pablo and Nina at the little goat Marzy, whose frolicsome disposition they were doing their best to repress.

"Are you all deaf?" exclaimed the Professor, beginning to get angry at the prolonged silence. " Must I speak louder? Have — you — such a thing as — a — spring — bal — ance ? "

A general shaking of heads and lifting up of arms was the only reply. The Professor began to perceive that his audience interpreted his orders too literally.

" Servadac ! " cried the Professor, directly addressing the Captain. " Don't you hear my question ? Why not give me an answer ? "

" I am sorry to say, my dear Master," stammered the Captain, after consulting with Procopius, " that there is no such thing as a spring-balance in Terre Chaude ! "

" What ? " cried the Professor, furious at the disappointment. " No spring-balance ! Then I may as well take up my papers and return to my observatory ! "

A general groan was the reply to these terrible words.

" Once more and for the last time," cried the Professor, on the point of starting, "have you no spring-balance?"

No reply.

"Well, find a spring-balance by this day month," said the Professor, half-way out of the Hall, "or —"

"We have a spring-balance!" cried a low voice evidently some distance off.

"What's that?" asked the Professor, suddenly stopping short.

"We have a spring-balance!" said the same voice.

"Who says so?" asked the Captain, vainly looking around for the speaker.

"Benni Zufo!" answered Nina, pointing at a man's form crouching behind a projecting rock.

"Where is the spring-balance?" asked the Professor in his shrillest tones.

No reply.

"Ben Zouf!" cried the Captain, half pleased, half angry.

"Present!" said Ben, stepping forward and giving the military salute.

"Why don't you answer the Professor?"

"May I take my place?" asked Ben in a whining school-boy voice that made even the Russians titter.

"Yes! take your place!" said the Captain. "All is

forgiven if you can tell us where to find a spring-balance!"

Ben came forward with a sheepish air on his face and a roguish light gleaming in his eye. He looked around very submissively, bowed very low to the Professor, crossed his arms over his breast, and assumed the air of a witness determined to testify to the truth, even if every letter was to cost him his life.

"Now, sir, where is that spring-balance?" asked the Professor in tones of thunder.

"Please your Professorship, I saw one at Dutch Isaac's."

"Are you certain?"

"I am, please your Professorship."

"Why didn't you tell us so at once? Why did you keep us waiting?"

"Please your Professorship, I was not here," said Ben in tones of injured but patient innocence. "I had tried to make myself useful, but was put out for my pains!"

"No more talk, Ben Zouf!" cried the Captain. "Go at once to the *Hansa!* Ask Isaac for the loan of his spring-balance! Get it, and return with it immediately!"

"Get it whether Isaac is willing or not, Governor?" asked Ben with sudden animation and straightening himself up. "Say but the word, and I shall fetch that spring-balance as sure as Montmartre is the finest spot in Paris!"

"No, no, Ben Zouf! No force-work with Isaac! If he is willing to lend, well and good! If not — stay — I'd better accompany you myself.. I'm afraid you would get into a difficulty with Isaac."

"I should like to go too, Captain," said the Count. "I am a little curious to know how Isaac is getting along in his lonely vessel."

"All right, Count! Come along! My dear Master, we shall be back in a few minutes."

"Before the Count starts," said the Professor, "I want him to order one of his men to cut me out of the solid rock a block measuring exactly one cubic foot."

"Certainly, Professor," said the Count courteously. "The machinist will do everything in his power for you with the greatest pleasure, only we must first furnish him with a measure exactly a foot in length."

"Of course, of course," said the Professor impatiently, "that's understood. What's the difficulty?"

"The difficulty, Professor, is that we have no foot-measure."

"No foot-measure either!" cried the Professor hotly. "What kind of people are you? I thought you had made some pretension to civilization!"

"Have we any such thing as a foot-measure, Ben Zouf?" whispered the Captain.

"No foot-measure among our own stores," answered Ben, loud enough for all to hear. "But I have no doubt Dutch Isaac has plenty of foot-measures. The old miser has everything — but charity!"

"I will go see Dutch Isaac myself!" suddenly exclaimed the Professor, throwing on his coat, pulling the hood over his head, and hastily quitting the Hall. "Come along, Servadac, and any one else that wishes to join us!"

He was instantly followed by the Captain, the Count, Procopius and, of course, by Ben Zouf, who could not think of remaining behind when there was so much sport in prospect. Hurriedly pulling on their overcoats, they ran after the Professor through the galleries, and soon found themselves descending, in Indian file, the icy road leading from the cavern to the sea-beach.

The temperature was very low, 30 below zero Fahrenheit, but nobody seemed to mind it. Beard, mustaches and eyebrows, were soon covered with crystals, the congelation of their breaths by the freezing air. Their faces were soon bristling with fine ice needles, glistening, white, sharp,

Like the bristles of the fretful porcupine.

GOING TO SEE DUTCH ISAAC.

Though it was by no means a new experience, the Count's party laughed heartily at each other's comical figures as they cautiously stepped on the slippery footway. The little Professor undoubtedly made the most fun. Wrapped up in his furs and skins, nothing of his face visible except his enormous spectacles, he waddled along like a fat Esquimaux with fishy eyes. He was continually slipping, and when he came down once or twice with a heavy bump, Ben was seized with such a fit of coughing that Procopius for a little while actually thought he was choking.

It was now eight o'clock in the morning. The sun was approaching the zenith, but his disc was now so much reduced in size by distance that he somewhat resembled a cool, white, wintry moon. His rays fell on the landscape, but they brought only a dim light and little or no heat. The rocks along the shore, and the rough flanks of the volcano itself, deeply covered with the snows formed from the last vapors in the Gallian atmosphere, gleamed with a whiteness of dazzling brilliancy. In the background, all the way up to the smoking cone that commanded the whole of this gloomy territory, stretched a hyperborean carpet, immense in extent, spotless in purity. But towards the northern slope of the volcano a great black zigzag rent disfigured the carpet. It was the lava hissing and flowing and moving, and here and there glowing with a lurid light. Further down it broke into a thousand branches, which, running at random and winding here and there according to the slopes and hollows of the mountain, finally united to fall into the Central Cavern, whence they hurried to the northern face of the mountain to take their final perpendicular plunge into the seething ocean.

Right above the cavern's mouth, nearly two hundred feet above the sea level, could be seen a dark hole, on each side of which a slender rill of lava plainly showed its devious track amid the dazzling snow. Out of it projected something like a flagstaff, which closer inspection, however, showed to be the Professor's telescope levelled at the southern sky from the Professor's observatory.

No line of demarcation separated the white beach from the white sea. High above this vast and dazzling whiteness and offering a strong contrast to its monotony stretched a cloudless sky of pale and lightly purplish azure.

In one particular part of the shore were the countless foot-tracks of the Gallians, who assembled here every day either to gather ice to be melted into fresh water, or else to put on their skates, very convenient seats being furnished by the numerous rocks around. Away to the right out on the frozen sea could be seen the countless curves made by the flying skaters over its glassy surface, intersecting, intertwining, entangling, and in short presenting the net-work pattern woven by water-insects reeling in circles on summer evenings over the silver surface of a placid lake.

A distance of two or three furlongs separated the shore from the little bay in which the two vessels were at anchor. The Professor, looking neither to right nor left, made straight for the *Hansa;* but the Captain called the Count's attention to a strange phenomenon. Instead of continuing at their original level with the ocean surface, the *Hansa* and the *Dobryna* had been lifted out of the water by the ice as it formed beneath their keels. They were now at least twenty feet higher than they had been a few months before.

" What do you think of that? " the Count asked of Procopius.

" It is interesting in the nature of its growth, though decidedly disquieting as to its result," was the reply. " The ice is forming below these vessels to an immense depth ; the crust therefore gradually thickens and by its comparative buoyancy lifts them up with a force that is actually irresistible."

" Will this upheaving action have any limit? " asked the Count.

" I can't say, Father," replied Procopius. " All I

13                    K

know is that at present the cold is very far from having attained its maximum."

"I should say so indeed!" exclaimed the Professor, suddenly facing his companions. "At least I should hope so! It would hardly be worth while to travel a distance of 200 millions of leagues from the sun and find after all nothing more striking than the pitiful temperature of the Arctic regions!"

Then, turning round just as suddenly, he started towards the vessel as rapidly as ever.

"I don't think the cold will be much worse, however," said Procopius to his companions. "The temperature of space, I understand, is not much lower than sixty or seventy below zero, a degree of cold which with some management becomes quite tolerable."

"Bah!" said the Captain. "A fig for such cold! As long as the wind holds off, I don't care how low the thermometer sinks. Don't you see it yourselves? In spite of the cold not a single cough or sneeze is heard day or night!—But, Lieutenant," he continued, addressing Procopius, "do you really think the vessels are in danger in case the ice keeps on accumulating under their keels?"

"They are in very great danger, Captain," said Procopius. "If they are lifted so high as to be in danger of toppling over, how are we to save them from complete destruction? Even if they rise no higher than they are now, how are we to save them when the thaw comes? Many a noble whaling-ship has been thus irrecoverably lost in the Arctic seas."

"But it won't do to lose these vessels," said the Captain; "they are our only refuge when the colds are past. Let us put our heads together to devise some plan to save them."

By this time the Professor had reached the *Hansa* and was beginning to ascend the icy steps lately cut by Isaac for his own convenience. But what could Isaac do when the *Hansa* would be lifted a hundred feet above the surface?

Only the outline of the vessel's hull was visible, enveloped as it was by a shell of ice three or four feet thick. That all was not dead, however, beneath this ice pile was sufficiently shown by a light bluish smoke curling out of a chimney that projected a foot or two above the surface of the hardened snow.

"The old miser must have hard work in trying to keep his carcass warm," said Ben Zouf, now joining the party.

"The work is really not so difficult as you think, Ben Zouf," said Procopius. "You see that coat of ice? Well, that serves the purpose of perhaps fifty folds of blanketing. It keeps in the heat and keeps out the cold wonderfully. I should not wonder if Isaac found his quarters tolerably comfortable."

"The old curmudgeon's usual luck, I suppose!" said Ben half bitterly. Then raising his voice, "Halloo!" he cried, "Shylock! Judas! Issachar! Come out here, and see your betters!" Hastily passing the Professor on his way up the ice-mound, Ben followed a little path crossing the deck, which Isaac's own hands had kept free from snow and ice, and began lustily pounding the caboose-door at the head of the stairs leading into the cabin.

"Hello!" he began crying again. "Do you hear? Come out here at once and receive in a proper manner the gentlemen honoring you with such an unexpected visit! Come! Don't stop to dress! We'll excuse the appearance of your shirt and collar."

He stopped for a moment to listen. No sign of any one stirring.

"Hello!" he resumed, howling with all his might. "Issachar! I say! Show yourself! We're impatient to feast our eyes on the charms of your beauteous phizmahogany!"

# CHAPTER VII.

## THE SPRING-BALANCE.

WHILE Ben was pounding, the rest of the party
remained shivering on the ice-bank outside the
vessel, kicking their heels together to keep their feet
warm.

Suddenly the upper part of the caboose-door opened a
little, and Isaac put out his head cautiously.

"Who's there?" he cried, looking around in great
alarm; then seeing the party, though probably not recognizing them in furs, he drew back quickly, exclaiming :

"Go away! There's nobody here! I have nothing
either to lend, sell, or give! Nothing whatever! Go
away!"

"Softly, friend Isaac," said the Captain a little im-
periously. "I hope you don't take us for thieves!"

"Oh! it's you, Signor Governor-General," cried
Isaac in a whining tone. "I had not the happiness
to recognize you at once, s' help me Father Abraham!
Excuse me! You are very kind indeed to honor my
poor vessel with your gracious presence!"

But he still kept the lower part of the door closed, and the upper part only half open.

"Come, Potiphar!" cried Ben, getting impatient. "Stow that patter! Open the door and welcome the gentlemen in!"

"Gentlemen," whined Isaac, opening the upper door a little wider, but ready to close it again at the least sign of danger; "this favor is altogether too distinguished for poor Isaac! To what am I indebted for it?"

"Oh, we just want to have a little talk with you," said the Captain, trying to keep his temper.

"I am very much flattered and gratified by the signal favor," said Isaac, still keeping cautiously behind the door; "please tell me what you want, and I will try to answer you the best I know how!"

"That's all very well, Isaac," said the Captain curtly, seeing his companions becoming impatient; "but you don't appear to notice that it is very cold out here. We are of opinion that we could enjoy your conversation with keener relish if seated comfortably in your cabin."

"You — you — want to enter my cabin!" stammered Isaac, opening the door very slowly and unwillingly.

"Exactly, Isaac," said the Captain, advancing with his companions; "that is precisely what we want. Please stand aside!"

"Gentlemen!" cried Isaac, still holding the door

only half open, "I protest—I have nothing to offer you—I am only a poor man, s' help me Father Abraham!"

"Oh, Haman! We're sick of that cackle!" cried Ben roughly, pushing open the door and laying a brawny hand on Isaac's breast. "Stand aside, and give way to the Governor and his friends!"

"Listen, Isaac!" said the Captain, standing at the head of the stairs. "We do not come at present to take anything from you against your will. But I now repeat what I have already told you several times—the instant the common interest will require an appropriation of the *Hansa's* cargo—that instant I shall not have the slightest hesitation in seizing it for the public good—paying you, as long as we have the money, the current European prices for your goods."

Then the Captain and his companions descended the steps.

"I understand it all," murmured Isaac to himself, closing the door carefully, and shuffling down the cabin steps after his guests. "You are not coming to take anything now. All right! As for the current European prices, all right too! my fine Captain. Your current European prices will find themselves snugly changed into current Gallian prices, or my name's not Dutch Isaac!"

The cabin was small, cheerless, cold and dirty. In one corner was a rusty stove, in which a few bits of coal were doing their best not to burn. In another was the miserable cot, serving equally badly for a seat by day and a bed by night. In a third lay a heap of coals and an empty scuttle. In the end of the room, opposite the entry, stood an old closet, its heavy doors carefully closed, bolted and padlocked. A few stools, a greasy deal table, a chair or two, an old barrel, and the commonest kitchen utensils, completed the furniture of an apartment anything but comfortable, but eminently worthy of its master.

The first act performed by the company on entering was done by Ben Zouf.

"Holy name of an iceberg!" he cried with chattering teeth. "It's colder in this pigsty than in the snow outside! Let us fire up a little!"

So saying, he hastily filled the coal-scuttle and began emptying its contents into the stove with no stingy hand.

"Blessed Father Abraham!" cried Isaac in consternation, seizing the scuttle and trying in vain to wrest it from Ben, "what is the Signor Ben Zhouf doing? Does he want to ruin a poor struggling man? Oh what unholy waste and prodigality! Don't squander the blessed combustible so, good Signor Ben Zhouf! I love that coal as much as I love the blood of my veins! For the love of heaven, let me have the scuttle!"

"Let go, you wicked old skinflint!" cried Ben beginning to feel angry. "Do you want to freeze your guests? If you don't let go at once, I'll put you outside and keep you there until we burn every morsel of coal in that pile!"

"Let Ben Zouf have his way this time, Isaac!" said the Captain quietly but decidedly. "He is used to be warm and comfortable, and there's no use in trying to prevent him. Besides, we shall pay you for all the extra coal burned while we are here."

At the magic word "pay" Isaac's nervous grip on the scuttle instantly relaxed. In a second or two he let go of it altogether; then, going over to the coal pile, he pulled out a memorandum-book and began jotting down items with the greatest care.

In a few minutes, thanks to Ben's intelligent management of the stove, a brisk fire made the temperature tolerable if not comfortable. All took seats as well as they could, except Isaac, who still remained standing in the corner, watching the coal and making his calculations.

"Isaac," said the Captain, endeavoring to assume a stern air, "put that book aside for a moment and listen to me."

Isaac put the book carefully in the breast of his old coat, crossed his arms, bowed his head, and stood before the Captain with the air of a criminal about to hear his death-warrant.

"We have come to ask a favor," began the Captain.

"A — a favor — Governor-General!"

"Yes, a favor in the interest of the community."

"But — I take — I have no interest in the community."

"Listen, Isaac, and don't cry before you are hurt! We are not going to roast you alive!"

"A fa — favor! Ask a favor of a poor struggling man like me! s' help me Fa —"

"Yes, Isaac," continued the Captain trying to keep a straight face, and speaking in tones of the greatest solemnity. "We have come here to ask you a favor. Keep still, until I explain its nature."

Concluding from the seriousness of the Captain's tones that a requisition was about to be made upon at least half his property, Isaac began to tremble with real alarm, though at heart as cool and as much on his guard as ever.

"We want you to lend us —"

"I have nothing to lend! I never lend!" interrupted Isaac, turning pale at the word, and almost shrieking in his anxiety.

"A FAVOR, GOVERNOR-GENERAL!"

"What! not even a spring-balance?" asked the Captain, with a quiet smile.

"A spring-balance!" repeated Isaac, hardly believing his ears, and evidently much relieved, though he still tried to throw into his words the despairing expression of a man compelled to loan his last dollar on bad security. "A spring-balance! Lend a spring-balance!"

"Yes!" cried the Professor impatiently, much disgusted with the unexpected delay. "Don't you know what's a spring-balance?"

"Doesn't he though?" cried Ben still busy at the stove. "And can't he use it too! Many a time I saw him weighing coffee and even money with it in Gourbi Island."

"Won't you have the goodness, Isaac, to lend us that spring-balance?" asked the Captain with much politeness.

"Lend, Signor Governor? *Lend!* S' help me —"

"Only for a single day, Isaac," interrupted the Professor, getting tired of the scene. "We shall return it to-morrow."

"Oh my good Signor Professor," whined Isaac, "my spring-balance is a very delicate instrument. The steel is easily snapped, especially in this cold weather. I hope you would not think of using it to weigh anything heavy."

"Nothing heavier than a chunk of the volcano!" cried Ben.

"Holy Father Abraham!"

"Better than that," cried the Professor; "we are going to weigh the Comet with it!"

"Merciful Heaven!" cried Isaac ready to drop, between sham alarm and real anxiety.

"Suppose, however, Isaac," said the Captain, "that we wanted your spring-balance to weigh nothing heavier than a pound?"

"Even a pound, Signor Governor," murmured Isaac, hardly knowing what to say, "even one pound — such weather as this — such a very delicate instrument!"

"But a pound won't weigh even a pound in Gallia," observed the Captain. "So your delicate instrument runs very little danger."

"That being the case — Signor Governor — I — I think I might risk it —" said Isaac feeling his way cautiously — "but lending — your Excellency — *lending* —"

"Well!" interrupted the Count bluntly. "If you won't lend it, will you sell it?"

"Sell it!" cried Isaac, as if somebody had asked him to sell his vertebral column. "Sell my spring-balance! How could I ever dispose of my merchandise? How could I make sure that my good customers should have their fair money's worth? My scales are lost. I have nothing left now but this poor delicate little instrument, exceedingly accurate and exceedingly just, and they want to take it away from the poor old struggling man! Hoo! Hoo!"

Here he pulled out an old handkerchief to wipe his eyes with, but while pretending to dry his tears he was all the time watching everybody eagerly through the holes.

"Hang the old curmudgeon!" cried Ben suddenly, striking the stove with a piece of coal and making noise enough to startle everybody. "I only wish the Governor would let me deal with him!"

But the Captain kept his temper. He was determined to exhaust every form of persuasion before resorting to anything like force-work.

"Isaac," said he, "your tears are rather premature. Put that old handkerchief away and listen! You are not willing to lend us your spring-balance?"

"Alas! Signor Governor, how can I?"

"Nor sell it?"

"Sell? Never!"

"Well, you may be perhaps willing to hire it?"

Again the little eyes gleamed like two coals of fire.

"Hire it," repeated Isaac slowly, trying to repress his eagerness. "Hire it — would you become security,

14

Governor-General, for not only its safe return, but also for whatever damage may befall it ? "

" Certainly ! "

" Would — would you mind leaving a deposit before-hand, to indemnify me in case of injury ? "

" Of course.   How much do you require ? "

" How much are you willing to give, Signor Governor ? "

" Well, the value of the instrument is at most a dollar or two.   Will twenty dollars do for a deposit ? "

" Twenty dollars !   Are you aware, Signor Governor, that it is the only instrument of the kind in this new world of ours ? "

" I am aware of it !   I know it only too well," said the Captain, showing some irritation in spite of himself.

" However," continued Isaac, watchfully eyeing the Captain, " seeing it is you, Signor Governor, twenty dollars may do for a deposit — that is, if the money is in gold, — none of your rag money for me ! "

" The twenty dollars shall be in gold."

" And you want to hire my balance — an article so extremely indispensable — you want to hire it for a day ? "

" For one single day."

" And for this loan you propose to pay — how much, Signor Governor ? "

While the Captain hesitated, the Count cut in.

"Five dollars, Isaac. Will five dollars satisfy you for the loan of your balance for a single day?"

"Gentlemen," whined Isaac, struggling hard to hide his joy, "you have everything in your own hands. You are great lords, but I am only a poor struggling man, and must therefore submit to whatever terms you may think proper to propose. Only the five dollars must be in gold too, and paid in advance!"

The bargain thus concluded, Isaac, turning his face aside to conceal his satisfaction, hastily left the cabin to fetch the instrument.

"The wicked old thief!" exclaimed Ben Zouf, again trying to let off steam by breaking a lump of coal on the stove. "Catch that fellow selling his birthright for a mess of pottage! Governor, I must say Esau has pulled the wool over your eyes this time!"

"I don't deny that he has had the best of the bargain!" said the Captain, looking a little ashamed of himself.

"Five dollars for hire, and twenty dollars on deposit for an old spring-balance worth at most a dollar or two — I can't understand it!" cried Procopius, apparently unable to master the situation.

"I'm afraid I'm losing my temper!" cried the Count, ordinarily so sedate and impassive.

"Messieurs!" began the Professor, but Isaac's sudden return left his remarks unsaid.

"Here's my instrument, my good gentlemen," said Isaac, holding it with ostentatious care in one hand, and stretching out the other for the money.

It was a spring-balance of the usual kind. A hook underneath held the object to be weighed, and a movable needle marked the weight on a graduated arc. It was exactly what they wanted, the absolute weight being shown by the spring alone, with the strength of which, as the Professor had observed, attraction had nothing whatever to do. On Earth this balance, if correct, would have marked a pound's weight for every object weighing a pound. But would it do so in Gallia? This is precisely what the Professor wished to determine by actual experiment.

The twenty-five dollars were counted over and deposited in Isaac's hand, which snapped on the gold like a rat-trap. The balance was then formally offered to the Captain, who nodded to Ben Zouf to take it in charge. Ben pretended as much unwillingness to take it from Isaac as if he dreaded infection. He ordered him to lay it on the table. Then, covering both hands with paper, he took it up, blew on it, rubbed it, scrubbed it, and turned it over again and again, all the time putting on as long a face as if he were engaged in an affair of life and death. Finally covering it up in fresh paper, and slipping it into the pocket of his watch-coat, he was following the others out of the cabin, when all at once he saw the Professor suddenly stop and hurriedly turn back, exclaiming :

"A spring-balance alone is good for nothing. Isaac, you will have besides to lend us—"

"Lend!" cried Isaac, starting and looking as if ready to faint.

"Yes, lend us a yard measure and a pound weight."

"Oh Signor Professor!" cried Isaac, this time in accents of perfect sincerity, "I am extremely sorry that I can't oblige you. I have not such things as a yard measure or a pound weight in my whole stock. They were both unfortunately left behind in my little tent at Ceuta! I can't say how much I regret the loss!"

His auditors felt convinced that for at least once in his life Isaac told the truth. But the Professor did not try to conceal his anger at the disappointment.

"How, Messieurs!" he exclaimed, flashing fiery glances at his companions, "did not you have better sense than to inveigle me into this hole on a fool's errand? I am now in a difficulty out of which I acknowledge I do not clearly see my way. But what's the use of telling you anything about it? Precious little good *you* could do!"

14 *                    L

So saying, he turned round and flung angrily up the cabin stairs.

His companions were following him quietly, when again Ben Zouf saw the Professor suddenly stop, again turn round, again brush past them with some violence, and again rush hurriedly into the cabin.

"You have some silver coin there, Isaac!" cried the Professor, rushing at the Jew and seizing him by the collar of his old overcoat.

"Silver coin!" cried Isaac, nervously trying to shut the drawer in which he was locking up the money that he had just received. "Silver coin! You must be mistaken, Signor Professor!"

"No mistake about it!" cried the Professor. "I heard the peculiar chink as I was ascending the steps. French coin, is n't it? Five-franc pieces?"

"Ye — s — that is — no — not at all!" stammered Isaac, much confused by the suddenness of the attack, and making every effort to shut the drawer.

But the Professor was too quick for him. He suddenly seized the button and pulled the drawer out far enough to get a glimpse of the money.

"Yes! there they are! I said so! Five-franc pieces! I must have them!"

And making a tremendous grab, he seized the money. But this time it was Isaac that was too quick. With a

"YOU HAVE SOME SILVER COINS THERE!"

sudden shove he pushed back the drawer, and nipped the Professor's hand so tight that its owner could not extricate it.

"Let go my hand, you barbarian!" cried the Professor, forgetting the pain in his anger. "I tell you I must have these five-franc pieces, and will have them!"

"Never!" shrieked Isaac, clenching his teeth together and pressing with might and main against the drawer. "You shall never get my money! I will die first!"

But the Professor, though puny of size and bare of flesh, had muscles of iron. Infuriated by the sight of the money, and smarting with the pain of his left hand, with his right arm he caught Isaac so tightly around the neck and gave him such a deadly squeeze that after a few desperate struggles the poor Jew had hardly breath enough left to gasp:

"Help! help! robbery! murder!"

The scene was so astounding in its nature, and the whole transaction had taken place in such a short time that the Captain and his friends looked on quietly for a few moments, hardly knowing what to make of it. But to Ben Zouf it afforded the richest fun. He clapped his hands with wild applause and even roared with delight when he saw Isaac getting black in the face.

"Go it, little Professor," he exclaimed, like a better at a dog fight. "Pinch him, old fellow! Squeeze him! Hug him tight! Wring his old neck off!"

But the Captain and the others, seeing things take such a serious turn, thought it was high time to interfere. Their first care was to free Isaac's neck; their next, to free the Professor's hand. Then, having given the adversaries a few moments for breathing time, the Captain quietly addressed the Professor.

"My dear Master, won't you allow us to arrange this little matter for you as well as the other?"

"Help, Signor Governor!" interrupted Isaac, so frightened as not to believe himself yet quite out of danger. "Help! Protect a poor struggling man! Defend my properties!"

"Keep still, Isaac, pray!" cried the Captain somewhat harshly. Then turning towards the Professor,—

"My dear Master," he asked quietly, "don't you want a certain number of five-franc pieces to help you in the solution of your problem?"

"Yes — Servadac — I do," answered the Professor, a little out of breath, and blowing on his pinched fingers. "I want in the first place forty five-franc pieces."

"That's two hundred francs he wants," murmured Isaac remonstratingly, "of my hard-earned properties!"

"I want besides," resumed the Professor, "ten two-franc pieces, and twenty half-franc pieces."

"Thirty francs more!" uttered the whining voice.

"Two hundred and thirty francs altogether," said the Captain. "My dear Master, will that be sufficient?"

"Yes," answered the Professor; "these seventy coins will be amply sufficient for my purpose."

"Now, Count," asked the Captain, "what have you to give Isaac as a pledge for the safety of the forced loan I am going to make on him!"

"My purse is always at your disposal, my dear Captain," said the Count. "Here it is. Only unfortunately it contains at present very little besides bank-notes."

"No paper! no paper!" cried Isaac. "Rag money has no circulation in Gallia."

"What kind of money, Isaac," asked the Count with a severe frown, "should have circulation in Gallia?"

"Look here, Isaac," said the Captain sternly. "No more nonsense! Your unfair and unreasonable selfishness has not as yet quite worn out our patience. But take care; don't provoke us too far! These coins we *must* have. We can't do without them, and —"

"Robbery!" shrieked Isaac in a loud voice. "Mur—"

But Ben's vigorous grapple around the neck put a full stop to such ejaculations.

"What do you mean, Jedediah?" he exclaimed angrily. "Do you know where you are and what you're howling about?"

"Let him alone, Ben Zouf," said the Captain. "Let go of him. He will come to terms of his own accord, without your interference."

"Never!" gurgled Isaac, hardly able to pronounce the word in more than a whisper. "Never!"

"We can't do without them, I was saying, Isaac," continued the Captain; "and now I am going to ask what interest you require for the loan of these seventy coins?"

"What, Signor Governor!" cried Isaac coming to himself in a moment, his voice relieved and his face radiant with satisfaction. "You want my two hundred and thirty francs only as a loan?"

"As a simple loan, Isaac, nothing more. What interest do you require?"

"Oh your Excellency," whimpered Isaac with a fawning voice, "money, you know, is money, and just now and just here it is more money than at any other time or in any other place!"

"No political economy, Isaac! Come to the point. What interest do you ask?"

"Well, your Excellency," replied Isaac, "taking everything into consideration, don't you think I 'm very reasonable if I ask only ten francs a day?"

"Ten francs a day for the loan of two hundred and thirty francs!" cried the Captain.

"Three thousand six hundred and fifty francs a year!" cried Procopius. "Sixteen hundred per cent.!"

"Old Skin-em-alive knows how to shave!" cried Ben. "Old Skinny would charge his dead father interest for the pennies put on his eyes to keep them closed! Governor, you should have let the Professor give the garrote another twist!"

"Too late for that now, Ben Zouf," said the Count quietly. "Say no more about it. A bargain is a bargain. Here is your principal, Isaac, and here is your two days' interest. Ten francs a day be it!"

So saying, he took some bank-notes out of his purse and laid·them on the table. Isaac pounced on them eagerly and counted them rapidly.

"Two hundred and fifty francs!" he exclaimed. "All right!"

He said no more about "rag money," partly because he was afraid of another twist on the neck, and partly because he knew that Russian paper was as good as specie. The enormous interest besides gratified his rapacity so much as probably to obscure a little his usual circumspection.

The seventy coins, all new and shining, were counted out carefully and placed in the Professor's hands. He pocketed them quickly, and instantly left the cabin, followed by his companions.

"In all probability, my dear Master," began the Captain, wishing to say something, "Isaac will get back his two hundred and thirty francs to-morrow?"

The Professor eyed him angrily.

"What two hundred and thirty francs are you talking about?" he replied snappishly. "I know nothing of two hundred and thirty francs. All I know is that I am now in possession of the seventy silver coins I wanted to weigh my Gallia with!"

# CHAPTER VIII.

## GALLIA WEIGHED.

A QUARTER of an hour later, the company was once more seated around the Professor in Central Hall, very curious to know how he was to set about weighing the Comet.

The seventy coins were arranged on the table in four piles: one containing the twenty half-franc pieces; one, the ten two-franc pieces; and the other two containing each twenty five-franc pieces.

"Now, Messieurs," began the Professor in a tone at once self-confident and satisfied, "the great shock having apparently so much disconcerted you as to deprive you of presence of mind enough to secure a yard measure or a pound weight, I have been obliged to devise out of my own brains a method of replacing these two articles, which are so absolutely indispensable if we are to calculate Gallia's attraction, mass, and density."

He paused a few seconds to watch the effect of this uncomplimentary exordium; but, finding that his audi-

tors did not appear to writhe much under the severity
of his remarks, he proceeded :

"Messieurs, it is hardly necessary to state that these
coins are perfectly new — they are still almost as bright
and unworn as they were on the very day they left the
mint. They are therefore capable of fulfilling every
condition required of them with rigid and unflinching
accuracy. Now, the first step will be to obtain the exact
length of a yard — a difficult matter unless you know
how to do it."

"Difficult!" interrupted Ben, perhaps in earnest but
more probably desirous of enlivening the proceedings,
"why, Professor, there's nothing easier than to find the
length of a yard!"

"You think so?" exclaimed the Professor, angry at
the interruption. "If you find me the exact length of
a yard I shall consider you a much more sensible man
than you are ever likely to be!"

"Everybody knows that three feet make a yard!"
said Ben sturdily. "Even a Savant is likely to know
that!"

"Three feet?" cried the Professor quickly. "But
what kind of feet? Yours, for instance, or Dutch
Isaac's? Three feet like the Jew's would make a yard
and a half. Three feet like yours would make two
yards!"

A universal roar of the audience told Ben he had come off second best this time. He laughed himself, however, almost as heartily as the others, while he quietly stretched out his legs and threw a comical glance at a pair of boots whose burly proportions furnished the point for the Professor's joke. Still, unwilling to give up and determined to watch his chances, he could not help saying:

"Thank you, Professor, I'll mark you one!"

"The Son of Montmartre," resumed the Professor, as soon as the general merriment subsided, "says it is an extremely easy matter to tell the exact length constituting a yard, or a *mètre* as we call it in France. Now I maintain, on the contrary, that it would be extremely difficult, if not wholly impossible, for us to ascertain the exact length of a *mètre*, had I not been fortunate enough to catch the noise made by Isaac as he was throwing the gold into his money-drawer. It is in emergencies of this kind that the gigantic power of the mathematical mind displays itself with startling effect."

Redoubled attention on the part of the audience. The Captain and his friends were beginning to feel that the Professor was really likely to effect his purpose.

"Messieurs," he resumed, "most of you must be aware that in the French coinage the decimal system is carried out as closely and thoroughly as possible. Of this coinage the FRANC is the standard. All coins of greater value are multiples of the franc. All coins of inferior value are even parts of the franc. Besides this, all coins are of an exact size, their diameters being rigorously determined by the law.

"To speak only of the coins before me — I know that the diameter of a five-franc piece is $\frac{37}{1000}$ of a *mètre ;* the diameter of a two-franc piece is $\frac{27}{1000}$ of a *mètre ;* and the diameter of a half-franc piece is $\frac{18}{1000}$ of a *mètre.* Now, as you see, I lay in a straight line ten of my five-franc pieces, which gives me the exact length of $\frac{370}{1000}$ of a *mètre ;* then, I continue this line with ten two-franc pieces, which gives me $\frac{270}{1000}$ of a *mètre ;* finally, I complete my line by twenty half-franc pieces, which gives me $\frac{360}{1000}$ of a *mètre.* I add the 370, the 270, and the 360 parts together, and I find that I have a line exactly one thousand-thousandths of a *mètre* long : that is, by drawing a line through the centre of these coins so arranged, I have found the length of a *mètre* or French yard rigidly and indisputably correct."

Very little more explanation was required to make all this perfectly clear, and loud applause testified the satisfaction of the audience with the learned Professor's success. Even Ben Zouf could not refrain from clapping his hands and exclaiming in profound astonishment :

"I LAY THESE COINS IN A STRAIGHT LINE."

" Seems to me after all that these Savants know something. I should have swallowed those coins myself sooner than make a *mètre* out of them ! "

" I dare say you would," said the Professor dryly; " but, Son of Montmartre, even to make a *mètre* out of coin would not be enough to turn an ignoramus into a Savant."

Marking off the exact length of the *mètre* on the table, the Professor took a compass, divided the line into ten equal parts, and so found the *decimètres*. Then cutting a rod exactly a *decimètre* long, he handed it to the machinist of the *Dobryna* to assist him in making his cubic or solid *decimètre*. The machinist, however, a skilful and intelligent man, possessing already a good idea of the length of a *decimètre*, had by this time finished the greatest part of his work.

This was simply to prepare a cubic block, a *decimètre* (nearly four inches) each way, of the hard metallic substance that composed the rocky walls of the volcano. He had made his block purposely a little too large, so that, to turn it into a perfect cube of the exact size, nothing more was now necessary but a little trimming off on each of the sides by means of the decimetric rod.

" To save time, Messieurs," said the Professor, " while waiting for our cubic *decimètre*, we shall now go to work

15 *

to find the exact weight of the Earth standard pound, or as we call it in France, the *kilogramme.* To do this will present just as little difficulty as to find the exact length of the *mètre.*

"The French coins, as already said, are not only of an .exact size, but of an exact weight also, rigorously determined by the law.

"One kind of coin will be enough to answer our present purpose. The five-franc piece weighing exactly the fortieth part of a *kilogramme* or 25 *grammes,* it is evident that forty of them put together will give us the weight of a thousand *grammes* or one *kilogramme.*"

"Hah!" cried Ben, "I should be greater than a Savant to do that!"

"Greater than a Savant!" exclaimed the Captain laughing. "You could not be greater than a Savant. No one can be greater than a *Savant!*"

"Beg your pardon, Governor," replied Ben, "a rich man is greater than a Savant! What's the good of knowing the weight of two hundred francs if I had not the two hundred francs to weigh? A Savant with an empty purse would be a poor calculator."

No one laughed this time at Ben's joke, probably because there was more truth than fun in it.

Here the machinist put into the Professor's hands the required cubic *decimètre* of rock made with an exactness quite sufficient for the purpose under consideration. He received it with much graciousness, and immediately resumed the interrupted lecture.

"Now then, Messieurs," he went on, "possessing as we do a *decimètre* cubic block of the material constituting the solid substance of our Comet, the exact weight of a terrestrial *kilogramme*, and also a spring-balance to weigh each of these articles in succession, we may consider ourselves in a position eminently favorable for finding the attraction, the mass, and the density of Gallia.

"In case you do not know it, or rather in case you have forgotten it, I must recall to your memory Newton's celebrated law : *The attraction exercised by one body on another is directly proportional to the mass of the attracting body, and inversely proportional to the square of the distance between them.* This principle I beg of you to keep carefully in mind."

Every one listened with the greatest attention ; even the Spaniards in a distant part of the Hall seemed to devour his words.

"Now, Messieurs," he went on, "here is a bag containing our forty five-franc pieces. It would therefore weigh exactly one *kilogramme* on the Earth. That is to say, if I were now on the Earth, and suspended, as I do now, this bag on this hook, the needle would point exactly at one *kilogramme*.  I hope I make myself quite clear?"

This question, though really meant for the audience, was directly addressed to Ben Zouf.  In proposing it, the Professor only imitated a custom of his illustrious master Arago, who, when delivering a lecture, invariably singled out the stupidest-looking person he found near him and carefully watched his countenance.  When the stupid-looking person seemed to understand him, he went no further into wordy explanations, being quite certain that he was also understood by the rest of the audience.*

Ben was by no means stupid-looking — far from it — but he was ignorant, which, in that case at least, came to exactly the same thing.  As he appeared, however,

---

\* On this subject Arago himself relates a very amusing incident.

One day in company with some ladies and gentlemen, the great astronomer had been just telling his audience of this custom of his, when a young man entering the room, immediately ran up to him, took his hand and shook it with the greatest cordiality.

"Oh Monsieur Arago," said he, "I am really most delighted to see you!"

"You have the advantage of me, my dear sir," said Arago, a little surprised; "really just now I cannot recall your name.  Indeed I'm pretty certain I have not the honor of knowing you."

"Not know me, Monsieur Arago!  How's that?  I always sit quite close to you at your lectures, and you keep your eyes fixed on me the whole time!"

"I HANG THIS BAG ON THIS HOOK."

to have understood everything so far demonstrated, the Professor continued:

" Now, Messieurs, being on Gallia when I hang this bag on this hook, this needle must tell me the weight of a *kilogramme* on Gallia. It does, you see. It descends a little, oscillates a little, and finally, settles at 133 *grammes.* Therefore, what weighs one *kilogramme* or 1000 *grammes,* on the Earth, weighs on Gallia only 133 *grammes,* or about 7½ times less. I hope I make myself clear!"

Giving Ben another sharp look and .finding his countenance beaming with comprehension, he continued his discourse.

" Messieurs, I probably may not have to remind most of you that the result thus obtained never could have been reached by the ordinary balance. You are doubtless well aware that the scale containing the coins and the scale containing the weight would exactly balance each other, the diminution of gravity being felt by both in exactly the same degree. I do hope I make myself intelligible."

Another glance at Ben eliciting a quick earnest nod, the Professor continued :

" Weight here being 7½ times less than on the terrestrial globe, we must of course conclude that the force of gravity is 7½ times less powerful on Gallia than it is on the Earth."

M

"There can't be a doubt about it," cried the Captain, delighted with the Professor's experiment. "Now then, my dear Master, knowing the force of Gallia's gravity, suppose you undertake her mass for us."

"Not her mass, Servadac," said the Professor; "we must find her density first."

The Captain looking a little surprised, Procopius undertook to explain in a rapid whisper.

"The Professor is right," said he; "knowing her volume already, as soon as we know her density her mass will be nothing more than an affair of a short and simple calculation."

"Right, Lieutenant," answered the Captain in the same low tone; "of course, you're right. I really had forgotten that!"

"Gallia's density, Messieurs," resumed the Professor, striking the table with one hand to command attention and taking up in the other the cubic *decimètre* of solid rock. "You know that this block consists of the strange substance you have found everywhere on Gallia's surface, even in your most distant circumnavigation. In all probability my Comet consists exclusively of this substance. Beach, strand, coast, mountain, north and south, east and west, all seem to be composed of this mineral, to which you, in your ignorance of the elements of geology, have not been able to assign a name."

"It was not from want of trying!" observed the Captain, half aloud.

"I think then," continued the Professor, "that I may feel myself justified in premising that Gallia is completely and solely composed of this substance from her surface to her core. You have here before you a block of this substance. Now what would it weigh on Earth? You know already that it would weigh there about 7½ times as much as it does here. You know that it *must* do so, the terrestrial attraction being 7½ times greater than the Gallian. I hope I still make myself quite clear."

Another rapid glance at Ben Zouf. But this time Ben's brow was knit, and he was scratching his head with a puzzled look.

"You don't understand, eh?" asked the Professor.

"N — o — o," answered Ben. "Not quite!"

"I thought as much!" said the Professor. "However, I have no notion of wasting my time in trying to enlighten puzzle-heads! Some people are blind enough not to see the sun at noonday!"

"Neither could you, if he was wrapped up in clouds!" grumbled Ben, though in rather low tones, for he was beginning to be a little afraid of the Professor.

"Let me weigh this block," continued the lecturer. "Doing so is really weighing Gallia herself on a small

scale.  See!  The needle marks 1333 *grammes*.  This
multiplied by 7½ gives 10 thousand *grammes*, or 10
*kilogrammes*, or 22 English pounds very nearly.  What
is the weight of a *decimètre* block of average Earth
material ?   As nearly as possible 5 *kilogrammes*, or
11 English pounds.  What is the irresistible conclusion?  Gallian density is actually twice as great as
terrestrial density, or as 22 is to 11 !  If attraction here
had been 15 times less instead of 7½ times less than
terrestrial attraction, both planets would have been
of the same density, whereas it is incontestable that
Gallia's density is actually twice as great as that of
the Earth !  What do you think of my Comet now,
hey ?"

In uttering these words he looked around on his
audience with such a majestic air, that he actually appeared to have suddenly grown to twice his ordinary
dimensions.   It was, in truth, enough to make any
man glow with a noble pride.  Not one man in fifty
million can say he has discovered a comet of twice the
density of the Earth !

But though a longer pause would be perfectly justifiable under the circumstances, the Professor resumed his
discourse in less than a minute.

"Now, Messieurs, I will take the liberty of reading
out for you the various items of Gallia's elements calcu-

lated so far. I shall confine myself as closely as possible to round numbers. Circumference, 2 thousand miles; Diameter, 6⅓ hundred miles; Surface, 1⅓ millions of square miles; Volume, nearly 150 millions of cubic miles; Density, double the Earth's; and Gravity, 7½ times less than the Earth's. We have now to calculate her mass, that is, to tell exactly how much she weighs.

"Nothing simpler than the calculation, Messieurs. A cubic *decimètre* of her substance weighing 10 *kilogrammes*, Gallia herself must weigh as many times 10 *kilogrammes* as her volume contains cubic *decimètres*. Now this volume being, as we know, 134 millions of cubic miles or 533 millions of cubic *kilomètres*, it must contain 533 quintillions of cubic *decimètres*. Multiplying this by 10, we have Gallia's actual weight to be 5⅓ sextillions of *kilogrammes*, or about 12 sextillions English pounds, equivalent to 5½ quintillions of English tons."

"Quintillions! sextillions!" cried Ben, with a loud laugh. "What kind of things are they, I should like to know!"

"Do you really wish to know what a sextillion is?" asked the Professor quickly.

"Well, I should not mind, Professor. I'm always ready for useful information," with a wink at Negrete.

"Where shall we begin?" asked the Professor.

16

"Come! Where shall we begin? Where have you stopped realizing to yourself the true value of a number? You don't know! Well, we shall soon find out. Do you know what a *milliard* is?"

"I think I do," answered Ben modestly.

"Now then, what is it? Be alive? What is a milliard? The exact value of a milliard?"

"It — is — a — very great number," said Ben, giving the best answer he could.

"I should think it was a great number, sir!" said the Professor sharply; "but we want something more definite than *a very great number!* Come! You can't tell? Well! let's see if I can't insense you into it! There are a good many minutes in a year, are there not?"

"Yes!"

"And a good many more in a hundred years, eh?"

"Yes, Professor; a good many more."

"And a great many still more have elapsed since the birth of Christ, about 18¾ hundred years ago?"

"Yes, Professor; a great many still more — beyond calculation probably."

"We'll see about that! Well, if you had been living in the days of Christ, and if you had been a clerk in the mint appointed to count coins at the sure rate of one to the minute, or sixty to the hour, or 1440 to the day, or more than 50,000 to the year, you would not have yet got through your milliard!"

"You're joking, Professor!"

"In 18,000 years from now you would be approaching your trillion!"

"I should have gone crazy long before that, Professor!"

"In 18 millions of years you would be getting ready for your quadrillion!"

"I am going crazy now, Professor!"

"In 18 thousand millions of years you would begin to think it was time for your quintillion! And as —"

"Enough! enough! Professor!" cried Ben, covering his head with his hands. "Don't tell me anything further about these dreadful numbers! My head is already giving way! I must run out before it splits!"

And he made for the entry.

"Don't go yet, Son of Montmartre!" exclaimed the Professor in soothing tones. "You have not yet heard about the sextillions!"

But Ben ran off, while the caverns rang with cheers for the Professor's glorious victory. He did not return for a quarter of an hour, and even then he approached no nearer than a distant buttress, behind which he could see and listen without danger of a new deluge of facts and figures.

In spite of his splendid triumph, however, the Professor soon began to look a little troubled. In Ben's absence he had nobody to expend his superabundant information on, and his countenance assumed an expression of decided uneasiness. Fortunately the Captain's wonderful intuition instantly came to the rescue.

" My dear Master," he eagerly observed, " hearing these marvellous calculations of yours reminds me of days long past and opportunities neglected forever. I hope my regret does not come too late. My friends and myself are very desirous to ask a few questions on certain very interesting subjects."

"Ask, Servadac," said the Professor, his countenance instantly losing its distressed look.

" Now that you have told us the weight of Gallia, my dear Master, will you not tell us the weight of the Earth?"

" Six sextillions of tons ! " instantly answered the Professor.

" How many Gallias would make the Earth?"

" 1728 Gallias."

"How many times is the Earth heavier than Gallia?"

" Nearly 900 times heavier ! "

" How many Gallias would make the Moon?"

" Thirty-five Gallias ! "

" How many times is the Moon heavier than Gallia?"

" Eleven times heavier ! "

" Compare Gallia's density with the Moon's ! "

" Gallia's density is four times greater than the Moon's ! "

" What is the Moon's absolute weight ? "

" Nearly 70 quintillions of tons English ! "

" What is the Sun's absolute weight ? "

" Two octillions of English tons," cried the Professor without stopping to take breath.

The Captain, now fairly run out of questions, here winked to Procopius, who immediately rushed to the rescue.

" You observed, Professor, did you not," he asked, " that gravity is $7\frac{1}{2}$ times weaker in Gallia than on the Earth ? "

" Quite correct, Lieutenant," replied the Professor graciously.

" Our muscular force must be therefore increased $7\frac{1}{2}$ fold ? " asked Procopius.

" Yes, yes, of course," replied the Professor rather impatiently.

" That must be the reason then why we move about here so easily, and lift great burdens with such facility ? "

" No doubt, no doubt ! " cried the Professor, beginning to get angry at being asked such simple questions.

16 *

Procopius glanced appealingly at the Captain, who again manfully entered the lists, armed to the teeth with another supply of puzzlers.

"My dear Master," said he, "we are all very curious to know what is the force of gravity on each of the other planets."

"What, Servadac?" cried the Professor, his countenance once more brightening up. "An old pupil of mine to ask such a question! You should be ashamed of yourself!"

"I am ashamed of myself," said the Captain meekly. "I neglected my advantages disgracefully, and I have been paying dearly for my folly ever since. But, my dear Master, won't you tell us the force of gravity on each of the other planets? My friends and myself are exceedingly curious to know."

"We're intensely excited on the subject!" protested the Count.

"Well, Messieurs," replied the mollified Professor, "since you want to know, I suppose I must tell you. The Earth's attraction let us call $1$ or unity. That of the Moon will then be $\frac{1}{6}$; that of Mars $\frac{1}{2}$; that of Mercury $\frac{4}{5}$; of Venus $\frac{9}{10}$; of Saturn $1\frac{1}{7}$; of Jupiter $2\frac{2}{3}$; and that of the Sun a little more than $27$."

"By that, of course, you mean, my dear Master," said the Captain, seeing the Professor stop, "that a terrestrial pound would weigh at least 27 pounds on the Sun?"

"Exactly, Servadac! Consequently a cannon-ball discharged with sufficient force to travel five miles on the Earth, in the Sun could hardly manage to crawl more than a thousand feet!"

"A first-rate battle-ground for cowards!" exclaimed Ben, from the lower end of the Hall.

"Not so good as you think," said the Captain seeing that the Professor was silent. "The cowards could never get away. They would be too heavy. A man weighing 150 pounds, once he fell, would have to lift 2 tons of flesh and blood before he could get on his pins again!"

"What's my weight here, Governor?" asked Ben.

"About that of a six months' baby, Ben Zouf. Probably 20 pounds."

"Yes, Ben Zouf," said Procopius, "and if Gallia had been smaller —"

"Smaller!" cried the irrepressible Ben, with a wink at the others and a glance at the Professor. "Smaller! Could anything be smaller?"

The taunt stung the Professor to the quick.

"Gallia may be small, sir," he cried in angry tones, "but the amount of brains in that cocoanut of yours called a head is infinitesimally smaller than the smallest element in Gallia's composition! A quintillion of such heads would not furnish brains enough for a goose of ordinary intelligence! A sextillion of them —''

But Ben ran out of the Hall in such comical alarm at the sound of this redoubtable word that the rest of the Professor's eloquence was completely lost in the laughter of the audience. The Captain took advantage of the opportunity to restore his old teacher to good-humor by plying him with another problem.

"My dear Master," said he, "one question more will be the last with which we shall trouble you to-day. It is suggested by your observation just made. Of what substance is Gallia composed?"

"Ah you wish to know that, Servadac!" said the Professor, gradually pluming his ruffled feathers. "Well, I dare say you do. It's worth knowing. Gallia's material must be pretty heavy since her density is twice as great as the Earth's."

"Yes, my dear Master; it must be very heavy. That is one great reason why we want to know what it is."

"It is a telluride," answered the Professor slowly and emphasizing each word; "but an exceedingly valuable one according to man's ordinary estimate. It is a gold telluride, not quite unknown on the Earth, but here it is much richer, for every seventy parts of tellurium there being thirty parts of pure gold."

"Thirty per cent. of gold!" cried the Captain, this time really surprised.

"Yes," said the Professor quite proudly, "and, by way of confirmation to this day's experiment, I shall give you another very simple calculation. Multiply 6 the specific gravity of tellurium by 70 per cent., and 19 the specific gravity of gold by 30 per cent.; add the results together and we shall have exactly 10, the specific gravity of our Comet as already ascertained by Isaac's spring-balance."

"A golden comet!" cried Procopius, as much surprised as the Captain.

"Something like a golden comet was guessed at by Maupertuis," said the Professor, "and Gallia shows that he was not so extravagantly wrong in his conjectures."

"If Gallia is thirty per cent. pure gold," said the Count, so far an attentive listener but now suddenly breaking silence, "her fall on the Earth would utterly derange the monetary system of every nation in the world."

"Your conclusion is perfectly correct, Count," said the Professor, with a grand air. "McCulloch says that the total coin actually in circulation in every part of the world except Asia amounts to 500 millions of English pounds sterling. Now multiplying Gallia's weight of $5\frac{1}{2}$ quintillions of English tons by 30 per cent., we shall have more than $1\frac{1}{2}$ quintillions of tons of gold. This, calculated at even the low rate of 100 thousand pounds sterling to the ton will give us — hum — hum — (calculating rapidly) — yes — would give the Earth that day at least 100 sextillions of English pounds sterling! Compared with this enormous sum, all the gold at present circulating on the Earth bears no greater proportion than the $\frac{1}{520}$th of a penny bears to the total English National Debt!

"Now, Messieurs," concluded the Professor, radiant with pardonable pride and glowing with exultation, "you look surprised, and well you may be so! But that's the kind of a comet Gallia is! I have the honor to wish you a very good-evening!"

The silence that prevailed in the Hall for a few moments after the Professor's departure was soon broken by Ben Zouf.

"What the little Professor says about quindrillions and trixtillions may be all quite true — at least *I* can't contradict him. But, Governor-General, what's the good of it all?"

"It's all of no good whatever, Ben Zouf," replied the Captain without a moment's hesitation. "It cannot possibly serve the least useful purpose that I can see. Such calculations, though wasting time and wearing out brains, benefit nobody. They don't make the least pretence to benefit anybody. But that is their greatest charm! That is the grand thought that consoles the Savant for all the ingenuity, the research, the time, and the labor he has expended in ascertaining that 500 trillions of red light waves enter our eyes in a single second of time!"

# CHAPTER IX.

## JUPITER.

WITH the Captain's candid opinion of the real value of the information just imparted to them by the Professor, his companions were in full accordance. What interest for them did Gallia's exact elements possess, her rate of motion through planetary space, her mass, her density, her attraction, or even the mineral wealth of her composition? What they desired to know was simply: Should she ever return to the Earth? and when might such return be expected? On these points the Professor had thrown no new light whatever, though it was with the expectation of hearing something definite and intelligible about them that they had listened with intense interest to information which otherwise they should have considered probably exceedingly dull and monotonous.

Still it would serve no good purpose to irritate the Professor. It was generally conceded that the only way to get anything desirable out of him was to keep him in good-humor.

Ben Zouf, however, was of a contrary opinion.

"Coaxing the little Professor," said he, "will never do him any good. He's too cranky, and too sharp besides! He can guess in an instant what you really want, and that's the very thing he'll never tell you!"

Against this heterodoxy the audience put in a general disclaimer. The Captain said Ben's opinion was worth nothing, being founded altogether on jealousy.

"Jealousy!" cried Ben; "on what account, Governor?"

"Everybody knows on what account, Ben Zouf! Gallia is so much superior to Montmartre!"

"Gallia is a fraud, Governor! You don't think so, but you'll find it out yet! Anyhow a sixtrillion of Gallias would not be as good as the smallest grain of sand belonging to old Montmartre!"

The company only laughed at Ben's exaggerations, and saw no reason, for the present at least, to discontinue what the Count called the "policy of the tickling process."

It was not often, however, that the Professor afforded them an opportunity for putting any kind of a resolution into practice. More than a month elapsed before the three gentlemen were summoned to the observatory to hear the monthly report. It is needless to say that they obeyed orders with an alacrity that richly deserved a better reward.

"Messieurs," said the Professor hastily to them as they entered, "I have the honor to inform you that to-day is the sixty-third of April (revised calendar), corresponding with the first of September (old or obsolete calendar). During the month which you call August but which I call the latter half of March, Gallia has made her 16 million 500 thousand leagues. She has still 81 millions of leagues to run before reaching her aphelion point, which she will touch in a little less than six of your months and in less than three of mine. You see we are advancing into depths of space into which human eye has never before penetrated, and in which I shall consequently find enough to keep every single moment closely occupied. Now then please to withdraw, allowing me to make the most of my unparalleled advantages. I will send for you again as soon as I shall have any important information to communicate."

No wonder that the Professor called his advantages unparalleled and desired perfect tranquillity in order to make the most of them. Never before had astronomer been favored with such opportunities, in the first place, for detaching himself most completely from all earthly considerations, and, in the second, for projecting himself most profoundly into the unspeakable sublimities of starry space. What glorious nights he enjoyed! How radiant the splendor of the glittering stars! Not even the faintest expiring zephyr, not even the most ethereal gossamer cloud crisped the sharp edge of their crystalline serenity! The resplendent book of the vast firmament lay open to his enraptured gaze, and his eye could never tire wandering over its enchanting pages.

The most dazzling of all these wonders at the present time was undoubtedly the great planet Jupiter. Every day he came nearer and nearer, and consequently grew more and more visible. He was now only 61 million leagues distant from Gallia, which is $2\frac{1}{2}$ times less than his shortest distance from the Earth, and for two months more the two planets were to continue approaching each other.

" Is there not some danger of a collision, Lieutenant?" asked the Captain one night, as the friends were walking up and down at the mouth of the cavern, smoking their cigars just before retiring.

"Well, collision is hardly the correct word, Captain," answered Procopius. "The Professor could no doubt have easily calculated the probable danger of a collision, and, as he has said nothing on the subject, we may presume that there is little danger of Gallia's orbit crossing Jupiter's at a critical point. The real danger lies in our proximity to an orb of such immense mass and therefore possessing such enormous power of attraction. You probably remember the Professor's words on this subject in his first lecture. Here they are in my memorandum-book: 'Jupiter is *par excellence* the grand muddler. He is always in the way of some planet or other, and is pretty certain to throw it out of kelter the very minute some unfortunate astronomer has made out its elements after much distracting and abstruse calculations.'"

"Do you really think, Procopius," asked the Count, "that the Professor took this danger into consideration when calculating Gallia's trajectory?"

"I am certain he did, Father," replied Procopius, "but I am also certain that, in spite of his vast mathematical and experimental knowledge, he may have made some mistake. The greatest astronomers have done so."

"Not to make a mistake I consider little short of miraculous," observed the Captain, "especially when we consider that the deviation of even a hair's-breadth in one direction would amount to thousands and thousands of miles in another. Would not the slightest modification of our course by the planet Mars, for instance, have been enough to set the Professor's calculations all wrong?"

"It certainly would, Captain," answered Procopius. "The slightest perturbation in her course by the proximity of Venus or Mars, would in all probability have retarded Gallia so much as to finally bring her within the sphere of Jupiter's attraction."

"What would be the result of such an untoward event?" asked the Count.

"The possible results are four in number," replied Procopius : "(1) Gallia, irresistibly attracted by Jupiter, would be precipitated on his surface to be instantly destroyed ; (2) or, captured only, she would become his satellite, possibly even a sub-satellite ; (3) or, deviating from her own orbit, she would follow some new one that would never bring her back to the Earth's ecliptic at all ; (4) or, finally, though not quitting her own track, she might be retarded so much in her velocity as to arrive at the critical point just in time to be too late."

"I believe in my heart," said the Captain, with a smile, "that, of these four formidable contingencies, my dear old Master dreads only two, the first and the second. As for missing the Earth, it would just suit him. Gallia would then either continue her regular course, revolving forever around the Sun in a flattened orbit, or else, whisked off to some other system, she might never stop until she had reached the soundless

17 *

infinities of the Milky Way.  I know him well.  Even when much younger than he is now, we could easily see that he was cut out for an unmitigated old bachelor. He never had a friend.  He had never time to make a friend.  He does not care a pin about the Earth. Little matters it to him where his body is, if his soul can only revel amid the wonders of starry space.''

As if in confirmation of the truth of these remarks, the Professor even now scarcely ever showed himself to friends who were very anxious to see him and who would be only too happy to treat him with every possible respect.  The most he would do was to reveal his existence every now and then by short bulletins indicative of Gallia's progress through interplanetary space. On the first of September she was announced to be at precisely the same distance from Jupiter as the Earth is from the Sun.  On the 15th, this distance had diminished to sixty-five millions of miles.  Jupiter could be easily noticed growing larger and larger among the other stars, and Gallia seemed to be making for him in a straight line !

News of this kind, dated and without note or comment, was anything but encouraging.  The three friends naturally began to feel apprehensive and to look at each other with rather disturbed countenances.  Too well they called to mind Newton's great law, as laid down by the Professor: *Attraction between two bodies is exerted in the direct ratio of their masses, and in the inverse ratio of their distances.* Jupiter's mass was enormous, and his distance was rapidly diminishing!

"What is Jupiter's size?" asked the Captain one day of Procopius, whom he had found deeply plunged in the Count's scientific books.

"His volume is between 12 and 13 hundred times greater than the Earth's. In other words, it would take between 12 and 13 hundred Earths to make one Jupiter. In fact, all the other planets, rolled together into one solid sphere, would not amount to half his size."

"And his mass or weight?" asked the Captain. "I am of course well aware that in estimating his power of attraction it is his mass or weight that must be taken into consideration rather than his mere volume."

"His mass is more than two hundred times greater than the Earth's," said Procopius; "that is, Jupiter weighs more than two hundred Earths rolled together into one solid ball."

"Why this great disproportion between his volume and his weight?" asked the Captain.

"Because," answered Procopius, "Jupiter is very unlike the Earth in many respects. His density is six times less than the Earth's; that is, Jupiter is not quite

as heavy as a globe of water of the same volume.
But though, for this reason, sometimes called the
*Watery Planet*, there is very little sign of water about
him. On the contrary, taking into consideration both
his extraordinary brightness. and his singular rarity, he
is most probably a small sun, in a state of cooling, it
is true, but none the less dangerous on that account
for Gallia to approach."

"I should think so indeed," said the Count; "tell
us a little more about him, Lieutenant."

"Well, he performs his revolution around the sun
in a little less than twelve years, travelling at the rate
of eight miles a second along an orbit more than five
times as long as the Earth's. He rotates once on his
axis in a little less than ten hours, the length of his
day, so that a point on his equator is whirled around
at the rate of about 8 miles a minute. The inclination
of his axis being almost perpendicular to the plane of
his ecliptic, he has been called the *Upright Planet*.
The chief consequences of this peculiarity are: the
equality of his days and nights the whole year round,
and the almost inappreciable variety of his seasons."

"How about his light and heat?"

"The average quantity of the sun's light and heat
received on every square mile of Jupiter is 27 times
less than that received on each square mile of the

Earth. This makes his extraordinary brightness still more wonderful, nay, even incomprehensible, unless we consider him to shine partly by his own inherent lustre."

"This novel theory of yours we shall take up for future discussion," said the Captain. "For the present I confine my curiosity to his satellites. They must make his nights very brilliant whenever they happen to shine all at the same time."

"That however they can never do," answered Procopius; "and for a very good reason: if they could, a night might come when none of them would appear at all. Their orbits are all nearly circular, and their motions uniform. Their diameters vary in length from that of the Moon to 1⅔ times her size, but their revolutions around their primary are much more rapid than that of the Moon around the Earth. The first, or nearest, revolves in 1¾ days, the second in 3½ days, the third in about a week, and the fourth in less than three weeks. This fourth, the most distant, often called *Callisto*, moves at a distance of more than a million of miles from her primary, or about four times further off than the first, usually designated *Io* by sentimental astronomers."

"Have not these satellites of Jupiter served for some important scientific discovery?" asked the Captain.

"I remember learning something about it in school, but I am sorry to say I forget it all now."

"Yes," answered Procopius, "it was by observing their eclipses that Roemer, a Danish astronomer, discovered the velocity of light in 1675. These eclipses did not always correspond with the predicted time, occurring earlier when Jupiter was in *opposition* or nearest the Earth, and later when in *conjunction* or at the greatest distance. Roemer was the first to suggest that this discrepancy was due to Jupiter's variation of distance from the Earth, and that light therefore, instead of being instantaneous, should take longer to come when Jupiter was further away. Bradley's discovery of the aberration of light has long since placed the correctness of Roemer's theory beyond all doubt.— These satellites are also very useful for ascertaining terrestrial longitudes; in fact," added Procopius, "Jupiter may be regarded as the great dial of a celestial clock, of which his satellites are the four hands announcing the time with perfect accuracy."

"I hope Gallia is not going to make a fifth hand," said the Captain hastily.—"But, Lieutenant," he continued with a smile, " you are so exceedingly kind that I am going to trespass a little longer on your good nature by asking your opinion on a discussion the Count and myself had the other day regarding the

READING FLAMMARION.

comparative age of the planets. Which do you consider the older, those between the Earth and the Sun, or those outside the Earth?"

"You must take me for another Professor Rosette," answered Procopius pleasantly; "but on such a subject to lie I am unwilling, and to guess I am ashamed. Therefore I shall either keep silent about it altogether, or read for you what Flammarion of Paris says on the subject in a strange book of his called *Stories of the Infinite.*"

"Read it by all means, my dear Lieutenant!" said the Captain. "I am ashamed to say I know nothing whatever of Flammarion or his book."

"I esteem him so highly," observed the Count, "that the last time I was in Paris I bought up every book bearing his name. I too shall be very glad to hear you read the quotation, Procopius."

The Lieutenant had by this time found the desired passage and immediately began to read :

"'The planets which are the most distant are also the oldest and the most advanced in formation. Neptune, 2¾ billions of miles distant from the sun, was the first to quit the solar nebula, billions of centuries ago. Uranus, revolving at a distance of 1¾ billions of miles from the common centre, is several hundred millions of centuries old. Jupiter, a colossal planet gravitating at an average distance of nearly half a billion miles away, is 70 millions of centuries old. Mars, 1½ times more distant from the sun than the Earth, is at least 10 times older. The Earth, 92 millions of miles from the sun, issued from his burning breast a hundred millions of years ago. Venus, ⅔ of the Earth's distance from the sun, is about ½ her age. Mercury, 10 times younger than Venus, is the nearest of all. The Moon's age does not admit of comparison with that of the other planets, as it is most probable that she sprang from the Earth herself.'"

The only observation elicited by this fantastical variation on Laplace's quite as fantastical nebular theory, came from Ben Zouf.

"If we're going to be nabbed at all I hope it won't be by old Jupiter! Mercury, being a younger man, would have probably less science and nonsense about him!"

During the latter half of September, Gallia and Jupiter were evidently drawing nearer. On the 16th of October the two heavenly bodies were to be at their minimum distance. Nobody apprehended a direct collision. If each planet rigidly pursued its own path, according to the Professor's calculation, no collision could well occur. The two orbits lay in planes diverging from each other by an angle of more than one degree. The real danger was to be apprehended, as already observed, from the enormous power of attraction exerted by the colossal planet. This really was a great danger, and in fact should prove inevitable unless the Professor's calculations were rigidly exact.

In spite of the general uneasiness, however, as the two heavenly bodies drew nearer, Jupiter's splendid appearance extorted the incessant admiration of the Gallians. His disc, reflecting the rays of a sun nearly 500 millions of miles distant, flooded the Gallian nights with a radiance surpassing that of the Harvest Moon. His bands and the other peculiarities of his surface revealed themselves sharply and definitely by an increasing variety of tints. His light was absolutely so powerful that his rays, reflected from Nerina's surface, revealed her presence, like a fluttering spirit star, in a part of the sky where, owing to her close proximity to the Sun, she should otherwise be totally invisible!

Who could be surprised if the Professor never quitted his observatory? Night and day his telescope was presented with deadly aim at Jupiter's devoted head. "Surrender your secrets or die!" seemed to be the motto of the merciless Professor. "So far," he went on soliloquizing with the radiant orb, "so far you have completely eluded our most patient investigations. Wrapped up in your distance of nearly 400 millions

18

of miles, you could laugh our puny efforts to scorn. But you never dreamed of one of us approaching you on the back of a comet! Nevertheless, so it is! We shall soon be only 30 millions of miles apart, and then I shall have you by the throat! We can already discern all your satellites, even the nearest, by the naked eye, a feat never accomplished by mortal man before, in spite of all the twaddle we hear about Kepler's teacher, the Siberian hunter, and the tailor of Breslau! Every human being on my Comet can see them now without any trouble. Even the children can distinguish Io's grayish tint, Europa's blueness, Ganymede's dazzling immaculate white, and Callisto's ruddy glow occasionally softening into a bright orange. You have stopped your twinkling, I see. You shall stop more than that before I am done with you! Don't imagine that *I*, like the ignoramuses down stairs (*en bas*), am afraid of you! We are getting nearer to you it is true, but we shall never be near enough to get entangled in the terrible tentacles of your attraction! I have calculated all that! Not the slightest danger of Gallia falling on your surface, or of being made a fifth satellite! Unfortunately, however, I am not yet able to say positively what power you may have in deflecting her course so much as to prevent her from returning to the Earth after a two years' revolution! I do not desire to return to Earth! I am now exactly where I wish to be, careering through space like a lightning flash, and so I wish to continue as long as the Creator leaves me life enough and intelligence enough to contemplate and appreciate his works! This is a most critical point in Gallia's existence. Sway her just a little, Jupiter, and she can never return to the Earth again! In such a case who knows what a glorious career awaits her! She may take us to Alpha Centauri — she may even enable me to contemplate more closely the mystery of Sirius's dazzling effulgence gravitating around a dark primary!"

Whilst thoughts of this kind chased each other through the Professor's busy brain, the tongues belonging to the other busy brains "down stairs" were wagging as loudly as ever.

"No use whatever in asking the Professor such a question," said the Captain in reply to a proposition of Procopius; "we shall soon find it all out with the utmost ease."

"How so, Captain?"

"We shall have only to watch the expression of his countenance on the 16th of October. If radiant and smiling, good-bye to the Earth forever! If cross and miserable, all right! Gallia's orbit has not been disturbed!"

"Your reasoning is probably quite correct!" said the Count; "you know him best. For my part, I hope sincerely he has made no mistake in his calculations."

"He make a mistake!" exclaimed the Captain. "Never! Don't trouble yourself on that point. When a boy at school he was nicknamed Little Calculus in Breeches (*Le petit Calcul culotté*), and he astonished even the great Arago himself by his keenness and intuition. If he says we are to return to the Earth, return we shall and no mistake!"

"Governor," said Ben hastily entering the room at this point, "I think I have made a discovery."

"Out with it, Ben Zouf!" said the Captain. "Favor us at once with your brilliant discovery."

"Thank you, Governor," said Ben with the serious air of a man who has expended profound thought on what he is going to say. "Does not the lightning-rod draw the lightning?"

"Well, suppose it does, Ben Zouf," replied the Captain, curious to know Ben's new kink.

"And is not Jupiter coming nearer and nearer to us all the time?" asked Ben.

"He most undoubtedly is," replied the Captain.

"And won't he destroy us all if he falls on us?"

"Unquestionably," answered the Captain. "Our total destruction would be as sure as fate."

"Well, Governor," said Ben, "I think I can prevent it."

"You can!" said the Captain, winking to his friends to keep a straight face. "How can you keep Jupiter off, if he thinks proper to come?"

"I shall quietly climb the mountain side," said Ben, with a knowing look, "and then I'll drop a few stones on it."

"On what?" asked the Captain.

"On the telescope," said Ben.

"On what telescope?"

"On the little Professor's telescope sticking out of the mountain side night and day, and drawing Jupiter down on us!"

A roar of laughter saluted Ben's brilliant thought. Even the grave Count was convulsed.

"Ben Zouf," said the Captain, gradually recovering from the fit and stopping every moment to wipe his eyes,—"Ben Zouf!—if I ever hear you say a word again about firing stones at that telescope, I shall bind you, legs and arms, and hold you tight till the Professor has made you understand the value of a sextillion!"

At this terrible threat Ben retired at once without a word, looking rather sheepish and crestfallen at his signal want of success in his first attempt to deal with scientific problems.

18 *  O

A bulletin from the Professor soon announced that on the first of October Gallia was only 43 millions of miles from Jupiter, less than half the distance of the Earth from the Sun.

" He is getting nearer fast," said the Captain. " His size is already monstrous. How much larger is he than the Moon ever appears to us from the Earth ? "

" He looks fully ten times larger," said Procopius.

" Ten times larger! how do you make that out ? "

" At the same distance from the Earth as the Moon is, he would appear to the Terrestrians as large as 1800 Moons put together. At present he is 180 times further off, and must of course look 180 times smaller."

" Lieutenant," said the Captain admiringly, " how proud your professor of astronomy must be at having you for a pupil! But to resume our lesson — what do you think these grayish parallel bands can be that we saw last night crossing his surface north and south of his equator ? "

" There you have me again, Captain," answered Procopius; " nobody can venture to say with anything like exactness what these bands or belts may be. I have no doubt that it is to their examination the Professor devotes most of his time in the observatory. I hope his labor will be repaid, but I doubt it. We are still too far from Jupiter to speak positively on the subject, and if we move much nearer we shall be inevitably dragged to his surface."

"I see that these belts, as you call them, are sometimes quite dark and sometimes quite bright at the poles," said the Captain. "The edges, however, are always bright. It is also easy to see spots dotting these belts here and there, and occasionally varying in size and shape."

"The spots are quite as puzzling as the belts," said Procopius. "Are they due to atmospheric disturbances? No one knows. Are they to be explained as accumulations of vapor, taking the form of clouds and whirled rapidly around the planet on the wings of something resembling the Trade Winds? No one can tell. Is Jupiter a body intensely heated as well as enormously surpassing the Earth in size? — in other words, is he a sun on a small scale and therefore entitled to an opaque atmosphere and to what are called spot zones? Pure conjecture! No one knows. No one is ever likely to know!"

Gallia moved on. The belted planet drew nearer. The Russians and the Spaniards at last were beginning to show some signs of uneasiness. Redoubled attention on the Captain's part to keep their spirits up was therefore necessary. He succeeded very well with his people ;

but his own apprehensions he was unable to calm. The Count too was a little restless, and, though in general a slight reserve kept him from close intimacy with the Captain, a sense of mutual sympathy excited by an alarming subject brought them frequently together. They were continually talking on the absorbing theme. Sometimes they tried to laugh at their fears and to speak of their return to the Earth as an undoubted fact. But very often they were seized by the opposite notion; — a return to the Earth was too absurd to think of — the remaining days of their life were to be spent in the midst of the boundless regions of the solar world — perhaps in the profoundest depths of the stellar universe! Did this new aspect of affairs render them very disconsolate? No. They never lost hope. They always endeavored to look the worst right in the face, to prepare themselves for it, to resign themselves confidently to whatever lot their Great Creator had in store for them. Even through the unfathomable womb of the Infinite, His all-seeing eye could easily track them, His almighty arm could readily shield them. This sublime hope generally succeeded in consoling them even when things looked blackest, and the friends would separate in pretty good spirits.

Next time they would probably meet in a more sanguine mood. Their hope of once more seeing the

Earth, their natural home, would again amount almost to a certainty. As long as they could catch a glimpse of her up there among the countless stars, sparkling like a bright gem on the dark mantle of night, they would wonder at themselves for ever renouncing the hope of visiting her again. Besides, as Procopius often assured them, this danger past all danger would be past. Saturn was altogether too far off to do harm, and on their return Jupiter, Mars, and Venus would be in another and more distant part of their orbits.

"To-night," said the Captain on the evening of the 15th of October, "we shall reach the nearest point. Only 30 millions of miles will separate the two planets. Let us hope for the best. We shall soon know all!"

No one slept that night in Alveario di Nina. No one could sleep. The Spaniards made too much noise with their dancing, singing, and castaneting. At the very first light next morning the Captain made some excuse for paying the Professor an early visit.

He was gone not more than a quarter of an hour altogether, but the delay seemed like a century to his impatient friends. At length they could see him hastily descending the mountain and joyfully waving his cap.

"Victory!" he cried.

The cheer replying to that cry from the mouth of the

cavern was one of the most joyous ever uttered by the lungs of man.

" How does he take it?" asked the Count.

" He is quite crushed and woe-begone!" answered the Captain. " I tried to cheer him up by congratulating him on the splendid result of his calculations. But he would not listen to me. He who should be the most triumphant of astronomers is now the most miserable of Gallians."

His Comet, instead of wandering off and getting lost forever in the intricacies of other systems, was bound once more to return to the Earth!

" Let us thank our Creator!" said the Count, taking off his hat and bending his knees. "A danger un-speakably great is past. We may now begin to hope!"

His example was immediately followed by the other Gallians. The next few minutes were devoted to silent but most fervent and grateful prayer.

# CHAPTER X.

## ISAAC PUZZLED.

THE Gallians had every reason to feel grateful. The moment had been extremely critical. If Jupiter's attraction had done no more harm than retard Gallia's velocity even by the short delay of fifty or sixty minutes, the Comet could never reach the Earth again. She might indeed reach the Earth's orbit at the proper point, but the Earth having passed in the meantime, her arrival would be too late. She would be 240 thousand miles behindhand, or no nearer the Earth than the average distance of the Moon. In how many cycles of ages would the same favorable conditions present themselves again? Thousands, millions, of ages would no doubt have to revolve before another contact was possible.

"But now," as Ben whispered to the Captain, when all, risen from their knees, were moving quietly to breakfast, "we've doubled the cape, and it's all serene!"

Two weeks later (November 1 ancient calendar, June 1 Gallian), a bulletin from the Professor announced the distance between Jupiter and Gallia to amount to more than 40 millions of miles, and that in 2½ months (old calendar) the Comet would have attained her greatest distance from the Sun.

"Two months and a half yet!" observed the Captain. "I should not be sorry if we were there to-day. I love the Sun, and it makes me miserable to be hardly able to recognize him in the sky. Only look at him! He looks for all the world like a little watery moon! It is now mid-day, and yet we can hardly see each other."

"No wonder," observed Procopius. "His light and heat can't be greater than the 25th part of the light and heat received by the Earth. He seems indeed to have hardly more effect on us than yonder Jupiter, whom his feeble beams strive in vain to eclipse."

"Yes," said the Count gratefully and warmly, "he may look small and weak, but he is still there! As long as we can see him we can feel ourselves in his power; I should rather say under his protection! Gallia is as obedient to him to-day as she ever was. Like the Prodigal Son, we shall soon begin to return to our father. We shall soon begin to feel the mighty heart of the solar system sending his pulsations of new light and heat through our own, and thrilling them with as much life, strength, and hope as ever!"

A burst like this from the Count, usually a man coldly reserved and dignified, produced a wonderful effect both on Procopius and the Captain. They instantly stopped grumbling, and the next time they were disposed to find fault they took care not to do so in the Count's presence.

Talking of grumbling, however, where has old Isaac been all this time? We have not seen him ever since the day he had rented the coins and the spring-balance, now fully two months ago. The following morning, as per agreement, Ben had brought back the articles safe and sound, and received in return the paper roubles that had been left in pledge. At the same time, Ben, full of mischief, took the opportunity to assure him that the Comet was pure gold, and that, if the little Professor was to be believed, as soon as they returned to the Earth gold would be just as plenty and just as valueless as dust in July.

This Isaac of course would not implicitly believe; anything that Ben said he would hardly believe at all. But he was very much worried. He had lately seen so many things running counter to all previous experiences that he felt it impossible to say what he really believed or did not believe. Gallia made of gold — why not? It must be made of something, and gold was just as likely as anything else! That little Professor certainly knew a great deal. Everything he had said so far turned out to be perfectly true. What if it was gold? The prospect was alarming — appalling!

The Gallians should either return or not return. If they did not, what was the good of gold? As well exchange his merchandise for the bits of rock found on the seashore. If they did return, such a sudden supply of the precious metal thrown at once upon the Earth would make gold so much dross. Why then should he part with his merchandise? What would he gain by its sale? Parting with it at once seemed useless; reserving it for the future was dangerous. What should he do?

Pondering over these problems gave him such hard work that he had kept himself altogether in his cabin for the last two months, never once entering Nina Hive to ask its inmates if they wanted anything in his line. The conclusion to which, however, he at last slowly came was : to sell his goods as usual, but to try to be satisfied with a profit of no more than 200 per cent.

Nobody ever missed him at the Hive. Nobody even mentioned his name, except little Nina who would now and then speak to Pablo about the poor old man who had nobody to talk to. To the others the idea of his existence hardly ever occurred. "Dutch Isaac," as Ben once said, "is one of those fellows whose absence is borne with wonderful ease. In fact, the further he is off, the more you want him to stay there!''

But the time was now approaching when the wants of the community required a new supply of his goods. The stores of oil, tobacco, coffee, sugar, etc., Ben reported one day to the Captain as running rather low. The Captain finding such to be really the case, at once made out a list of the necessary articles, provided himself with a supply of money from the treasury and, attended by Ben Zouf, started for the *Hansa*.

Isaac of course saw them coming down the mountain road, and had time to make every preparation for receiving them. By this time his resolution was fully decided on. Sell? Certainly. Comet gold, however pure, could not be as good as gold *coin*. Even on the Earth, some time should elapse before the Comet gold could be brought to market. Therefore sell! but not at too high a price. "No, no," soliloquized Isaac; "don't play too dangerous a game, my friend! If you drain these people dry before you have disposed of all your merchandise, what are you going to do about the rest of it? As long as they have money, they will certainly pay for what they take. The Captain, with all his gasconading, is what simple people call an honest man. I rather like an honest man. He is very nice to sell to. Any day I would prefer making fifty per

cent sure off an honest man than run the risk of making
nothing at all off a rogue! The Count too is 'honorable' and 'generous,' as long as the money lasts. But
when it runs out, what will they do? Will their 'hon-
esty' compel them to lie down and quietly starve to
death while plenty of food is rotting in your vessel?
Not likely! Even 'honest' men are not such jackasses
as that!

"I know however what I shall do. By asking no
more than 200 per cent profit I shall stave off the dangerous moment for a good while. It will come at last,
I know. Their money all gone, they will come quietly
here and say: 'Dutch Isaac, we want food. We can
buy no more, as you have all our money. But we are
not going to starve! Stand out of the way! We shall
have food by foul means since we can't by fair!'

"At such a moment, Isaac, will you know what to
do? Certainly I shall. In the first place, I shall be
as cool as I am now. In the second, I shall throw up
my hands in surprise and exclaim: 'Foul means, my
dear friends! No need of threatening old Isaac with
such an expression! Money? Who wants money?
You're starving, you say. But I say you shan't starve
as long as old Isaac can prevent it! But the Governor
is a gentleman! The Count is a gentleman! You are
all gentlemen! You would despise taking his mer-

chandise from a poor man without offering him some equivalent. Well, let the Governor and the Count sign this little paper, and you can have all the merchandise you like and at the old prices too, except a slight nominal interest. I ask the Governor's and the Count's signature merely to gratify their fine sense of honor, for, being gentlemen, they would scorn to be beholden to a poor man for a favor without doing everything in their power to return it!' There I shall have them on the hip! They accept my terms at once. In their surprise they will scarcely look at the paper they sign. But once back on the Earth, they will learn the secret of my 'generosity.' The Captain has some rich relatives! Besides he will find himself such a famous man as to have little difficulty in meeting his paper. As for the Count, I know all about him already. He has immense estates near Voronetz, on the Don, adjoining the great Danischeff property. No danger of *his* notes being protested! Isaac, my son, s' help me Father Abraham! you 're a match for them all, if, as the Gentiles say, you only keep your top eye open! But — hush! there 's the Governor's step outside! Be on your guard!' "

In a few seconds a knock was heard at the door. Isaac hastened to open it, and, bowing low, pretended to receive the Captain with the greatest joy and respect.

19.*

"O Signor Governor-General!" he cried in as soft fawning tones as his grating voice permitted, "this honor to a poor destitute man! S' help me Father Ab—"

"Isaac," said the Captain unceremoniously cutting him short, "we want new supplies of coffee, tobacco, oil, and other articles in your line. Ben Zouf will accompany me here to-morrow to make a selection of what we require and to pay you for it."

"Mercy! my good Governor-General, mercy!" cried Isaac, employing as usual his stereotyped stock phrase whether there was any reason for it or not.

"What are you mercying about?" asked the Captain, trying to keep his temper. "I said 'pay,' did I not? 'Pay' means giving a fair value in exchange for goods received, does it not? What do you mean then by asking for mercy?"

"Oh Signor Governor!" replied Isaac in a voice trembling like a beggar's asking for bread, "I understand you very well. I always said your Excellency would never allow a poor merchandising man to be robbed of his properties merely because he had got into a little difficulty!"

"There is no thought of robbing you! You shall be paid full value for everything."

"P-a-i-d, Signor Governor? Paid — in — in — ready money?"

"THIS HONOR TO A POOR MAN!"

"Yes, paid in ready money."

"Because, you know, Signor Governor, it would be quite impossible for a poor man like me to give credit— particularly —"

He stopped, expecting the usual interruption, but, seeing that the Captain was disposed to listen, he went on with what he had to say.

"Particularly as — yes — your Excellency knows it as well as I do — we have here among us very honorable gentlemen — that is, very solvent gentlemen — fully able to pay as they go — Signor the Count for instance — they say he owns half a province —then there's the Signor Governor himself —"

He stopped again, seeing the Captain give an impatient start, but finding nothing came from it, he resumed:

"And your Excellency knows well that if I gave credit to one I could not refuse it to another. This would lead to jealousies and unpleasantnesses very disagreeable to a man of peace like your Excellency — so I think that for the general good I had better trust nobody!"

"I think so too, Isaac."

"Signor Governor, now you talk like a good business man! S' help me Father Abraham! I like a good business man! I prize him like the apple of my eye! But will your Excellency do me the favor of saying in what kind of ready money I am to be paid ? ''

" In gold coin, silver coin, copper coin, and, when the coin is all gone, in good bank-notes."

" Paper money ! '' gasped Isaac, as if ready to drop. " The very thing I dreaded all the time ! ''

" Isaac, don't be an ass ! Have you no confidence in the Bank of France? the Bank of England? the Bank of Russia ? ''

" Oh Signor Governor, I never could believe in paper ! Rags can never make good money. Gold and silver is money all the world over ! Gold first of all, and then — well then — if I can't get gold — well, silver. But no rags ! No rags ! ''

" All right, Isaac ! '' replied the Captain, trying to talk as pleasantly as possible. " I have told you already you will be paid in current gold — in current silver —''

" In gold ! Only in gold ! '' cried Isaac, cravingly like a hungry man for food. " S' help me Father Abraham, all other kinds of money are only dross ! ''

" Well, gold be it, Isaac. Fortunately it is gold coin that is most abundant in Gallia just now, Russian gold, French gold, English gold —''

" Oh the nice good golds ! I love them all so dearly ! '' murmured Isaac with suppressed enthusiasm, his fingers clinching convulsively on some imaginary treasure. "But Signor Governor," he added, seeing the Captain about to withdraw, "won't your Excellency permit me to ask one little question?"

"Certainly, but be quick!"

"Shall I not be allowed the right, Governor-General, of putting my own price on my own properties?"

"Master Isaac, you forget, I'm afraid, that I have the right to put a maximum rate on your goods to prevent extortion. But I confess I do not like these revolutionary proceedings, and I am determined never to have recourse to them unless when compelled by extreme necessity. You shall, therefore, be paid the regular European prices for each article, not a sou less. Of course, you would never think of asking a sou more?"

"Oh mercy! mercy! good Governor-General!" cried Isaac, now terribly alarmed; "won't your Excellency allow me to take my advantage of the rise in the market? That is the strict law of trade, you know! I alone have the right to dictate the price since I alone have the properties! The law, your Excellency! and it can't be opposed! To oppose it would be robbing me of the dearest of the seller's unquestioned rights!"

"Each article at its current European price — no other!" repeated the Captain quietly.

P

"What, your Excellency! Here I have an opportunity to corner the market —"

"The very opportunity you must not make use of!"

"Never, s' help me Father Abraham! will such a
splendid opportunity —"

"Of flaying your fellow-creatures alive occur again!
I know it — at least I hope so! But try to talk a little
sense, Isaac. You seem to forget that, situated as we
all now are, in circumstances unparalleled in human
history, all conventional regulations cease, and self-
protection becomes the final law! In virtue of that
law, as the head and protector of this community, I
have the undoubted right to seize your merchandise for
the common benefit —"

"Seize my merchandise! Seize my lawful properties! Is that Christian justice? Is that —"

"Isaac," said the Captain quickly, "I find I am only
wasting time in trying to make you understand the simple truth that exceptional conditions allow exceptional
measures. Don't mind my arguments therefore, but pay
good attention to what I say. Try to be satisfied with
what you get. Be thankful that you get anything.
Don't irritate us into such a state of feeling that we
should not scruple to compel you to give us up everything for nothing!"

"For nothing! Holy Father Abraham! My goods
for nothing! —"

"That will do now, Isaac," said the Captain, hastily opening the door, and ascending the cabin steps. "European prices! The regular European prices! Good-morning!"

For the next hour or two Isaac was as miserable as miserable could be. Sinking on the old bench, he beat his head, tore his hair, howled like an angry schoolboy under the rod and, as no one was present, probably shed a few genuine tears. But suddenly a bright thought struck him. He started up quickly and began pacing his narrow cabin with a bold decided step.

"Ah, you plundering Gentiles!" he soliloquized, "you wish to cheat the poor Jew man, do you? At European prices, eh? Very well! European prices let them be! Let us see what you'll make of it!"

At an early hour next morning the Captain, Ben Zouf and two Russian sailors knocked at the cabin door. It was instantly opened by Isaac, who welcomed his guests with a great deal of bowing and muttering.

"Hello, Pharaoh!" cried Ben, slapping him on the back, "how is the old fraud getting along?"

"I am very glad to see the good Signor Ben Zhouf," said Isaac, half in earnest.

"We're coming to get skinned this morning, Belshazzar!" continued Ben; "but don't cut too deep, you old reprobate! Leave a little for another time!"

"You shall have all my goods, Signor Ben Zhouf, at the lowest living profit —"

"European prices!" observed the Captain, taking a seat and pulling out a cigar.

"Certainly, European prices," said Isaac acquiescently. "Now what can I accommodate you with, my good Signor Ben Zhouf?"

"To-day, Levi," said Ben, reading off his memorandum, "we want 30 pounds of coffee, 30 pounds of sugar, and 25 pounds of tobacco — and be sure to give us a good article, skinflint, or I'll break every bone in your carcass. But above all things, give us the right weight! I'm quartermaster-sergeant, and know all about it! Don't imagine you can humbug me!"

"Quartermaster-sergeant!" said Isaac, pretending to look surprised. "I thought you were his Excellency's aid-de-camp, Signor Ben Zhouf!"

"Yes, Methuselah, aid-dè-camp on state occasions, but full quartermaster-sergeant when we have to deal with a cunning old fox like you. Come, be alive! Don't keep us fooling here all day!"

"Thirty pounds of tobacco, did you say, Signor Ben Zhouf?" asked Isaac.

"No, you old curmudgeon! only twenty-five pounds of tobacco, but thirty pounds of coffee and the same of sugar."

"All right, Signor Ben Zhouf," said Isaac, lifting the trap-door and descending the ladder that led to the hold.

He was back in a few minutes, carrying five packages of tobacco, all fastened, and stamped, and sealed, strictly according to the French law.

"Here are five packages of the best tobacco," said he. "Each weighs five pounds. That is twenty-five pounds in all; which at six francs a pound makes exactly one hundred and fifty francs."

"Are you satisfied with that price, Isaac?" asked the Captain.

"I must be satisfied, Governor," answered Isaac, well aware he was asking double the ordinary price; "a poor man has no resource but to submit."

"Very good!" said the Captain. "Now then, let us see you weigh these packages."

"What's the use, Signor Governor?" pleaded Isaac. "You see these bands? They are untorn. These stamps? They are unbroken. These figures? They are unchanged —"

"Talk, talk, talk!" cried Ben, impatiently interrupting him. "Have you not heard the Governor? Hook them on and let us see them weighed!"

Isaac took another dive into the hold and returned slowly with the spring-balance in his hands.

20

He suspended one of the five-pound packages to the hook.

"*Ach du guter Himmel!*" he shrieked, looking at the needle.

It registered only about ten ounces for a five-pound package!

Ben was so amazed that he suddenly lost his power of speech.   Even the Russians exchanged angry glances at such an outrageous piece of knavery.

The Captain remained perfectly tranquil, well aware, of course, that the change of weight was due to Gallia's comparatively slight gravity.   But instead of explaining, he assumed the most serious countenance and quietly addressed the distracted merchant who was hastily weighing one package after another with invariably the same result.

"Now, Isaac, I was right you see in asking each package to be weighed.   You will of course add whatever is required to make the weight all right."

"Mercy, good Governor-General!" shrieked Isaac, clasping his hands.   "Don't ruin me!   Something is wrong!   Some evil spirit —"

"Yes, you old hypocrite!" interrupted Ben angrily, "something is very wrong!   The evil spirit is your own!   Look!" he added turning to the Russians, "the old scoundrel wanted to do us out of our tobacco!"

HE SUSPENDED ONE OF THE PACKAGES.

The two Russians lifted their hands in perfect amazement, quite horrified at such supernatural depravity.

"Mercy, good Signor Ben Zhouf!" was all Isaac could say, as he threw himself at Ben's feet and shed abundant tears, some probably real.

"Shut up, you infamous old Bedouin!" cried Ben, quite indignant. "Make up at once for the deficiency to the last grain, or we shall go down and help ourselves!"

Isaac continued to object frantically, though he began to feel it was no use. He *should* stick to his own balance; the Gentiles would not listen to any other arrangement. Oh if he had only an ordinary pair of scales! Five pounds would then weigh five pounds — neither more nor less — not less certainly. But having nothing but his spring-balance, he had to extricate himself out of his difficulty as well as he could.

A fresh appeal to the Captain. Perfectly useless.

"This is not our spring-balance, you know, Isaac," said Servadac quietly. "If it were, you might object with some reason. It's your own. It is the very spring-balance you have always used in dealing with your customers. You buy with it, so you must sell with it. When we pay for a pound, a pound is the least we can expect."

Further negotiations being evidently vain, and Ben appearing disposed to take the adjusting operation into his own hands, Isaac had nothing left but to comply. But with what reluctance! He had actually to return to the hold three separate times before he had the full amount — 37½ packages instead of 5. And so it was with the coffee and the sugar, only, these not being in packages, carrying them up in boxes and bags was still more difficult. What fun it was for Ben and the Russians! Ben grinned, but the Russians roared till their sides ached. How politely they ran to help him when the packages or bags slipped from his overloaded hands! How nicely they piled them up in a shapely pyramid! How, when they had almost laughed themselves sick, some shallow joke of Ben's would start them off again!

"If you like a little smoke, Beersheba," he would say at one time, "come over to-night to my cell in the Hive! Don't bring any tobacco along! There will be plenty there for all, but no one will be more welcome than you!"

Then pretending to look distressed, "Poor Aminadab!" he would say with a sigh, "his generosity will be the death of him! See how he totters! Suppose we go down, boys, and clear out the whole hold! That would save him further trouble!"

But he threw them into fits when he told Isaac to

"bring up that horse and wagon! or if he had such a thing as a brewer's dray down there to fetch it along! they would be sure to return it," etc., etc.

Isaac bore all this "chaff" without a single word in reply, except an odd grunt now and then sure to excite the renewed hilarity of his merciless tormentors. He worked away grimly, and, in about an hour and a half, more than a hundred packages of tobacco, coffee and sugar were piled on the ground, ready to be taken away. Ben, opening his purse, counted out six hundred francs in gold and asked Isaac for a receipt. Isaac counted the money carefully twice over, and, seeing there was no help for it, began scrawling something on a dirty bit of paper, when the Captain at last thought proper to interfere.

He had allowed things to go so far more for the sake of amusing himself and punishing Isaac a little than for any other precise purpose. He knew indeed in his heart that a good deal of the Jew's grief was only affected and that his loss was very far from being equal to what he pretended; still he had such a regard for the observance of even the outward forms of heavenly justice that he would not allow even a rogue like Isaac to imagine himself cheated.

He therefore ordered Ben Zouf to pay over 4500 francs for what had really cost 4500 francs and told

20 *

Isaac to make out the proper receipt.  Ben started a little, but did not make much difficulty about obeying orders, having already a pretty clear idea of the real state of the case.  The Russians looked at each other open-mouthed, and tried in vain to comprehend this new turn of affairs.  But as for Isaac himself, it took him at least five minutes to recover from the profound astonishment into which the sight of the 4500 francs had instantly thrown him.  At first he felt a little dazed like ; then, the truth beginning to dawn on him, he felt inclined to be spiteful.  But the glitter of the pile of gold had a sedative effect on his nerves, and, at last recollecting that he had not thanked the Governor for this most unexpected and welcome favor, he hastily started up and, seeing he was no longer in the cabin, ran up the steps to overtake him.

But the Captain by this time was too far off.  The two Russians bearing between them a hand-barrow piled high with the merchandise, were slowly and cautiously descending the ice-road leading down the vessel's side. Ben was carefully watching the whole operation, lending a hand now and then to steady the men down the slippery path or to prevent a loose package from rolling off. As soon as they were fairly down on the shore where the footing was good, he turned himself into a military band to encourage his toiling comrades.  As Isaac slowly returned to his cabin, he could easily hear some of the simple words with which the sprightly Orderly endeavored to imitate the noisiest musical instruments.

His song is of course untranslatable, its merit lying more in the spirit than the words, but more in the singer than either. The following doggerel, however, may give the reader some kind of an idea of the nature of

### BEN ZOUF'S BATTLE-SONG.

At the bugle sound
How the pulses bound!
Too toototootoo too too too! (*Imitating the Bugle.*)
And the trumpet blast
Makes the blood run fast!
Tan tantarantan tan tan tan! (*Imitating the Trumpet.*)
Oh the shrilling of the fife
Sets me thrilling with new life!
Pee peepepeepee pee pee pee! (*Imitating the Fife.*)
And the rattling of the drum
Makes my breath go and come!
Rub adubadubdub rub dub dub! (*Imitating the Drum.*)
But neither Bugle sweet
Nor Trumpet's wild repeat
Nor Fife's enkindling heat
Nor Drum's arousing beat
Can ever stimulate me like the Cannon's swelling roar!
Boom boobaboomboom boom boom boom! (*Imitating Cannon.*)
Can ever captivate me like the Cannon's stunning roar!
Boom boobaboom boom, etc. (*Imitating Cannon.*)
Can fascinate, intoxicate,
Can subjugate, infuriate
Like Cannon's deadly roar,
Like Cannon's savage roar.

Boom boobaboomboom boom boom boom!
Can ever petrify me like the Cannon's maddening roar!
The Cannon's fiery roar,
The Cannon's frenzied roar!
(*Con furia*) Electrify, delirify, barbarify, demonify,
Like Cannon's raving roar,
Like Tiger Cannon's roar!
Boom boobaboomboom boom! boom! boom!

# CHAPTER XI.

## SATURN.

THE Gallian days slipped quietly past, but they were no more peaceable than the Gallians themselves. No quarrels, misunderstandings or ugly passions of any kind disturbed the harmony of the little world. Even the old innate faults of humanity the new colony seemed to have mostly left behind. With the single exception of Isaac, the personification of cupidity and selfishness, no ugly blotch disfigured this blest abode of innocence and harmony. As for the Professor, he was cranky and eccentric, but that was all. There was no real harm in him! Leaving out his vast scientific knowledge and wonderful powers of calculation, he was simply an over-grown child, passionate, inconsiderate, too much absorbed by the present to think seriously either of the past or future.

In fact, so far as enjoyment of the present went, the Russians and Spaniards were just as much children as Nina and Pablo. Did they ever think of the Earth? Of course they did. It was in talking over the Earth and its recollections that they spent most of those long six hours of every day's occurrence, when it was too dark to remain outside and too early to go to bed. But they spoke of it as Australian emigrants often speak of their native land; their present separation from it was merely temporary, and their future return a certainty on which it was not worth while to waste a doubt. How they were ever to get back, how the safe transfer should be effected, how the consequences of the terrible shock were to be avoided — these points they never troubled themselves with discussing. Even the Captain, the Count and Procopius gave themselves very little present uneasiness with regard to these tremendous questions. That the day for decided action would come they felt pretty confident, but they shrank from undertaking to devise the means of overcoming the enormous danger that day should bring. If we said they were afraid of looking these awful dangers square in the face, we should say nothing but the truth. By silent consent they seemed to defer serious consideration of the subject as long as possible, knowing well that all present arguments were premature and that the question would lose no importance by delay.

This confident anticipation of being one day afforded a chance to revisit Mother Earth, was highly useful to the Captain and his friends in more ways than one.

It banished completely all moping, melancholy, and despair, and saved them an immense amount of trouble besides. They had not to distract themselves regarding means of support in the distant future, nor occupy themselves too seriously with the clothing question, or the agricultural question, or the animal question. In fact, they found themselves completely free from numberless questions sure to obtrude themselves in case Gallia was likely to be their permanent abode.

Not that they did not now and then find themselves warmly discussing what they should have to do in such a contingency. At present, of course, little could be done anyway. But in eight or ten months more the solar heat would be strong enough to make the ocean free and the land available. Then would be the time for the *Dobryna* and *Hansa* to carry back the men and animals to Gourbi Island. Its fertile portions ploughed, dug, harrowed, sowed with a rapidity rendered necessary by the shortness of the Gallian summer, mowing, reaping, and every other harvest operation could be readily got through before the return of the long and dreary winter. During the continuance of the fine weather the little colony would enjoy the healthy and stimulating life of hunters and husbandmen, and, summer over, they would return once more to the bowels of their volcano. Veritable birds of passage, with the change of season they should change the scene and mode of their existence.

"But during the summer," said the Captain, "why not start on some new exploring tour? I am confident that much of Gallia is still unknown to us. Who can tell? Perhaps we should discover a coal-mine or some other store of fuel that would save us the necessity of passing the long winter in the gloomy caverns of a volcano."

"Yes," said the Count, "if we had plenty of coal, though silos would be out of question, we might easily construct such dwellings as would permit us to spend the winter as well as the summer in Gourbi Island."

"A coal-mine or anything of the kind," observed Procopius, "can hardly be expected to exist in Gallia. Nevertheless, we should make every attempt to discover anything at all in the shape of a fuel supply. We have nothing indeed to complain of so far, but I often have my doubts regarding the durability of our volcano. Our existence here hangs on a thread."

"I understand your allusion, Procopius," said the Count. "You mean to imply that our volcano might be suddenly extinguished some day. Gallian fires, no doubt, can hardly be called inexhaustible. The first time we approached Terre Chaude, you both remember, there was no sign of a volcano to be seen. The eruption therefore must have burst forth suddenly. Now, what bursts forth suddenly may just as suddenly come to a stand-still."

"What should then become of us?" asked the Captain. "As for myself, I see one solution of the question, and only one. It would be to descend deeper and deeper into the abysses of the volcano until we should reach a spot low enough and warm enough to afford some kind of protection against the terrible colds of space."

"If this 'fate ever befalls us," said Procopius, "we shall be in exactly the same condition as an inhabitant of the Moon finds himself to-day — a dweller in a dreary land of cinders and ashes! Can the Moon be no more than a larger Gallia? Is it really true that every world in the universe must be in one of the three conditions — of preparation, as Jupiter — of perfection, as the Earth — of extinction, as the Moon?"

"Keeping to the main question, Procopius," said the Count, "have you ever noticed any sign of change, either way, in the flow of our eruptive matter?"

"Never, I must acknowledge, Father," was the reply; "its action is still as regular, calm, and steady as it was the first day we visited it together."

"Such has been my experience too," said the Captain confidently; "in any case it is time enough to cry out when we are hurt."

21          Q

"No wonder, Captain, that your motto is *Never despair*," said Procopius. "I wish I could look on things as sanguinely. I should then be completely free from an apprehension that I confess often makes me feel anything but comfortable."

"What is it?" asked the Captain and the Count, struck by the unusual gravity of Procopius's tones.

"Gallia may be only one of the wrecks of a greater planet that once exploded prematurely," said Procopius. "If so, why may she not explode again?"

"Prophet of evil, hold thy peace!" said the Count in Russian, the language he often used when very much in earnest.

"Oh come, Procopius!" said the Captain, trying to laugh. "We have enough of real evils! Don't freeze the very blood in our veins with your horrible gorgons! Dante's Inferno is side-splitting fun in comparison with your conversation this morning!"

A despatch from the Professor, dated the 45th of June (December 15th), informed the Gallians that their world, now moving at the diminished velocity of 11 or 12 million leagues a month, was 216 million leagues from the sun, and had nearly reached the furthest extremity of her orbit's major axis. The despatch concluded with these words:

"Look out for Saturn!"

In telling them to "look out," the Professor, however, did not mean to imply that Gallia was again in the danger that had threatened her when in proximity to Jupiter. For in fact she was in no danger at all. Instead of 31 million miles, the distance which had separated Gallia from the Jovian world, a safe distance of at least 400 million miles separated her from the Ringed Planet. No peril therefore need be apprehended beyond the little that had been calculated and allowed for.

By urging his friends to "look out," he merely wished to call their attention to the exceptional opportunity for contemplating this wonderful planet — an opportunity never granted before to mortal eye. Saturn showed himself fully as plainly to the Gallians now as he would to the Terrestrians by coming twice as near.

"I feel like asking the Professor some questions about Saturn," said the Captain after reading the despatch. "Let us pay him a short visit. By a little dexterous management, we may get him to talk to us."

They went up to the observatory; but that was all they had for their pains. The Professor would not even look at them. He kept his eye glued to the telescope all the time they stood there, and only showed he was aware of their presence by signalling to them with his hand to go away.

"Lieutenant," said the Count on their return, "you will have to be Professor for us this time. We all want to know something about Saturn."

The *Dobryna's* library fortunately contained elementary works enough on astronomy to be of great help to Procopius in the little *conversazione* at which he presided that afternoon.

Besides the Captain, the Count, and Ben Zouf, the audience consisted of three Spaniards, two Russians, and the two children Pablo and Nina. The Captain, as their teacher, wished his pupils to learn all the astronomy they could under such favorable opportunities.

"In the first place," began Procopius, starting the subject, "were Gallia to change places with Saturn, the Earth would be completely invisible to our naked eye."

"I hope Gallia won't do anything of the kind," said Ben. "I should be sorry to lose sight of the Earth! As long as we keep her in view, we are all right!"

"If you have not already carefully examined Saturn, Messieurs," continued Professor Procopius, "I should advise you to begin this evening, and don't be satisfied with merely using the naked eye. We have plenty of telescopes, one belonging to the Captain, the others to the *Dobryna*. Do not be chary of their use.

"Saturn gravitates in space at a distance of more

than 400 million miles from Gallia, and at a mean distance of 872 million miles from the sun. So you see we have not yet got quite half-way. At this immense distance from the centre of the solar system he receives only about the hundredth part of the light and heat bestowed on the Earth.

"The dry figures denoting his elements must not detain us more than a few moments. His year is nearly as long as thirty Earth years, all that time being required to perform one revolution around the sun. His orbit is nearly 5500 million miles in length, and he traverses it at the rate of more than 21 thousand miles an hour. His circumference is about 220 thousand miles, his surface 16 billion square miles; and his volume is 190 trillions of cubic miles. Though three times smaller than Jupiter, therefore, he is more than 720 times larger than the Earth. But in spite of this great superiority of bulk over the Earth his mass is not 90 times greater. His consistency in fact does not seem quite equal to that of water —"

"Hem!" coughed Ben Zouf incredulously, and he whispered to a companion, "Likely story! Don't believe it!"

"His days are only 10½ hours long, but, owing to the great inclination of his axis to the plane of his orbit, his seasons last more than seven Earth years each.

21 *

"But what must afford especial delight to the Saturnians — if there are any Saturnians —"

"Why are there not?" asked unbelieving Ben in an undertone.

"Is the splendor of his nights, illuminated as they are by no less than eight moons. Their names, beginning with the innermost, are Mimas, Enceladus, Tethys, Dione, Rhea, Titan, Hyperion, and Japetus. Their periods of revolution, like their distances, are of course all unequal, from that of Mimas, who takes only 22½ hours, to that of Japetus, who takes 79 hours to revolve around his primary. Japetus's distance from Saturn's surface is about 2⅓ million miles or ten times the distance of the Moon from the Earth, but Mimas and the three following are much nearer to their primary than the Earth's satellite is to hers. These moons too must be far more dazzling than the terrestrial moon, not only because they are much brighter, but because the feeble sunlight seems to bring them out in stronger relief.

"But Saturn's greatest glory, and what must make his nights lovely beyond conception, is his famous triple ring. Examine him carefully this evening. Seen from Gallia, the planet looks like a monstrous diamond set in a triple circle of pale gold. He is more brilliant than even Venus at her brightest; in fact, he looks almost as large as the sun, though, of course, he bears no comparison in splendor. Let us say a word or two about the ring.

THE RINGED PLANET.

"An observer on Saturn, standing directly under the ring, which spans the heavens at a distance of about 12 thousand miles over his head, can see no more than a narrow band probably not more than a few hundred miles in width. It resembles a glittering silver thread stretched across the sky from horizon to horizon. But, quitting this position, let him move a few degrees north or south and he will behold three concentric arcs detaching themselves slowly from each other. The nearest, darkish and semitransparent, is about 9 thousand miles broad; the middle one, brighter than the planet itself, has a width of nearly 18 thousand miles; and the outermost, of a dusky gray, is more than a thousand miles narrower than the innermost. The intermediate ring, therefore, is not only the brightest, but it is actually wider than the other two put together."

"Are these rings stationary?" asked the Captain.

"No," answered Procopius; "they manage to whirl around the planet in their own plane once in every 10½ hours."

"What, Professor!" cried Ben, still incredulous. "Rings of such an enormous size, of no greater solidity than water, to roll around at such frightful speed without flying into a million — a sextrillion of fragments! Another likely story!"

"Your surprise is natural, Ben Zouf," answered Pro-

copius quietly. " I did not however say Saturn's *solidity*
was less than that of water ; I said his *density* — a very
different thing.  Many kinds of wood, for instance,
have less density than water, yet they are very solid,
and have much cohesive power.  Still with every possible allowance the great difficulty you have pointed out
remains as obvious as ever.  What prevents these rings,
subjected as they must be, to incalculable centrifugal
power, from instantly flying asunder?  I must candidly
say, I don't know.  Nobody knows.  People can guess,
but a guess is no reply.  Some will say that in allowing
these rings to exist, the Omnipotent Creator has been
willing to give human beings a glimpse into the gradual
formation of the heavenly bodies.  These appendages,
they tell you, are the remains of the great nebula which,
solidifying and concentrating itself by degrees, has at
last become Saturn.  As to how the rings themselves
have also become solidified, no explanation is however
attempted.  That they are solidified, I think, cannot
be doubted.  If they break, they would probably either
all fall in bits on Saturn's surface or, flying off at a
tangent, finally become new satellites, increasing the
band of eight that already exists.

" Leaving speculations, however, and coming to
probable certainties," continued Procopius, " we may
say pretty positively that to those Saturnians living

between the 45th parallel and the equator the triple ring must present a variety of very wonderful phenomena. Sometimes it is a vast silver arch enveloping half the sky, but broken at its keystone by the planet's projected shadow. Sometimes it shows its entirety, like a series of semicircumferences without break or interruption of any kind; at other times again, and even pretty often too, these rings eclipse the sun himself, who then makes his appearance between the bars at certain calculated mathematical intervals, to the intense delight no doubt of the Saturnian astronomers. If to these phenomena we add the rising, the marching, and the setting of the eight satellites, some in quadrature, some full, some presenting silvery discs, some only horned crescents, we can easily conceive what spectacles of transcendent beauty may be revealed night after night to the Saturnian observer.

"We Gallians have no opportunity of beholding anything approaching the splendor of such spectacles. We are too far away. Terrestrial astronomers at this very moment with their powerful telescopes can see Saturn probably a thousand times more plainly than the keenest-sighted among us. Even the Professor above in his observatory works at a disadvantage in comparison with astronomers in Ireland, in Paris, in Rome, in Harvard. Everything that I have said about Saturn, I have taken out of books belonging to your own library. Even the *Dobryna's* telescopes cannot show you much. No matter for that! We can easily console ourselves for not making a nearer approach to Saturn. We are gone far enough into the regions of eternal twilight. If we went further we should be so much the longer in getting back — that is, if we ever get back at all!"

This sentiment was received with the heartiest applause particularly by Ben Zouf, and the Captain asked the Lecturer to wind up by telling them something about Uranus and Neptune.

"Of Uranus I can say very little," said Procopius. "You can distinguish him yourselves to-night as a star of the sixth magnitude without much difficulty. But even with your best telescope you can see none of his eight moons. We know that he is about 75 times larger than the Earth, that his density is about that of water, that it takes him 84 years to revolve around the sun, from which he is so remote that the orb of day can never appear more brilliant than an exceedingly bright star.

"As for Neptune, the last planet of our solar system (till another is discovered), we cannot see him at all. The Professor no doubt with his superior telescope sees him plainly enough. But as there is little use in questioning the Professor just now, we must fall back for information in our old friends the books.

" These tell us that Neptune's existence was suspected long before it was ascertained. Bouvard started the idea in 1820 by observing some unaccountable perturbations in Uranus. Leverrier and Adams took up the scent, and separately tracked the planet to the part of the sky where he should be found. Galle and Challis actually found him there in the summer of 1846. It was however soon discovered that Lalande of Paris had already seen him in 1795, and recorded him in his Catalogue, though never suspecting him to be a planet. He had even noticed his displacement among the other stars, but, by attributing it to imperfect observation, Lalande missed forever an immortal discovery. Neptune's mean distance from the sun is more than $2\frac{1}{2}$ billions of miles, and he takes 165 years to accomplish his revolution. He sweeps through an immense orbit, 30 times greater than that of the Earth, with a velocity of 12 thousand miles an hour."

" Beg pardon, Professor," said Ben, " but what did you say was Neptune's distance from the sun ? "

" More than $2\frac{1}{2}$ billions of miles," answered Procopius.

" How much further off is that than we are at this moment ? " asked Ben.

" Nearly six times further off."

" Billions, billions," said Ben reflectively ; " it makes my head ache trying to realize these terrible numbers."

"No wonder," said Procopius; "but a billion miles is a mere speck in comparison to the distance from here to the nearest fixed star."

"Which is the nearest fixed star?" asked Ben.

"One of the nearest fixed stars," answered Procopius, "possesses additional interest for us just now from the fact that it is in all probability the very star to whose system Gallia would attempt to attach herself in case she succeeded in withdrawing from that of the sun. It is *Alpha Centauri*, easily visible in the southern heavens. Its distance is so great that its light, though travelling at the rate of 12 millions of miles a minute, is three years and a half in reaching the Earth. In other words, it is no less than 20 trillions of miles away."

"How have such vast numbers been got at?" asked the Captain.

"To reach them is no easy matter, as you may well suppose," answered Procopius. "Time, patience, close observation, and, above all, a clear, cool, logical head, are the least indispensable requisites for attacking such problems. As a consequence, very few of the distances of the fixed stars have been calculated at all — ten or twelve at most. The results most agreed on are the following, which I have jotted down in my memorandum-book:

Vega is at least 125 trillion miles distant.
Sirius     "      130   "      "      "
Polaris   "      280   "      "      "
Capella  "      440   "      "      "

"But, after all, these numbers give the mind hardly the faintest idea of the ineffable immensity of such distances. Let me read you a passage on the subject I lit on by accident in some astronomical work, and which struck me so forcibly at the time that I immediately copied it off, translating it into Russian. For the details of course I do not vouch, though I have little doubt that in the main they are quite correct.

"'We see,' says my author, 'by means of light, but, as light requires some time to travel, we do not see instantaneously. An eye, for instance, as far off as the sun, and able to see at that distance, does not see the events that are actually transpiring on the Earth, but only those that took place eight minutes previously. Placed in Jupiter, the same eye could not see events until three-quarters of an hour after they had taken place. Let us extend this idea further. Suppose a being with an all-penetrating eye has taken a stand on *Alpha Centauri ;* he sees events transpiring before him that had really taken place three years and a half before. Transport him to Capella ; he is an eye-witness of the great battles and other striking occurrences of the first

22

years of the present century.  Set him back to a star ten
times more distant ; he is in the middle of the Crusades,
and can easily recognize Godfrey, Richard, Saladin,
Barbarossa, or Saint Louis.  Set him further back yet to
a star which light takes 18 or 19 centuries to reach ; he
sees the sun darkening, the Earth trembling, the dead
rising from their graves, and the other awful phenomena
attending the ineffable tragedy of the DEATH OF CHRIST.
Transport him still further back, away to the regions of
eternal darkness, which the light of the sun requires six
thousand years to reach ; he surveys the vast desolation
of the Universal Deluge.  Further back, back, back still,
since space is infinite ; he beholds the Earth crawling out
of Chaos, and Life beginning to develop.'  In fact,'' concluded Procopius, closing his memorandum-book, ''all
facts are stereotyped somewhere in space, and nothing
once accomplished in the universe can ever be effaced
from its everlasting tablets.''

''The writer of that passage was as great an enthu-
siast for science as my old Professor,'' said the Captain ;
''and I must confess it has given me some kind of an
idea of his strong desire to traverse the stellar universe,
contemplating all its wonders, without ever troubling
himself with a thought on the dangers or inconveniences
of such a journey.''

''If he only lived long enough on the Earth,'' said

Procopius, "he could accomplish such a journey without any serious danger or inconvenience at all."

"I understand you, Lieutenant," said the Captain. "You mean that if the human race lasts long enough, the Earth herself will give it an opportunity of visiting every portion of the universe."

"Exactly, Captain. We are told that the sun himself, instead of being stationary, is revolving around some great centre, dragging his host of planets along with him in the direction of the constellation Hercules."

"At what rate?" asked the Count.

"At the rate of nearly 200 million miles a year. But so slow is this motion in comparison with the distance of the constellation that an observer, beginning at Adam's time and watching carefully ever since, could not yet determine whether the sun moved in a curve or in a straight line. The curve of the mighty arc would be actually inappreciable."

By this time Ben's eyes began to look very heavy. The children, carefully covered up, were fast asleep on the benches. The Spaniards and the Russians had noiselessly withdrawn. Nevertheless the Captain and the Count had found Procopius so interesting that they wished him to continue the *conversazione* a little longer.

"The observer may not be able to notice much change in six thousand years," said the Count. "But if he continued his observations, the day should surely come at last when he could notice some change in the relations of the stars to each other."

"Certainly, Father," answered Procopius; "the forms can't help changing in course of time, since the stars composing them move or seem to move with unequal velocities. Some astronomers, I find, have even given themselves the trouble to calculate what shapes some of the constellations will assume 50 thousand years from now. They have even drawn these shapes mathematically on paper. They show you the well-known quadrilateral of the Great Bear taking the shape of a long cross, and Orion, no longer a pentagon, becoming a somewhat irregular parallelogram."

"The effort to conceive futurities of this nature," observed the Count, "I should consider to be just as distressing to the mind as the effort to conceive the just value of high numbers. For my part, I prefer to keep to the present. What would be the consequence, for instance, Procopius, if, breaking away suddenly from the solar system, we were whirled off into the immense fields of space?"

"To such a question, Father, no answer deserving the name can be expected. We should probably be dazzled by the sight of wonders of which our solar system can give us no idea. We might find, for example, planetary systems which are not always governed by a single sun — regions of the universe, in fact, whence the monarchic idea was excluded altogether. We might find two suns, three suns, even six suns, depending on each other, and gravitating around each other, with a complexity the most astounding. We might find red suns, yellow suns, blue suns, orange suns, indigo suns. We might have an opportunity of admiring the effect of these different colors reflected all at the same time from the surface of the various planets. Who knows if we should not have even days of different colors succeeding each other? Might we not even be so favorably situated as to have each and every one of Gallia's days consisting of as many colors as make up the spectrum?"

"Come, come, Procopius," said the Captain, smiling, "are you not giving rather loose reins to your imagination? One thing, in fact, I have always noticed. You scientific men, who pride yourselves on the closeness with which you always stick to dry facts, and particularly on the cold sneer with which you always regard the wild flights of imagination's shadowy steed, are only too often tempted to bestride the animal yourselves! And when you do, the Lord only knows when you are going to pull up!"

"Captain," said Procopius pleasantly, "your re-

22 *                R

mark, though full of truth, just now is not quite applicable. In the first place, I am not a scientific man; and in the second, I am trying to answer an imaginative question the only way it can be answered — in an imaginative way. Gallia is never to see any of these wonders. She is never to lose herself in the conglomerations of the Milky Way, in the mystic clouds of the so-called Star Dust, nor in the glimmering worlds of nebular vapor whose weird and startling shapes telescope has never yet decomposed. No. Gallia, dear friends, I am happy to say, is never to quit the solar system, never to lose sight of our glorious Sun; and her little promenade of 1500 million miles through the universe is no more to be compared to the distances separating her from the countless orbs of space than —"

"Than a coral insect to the Pacific Ocean!" said the Captain, seeing Procopius hesitate for a comparison, and fully appreciating every word he had said.

# CHAPTER XII.

## THE HOLIDAYS.

A S Gallia moved on, though with diminished velocity as she approached her aphelion point, the cold sensibly increased, the thermometer now marking 64° below zero. We need hardly say that alcohol thermometers alone were now employed, the cold for some time having reached the point at which mercury freezes.

With the increase of cold increased likewise the danger for the *Dobryna* and the *Hansa* that Procopius had apprehended. The icy layers had kept on increasing with irresistible force beneath their keels and lifting them higher and higher over the surrounding levels. Every day the change in their altitude could be detected. They were now at least fifty feet higher than the surface of the Gallian Sea. And this upheaving force of the ice no human power could prevent or counteract.

The chiefs grew seriously uneasy at the prospect of the doom inevitably awaiting the vessels. Procopius was particularly disturbed. All the *Dobryna's* effects he had removed long ago; nothing now remained but her masts and machinery. For these there was no help, but it was the loss of her keel that he particularly regretted. In case of a certain contingency, the possibility of which always haunted him, it might make a tolerably safe refuge for the little colony. Besides, if she was destroyed, how could they ever remove from Terre Chaude? The *Hansa's* danger was just as great. Badly balanced on her airy pedestal, she leaned over already at a dangerous angle.

Isaac was warned, but at first the danger he either did not or would not see. Never should he abandon his vessel, he protested; he would watch her by day and would watch her by night! But latterly he had been noticed, whenever he thought himself unobserved, to leave his vessel stealthily, in order to get a good look at her. He took several views, and varied them by varying the points of observation. But from no point were they assuring; so at least concluded the Gallians watching him from Nina Beehive, who could see him tearing his hair and beating his breast. Some of them could even imagine they heard his oaths and imprecations, for, like many others who lightly use the name of God, when deeply irritated he could be a terrible blasphemer.

It was clearly time for the Captain to interpose.

Neither Isaac's life nor Isaac's cargo should be lost without an effort to save them.

"Isaac," said Servadac, one day approaching the Jew so suddenly that Isaac started at the sight of him. He had been probably so absorbed in the contemplation of his vessel's danger that he had not heard the Captain's footsteps. "Isaac, your vessel can't last much longer in her present condition. I am now come to ask you for the last time, are you not willing to leave her?"

"Never!" cried Isaac, howling like a wild beast as he ran up the dizzy stairs of ice. Then crossing the deck and plunging into the cabin, he bolted, barred, and locked himself up with as much determination as if he really believed that by these means he could forever keep out all intruders.

Early next morning a vigorous knock was heard at his door. He did not answer. Another. No reply. The third knock was made by a log of heavy wood, which, wielded as a battering-ram by two stalwart Russians, burst the door into splinters and showed Isaac the Captain and his men ready to remove to a place of safety a valuable cargo and its owner too whether he liked it or not.

Here, as before, it would be neither instructive nor agreeable in any way to give the reader even a tenth

part of Isaac's protestations, exclamations, or imprecations. To listen to him you would imagine him to be
one of his ancestors just caught by a robber king of the
middle ages. Still neither his teeth were to be drawn
one by one, nor his limbs to be racked, nor his "properties," dearer than tooth or limb, to be taken away.
On the contrary, his goods were to be removed to a
place of safety, and himself to be conducted to comfortable warm lodgings, where not only should he be abun-
dantly fed and cared for, but also allowed every opportunity to watch over his merchandise and sell it at a price
which everybody knew brought enormous profits.

Negrete and the others only laughed at his howls, but
Ben Zouf's hot blood began to get hotter, and he hinted
a notion of bringing him to reason by a quiet tap on the
head.

But here, as before, Isaac knew exactly what he was
about. Not a tear did he shed, not an insult did he fling,
not an imprecation did he vociferate, of which he had
not carefully calculated the effect. Unless he made these
ungodly Gentiles see that it was all force-work, they
would be wicked enough to charge him for their labor.
Whereas by the well played farce of "remonstrative
action," he could get it all done, as it had been done
some months before, without its costing him a single
cent.

Ben Zouf probably saw through him. Anyway he knew how to deal with him. Next morning Isaac was delivering the usual string of epithets more loudly and volubly than ever against "abductors," "kidnappers," "nigger-drivers," etc., and protested that he *would* remain in the *Hansa* as long as he lived, preferring to be torn limb from limb rather than abandon the vessel or his lawful "properties." Ben interrupted him in a pause of the harangue by quietly observing :

"You're quite right, Bendigo. Stick to your vessel to the last. The Governor has decided not to disturb you."

Isaac started as if he had been shot, gave Ben a keen glance of his cunning eyes, and kept a wonderfully quiet tongue during the rest of the day.

He accomplished his purpose however with perfect success. The goods were all stowed away most carefully, at the expense of the Gallians, not at Isaac's. The labor was long and hard, but the Spaniards and Russians worked with much activity and cheerfulness. Warmly clad and well muffled up, whenever muffling was necessary, they endured the low temperature with singular ease. They were however carefully cautioned not to touch any metal with the naked hands. If they did so, their fingers would be destroyed in exactly the same way as if the metal had been red hot. But fortunately the whole job was got through without the slightest accident worth mentioning, and by the end of the third day all the *Hansa's* merchandise was safely stowed away in the capacious caverns of Alveario di Nina.

Did Isaac remain behind, as he had solemnly sworn to do? Not much, as Ben Zouf expressed it. He followed the last load to its destination, and made himself quite at home in the volcano, as naturally, and as quietly, as Ben Zouf himself. More than that. Early next morning he went back to his vessel, and soon returned laden with a heavy cargo. In fact all that day, and the next, he spent in trips between the Hive and the *Hansa,* always returning loaded with old ropes, rusty iron, rotten sail-cloth, bits of chain, broken pulley-blocks, and other articles abandoned by Ben Zouf as useless, but picked up carefully by Isaac to be stowed away with the rest of his " properties " in the nooks and corners of the especial gallery placed at his disposal.

What he did beyond this attracted no notice. It must be acknowledged that he was never in anybody's way. He was hardly ever seen. He slept in the midst of his property, and troubled nobody for his food or drink. A little alcohol lamp cooked his meals, which it would be an exaggeration to call even modest. The other Gallians had nothing whatever to do with him, except when they came to buy his goods. Seldom did such visits result without a trade. One thing, indeed, was quite certain. Slowly, but surely, every morsel of gold in the little colony was finding its way into Isaac's money-drawer, the key of which Isaac never parted with day or night.

Christmas was now approaching, and in a week or two another festival would be on hand — New Year's, the anniversary of Gallia's encounter with the Earth. Not a single one of the thirty-six human beings she had then swooped off was now missing. They were all still on deck, as the sailors say, and, in spite of the wildest vicissitudes, in perfect health and strength. The temperature had, indeed, diminished to a very low degree, but progressively and harmlessly, without abrupt extremes, without cutting winds, without even an air-current bad enough to give a cold. No climate could be much healthier than Gallia's. And there was no sign of anything like an abrupt change ever occurring in the state of the elements. It was, therefore, quite probable that on Gallia's return to the Earth she would bring back her full list of passengers safe, sound, and flourishing.

In such a cheerful state of things the Captain did not like to let the holiday season pass without some appropriate celebration. He spoke very decidedly on the subject to the Count and Procopius, as they were one day talking over the state of things in general.

23

"We must not let our people," said he, "lose all interest in Earthly matters. They are still children of the Earth. They are some day to return to the Earth, but even if they never return, it will be useful to attach them to our dear old mother world by at least memory and grateful recollection. In that old mother world our fellow-beings will be soon celebrating Christmas and New Year's happy days with all imaginable solemnities and rejoicings. If the Terrestrians are right, we should imitate their example on our Comet. In fact, we Gallians have even greater cause for warm gratitude and heartfelt thanksgiving. Our safety during this wonderful year has been a standing miracle. Let us unite ourselves in spirit with our terrestrial brethren in their festivity, and let us make distant regions of space, where such sound was never heard before, ring with the angelic chorus of Christianity: *Glory to God in the highest, and on Earth peace to men of good-will!*"

"I approve of the idea most heartily, my dear Captain," said the Count warmly. "Whether our stay here is to be a short one, or to last for the rest of our lives, we must never forget that we are children of Mother Earth, both with their advantages and their responsibilities. All the grand memories of our former life we must always carefully cherish. The peculiarities of one people, or of one country, need, of course, never be regarded here, unless under very exceptional circumstances. But the memory of the great events in the Earth's history that affect humanity at large, should never be allowed to die out. The first of these, most undoubtedly is Christmas, which, however, in my opinion, is more becomingly celebrated by a quiet, serious, and rather internal expression of deeply felt sentiments, than by any external noisy demonstration. New Year's is quite another matter. It is older than Christmas — it is the oldest of all festivals. Celebrating, as it does, the establishment of *Life* in *Nature*, it cannot be too jubilant; action, fun, noise, every exciting phase of life, within proper bounds, should not only be permitted, but encouraged. Therefore, my dear Captain, I applaud your idea most warmly. Let our stay in Gallia be of short or of long duration, we must never forget to celebrate the two great anniversaries that remind us so forcibly of the two natures of man — his body perpetually dying, though perpetually renewed, and his soul ever young, unfading, immortal!"

Procopius expressed himself quite as earnestly on the subject, and after awhile the conversation became more general.

"Don't you think, Count," asked the Captain, "that our friends the Terrestrians will be exceedingly interested in the celebration of the New Year's that is to come twelve months after the next? Don't you think that they know enough of Gallia by this time to be a good deal concerned as to the issue of a second contact?"

"I have very little doubt on the subject," answered the Count. "I see no reason why the great observatories particularly are not greatly excited about the new Comet. It is pretty certain that at this moment they are making every effort to catch a glimpse of us from Paris, from Pulkowa, from Boston, but especially from Parsonstown in Ireland, where the finest telescope is still to be found."

"Gentlemen," said Procopius, "I cannot say that I quite agree with you on this subject, nor can I say either that I quite disagree. You must remember that not only on the very night of the collision, but also for several weeks before, very heavy mists had obscured the Earth, completely cutting off the astronomers from all observation of the sky. Gallia therefore had plenty of time to approach unannounced, unseen, and to make her full swoop without anybody knowing anything about her except the Professor, whom some atmospheric peculiarities seem to have exceptionally favored at Formentera. How do we know if these mists disappeared rapidly enough to allow a glimpse of the Comet on her way to the sun? Remember that it is only in a very limited portion of her orbit that a comet is visible at all.

Then how very small our Comet is! Her diameter is more than three times less than the Moon's, so that, at the same distance, that is, a quarter million of miles' distance from the Earth, she would not present a surface one-eleventh times as great. Imagine her size then when millions of miles away! Besides, there is no reason whatever for supposing Gallia to be supplied with a comet's usual appendage — a tail. We can see no sign of one. The Professor never spoke of one. In fact, from the solid constitution of Gallia, there could hardly be one. But I see you are getting impatient and wish me to come to the point at once. It is simply this: some astronomers probably know a little about us on Earth, but the most of them know nothing at all. Not one of them, I am pretty confident, has ever thought of connecting Gallia with the disappearance of a small portion of Gibraltar, of a rocky islet of the Balearics, or even of a tolerably large portion of a deserted region of the northern African shore. All these they have tried to account for in more or less satisfactory ways. 'Sinking of the land level,' 'Elevation of the sea level,' 'Tidal Wave,' 'Undermining,' 'Forces of Shrinkage,' 'Caving in,' and other favorite phrases, as commonly used as they are destitute of definite meaning, will amply account to the world at large for the sudden loss of some territory without having recourse to

23 *

the wild theory of a comet.   Consequently we Gallians
give very little trouble to the world at large.   No one
remembers us now except our very intimate friends,
whom however our sudden disappearance must have surprised quite as much as grieved.   As for Gallia herself,
with all due respect to the Professor, I do not think
a single astronomer on the Earth troubles himself
seriously about her.   A few obstinate calculators, it is
true, may have discovered the period of her contact
and predicted that event.   But these are in such a
minority and the world at large has so many other
events to trouble itself with that, if we received a mail
from the Earth to-day, I should venture to say we could
not find a single allusion to Gallia beyond an odd squib
in the corner of some country newspaper.''

The Count and the Captain looked at each other in
silence for some time, not knowing what to think of
Procopius's strange notions.   But as they had generally
found him to be possessed of a clear head and sound
sense as well as of a large share of practical scientific
knowledge, they were somewhat disposed to consider
his observations as rather plausible.   At all events
they could not think of answering them until the
holidays were over.

First came Christmas Day, December 25th.   According to the Russian calendar the anniversary of Christ's

birth would not come till eleven days later, but the Count, strictly following up his own remarks about the suppression of all national peculiarities, in order to celebrate the great common points of faith with greater harmony and effect, ordered his people to join the others in the celebration of the great Christian festival.

To carry out the idea according to its spirit, every Gallian without exception should be present. Accordingly on Christmas eve the Captain and the Count called in person on both the Professor and Isaac, presenting the kindest regards of the Gallian world and inviting them to assist next morning at the solemn festival and thanksgiving. They found Isaac half asleep on an old table that served as a bed, and rather poorly covered, though he had splendid blankets by the horseload. His reply to the invitation was not unexpected. It was "No!" pure and simple, only much surlier and more snappish than any such occasion called for.

With the Professor, to their great delight, they were far more successful. They found him still at his telescope, watching the heavens carefully and recording his observations by the light of an ingenious astronomical lamp which he had invented for the purpose. He scowled at being disturbed by visitors, but on learning the object of their visit he was visibly pleased.

"Certainly I will join you," said he, "in the first general expression of homage to the Great and Good Creator that has ever been presented from the surface of my Comet. Gallia is now a recognized and particularly favored portion of the universe by being made the abode of Life. Of how few mighty planets, of how few gigantic worlds, can this be said! Gallia therefore should be proud of the distinction — Gallia, I mean, should be grateful for the favor, and grateful she is! In everything concerning Gallia I will cheerfully take part. To-morrow's great festival being religious, as it ought to be, I will do my best to take a religious part with you in celebrating it. I shall be down with you at four o'clock in the morning, and though I have almost forgotten my religious duties, I am willing to take whatever part you assign me. I will pray a prayer, read a prayer or sing a prayer. I will preach a sermon, read a sermon or listen to a sermon. I will write a hymn, sing a hymn or take part in a hymn. You stare at my unusual amiability to-night, Servadac. Thank the festival for it! Happy Christmas to you both! I feel something like I felt when a little boy with my widowed mother long ago in Lorraine. Good-night, Messieurs! Happy Christmas!"

The Captain and the Count retired perfectly enchanted with the Professor.

" He can be a capital fellow when he takes the notion ! " said the Captain admiringly, but the Count's observation was different :

"What shall we give him to do? "

This reminded them that they had not yet definitely settled on any particular programme of the proceedings. Not a moment therefore should be lost. After some consultation, Procopius and Ben Zouf taking part, it was determined that the exclusively religious portion of the exercises should be short, simple, and of such a nature that all could join in heartily. The Hymn of the Nativity should first be sung by the assembly. Then a prayer or anthem would be read by the five chief men of the colony, beginning with the Professor and ending with Ben Zouf. Then the Captain would close the proceedings with a short impressive discourse, reminding all present of the great mystery of the Redemption, of God's ever-watchful Providence, and of man's duty to be always kind, forgiving, and merciful to his fellowmen. Then all were to go to breakfast together, but the rest of the day was to be spent rather quietly, and all were to be encouraged, in case they had any quarrels, to make them up immediately and to forget all about them at once and forever.

This programme was carried out as strictly as could be expected. At four o'clock, Christmas morning, all the

S

Gallians, except Isaac, were punctually assembled at Central Hall. At a signal from the Captain, all struck up together the grand old hymn, *Adeste, Fideles*, and, having been already well trained, the Spaniards especially, they sang it in very good style, and most assuredly with a good deal of fervent expression. Pablo's and Nina's sweet voices in particular enriched the harmony as with the melodious swellings of an æolian harp. Then all knelt down, and the Professor proceeded to read out of a prayer-book, presented by the Captain, the following anthem, formerly chanted in the Roman Catacombs by our Christian ancestors :

" O Wisdom ! proceeding from the mouth of the Most High God, extending throughout the boundless universe, disposing all things firmly and sweetly, vouchsafe to teach us the ways of prudence !

" This day we know the Lord has come to save us. This morning we see His glory. The Earth is the Lord's, and the fulness thereof ; the countless stars, and all that therein may dwell ! We bless His holy Name, which is worthy of praise and glory forever ! "

"*Amen !*" responded the assembly with one voice.

The Captain read the second anthem :

" O Adonaï, Creator of the human race, its Lawgiver on Mount Sinai, its Preserver in all places, its Redeemer forever and ever, extend Thy right arm over Thy wandering children, and direct them to the home Thou hast prepared for them since the beginning of Time!"

"*Amen!*" as before broke from the crowd.

Then came the Count's turn :

"O Root of Jesse, standing as a mighty sign to the nations! in whose presence the countless worlds come and go with never-ending regularity! look on Thy children struggling in captivity, and set them graciously free.

"O Mighty Key of the Infinite! who unlockest and no one shutteth, who shuttest and no one openeth, mercifully regard Thy servants sitting in the darkness and shadow of death!"

"*Amen!*" once more resounded fervently through the Hall.

Procopius now took the book :

"O Splendor of the Orient! whose breath hath enkindled the sun, whose smile hath spangled the sky with stars, dispel all gloominess from the hearts of Thy servants, and let Thy holy light illumine them forever!"

"*Amen!*" swelled loud and earnest as before.

Last of all came Ben Zouf :

"Eternal King! who hast formed man's body of matter, and his soul of Thy own eternal essence! Emanuel, the Merciful One, who knowest the dangers continually threatening both! However abandoned or deserted we may appear to be, we know that we are not lost, for Thy creatures are ever safe within the compass of Thy all-protecting hands! Blessed be Thy holy Name forever and ever!"

"*Amen!*" again reverberated through the caverns.

The Captain now signalled the assembly to take seats but the Russians and Spaniards remained kneeling.

"The Little Madonna!" they exclaimed with one voice. "We want the Little Madonna to say a prayer for us!"

The Captain went over to where Nina was kneeling, and, taking her hand to encourage her, whispered softly:

"My dear little daughter, recite aloud the short prayer I have taught you and Pablo to say every night and morning."

"Am I to pray 'Our Father' also, Padrecito?"

"Yes, Nina. 'Our Father' first, and then your own prayer."

The little thing, without any hesitation, knelt down at once beside the Professor's chair, and in her sweet, touching voice recited the sublime Prayer as an angel from heaven might have repeated it.

"AMEN!" cried the chorus with an energy really startling.

Then amid the profoundest silence, broken by nothing but the stifled roar of the lava cataract, the child, with clasped hands and bending head, recited the following prayer :

"O Almighty God, infinitely Merciful, infinitely Just, who hast made the Earth and the Sun, the beautiful Moon and the Stars, the animals and the human beings Thy especial servants, extend Thy mercy to Thy poor creatures now far removed from all human aid. Though distant from our own world, we are not distant from Thee. Make us resigned to Thy holy will and banish despair forever from amongst us. Let us love each other as brothers, and be just and merciful to each other as the children of the Most Just and Merciful One should be. Have mercy on the little planet that enables us to see so many of Thy wonders with our mortal eyes, and guide it ,at last safely into its destined haven. Bless the good Professor, the good Count, good Procopio, good Benni Zufo, my dear Padrecito, my brother Pablo, and my good friends the Spaniards and the Russians."

Here the child made a slight pause, being probably out of breath.

"AMEN !" cried the chorus of voices with greater depth of intense feeling than ever.

"And O dear Merciful God," resumed Nina in a

24

voice tremulous with emotion, " have a little mercy also on poor old Isaac, who lives all alone, all alone, and who is always talking to himself, because he has no little child to talk to!"

"AMEN!" cried the voices still loud and fervent, but the Captain's quick ear had caught an unusual element in the chorus coming from a dark and distant nook within which he had no doubt Isaac was secretly hiding.

What we have said will give the reader a sufficient idea of the other exercises with which the great festival of the Redemption was celebrated. They were all carried out in the same reverential, subdued and grateful spirit that the human soul so naturally sinks into, when the proper occasion comes to evoke it. But Christmas once over, immediate preparations were set on foot for celebrating New Year's with more noise, laughter, excitement, and general animation.

Ben Zouf was unanimously appointed Grand-Master of Ceremonies. He instantly considered himself bound to devise an attractive programme, full of variety as well as of general interest. A little reflection, however, soon convinced him that variety in amusements was a scarce article in Gallia. His decision therefore as to the items of the programme did not take long to be arrived at.

THE BILL OF FARE.

The day was to open with a grand monster breakfast, which was to embrace as far as possible all the chief features of a joyous social gathering. The mid-day entertainment was to be a grand skating-match in the direction of Gourbi Island. And the great feature of the evening was to be a return to Terre Chaude by torchlight.

"The first thing to be attended to," said Ben, "is to see that the breakfast is all right. If it is, our promenade will be a big thing on ice, not to talk of the torchlight procession to wind up with."

The composition of the bill of fare became therefore all at once a question of vast importance. Many a long colloquy did Ben and Mochel hold together, consulting, devising, correcting, improving, altering, and suggesting. They all ended at last in a complete and highly successful fusion of the French and Russian cookery systems into a new Gallian system, which, while carefully avoiding the defects of either, most intelligently united the respective advantages of both.

On the evening of December 31 everything was ready. Such viands, as preserves, game, pies, galantines, pickles, relishes, custards and other delicacies that could be eaten cold, were arranged in rows on the grand table of Central Hall and made a most attractive and appetizing display. As for the hot dishes, the morning would be time enough to cook them, the lava ranges affording admirable opportunities for preparing everything at the shortest notice and in the most exquisite style.

Once more the question was proposed : Should the Professor and Isaac be invited? and after a few minutes' debate unanimously decided in the affirmative. Procopius was delegated to wait on Isaac, and the Captain on the Professor. Procopius was hardly gone when he was back again, Isaac's " No !" being surlier and more snappish than ever. The Captain met with no better success ; the Professor was too busy even to notice his presence.

What was to be done now? The Count instantly volunteered to go himself or, better still, proposed sending Pablo to the Professor and Nina to Isaac, with formal notes requesting the honor of their company at the festival of the New Year.

But against anything like this Ben Zouf, Procopius, and even the Captain decidedly objected. Why expose the Count to the same insults as had met the others? As for notes to be sent by Pablo and Nina, writing them would be a mere waste of time. Everybody had done his duty, except these two stiffnecked men. They deserved no further attention. Why take further trouble with them? Still the Count persisting, a compromise resulted in letting Isaac severely alone and sending Pablo to the Professor.

He soon returned with the following unsealed note:

" To the Invitation Committee.

" Palmyrin Rosette begs to inform the gentlemen composing the committee above named that he has received their notice requesting his presence at what they call the ' Festival of the *New Year.*'

" In reply P. R. begs to state that he does not understand exactly what they can possibly mean by such a phrase. To-day being the 125th of June and to-morrow being the 1st of July, the use of the term ' *New Year* ' he considers utterly unintelligible, unless possibly the invitation is sent six months ahead of time. Such thoughtfulness on their part, if sincere, is beyond all praise. Indeed it is the only alternative that relieves their note from being a gratuitous, stupid, and malicious insult.

" Interpreting their note therefore in the only possible sense consonant with good breeding and ordinary intelligence, P. R. begs to inform the Committee that in six months from now he will gladly coöperate with the gentlemen to celebrate the great ' New Year ' festival in whatever manner they may deem most appropriate."

The reading of this characteristic note was greeted

24 *

with thunders of applause, even Ben Zouf being too much amused with its contents to be angry with the writer.

The *déjeuner à la fourchette* next morning was a grand and glorious success. All took their places at ten o'clock precisely, or two hours before sunset. The Count was at the head of the table; Negrete took the foot. The Captain and Procopius, with Nina between them, sat at the Count's left hand; the others were assigned the seats where they found themselves most at home.

The repast itself was a perfect masterpiece. In the solids Ben and Mochel had really surpassed themselves. Everything from the soup to the *pâtés de foie gras* was simply exquisite. A dish of partridges in particular, prepared according to some receipt Mochel had learned from an English *gourmand* in Calcutta, was delicious enough to dissolve the papillæ of the tongue and thrill with ecstasy the very lining of the stomach itself. What shall we say of the wines? The Count was no epicure, but he had often found himself the host of epicures. He had thus learned how to gratify the most luxurious tastes. Wines of Gascony: Château La Tour Blanche, Château Yquem, and Château Margaux; wines of Burgundy: Nuits, Clos de Vougeot, and Chambertin; wines of Champagne: Clicquot, Verzenay, Roederer; wines of Spain: Malaga, Alicante, Benicarlo; flowed

THE DÉJEÛNER.

in the greatest abundance, and were drunk with the greatest gusto. Even Nina was able to sip at a glass of exquisite Montepulciano; and some of the Russians, not caring for wine, had plenty of Kummel to make merry over.

Of the general enjoyment we must allow the reader to form his own conception. Every one was perfectly happy. Everybody made a speech, sang a song, danced a dance, and proposed a toast. The most successful of the speeches was that made by Mochel the cook in response to his health drunk with the utmost enthusiasm. He undertook to deliver it in French, and, as nobody understood a word he said, all thought it their duty to greet every observation with the most vociferous applause. The best song was sung by Ben Zouf — the *Zouave Chorus* already given in a previous part of this history — his audience encoring him no less than five times. The best dance was of course danced by the Spaniards, who performed a *fandango* in a style that could have never been learned out of Seville. Nina and Pablo also executed a little saraband with a grace and youthful enjoyment that afforded the spectators exquisite delight. But the best toast was that proposed by the Captain, for whom it had been tacitly and by common consent reserved for the last. It was "May our next New Year's be celebrated on Old Mother Earth!"

Words cannot describe the enthusiasm enkindled by the simple enunciation. Again and again the caverns rang with the most frantic " hurrahs ! " The tempest of sound was so great that the birds, not knowing what to make of it, commenced devouring the wrecks of the dinner before the dishes were removed, instead of respectfully waiting till they were helped, as they had been accustomed to do. The Captain did not accompany his toast with many words. They would be simply wasted. He sat down once or twice, but he was instantly called up to repropose his toast. It was again received with the same enthusiasm as before, the whole company shouting, cheering, and waving their glasses for at least five minutes.

When such a lull at last occurred in the storm that he felt he could make himself heard, he cried out :

"According to an understanding entered into with our distinguished Master of Ceremonies Ben Zouf, I take advantage of this opportunity to remind you that it is now time to take our excursion on the ice ! We have been more than four hours at breakfast ! "

The words produced a magical effect. Instantly every seat was quitted, and every form was seen retiring to its room to muffle itself up carefully in preparation for the exciting promenade.

At four o'clock all were ready. It was still quite dark,

being really one hour after the Gallian midnight, but in two hours the sun would rise again, and the stars, not to mention Jupiter, Saturn, and little Nerina, gave so much light that the Gallians could move about on the frozen sea without any serious inconvenience.

All started together, some singing, some chatting, some laughing, all in the best of spirits, and fully determined on having a " good time." Hastening out of the shadow of the mountain as quickly as possible, they soon reached that part of the ocean that was directly illuminated by the falling cascades of red-hot lava.

It was an entrancing scene. The stars blazed in the dark sky overhead. The ocean gleamed grayish for some distance all around. Then impenetrable blackness in every direction, save where the fire-current tumbled down the mountain side like a red river of melted iron blazing, sparkling and shimmering as if it flowed out of some gigantic furnace.

In the spot where the red glare was strongest, they continued to skate for an hour or so, presenting such fantastic figures as they alternately flashed into light or vanished into darkness, as were never surpassed in weird-like or grotesque effect by Doré's marvellous pencil.

But the sun, suddenly rising in the west, now gave the party the vast sea for a skating-ground. Instantly forming themselves into various groups depending on hazard or choice, they all simultaneously turned their faces to the north-east, and, like a flock of graceful sea-birds, started immediately in the direction of Gourbi Island.

The Captain, the Count, and Procopius kept together, preferring circular to straight-line skating. Negrete and the other Spaniards had now become by continual daily practice such magnificent skaters that they really seemed able to move as they pleased over the glassy surface of the deep. We compared the whole company a moment ago to a flock of graceful sea-birds. In this, however, we rather underrated the Spaniards. Never did sea-gull poise himself more easily on air, never did he circle round his companion in smoother curves, never did he suddenly dash forward in longer lines of unerring straightness, than even the least expert of these extra-ordinary skaters. The Captain and his companions frequently stopped, struck with wonder and admiration. The marvellous dancers had become skaters just as marvellous. What muscles of steel were theirs, and under what perfect command! One or two feats they performed in particular which the Captain in all his travels had never seen even attempted before. When skating around, waltzing, twisting, and spinning like whirligigs, at a signal they would suddenly become per-fectly motionless, still and stiff as statues. Then starting once more on a great run, they would lean over gradually, bending lower and lower, until the head was within a few inches of the ice; then just as you had concluded that they were lying down to take a rest, you would discover them still in motion, and gradually rising higher and higher from their horizontal position, until at last they became as vertical as ever. The Russians, following a custom of their country, formed in Indian file, and, keeping themselves in a straight line by means of a long stiff pole carried under their left arm, they launched off at an enormous velocity, and in immense curves, until they at last gradually faded out of view.

Pablo and Nina, arm in arm, kept fluttering about the Captain's group, laughing, chatting, shouting, now coming up close to their friends to tempt pursuit, now darting off with lightning speed, and making the welkin ring with their joyous cries of triumph.

Ben Zouf was everywhere. Sometimes, in the midst of the Spaniards, he imitated their most daring exploits with a boldness and confidence often crowned with success. Sometimes, making a bee-line for the Russians, and suddenly seizing the last man, he would grasp the pole and give it such a pull as very considerably altered the nature of the contemplated curve. Then, shooting off at a tangent, he would stealthily approach Pablo and Nina from behind, and, suddenly stooping, carry off the child from Pablo, who would, of course, make every effort to rescue her. After surrendering her at last, Ben would often approach the Captain's group, ask respectfully for orders, and, if he received none, spend a few minutes pleasantly chatting with the children, or entertaining the elder portion of the company with an account of some of his comical exploits.

Three times had he already approached the Captain for orders, and three times had he been told that the Captain had just then no orders to give. The fourth time he came up directly, without stopping to play with the children, as if to be in readiness to execute the orders which this time he was quite confident of receiving. He was not mistaken.

"Do you know what o'clock it is, Ben Zouf?" asked the Captain.

"Yes, Governor, it is eleven o'clock at night. In one hour the sun will set."

"How far are we from Terre Chaude?"

"Twelve or fifteen miles at least, Governor. Yonder are the peaks of Gourbi Island. They are far more easily seen than the summit of our volcano."

"It is time to return, Ben Zouf. Call our people together. The instant the sun sets, light torches, and start for Terre Chaude."

"All right, Governor!"

The Spaniards were still floating around on the verge of the horizon. The Russians had disappeared altogether. But Ben, knowing what direction they had followed, instantly started after them. In less than three-quarters of an hour the whole party, grouped once more around the Captain, began quietly moving south.

"We started as skirmishers," said the Captain, addressing them, "but we must return in close order, or somebody may get lost in the darkness. Have your torches ready to light as soon as the sun sets."

The torches, slung over their shoulders at starting, they now loosened, and held in their right hands ready for kindling. This was, of course, all done without interrupting their southern movement. To stand still even for a short time was highly dangerous; a serious chill might be the result, for, though there was no wind, the air was intensely cold. The sun was setting rapidly, and, through a peculiarity of the Gallian sky, seemed to set still more rapidly. No clouds by enlarging his size apparently retarded his vertical plunge. No refracting vaporous air, as on the Earth, enabled the spectator to see him for some moments, even after he had really sunk below the horizon. No gleam of green light reached the eye through the transparent waters of a heaving sea. As soon as his edge touched the horizon, owing to the perfect reflection of the glassy surface, the globe of

pale fire seemed to be a double sun.   Half-way down, he
was himself again.   Three-quarters down, he was only a
lurid spindle.   Then he disappeared as rapidly as if he
had fallen through a trap, and all light vanished from
the sky as suddenly as when somebody turns off the gas.

Faint and dim as had been the sunlight, for a few
seconds after his setting the darkness was most profound.
But the blazing torches soon lit up the scene.   Ben, as
Grand Master of Ceremonies, bore the brightest light,
and, preceding the party by a few hundred yards, carefully led the way.   His torch-flame, streaming behind
like a warrior's plume, was easily kept in sight by the
leaders.   And as for the stragglers, they were kept well
up by a few torchbearers especially appointed by the
Captain for the purpose.

The party had not been moving more than a quarter
of an hour in the darkness when the leaders saw Ben
turning back and waving his torch by way of signal.

"What now, Ben Zouf?" asked the Captain, springing forward half-way to meet him, being very unwilling
to allow the party to come to a halt for a single instant.

"Terre Chaude right ahead!" cried Ben, touching
his cap.

The Captain, shading his eyes from the glare, could
easily see where the atmosphere above reflected the
light of the burning crater, and where the lava river

"TERRE CHAUDE RIGHT AHEAD!"

below came down the mountain side, resembling in the distance a great, crooked, twisted, red-hot iron bar of very unequal thickness.

"All right, Ben Zouf!" said the Captain, slowing up for his party, while Ben, turning on his heels, instantly moved forward to resume his duties as courier and guide. The red hot river soon grew visible enough, though, owing to the smoke and glare of the torches, the moving crowd could not always easily discern it. On they moved with increased vivacity and animation. On reaching the skating-ground of six or seven hours before, however, the lava stream struck them all by its very peculiar color. *It was a dazzling blinding white, instead of a dull lurid red.*

Suddenly a vivid light, like a lightning-flash, rendered everything visible for miles all round. Even the spars of the two vessels seemed tipped with flame. At the same time a great blaze burst upwards from the summit of the volcano, shooting bits of glittering lava by the millions up to an immense height in the sky. For an instant, glare more intense had never been shed by the most dazzling meteors. Then burst on the ear the sound of the great explosion, deafening, stunning, ear-splitting, blood-chilling, heart-stopping.

Then dead silence all around, and intense darkness in every direction, save where the lava current still checkered the mountain side. But even that was growing dimmer and dimmer.

Ben Zouf's torch was now seen approaching rapidly through the gloom, diminished to a mere speck by the precipitancy of his speed.

" Governor! " he cried in a voice so hoarse as to be hardly recognized.

" What is it all? " asked the Captain, instantly dashing forward.

" THE VOLCANO IS EXTINGUISHED ! "

A terrible shriek of despair rose from the little band. In spite of the Captain's positive injunction, all paused to look. No glow was now visible over the crater. The lava river was becoming fainter and fainter in its outline. And, worst sign possible, the fire near the mountain summit was no brighter than the dying glimmer at the base !

" Onwards ! " cried the Captain, instantly snatching up Nina and muffling her up as carefully as he could while Ben took Pablo by the hand ; " for Terre Chaude with all possible speed ! "

Could the eruptive material have become suddenly and completely exhausted ? Had the oxygen met depths in the interior of Gallia beyond which it was unable to penetrate ? Was there an end to all hope of new volcanic action ? Was freezing to death their inevitable and early doom ?

"Onwards!" cried the Captain again, as he writhed in agony under these torturing questions.

The velocity of the party was now so great that some of the torches were extinguished. But Ben Zouf's still waved ahead like a gonfalon. The great blackness of the mountain now began to shut out the stars in front and on the left. Soon at its base, the skates were off in the twinkling of an eye. Ben's torch and a few others showed the way up the mountain road.

Plunging into the open portal, tearing through the well-known galleries, the whole party soon reached Central Hall ——

It was dark as pitch, and the temperature was already of an icy chill! Silent as the grave too was all around! Procopius hurried to the opening beyond which the cataract had till lately been falling like a fiery screen. No sign of fire there now, above or below!

Looking upwards, he saw the cold white stars gleaming in the pitch-black sky. Leaning over the precipice and dropping a stone downwards, he listened intently. Down, down it went, its course easily tracked from rock to rock, down, down, and then — no splash! A long continuous sound, as if made by a body moving slowly over very smooth ice.

The lagoon, till then kept liquid by the current of lava, was frozen solid!

25 *

# CHAPTER XIII.

## DE PROFUNDIS.

HOW the Gallians passed the rest of this terrible
night, or rather the few hours that remained of it,
can easily be told.

First. A great fire was kindled as soon as possible by
means of all the old boxes, barrels, boards, planking
and other combustible trumpery that could be found.
Messengers were instantly despatched to fetch whatever
fuel might be still found lying about the ships. Ben
was sent up to the observatory with orders to bring the
Professor down to Central Hall at once, and was strictly
enjoined to carry him down by main force if he was
unwilling to walk. Ben, however, had no trouble.
The poor Professor soon made his appearance, as meek
as a lamb, hardly able to move, and nearly dead with
cold, though out of all shape with the five suits of
clothes in which he had somehow contrived to array
himself. He would have come down long before if he
had been able to make his way in the darkness.

Secondly. All were to wrap themselves up as carefully

as possible, and then, taking seats around the table, to eat a good abundant warm meal which Mochel and Ben Zouf prepared in a surprisingly short time. They had not eaten anything for eight or nine hours, and, besides serving as a great relief to the gnawing of the stomach, good food is a well-known preservative against bodily fatigue and depression of spirits.

Thirdly. The fire, which of course had not been kindled in Central Hall, but in a blind gallery leading out of it, afforded heat enough to the worn-out party to take a few hours' repose with perfect safety. To the chief danger of the moment, want of sufficient ventilation, the Captain attended carefully himself, and so watchful was he on the subject that he was perhaps the only Gallian who never closed his eyes once during that ever-to-be-remembered night.

At the breakfast-table next morning, he spoke to his companions as follows:

"A terrible night has passed without doing us the least harm, thanks to Heaven in the first place and in the next to our good friends who kept the fire so well supplied. Your eyes indeed look red from smoke and many of you are rather pale for want of pure air. But taking everything into consideration, very little real injury so far has befallen even the weakest of us. Safety, however, by artificial fire is impossible. Fuel could never be procured in sufficient supply — not to mention other objections which I shall omit for the present.

"Let us look at our danger squarely in the face. What is the cause of this danger? Cold, and cold alone. Nothing else whatever. We have provisions enough to last us as long as we shall remain in Gallia. We have potted meats and other preserved food in sufficient abundance to dispense, if necessary, for a long time with cooking altogether. What then do we require? Heat! but not great heat; barely enough to keep our blood circulating. This heat, the Count and the Lieutenant think, is still to be found further down in the depths of the mountain. How much further down no one can tell. But there we are going to look for it! Now are you willing to accompany us?"

For a few moments there was a dead silence in the crowd, hardly broken by the faintest whisper.

Then little Nina's childish voice was heard:

"Dear little father, I am not afraid to go where you go. And Pablo will accompany me, won't you, Pablo?"

"I will go wherever the Signor Governor orders me to go!" said little Pablo quite resolutely.

"We will all go, Governor!" cried the others with one voice. "Ask us no questions! Tell us what to do, and it is done!"

"All right, friends," resumed the Captain. "Your confidence is gratifying, but I expected no less. Now listen! We propose to descend into the real interior of the volcano. Here we are not at all in its interior— we are only near an opening over which the chief lava current fell like a cataract. We must go much lower down. Now the trouble is this. We cannot get down unless through the open chimney, and the only possible road to the great open chimney is by the crater outside. But I know enough of the crater to assure you that no mortal foot could ever descend the chimney by that journey. The walls are too steep, too slippery, and too hard to be descended with safety, and they never could be ascended at all! Once down, there we should stay!

"Clearly some better road than the crater must be sought for reaching the central chimney — and that road we think we have discovered. Lieutenant Procopius, whilst taking observations for the purpose of constructing a chart of the Nina Hive, came upon several galleries of which most of us never suspected the existence. One in particular struck him as being always extremely warm, though lying at a long distance from Central Hall. Owing also to its distance from the noise of the falling lava, he was often able to catch a peculiar flowing noise, which he considered to be caused by the upward rush of the condensed vapors and the volcanic matter, at some point not far off, twenty or thirty feet at the utmost. A tunnel from this gallery, excavated in the direction the Lieutenant will point you out, he is confident will strike the main chimney at a point from which further descent will be a comparatively easy matter.

"Now then, I ask no questions! This tunnel is to be made! To the work at once!"

To the work they went at once and with a will. Every pickaxe, shovel, spade, and mattock in Terre Chaude was put into instant requisition. But it was soon found that such implements could not produce the slightest effect on the flinty walls. Holes had to be drilled into them with cold chisels, filled with gunpowder and plugged tight. When exploded, little bits of rock were broken off. The work was slow, disagreeable, and dangerous; but the men were enthusiastic, and so much progress was made that at the end of the first day Procopius announced that he considered half the task accomplished.

The second night was a most wretched one to the Captain, the Count, and Procopius. In spite of their weariness they would not lie down. They preferred staying up to watch the fires. The Count in particular was in unusually bad spirits.

"I'm afraid your labor is all you will have for your pains, Procopius," said he. "This tunnel project will probably end in nothing at all. What then is to become of us? Fuel enough to keep these fires burning must run out in a few days. This volcano will be our tomb!"

Procopius made no reply, knowing by experience that when the Count was in a bad humor, talking usually did very little good. But the Captain would not let the conversation drop.

"Count, my dear friend," said he, "you cannot be in earnest. Where is your habitual confidence in Heaven? I know it has often kept me from sinking into absolute despair."

"Yes, Captain," answered the Count in some confusion, "but Heaven may not grant to-day what it granted yesterday. We are not to scrutinize its decrees. Yesterday the Heavenly Hand was open; to-day it is closed —"

"Only half closed, Count," said the Captain. "And even this may be only to give us an opportunity to exercise our courage, our intelligence, our perseverance. For my part, I cannot believe that this eruption has ceased forever. I cannot believe in the total extinction of Gallia's internal fires."

Here Procopius thought he could put in an oar with some effect

"The Captain means," said he, "that Gallia's internal fires, possibly finding some other outlet besides Terre Chaude, may have sought that issue in preference. He is therefore probably correct in refusing to believe that the preference for such other outlet may be much more than temporary. In fact, the sudden cessation of our volcano is by no means a conclusive proof that the minerals whose combination with oxygen gave rise to the eruption are exhausted. But if the Count means it must be an exceedingly difficult and doubtful task to reach the spot in Gallia's depths where the combination, without making heat enough to cause an eruption, still does make heat enough to enable us to endure the terrible colds of space — then the Count is right too."

By long rambling sentences of this kind, Procopius generally put an end to disputes; but here there was no time to test his experiment.

"Somebody walking outside!" said the Count quickly. "Who can it be at such an hour as this?"

"It must be the Professor," answered the Captain; "at least he is the only one of our people missing. He is a man of extraordinary activity of brain. He cannot rest idle a single moment. Without a single soul to help him, he carried down his big telescope from the observatory, and in spite of all my opposition actually planted it at the great opening of Central Hall! There he has spent all the day; and there, I am sure, he would spend all the night too, but for the cold —"

The Professor's entrance cut short all further remarks. In spite of his five suits of clothes, he looked like a frozen corpse, and he was hardly able to put one foot before the other. The fire within his little body was however far from being extinguished. His temper was as hot as ever, and suffering had not improved his patience. That he was in the worst possible humor his disjointed grumbling remarks showed, though his teeth chattered so fearfully that many of his words were lost.

"The imbeciles! Call this den, this hole, this dungeon, this plombière, this gehenna, this Mamertine prison, this ice-pit a *Terre Chaude!*" he growled as he entered, indifferent apparently as to whether he was heard or not. "*Terre Chaude* indeed! And to crown the stupid joke, an *Alveario!* A precious bee-hive! Full of the laziest of lazy drones! I'm the only bee myself among the lot, and I should never stop working night or day if I only had a place to work in! Why did not that *bête* Servadac let me stay quietly at Formentera? It was pretty cold there too, but at least I never made an ass of myself by calling it a Terre Chaude!" etc., etc.

So he mumbled and grumbled while he stretched himself down in the warmest corner he could find; but his

26

restless spirit was soon wrapped in slumber, and his sharp tongue was heard no more.

The whole scene greatly amused the Count. A slight smile even flitted over his cold features — the first for more than twenty-four hours.

But the watchers were destined to have another visitor that night. In saying the Professor was the only one of the Gallians missing, the Captain had made a very natural mistake. Isaac's face was so seldom found among the others that nobody ever thought of looking for him. In he came now, however, the very last, to warm himself a little, and perhaps to take a few hours' sleep in the genial quarters of the blind gallery. In spite of his long and lonely hibernation in the *Hansa*, the day's cold had told terribly on him. He evidently suffered more than the Professor. He was almost bent double, and he moved along with nearly as much difficulty as if he had been stricken with paralysis. He was white with paleness, if such an expression is permissible. His teeth chattered audibly, and his whole frame was shaking as if from an ague fit.

Approaching from a quarter where he could be easily seen by the Captain and his companions without being able to see them in return, he evidently considered himself unobserved, at least he acted as if he did — or rather, now that we think over the matter more carefully, he probably acted as if he knew he was observed.

"Drag me from my comfortable home in the *Hansa!*" he hissed as he shuffled nervously along. "Stick me in a hog-pen like this! Expose my properties to thieves and cheats! That's what they call Christianity! S' help me Father Abraham, a rat from the *Hansa* would run in disgust from such an ice-well! All day in the dark watching my properties — trying to cook a bit of food in the dark — the fire too cold to burn enough to give light or heat — all day long my heart freezing — my teeth worn to stumps with chattering — why did n't that popinjay Captain let me stay in the *Hansa?* — there everything was under lock — good locks — very good locks! — and good keys!" — taking a bunch out of his pocket and looking at them dolefully — "now good for nothing! I could sleep as much as I pleased! I could cook my little foods! I could count my little moneys! — very little moneys! — but oh this good fire! S' help me Father Abraham, it makes me a young man again! But I can't stay long! I must go back to watch my properties! — though I nearly fainted to death there just now — oh the cold and the dark! — and the dread of robbers! — why not leave me in the *Hansa?* This Captain is what the Gentiles call a just man — just! — if he had a particle of justice in him he would have left me in the *Hansa!*" etc., etc.

So moaning and groaning, he too soon found a warm corner, and the only sounds heard during the remainder of the night by the watchers were the occasional mutter of a dreamer, and the crackling and crumbling of a burning log.

Next day the work at the tunnel was renewed with such energy, skill, and success that, before night had come, Procopius by skilful tapping was able to declare positively that the grand chimney could not be more than a few feet distant. After another hour's patient drill-work, he declared he could hear great pieces of loosened rock, not only detach themselves outside, but even in their fall slip along a sloping floor and strike against angular projections. The chimney then must be inclined, and the descent practicable; next morning, however, would be time enough to break down the last obstruction.

That night was passed much more pleasantly than the previous one. The Count, very hopeful, was easily compelled by the Captain and Procopius to take a rest. The Captain too, paying no attention to exclamations, had enforced the presence both of the Professor and Isaac in the dormitory at a comparatively early hour, where he soon enjoyed the gratification of seeing both sunk in a deep and peaceful slumber.

Procopius's calculation was right. It *was* the central

"A SPLENDID STAIRCASE!"

funnel, and the descent *was* sloping. An exploring expedition was instantly organized, consisting of Procopius, the Captain, and Ben Zouf. The Count, left in charge of the others, superintended the removal of the *débris*.

In the beginning of the descent at least, there was little danger of a fall, the inclination never exceeding forty-five degrees. The walls, besides being a convenient distance apart, were broken, indented, full of projections for the hands to hold by; and the floor was strewed with too much ashes and cinders to be either too straight or too slippery.

"All this proves pretty conclusively," said Procopius, "that the eruption has had a recent origin. The lava has no more than burst a passage for itself, and has not had time to wear off much of the angular projection of the walls. In all probability it was the oxygen obtained from the Earth that caused the whole explosion."

"A splendid staircase, gentlemen," said Ben, "only please excuse the carpet!"

They descended watchfully and with every precaution. The "steps" gave out here and there. Now and then, also, large openings would branch off to the left and right into which Ben always ventured, brandishing his torch, while his companions waited outside. But he invariably returned in a few moments. No thoroughfare. Nothing like the endless ramifications of the Alveario. Downwards, therefore, was still their only course.

After about half an hour's descent, an inspection of the Captain's aneroid barometer showed that they had reached a perpendicular depth of between 5 and 6 hundred feet, their course being mostly southwards. A look at a pocket thermometer too showed Procopius that the temperature was decidedly on the increase. The glass did not rise at the gradual but slow rate of terrestrial thermometers let down into very deep mines. On the contrary, it rose with comparative rapidity, and every few feet they descended it rose still higher.

There could be no longer any doubt as to the real state of things. The lava had no longer sufficient force to rise and overflow as it had done lately; but it was bubbling and seething red-hot at no very great distance further down, whence it was transmitting its heat very decidedly through the metallic structure of the mountain.

"Six hundred feet below sea-level!" announced the Captain.

"20 degrees Fahrenheit!" announced Procopius.

"A temperature of twenty degrees, though an immense improvement on the Bee-Hive," observed the Captain, "would never suit people compelled to pass many months in a place where they could take no exercise. Let us go lower. The air is still good, and everything promises well."

The air in fact was remarkably pure. Entering by the central chimney and the great lateral opening, it seemed to be sucked down, as it were, into these depths where the effort of breathing was far easier than in the smothering recesses of the blind gallery.

After a quarter of an hour's easy descent, a halt was made and progress investigated.

"Nine hundred feet below sea-level!"

"52 degrees Fahrenheit!"

"Fifty-two will suit admirably," said the Captain. "No need of going any further."

"Glad to hear it, Governor," said Ben, wiping his forehead. "I'm so warm there's hardly a dry stitch on me. But that's not the trouble. Listen! Don't you hear that boiling, hissing, and steaming noise there below? I do plainly. The red-hot lake is not far off. Let the chilly fellows go down deeper if they like. For my part, I consider even where we are too hot already!"

"Let us make an inspection of what we have come to!" cried the Captain. With torches fresh trimmed and resupplied with oil, the inspection was made and soon accomplished.

Truth compels us to state that it was not exceedingly satisfactory. The great chimney had here become somewhat wider than elsewhere. The place was therefore large enough to hold the whole colony, but that was about all that could be said in its favor. Here and there indeed were slight recesses that might serve for storing provisions, but private apartments or comfortable nooks could not be thought of. Even a little niche large enough for Nina was discovered only after a long search. Life here should be *à la commune* in the fullest sense of the term. The expanded chimney should be at once kitchen, dining-room, sitting-room, and dormitory. After burrowing for awhile below the surface, like rabbits, the Gallians were now to grub in the mountain depths, like moles, but without the compensation of a mole's long winter sleep.

Still, the situation could be worse.

The light question did not present much difficulty. There was still plenty of oil among the stores, and even of spirits — so useful in cookery — the supply was by no means scant.

Then the absolute imprisonment of the colony in this dungeon the whole winter long was not absolutely necessary. If clad warmly enough the Gallians could vary the monotony by making occasional excursions, some days up no further than the Alveario, but on others they might venture to the sea-shore and even to their old skating-ground.

In fact, when the Captain had discussed the matter a little with his comrades, it was readily ascertained that these excursions need not be simple promenades undertaken for the sake of pleasure or variety — they would be acts of absolute necessity. Plenty of water, for instance, would be required. The only way to obtain it would be by transporting blocks of ice from the shore, first up two or three hundred feet above the sea-level to their old quarters, and then down the sloping chimney to a depth of twelve or thirteen hundred feet. Such labor as this would be no child's play and every Gallian would be compelled to take it in turn.

"Everything considered," observed Procopius, as they wound their way slowly upwards, "our people here will be no worse off than most of the winterers in the arctic regions. There, whether in the whaling-ships, or the station-houses, or the forts, or the Esquimaux huts, there is no multiplication of apartments or private chambers ever thought of. One large room well protected against cold and damp is made to serve every purpose. Corners are particularly warred against. One large apartment is most easily lighted, heated, and ventilated ; consequently it is considered healthier in every respect."

The Gallians meanwhile, having cleared away all rubbish and made the tunnel a perfectly convenient approach to the grand chimney, were assembled in the blind gallery, quietly awaiting the return of the explorers. The cold elsewhere was too intense to be borne by any one not engaged in active bodily exertion. The Count, a little uneasy at the protracted delay, was just sending Negrete and another Spaniard in search of the absentees, when joyful shouts announced their safe return.

The Captain's verbal report, giving in a few words the chief points of the place of refuge just discovered, was received with loud cheers. Immediate preparations were made for instant change of domicile. Considering the number of the community, the length of the journey, the quantity and variety of the articles to be transported, perhaps no other removal was effected more rapidly — especially when we remember that it was all done in the absence of sunlight. In one day almost every change was made that had to be made. Wise arrangements rendered every labor comparatively easy.

The first proceeding was to place at proper intervals stationary lamps along the galleries to the tunnel, and from the tunnel down the descent as far as the intended resting-place. These lamps were given in complete

ISAAC'S NOOK.

charge to certain Gallians appointed by name, who were held responsible for keeping them in order, and extinguishing them at the proper time.

Ropes, securely fastened at the end of the tunnel, served as a handrail all the way down, and afforded considerable help on the return. By means of other ropes playing in pulleys at the head of the descent, temporary sleds, carrying an immense load of articles, were let down the incline and, with proper guides stationed here and there, safely reached the final landing. In spite of the rough road, the great haste, the unavoidable confusion, very little was broken or lost, a pepper-caster and a bottle or two of pickles being the only articles reported by Mochel as missing. Of course it need hardly be mentioned that it was only the most indispensable articles of furniture, etc., that were removed ; the rest were allowed to remain undisturbed, not to be called on until absolutely needed.

The Professor, as might be expected, refused positively to go down to the "bottomless pit," as he called it. In vain did the Captain seek to bribe him to make the attempt by offering to send down the telescope to keep him company. "No telescope wanted down there," he said. "No discoveries possible in the infernal regions." The Captain, finding words useless, was obliged to have recourse to what he called the *grand moyen.* At the word of command, Negrete laid hold of the little man, hoisted him on his brawny shoulders, and, despite his struggles, screams, and fierce resistance, deposited him soon safe and sound in "pandemonium."

Isaac gave quite as much trouble. He would not leave his "properties," and he would not allow his "properties" to be removed. The Captain indeed was quite as unwilling to have the goods removed; it would be both an enormous labor and a useless task. But Isaac himself should go below; and on Negrete's shoulders he was soon put below. But putting him there and keeping him there were two different things. The instant his movements were free, he was back again freezing to death among his dear "properties." Again Negrete was called into requisition, and again he failed. At last the Captain had to make a compromise. Certain openings branching off the main chimney have been spoken of as examined by Ben Zouf when the explorers were making their first descent. Into one of these recesses, about twenty feet square, and very cold and dismal, the light, loose and valuable articles of Isaac's stock were hastily carried. There he proposed, by means of a little spirit-lamp, stove, and heavy curtains hung across the entrance, to keep himself from freezing to death; at all events there he could have the consolation

THE REMOVAL.

of watching over his dear "properties," and of selling them to whoever chose to buy.

As to the animals — many of them had to be sacrificed ; there was no room for them below. To abandon them in the upper galleries would be to condemn them to the cruelest of deaths. They were, therefore, slaughtered without delay; little further trouble was necessary regarding their flesh, the excessive cold keeping it in a perfect state of preservation.

Among the animals not thus sacrificed Zephyr and Galette were of course included. The Captain and Ben loved them too much to consent to their death unless under circumstances of the most absolute necessity. An opening like Isaac's was turned into a stable for the poor beasts, where they were visited every day by Ben, who gave them plenty of food, and did everything to keep them warm and comfortable.

The first night passed in the subterranean abode was rather cheerless. Nobody was in good-humor, except Ben Zouf and Nina. The child, feeling the universal depression, did all she could to remove it by redoubled cheerfulness. She talked more than ever, smiled more than ever, and, before retiring to her little nook, ran round the whole circle, taking everybody's hand, kissing it affectionately, and wishing all a *felicissima notte !* But Ben surpassed himself. After doing as much all day

27

as any five others, before closing his eyes for the night, he made the rounds carefully, and saw that every man was comfortably fixed and properly supplied with covering. For every one he had a word or a joke, or something to make them laugh.

"What have we to complain of after all, Nunez?" said he to one of the Spaniards who was grumbling a little. "We have merely shifted our quarters from the first story to the cellar. You spoil your good looks by growling. Rather say *Va bene* like little Nina, or *Ol dry* like the Professor when he talks English!"

But a few weeks' judicious work made a great improvement every way. On the night of the 15th, when the ceilings blazed with chandeliers and bright lamps lined the walls, when the Gallians, now quite at home in their new quarters, were divided into different groups, talking, playing cards, smoking, dancing, etc., the general effect was decidedly cheering. Here everything was bright and pleasant, and even warm — about 60°, the lamps having somewhat increased the temperature — whereas outside, as Procopius had ascertained that evening, the alcohol showed a cold of more than 100 degrees below zero.

Our three friends, however, if more hopeful, were anything but gay. Gloomy thoughts would intrude. If this volcanic heat should fail, if Gallia should miss her appointment, if anything should occur to make another dreary wintering inevitable, was it possible to discover fuel or combustible of any kind in the Comet? Such discovery was extremely unlikely! Coal, the wreck of primeval forests overwhelmed in the geological epochs, and mineralized by the long lapse of ages, need not be looked for in Gallia! In such eventualities then, what should be done?

" Questions like those, Procopius," said the Captain, " in my opinion, if not useless, are exceedingly premature. Let those terrible times you hint at come along! When they do, ideas will also come along! As for my part, I can never tell what to do until the moment comes for doing it!"

"The wisest are like you in that respect, Captain," said the Count. "In presence of danger, the mind, under unusual and highly stimulating pressure, merely gives vent to an idea that would otherwise have lain dormant forever. — Have you any reason, Procopius, to apprehend a final extinction of Gallia's internal heat before the return of summer?"

"None whatever, Father," was the reply. "On the contrary, I consider the inflammation of volcanic substance here is of a date quite recent. Before Gallia's encounter with the Earth, she had no atmosphere; consequently it was only the collision that made the combination of oxygen with volcanic matter at all possible. The present cessation I consider to be in all probability only momentary. My opinion, in fact, is this : the plutonic forces in Gallia's interior have only just begun to operate. Far from fearing the extinction of central heat, another eventuality, much more dreadful for us, circumstanced as we now are, is what should give us the most alarm."

"Which is —— ?" asked the Captain.

"A new and sudden eruption catching us without a moment's warning ! "

"Your gloomy anticipations, Procopius, give me the horrors," said the Count somewhat impatiently.

"Such a calamity is possible, no doubt," said the Captain musingly. "But against it all struggling would be vain. It would be all over before we felt the blow that struck us ! "

" I give expression to my apprehensions, dear friends," said Procopius, "simply in order to be better on our guard. For I can say positively that, by watching carefully and observing certain signs, such a surprise is impossible. Now let us retire. This very night, January 15th, Gallia passes her aphelion. She is now 220 million leagues from the sun; but to-morrow she is homeward bound. Good-night ! "

# CHAPTER XIV.

## HOMEWARD BOUND.

WITH the exception of the English garrison of the Rock Fortress, every soul in Gallia was now leading a Troglodyte life in the caverns of Terre Chaude, nearly a thousand feet below the level of the sea.

Of this English garrison the Captain and his companions sometimes felt inclined to have a little talk. How had General Murphy and his men borne the first half of the Gallian winter? In all probability far better than the Terre Chaudians. For heat enough to .keep themselves from freezing they were dependent on no volcanic action, as they had sufficient coal to last for several winters. The same might be said of their stores of provisions of all kinds. Sheltered within the enormous walls of their rocky fastness, well fed, well clad, they could bid defiance to the last extremities of cold. In fact, as Ben Zouf said, the only trouble likely to befall these stall-fed Englishmen was the difficulty of keeping buttons on their waistcoats. They popped off every day, he had· no

27 *

doubt, like corks out of ginger-beer bottles. The
Captain thought the famous game of chess was finished
by this time; Procopius's opinion was different; the
Count stopped the argument by saying that if it was not
finished yet, it would be likely to last some time longer.
All, however, including even Ben Zouf, who dearly
liked poking fun at an Englishman, unanimously agreed
that the manliness and determination with which the
plucky little garrison stuck to their post through thick
and thin were worthy of the highest praise, and that
England had every reason to be proud of such soldiers.

If the worst should come to the worst with the Terre
Chaudians, that is, if they could not possibly remain
where they were without the certain prospect of per-
ishing from cold, the Captain assured his companions
that he should not have the slightest scruple in ap-
plying to Gibraltar as a place of refuge. No doubt
they would be there warmly welcomed and well treated,
in spite of the scant hospitality shown to them on the
occasion of their first visit. The English, said he, are
not the kind of men to let their fellow-creatures perish
without first affording them every relief in their power.

The Count and Procopius shook their heads at such
a notion. Not that they entertained the least doubt
regarding the friendliness and ungrudging bountifulness
sure to be displayed by the English in a case of un-

doubted distress. But look at the length of the journey! Over an immense sea of ice! Without shelter, heat, or locomotive power for the sick or disabled! The probability was that the attempt would end in a line of human corpses stiff and stark, and not even reaching half-way! No. Every possible extremity should be endured at Terre Chaude before a journey of such fearful risks should be so much as even contemplated!

Procopius and the Count being probably right, the Captain prudently turned the conversation.

The change of domicile was borne pretty well for at least a month. The novelty of the situation, the necessity of hard work to make things somewhat orderly, and the sense of rest so keenly felt after hard labor of any kind, made the new quarters quite tolerable for some time, and perhaps even somewhat enjoyable.

But towards the middle of February, the terrible monotony began to tell on the spirits of the little colony. The torpor that was gradually crawling over their bodies began to prey on their minds. The leaders of course did everything in their power to ward off an apathy that was sure to be attended with fatal results.

A closer communion of daily life was warmly encouraged. At certain hours of the twenty-four, conversations were started at which all were expected, if not even compelled, to take part. The most interesting books on all subjects, especially history, travels, and science, were read aloud and intelligently commented upon. Procopius, aided by the Captain, the Count and Ben Zouf, started a series of lectures on the natural sciences, and, in spite of rather meagre apparatus, succeeded pretty well in rendering the great laws of nature tolerably familiar to the generality of the audi-ence. The Captain kept public school every day for two hours, and, well assisted by his intelligent pupils Nina and Pablo, was pretty successful in teaching the Russians and Spaniards not only to read and write French but also to know a little arithmetic. Every one had to pay a visit at least once a day to the Al-veario in spite of the cold, but going outside was not encouraged. For that there would be plenty of time some four or five months hence when the gradual ap-proach of the sun would begin to mollify a little the extreme severity of the temperature. Plays of all kinds were acted, at which species of amusement the Spaniards revealed wonderful innate capacity and obtained great applause. There was a good deal of dancing too, only the great slope of the floor gave the performers much difficulty in keeping their places. They were continu-ally slipping down hill.

The evenings always concluded with music; then after a hymn at which all took part and a devout general recitation of the Lord's Prayer, the lights were extinguished and the little colony endeavored to make the best use it could of the eight hours allotted for undisturbed repose.

In all these tolerably successful attempts to prevent the spirits of the Gallians from falling into a state of torpor sure to result in death, it is almost needless to say that Isaac took no part whatever. What would he have gained from them? For him they did not possess one single element of interest. To him in fact they would be simply time wasted. To arouse *his* dormant energies no outside stimulant was necessary. No danger of *his* ever falling into the sleep that knows no waking, as long as he had his beloved gold pieces and his beautiful bank-notes to count over and over again, to handle, to examine, to inspect, and to calculate the interest of in case he was offered a good safe investment. This investment, however, he was grieved to think, seemed just then to be very slow in presenting itself, while meantime the valuable days were slipping rapidly away without bringing any new and welcome addition to his pile.

Another Gallian not in the slightest danger of falling a victim to despondency was the Professor. What his money-bags did for the miser in the way of consolation was nothing to what his figures and his diagrams did for the calculator. He was never idle for a single

V

instant. Even at meal-times he was thinking over his logarithms. Never, in fact, had his moments flown more rapidly than they did from the instant he felt himself at home in what he had at first called *Abaddon's lowest tartarus.* He was now on a new tack which for the time gave him a most intensely interesting occupation.

Of Gallia he knew all that could be known; Nerina was now the absorbing object of every thought and act. As lord of the planet, his claim naturally extended to the satellite; it was his bounden duty therefore, as well as his fiercest delight, to find out all the peculiarities of an asteroid which had now, through a wonderful combination of startling events, become his own undoubted property.

The first problem was to ascertain her weight.

For this, in the first place, a few exact observations as to her precise position in certain portions of her orbit were absolutely necessary. Then, well acquainted as he already was with Gallia's mass, nothing more would be required for his purpose than a room, or cabinet as he called it, where he could work out his figures without dread of being disturbed by importunate or idle curiosity. He had broached the subject to the Captain the first moment the hurry of the removal admitted a little breathing-time.

"You shall have a cabinet by all means, my dear Master," said the Captain. "It will not be as comfortable as I could wish, but it will allow you at least to work in peace and quietness."

"That's all I want, Servadac," said he, turning away. "You are very kind."

"Dear Master," said the Captain, wishing to take advantage of the favorable opportunity, "I have a mind to ask your opinion regarding an idea that has just struck me."

"An idea, Servadac? Well, let us hear it."

"Your calculations regarding the exact length of Gallia's revolution period are no doubt accurate in the highest possible degree," said the Captain; "but, my dear Master, it is hardly necessary to remind you that even half a minute too late or too soon would be enough to prevent Gallia from meeting the Earth at the all-important point."

"Well?"

"Well, my dear Master, don't you think a little re-vision of your calculations would be advisable?"

"Revision? Not at all. Quite useless."

"Procopius would be delighted to undertake all the really tiresome part of the difficult task."

"I want no help whatever in anything I undertake to calculate," said the Professor curtly.

"Still, it would do no harm, my dear Master —"

"It would do no good either, Servadac. I never make a mistake. I use too many counteracting checks to allow a mistake to be possible. This importunity of yours is therefore quite uncalled for."

The Captain felt the rebuff, but, never forgetting the necessity of keeping the Professor in good-humor, he suppressed every sign of impatience in his reply.

"My dear Master, a man with such an active brain as yours must find employment, or give up the ghost. The revision —"

"Servadac," said the Professor severely, "don't trouble yourself about finding me employment. That I am quite capable of doing for myself. I never revise my calculations, sir. When I announce them as just, they *are* just, and beyond all revision! However, I have no objection to inform you that what I have done for Gallia I am now about to undertake for Nerina."

"Nerina!" said the Captain heedlessly; "why, my dear Master, Nerina being a telescopic asteroid, her elements must have been calculated long ago."

By their effect on the Professor's countenance, he instantly saw the harm done by his unlucky words, and he could have cut his tongue out for uttering them.

"Servadac," said the Professor in tones of suppressed

wrath, "Nerina being — as you say — in one sense, a telescopic planet, it is quite possible that her elements have been already calculated. Her daily motion, the length of her sidereal revolution, her mean distance from the sun, her eccentricity, the length and mean longitude of her perihelion, the longitude of her ascending node,— all that may be old work, and likely enough has been done long ago. Nevertheless, it has to be done all over again. Nerina, sir, is a telescopic asteroid no more! She is a *moon,* sir, *my* moon — at least a moon of *my* planet! She must therefore be studied as a moon, and I am sure I don't know what law forbids the Gallians from learning as much regarding the Gallian moon as the Terrestrians have learned of the Terrestrian!"

I am sorry these words must give the reader only a faint idea of the lofty contempt already entertained by the Professor for everything not rigidly Gallian. If Gallia had any native inhabitants of her own, I have no doubt he would consider them infinitely superior to all other created beings in God's mighty universe.

"And now, Servadac," he went on, "having convinced you of the vast importance of my contemplated labors, I end as I began by asking the favor of finding me a working cabinet as quickly as possible."

"My dear Master, I shall see to the matter the very

28

instant I have given some orders to Ben Zouf regarding the provisions, and more to Negrete regarding the transportation of some particular pieces of furniture."

"Oh, I'm in no hurry, Servadac," said the Professor grandly. "Take your own time. I shall be perfectly satisfied if my cabinet is ready in an hour!"

It took four hours' hard work, however, before the Captain had everything arranged to anything like his satisfaction. By the end of that time a nook was nicely screened off from "Pandemonium," in which there was found plenty of room for the Professor's table, arm-chair, black-board, books, papers, and other necessary articles. A student-lamp, provided with the best oil, gave him excellent light. Everything in fact was done that could be done to make things comfortable, but the Professor fumed audibly at the delay, and took his seat at last with the air of a highly-injured man.

His sense of the injustice, however, with which he was treated seemed only to quicken his industry. He commenced his work at once. Every day he went regularly up to Central Hall and even outside, in spite of the terrible cold, to take observations regarding the various positions in her orbit occupied by Nerina. Then shutting himself up in his cabinet, he drew his diagrams and made his calculations, and never, except at meal-times, made his appearance in public.

For the next several months the public life of the community was unmarked by any noticeable incident. As already mentioned, every one was compelled for the sake of exercise to make a little excursion every day as far as Central Hall, but very few ever thought of going out in the open air except those especially appointed to cut ice for fresh-water purposes.

A few excursions in a contrary direction, however, namely downwards, were undertaken by the Captain and his companions. But from these explorations very little resulted beyond the discovery that the chimney grew narrower and steeper in its descent, and that the lava, hot enough to be in a liquid state, was still at a considerable distance below. This lava was also so quiescent as to give a high degree of probability to the surmise that the volcanic matter was escaping through openings to be found elsewhere in Gallia's surface.

As the months dragged on the situation did not improve. In spite of all they could do, the Gallians still found a physical and a moral torpor stealing irresistibly over them. The first two months' battling against it was tolerably successful, but towards the middle of April the awful monotony of the underground life began to affect even the indefatigable Ben Zouf himself. The readings could not keep the listeners awake. The conversations were limited to three or four participants, and even then they were carried on in such a low voice as to become exceedingly dull and lifeless. The plays aroused no enthusiasm, the actors being often as sleepy as the audience. The school-hours had to be shortened, from the difficulty of keeping the scholars awake. The Spaniards were the first to sink, and the Captain gave himself incredible pains not merely in forcing them to take a little exercise, but actually to take a little food. The Russians held out better, and really did most of the hard work.

Procopius, the Count, and Ben Zouf still continued, of course, to second the Captain in every effort to ward off the fatal lethargy that threatened the speedy destruction of the colony. But even these felt the deadly torpor gradually crawling over them. It showed itself especially in the mornings by an extraordinary and almost irresistible desire to keep on sleeping. To get up on one's feet early enough to properly resume the ordinary avocations of the day required such a determined and persevering effort of the will that the Captain feared the morning would soon come when nobody would get up at all. Another symptom gave him considerable alarm even in his own case. The general repugnance to taking nourishment was becoming stronger every day. Shut up in the bowels of the planet, like tortoises, were the Gallians indeed to imitate the hibernation of tortoises by fasting and sleeping in a torpid state till the return of spring? And how long was the hibernation really to endure? Once they yielded to the overwhelming drowsiness of mind and body, who could say if the genial touch of spring would ever succeed in wakening them from the fatal sleep of winter?

For the escape of the colony from some such dreary doom, they were indebted, after Heaven, to the liveliness, spirit, cheerfulness, and incessant, self-denying devotion of little Nina. As if by instinct the child rose at once to a full realization of the dangerous crisis and its requirements. She was here, there, and everywhere at the same moment. Now encouraging her friend Pablo to rouse himself, in the next instant she was in another part of the Hall strumming the guitar to prevent some poor Spaniard from falling asleep at meal-time. For everybody she had a word and a laugh, fluttering backwards and forwards unweariedly, like a beautiful butterfly in summer-time. She brought a tempting morsel of food to one, and to a second a nice cup of soup. She made a third laugh at one of Ben Zouf's jokes, and set the ears of a fourth tingling with pleasure by a little Italian song. Regarding the Captain she was particularly watchful, and, as if conscious that it was on him that the lives of all depended, she never let him oversleep himself in the mornings. With greater pro-

28 *

priety than ever she could be now called the real life
and soul of the community, keeping its spark of existence alive, as it were, by her superabundant vitality.
Changing the comparison a little, we might say that
every one of its members without exception felt himself
beneficently affected by the visits of this bright little
creature, who, like a taper, seemed to possess the property of enkindling light and movement in others without
impairing in the slightest degree her own brilliant
radiance. The " Little Madonna," till of late so orna-
mental, so attractive, so purifying, so tranquillizing, now
gradually seemed to become so sympathizing, so consoling, so assuaging, as to be called the " Little Sister."
In a word, this dear child only nine years old proved,
under Heaven, as mentioned above, the chief and perhaps the only antidote against the terrible despondency
that would otherwise, during the two dreary months of
May and June, have crushed the life out of the entombed
Gallians.

Towards the beginning of July, however, this despondency began to relax its deadly grip on the little
community. Rising at a regular hour in the morning
was felt to be somewhat easier; the desire for continual
sleep during the day was not quite so oppressive ; and,
above all, food began to be taken, if not with pleasure,
at least without repugnance.

Was this happy change due to the reaction of the human system against an unnatural and long-continued strain? Or, was it owing to the influence of the sun who, though still far, far away, was now getting near enough to allow some of his beneficial effects to be felt? It was probably the result of both these causes, though of the latter no doubt in a more eminent degree.

So at least said Procopius, who now kept count of Gallia's time and course as carefully and intelligently as he had formerly kept the log of the *Dobryna*. By means of the notes, figures, and diagrams furnished by the Professor during the first half of the Gallian revolution, he had constructed new diagrams for himself, made out an ephemeris, and drawn an orbit on which, as on a chart, he tried to follow with more or less accuracy the Comet's progress on her home voyage through planetary space. He was, therefore, now able to inform his companions that Gallia had some time since crossed Jupiter's orbit, and, though she was still at the enormous distance of 197 million leagues from the sun, that, by virtue of one of Kepler's laws, her velocity was rapidly accelerating. In four months more she would be entering the Zone of the telescopic planets, at least fifty million leagues nearer.

The general improvement, though for some time hardly perceptible, still continued. Torpor gradually but surely gave way to vigor, silence to the hum of life, and dull repose to brisk and bustling movement.

Every name was now cheerfully responded to at roll-call in the upper galleries. Visits to Central Hall, instead of being matters of form impatiently hurried through merely to discharge an irksome task, lasted longer and longer every day, and were made occasions of pleasant and healthful exercise. The Captain and his companions often made excursions to the sea-shore. The cold was still intense, but the atmosphere was as calm as ever. A feather fell to the ground in almost as straight a line as that made by a stone. Not a particle of snow had been drifted during the long winter. The footmarks were still as sharply defined as they had been six months before.

In one point alone a decided change was noticed — an extraordinary change in fact — but still neither surprising nor unexpected. The upward movement of the ice lying under the vessels had continued without interruption. The ice cones beneath the keels could not now be less than a hundred and fifty feet high. There the *Dobryna* and the *Hansa* could indeed still be seen, perched on the summit of these inaccessible cliffs; but their destruction was certain; no power could save them.

" Fortunately for our ears, Dutch Isaac is not along ! " said Ben Zouf at this sight. " How they would ring

THE CAVERN BY THE SEA-SHORE.

with his peacock squawks!—but, to do him justice, that's all there is of the peacock about him."

The next two months, July and August, brought Gallia within a distance of 164 million leagues from the sun. During the short nights the cold was quite as severe as ever; but during the daytime the sun, crossing the meridian a little north of Terre Chaude, sent forth heat enough to show a decided increase of twenty degrees. His cheering rays produced an extraordinary effect on the Gallians, who now came down to the mouth of a sheltered cavern by the sea-shore, where they could bask in his cheering influence for the space of two or three hours every day. In this they were faithfully imitated by the birds. To the general surprise, these poor creatures, after passing the winter in such a state of torpor and silence that every one believed them dead, now suddenly made their appearance in numbers seemingly as great as ever.

This return of spring—if the use of the term may be permitted for a period when the cold was still very severe—was not long about restoring the general health of the Gallian colony; and with renewed health came renewed hope and confidence. From day to day the sun's disc showed itself perceptibly larger in the sky; from night to night the Earth's silvery surface kept increasing in size among the stars. Both were cheering sights, but the Gallians rested their weary eyes with greater pleasure on the pale but sparkling orb that was once their home. Sometimes they extemporized midnight excursions from the Lower Hall to the sea-shore for no other purpose than to afford themselves the pleasure of a long lingering look.

"Small as yon speck of light seems among the other stars," said Ben Zouf one night to the Count, "Montmartre is still there as large as life! And that's a great comfort!"

"You are quite correct, no doubt, friend Ben," was the Count's reply, "but Montmartre is still a long way off."

"We're going there right straight, are we not, Count?" asked Ben apprehensively, a little dismayed at the Count's grave manner.

"Yes, Ben Zouf, as straight as straight can be."

"Because, Count, if we get switched off the track, could not we take some measures to get switched on again?"

"No, Ben Zouf; to change our course one jot or tittle is beyond the ability of united humanity. It is on the will of the Creator exclusively that the geometrical arrangement of the universe depends. Miserable indeed is the plight which we should be in, if His infinitely wise arrangements could ever be interfered with in the slightest respect by short-sighted but self-confident man!"

# CHAPTER XV.

### THE PROFESSOR MISCALCULATES!

THOUGH September brought more heat, the Gallians did not yet think it prudent to quit the gloomy caverns of their subterranean abode for the comparatively cheerful quarters of the Alveario. The bees were afraid of being frozen in their honey-combs. The volcano had not yet shown the slightest sign of renewed activity — a fact to be interpreted favorably or otherwise according as it showed a probability of the eruption coming on so gradually as to give every one time to get out of the way, or so suddenly as to render all escape impossible. The results would of course be widely different. In the latter alternative, instant and complete destruction; in the former, a resumption of the old, comfortable, and comparatively even joyous, existence in the upper galleries of the volcano.

"The worst is now over, for awhile anyway," said the Captain to Ben Zouf one day as they were talking on the subject.

"Ugh!" said Ben with a grimace and a shudder,

"those terrible seven months! I hope I shall never have such a time again! I don't think I could have ever worried through it but for that wonderful little creature Nina!"

"She is truly wonderful, Ben Zouf," said the Captain warmly. "She is really a smile from Heaven upon us!"

"We shall have to take good care of her, Governor, when we get back again!"

"We will adopt her, Ben Zouf!"

"Bravo, Governor. She will be the flower of Montmartre. You will be her father and I her mother!"

The Captain laughed as he said :

"We must be a married pair then!"

"Governor," replied Ben with much gravity, "we were a married pair years ago, and no power on earth can sever us!"

The days wore away.

Early in October, though Gallia's distance from the sun was still three times greater than the Earth's, the cold relaxed so much in severity as to be endured even in the night-time without much discomfort, owing to the utter absence of anything like wind. The mercury now never sank lower than 28° or 30° below zero, Fahrenheit. Excursions were made twice a day to Central Hall, and by degrees the colonists ventured even down to the coast, often remaining there till evening. Skating too was resumed with some of the old spirit, the poor prisoners feeling like birds just escaped from a cage, as they skimmed lightly over the glassy expanse. The Captain and his friends now felt themselves drifting occasionally into some of their old arguments and discussions. The subject, however, that turned up oftenest now was — How to make the connection? Even granting Comet and Earth to meet at the right point and exact moment, how were the consequences of the shock to be avoided? How was the safe transfer of the passengers to be effected? That these questions were still too difficult to be answered was shown by their being always changed by universal consent for something more tractable; but that they continually occupied every waking thought was evident from their constant recurrence at almost every conversation.

One of the most noticeable faces that now began to figure around was the Professor's. After vanishing almost completely from general observation for five or six months, here he was again, as lively, as important, and, as Ben irreverently expressed it, every bit as "fussy" as ever. His telescope had been lately installed in the observatory, where he once more devoted to astronomical observations every moment that the severity of the temperature permitted. The six months of winter had passed over him like lightning, immersed as he was in incessant calculations, and he was now desirous to ascertain if his results corresponded with new observations to be taken of Nerina in several points of her orbit. What these results were nobody knew; nobody indeed had asked, for nobody was foolish enough to draw upon himself the mortification of an undoubted rebuff.

The telescope had been hardly more than a week or two in the observatory, when the Captain began to notice in the Professor's countenance a constantly increasing shade of dissatisfaction. He watched him regularly every morning hurrying up the winding tunnel of the main chimney and thence, through Central Hall, making all possible speed towards the observatory. He watched him again when five or ten minutes later he came running out and heading straight for his cabinet. In about an hour he would appear again to vanish into the observatory, whence he would once more soon emerge to dive again into the cabinet, where this time, however, he generally spent the rest of the day. Occasionally he went neither to cabinet nor observatory, but prowled around, muttering to himself, stopping every moment to think, or rain oceans of figures into his memorandum-book.

The Captain's eye was not the only one that was

strongly attracted by the Professor's strange movements. Ben too watched him as a cat watches a mouse. He even made up his mind two or three times to ask the redoubtable Professor what was troubling him. But though physically as brave as a lion, he was easily overawed by the Professor's terrible eyes scowling through those terrible glasses. At the decisive moment his heart sank within him; he could utter no more than "Hem!" and even that was half disguised as a cough; then he turned away quite discomfited and heartily ashamed of himself.

"It's not exactly afraid of him I am," he would mutter to himself by way of consolation; "it's about Montmartre I am concerned. Who knows, if I vexed him, but that would be the very spot he would select for landing his confounded Comet on!"

But the Captain and his companions were soon seriously disquieted by the Professor's unusual state of silent irritability and even suffering. It must proceed, they knew well, from some momentous cause. What could it be? Some error in his calculations? Did Gallia's movements disagree with her ephemeris? Was there — here lay their greatest trouble — any danger of the Comet's missing the Earth at the appointed time and place?

These conjectures were partly right and partly wrong.

The Professor was at the present moment the most un-happy astronomer living. His calculations and his ob-servations would not agree. Time and time again he would dash into his cabinet, fully confident that he had detected his error. Though half frozen with his prolonged stay in the observatory, he would instantly set again to work at his figures and diagrams with all his old spirit. But it was to no purpose. In ten or fifteen minutes he would fling his pencil furiously against the wall, and commence to tear out the little hair still left him.

"Confusion!" he would exclaim almost loud enough to be heard outside. "What's the meaning of this? What is she doing there? How the Hades did she get there? The Satanic little wretch has no business there! She's not up to her time! If she's right, everything is wrong, and Newton must have been as mad as a March hare! Are the laws of universal gravitation the laws of universal humbug? Wrong myself? Impossible! *My* calculations are never wrong! They *can't* be wrong. It's that infernal piece of im-pertinence that won't come right! But I'll fix her yet!"

Then burying his head between his hands, he would remain as long as five minutes plunged in the deepest and closest thought.

"IS UNIVERSAL GRAVITATION UNIVERSAL HUMBUG?"

"Something *must* be wrong!" he would say at last. "What is it? Either myself or the universe! It can't be myself — my calculations are too careful! Still — still — possibly — let's try it again!"

Then he would start once more for the observatory, but only to return once more to his cabinet with invariably the same result.

The Captain and his friends grew more and more uneasy. The Professor could neither eat, drink, nor sleep, and was fast dwindling away into a shadow.

Such a state of things could not, of course, last long.

One morning — it was the twelfth of October — immediately after breakfast, Ben, having some work to do in the Alveario, had hurriedly ascended the main chimney, and was approaching Central Hall, when all at once he heard a sudden yell, in which he thought he recognized the Professor's voice. Fearing he had hurt himself, and was crying out for assistance, Ben rushed into the apartment at full speed, but he was instantly brought to a complete stand-still.

The Professor was hopping around the room, wild with excitement, clapping his hands, and screaming " *Eureka! Eureka!*" with all his might.

Ben was a little frightened.

" Can I do anything for Monsieur the Professor?" he asked timidly, and keeping off at a good safe dis-

29 *

tance. He had often heard that lunatics can give very severe bites.

"*Eureka! Eureka!*" was still the Professor's sole reply; at sight of Ben, however, he had stopped dancing.

"*Eureka?* Monsieur the Professor," said Ben, "*Eureka?*"

"Certainly *Eureka!*" cried Rosette, "don't you know what *Eureka* means?"

"Not very well, Monsieur the Professor."

"Of course you don't! Just like the ignoramus you are. Go find out!"

Ben instantly sought the Captain.

"Something new, Governor," said Ben touching his cap, "but not quite unexpected."

"What is it, Ben Zouf?"

"Professor's gone crazy!"

"What!"

"I have just found him pirouetting around the room like a ballet-dancer, and shouting something *Eureka!*"

"*Eureka?* Are you sure? He has found it out then! What has he found out?"

"Indeed, Governor, I don't know. Something about his Comet I suppose. But here he comes to answer you."

But the Professor did not seem disposed to answer

anybody. He did not even look as if he was conscious of anybody's presence. He had, however, lost his uneasy expression altogether, and now with head bent and arms folded, he moved along slowly in the direction of the cabinet, apparently engaged with himself in a very earnest colloquy.

The Captain had not the courage to ask him a question, but, by following him pretty closely, he managed to pick up a few disjointed sentences.

"Yes!" they heard him mumbling, "of course — that's it! It can't be anything else! Oh the infamous scoundrel! Shan't I make him quake for it! But — proceed cautiously — on such a subject no doubt must exist! How to get him to confess? If he chooses to deny, I'm as much at sea as ever! He is deep and sly — but I must be deeper and slyer! Hang the old swindler — I should have known him better! Oh how my fingers itch for his throat!"

Here he vanished into the cabinet, and for two or three hours no more was seen of him.

But that very day at dinner everybody noticed a wonderful change in the Professor. He ate and drank with the others, and seemed to enjoy their society. His temper appeared to be improved quite as much as his spirits. He showed himself extremely affable towards everybody, laughed at Ben Zouf's jokes, tried to make

jokes himself, patted little Nina on the head, and —
most amazing and astounding of all — began to treat
with the utmost courteousness and respect the most
unlikely man of all the Gallians to evoke either — in
fact, our slippery friend Dutch Isaac.

Nobody knew what to make of it. Looks were exchanged, and heads were shaken, but no rational conclusion was arrived at. Ben, indeed, touched his forehead
significantly; the Professor's labors, he said, were
softening his brain. But nobody was more astonished
at the phenomenon than Isaac himself. Remembering
very well that the Professor had always treated him, not
only without ceremony, but with undisguised contempt,
he was now the more puzzled in attempting to account
for these respectful advances and this evident desire to
ingratiate. He pretended, however, to notice nothing,
and kept, if possible, a closer watch than ever on everything going on.

The Professor's doings, it must be acknowledged,
were exceedingly strange. The first thing he did every
morning, for instance, was to call on Isaac in the gloomy
hole where he kept his goods. He inquired carefully
for the state of his health, showed extraordinary interest
in the details of his business, hoped he had made good
sales and particularly had realized good profits. He
encouraged him not to be too squeamish about taking

every advantage of the present opportunity of enriching himself, and even took the trouble to teach him an exceedingly short method of calculating interest that astounded Isaac by its simplicity and correctness.

But the old fox was not to be fooled without at least knowing what for. As Ben said, whoever expected to draw the wool over Dutch Isaac's eyes should get up early and sit up late. The miser's keen instinct began to warn him that the Professor was after his money. Now Isaac had not the least objection to lend money on good security and at a good rate of interest. Count Timascheff, the owner of a whole district, and a close relative of the proud Danischeffs, might have as much money as ever he asked. The Captain, poor of course as every Gascon must be, could not get a cent — except, perhaps, a little, for the sake of policy. But as to the Professor — who in the world ever thought of lending money to a Professor?

Accordingly, in reply to Rosette's profuse expressions of unbounded interest, Isaac answered only in the driest monosyllables ; and pretty soon he even began to keep his mouth shut altogether.

Besides, just at this very time, Isaac found himself compelled by circumstances to think of something very different from lending money, namely, spending money — in other words, shedding his heart's blood. In looking over his merchandise, he found he had not a particle of coffee left for his own use. The price had been so good that he had sold it all to Ben Zouf, forgetting to reserve any for himself, except a very small store which was now completely used up. As he could not possibly get along without his coffee, no resource was now left but to apply to Ben Zouf, the head steward and quartermaster-general. The provision store being common property, why should not his, Isaac's, claims be heard as well as another's? One morning then, after listening for some time to the Professor's eloquent protestations of interest with the most freezing silence, he suddenly started up, and hastily told Rosette he was sorry to interrupt such a flow of oratory and learning, but that he had some important business on hand which should be instantly attended to.

He found Ben busily engaged in arranging things in the provision cellar.

"Ah, Signor Ben Zhouf," he began in his most wheedling tones, "I have the honor to bid you a very good-morning!"

"That you, Bendigo? Good-morning! What's the matter? Coming to force money on me? No use. I'm too rich already and you are too poor!"

"Ah, Signor Ben Zhouf, you be the funniest man — ha! ha! ha! — you kill me with your jokes!"

"Stow your jaw, Meshach, and tell me what you want."

"Very little, my good Signor, only one small pound of coffee out of the general reserve."

"A pound of coffee? For yourself? Not much!"

"It is not much indeed, Signor Ben Zhouf," said Isaac, misunderstanding Ben's slang. "You speak very truly."

"I speak very truly when I say you can't get any!"

"What! Is the coffee all out?"

"Oh no; we have several hundred pounds still on hand."

"Well then, my good Signor, can't I get one little pound for my own consumption?"

"Not likely, Saul, not at all likely," said Ben, shaking his head.

"Only one small pound of coffee!" persisted Isaac; "it would raise the cockles off my heart!"

"Heart! You have n't one, you old reprobate! If you ever had one, you sold it long ago!"

"The good Signor will have his little jokes. He! he! he! But it's so cold over there in that cell of mine that I can't do without a little coffee."

"Count your money, Ezekiel! That will keep you warm!"

"The little money I have is soon counted, Signor Ben Zhouf, s' help me F —"

"All this cackle is useless, Bendigo! I'll give you no coffee without a written order from his Excellency!"

"Why, Signor Ben Zhouf, I have so much confidence in his Excellency's justice —"

"Justice!" interrupted Ben, locking up the boxes and going off to see the Captain. "If there's anything like justice done, you'll never get a grain of coffee."

Ben was hardly out of the store, when the Professor, who had been within ear-shot all the time, popped in, and took the vacant chair.

"O you want coffee, don't you, Monsieur Isaac?" he asked in the softest tones.

"Yes, one small pound, Signor Professor."

"Your own is all gone then?"

"Alas! yes, Signor Professor. In my anxiety to do as much good —"

"Yes, yes, I know," interrupted Rosette. "You can't, of course, do without your coffee. Neither can I. It's a fine stimulant. It heats the blood!"

"Yes, Signor Professor. It warms up the veins! In that den of mine it keeps me from freezing."

"Monsieur Isaac, you should get your coffee as well as the rest of us."

"You speak like the holy prophet Daniel, Signor Professor! Supposing I did sell the coffee. Should that prevent me as a member of this community from being allowed my own particular share?"

"Not at all, Monsieur Isaac. Your rights are incontestable. Now how much coffee do you want?"

"Only one small pound, Signor Professor. Not a grain more. I am so very careful. It will last me ever so long. I am not a Prodigal Son!"

"And—how—are you going to—weigh the pound?" asked the Professor so carelessly as to throw Isaac completely off his guard.

"With my spring-balance, Signor Professor," answered Isaac, now so far forgetting himself as to accompany his words with the slightest possible sigh.

The Professor's sharp ears had caught the sigh, and he was now hot on the scent.

"With your spring-balance of course," he resumed. "There's no other balance here I believe?"

"Not one, alas!—I mean there's not another one!"

"Ah Monsieur Isaac," said the Professor, smiling with his lips whilst his eyes went through the Jew like an auger, "you are going to make considerably by your bargain. Instead of one pound you are going to get seven and a half."

"I understand, Signor Professor, "seven and a half, only—"

30

"Isaac Ben Isaac," interrupted Ben, hastily returning, "his Excellency will not let you have any coffee —"

"How won't let me have any coffee?" screamed Isaac.

"Will not let you have any coffee," continued Ben slowly and monotonously, "unless you pay hard cash for it down on the spot!"

"Pay for the coffee! *Guter Himmel!*"

"Pay for the coffee. Give back some of the money you took from us. What! You want your own coffee and our money too? You imagine we're all Babes in the Wood! Come, let us see the color of your yellow boys, or clear out!"

"Make a poor destitute man like me pay for his share of the coffee, when another —"

"Yes, but you're not another, you know! See the distinction? But I have no time to stand here higgling! will you pay or will you not?"

"Have a little compassion on a poor destitute man! S' help me —"

"Clear out! I'm going to shut up shop! Vanish!"

"If I must — I must," gasped Isaac, seeing he could not get any better terms out of Ben.

"Be lively then! Where's the balance?"

"How much am I to pay for the pound?" asked Isaac.

"The same price as we paid you," answered Ben. "So the Governor says. That's not what *I*'d ask, you may be sure! Though what's the good of flaying you alive? Your old skin would not be worth the trouble!"

Isaac, every motion of his still closely watched by the Professor, put his hand into an inside pocket of his old gabardine, making some pieces of money jingle by the action.

"How much am I to pay for the pound?" he asked.

"Seventy-five francs a pound, the price current at Terre Chaude," answered Ben. "But what difference need the price make? More money less money, all the same! Once we get back to the Earth, gold won't be worth more than its weight in sand!"

"Ah good Signor Ben Zhouf, you cut my heart by saying such things! — Now give me the coffee — and here's your money!"

Taking out the gold pieces one by one, he held them awhile in his left hand looking at them tenderly. Then he patted them, kissed them, and rubbed his hands over them again as if their electric touch gave him an exquisitely delightful pleasure. Then he counted them quickly, and handed them at once to Ben Zouf, with the resigned air of a convict mounting the scaffold. Ben counted them over twice, apparently with the greatest care, though there were only seven of them altogether, and piled them on his desk.

"Yes, Shylock, money's all right. Now let us have your spring-balance to weigh the coffee!"

With another deep sigh, still watchfully noticed by the Professor, Isaac put his hand into an old knapsack hanging at his side, and drawing out the spring-balance, handed it to Ben.

Suspending a deep pan to the hook, and noticing where the needle pointed, Ben plunged a scoop into the coffee-chest, and poured into the pan just as much coffee as was necessary to bring the needle one pound lower down.

"There's your coffee!" said Ben hastily. "But you will have to wrap it up yourself."

Isaac watched the whole operation with the greatest care.

"The needle is not quite down on the figure, Signor Ben Zhouf," said he, somewhat hesitatingly.

"Yes, it is, Mordecai," said Ben, "you have your just weight."

"Not exactly, Signor Ben Zhouf," said Isaac, looking about and seeing nobody, "because — to be quite right — the needle should go a few points lower!"

"What!"

"The spring often gets a little weak, Signor Ben —

it is such a very delicate instrument — and then it marks more than the right weight —''

Like a cat pouncing on a mouse, or rather like a Numidian lion swooping on his prey, the Professor instantly had the Jew by the throat. Shaking him furiously, pulling him, knocking him here and there, he chuckled him, he almost strangled him.

"Ha! you infamous scoundrel!" he screamed as he knocked his head against the wall, "I've caught you at last! But I'll teach you not to fool me again! Take that, you thieving hypocrite! and that, and that! I wish I could knock the breath out of your old carcass altogether, so that you could never again deceive anybody by your infamous lies!"

"*Hilf!*" gurgled Isaac, half choking. "*Hilf! Du guter Himmel!*"

"I'll *hilf* you, you infernal villain!" cried the infuriated Professor, swinging him around wildly, and tightening his grasp on Isaac's throat, until the poor Jew's eyes were beginning to start from their sockets. Physically, Isaac was a larger and heavier man than his opponent, but the Professor, though lightly built and small of frame, was exceedingly wiry, and his tremendous nervous energy for awhile gave him irresistible strength.

The struggle continued. In vain did Isaac try to

30 *                         X

shake off his adversary by running around the room, dragging him over the boxes, barrels, and cases. The little Professor held on with the grim tenacity of a bulldog. Every moment he found his right hand free, he tried to plant a facer on Isaac's nose or eyes. In this, however, he did not always succeed, for, though the Jew did not attempt to strike back, he showed a wonderful dexterity in warding off ugly blows.

Ben was delighted. For a whole year's pay he would not spoil such a lovely fight by offering the slightest interference. He did not care much which whipped, and, though he most heartily detested Isaac, he would not be a bit sorry to see the Professor get an eye or two well blackened.

At the first onset, he jumped up, and, pulling the furniture out of the way, he clapped his hands together to keep up the fun, danced around, and tried to stimulate the attacking party, like street boys at a dog-fight.

"Go for him, little Professor!" he would cry. "That's your sort! Give it to him! Short and sweet! Now for his lamps! Take a better aim next time, Professor! Ha! Right on the smeller! There goes the ruby! Now for a double up!"

But seeing Isaac's tactics to be entirely of the defensive order, and strictly confined to running about and crying for help, he took a seat and proceeded to enjoy the fun philosophically.

Stools and chairs were knocked over, the coffee was scattered about the floor, the gold pieces were flying in all directions, the spring-balance was bent up out of all shape, the Professor's shins were all rasped by being dragged over the sharp-edged boxes, but still the struggle continued. Isaac had succeeded in loosening the clutch a little off his throat, and was crying out louder than ever; the Professor, though still maintaining his full grip, was beginning to puff for want of breath; Ben Zouf's roars of laughter were growing wilder and wilder with the intensity of his enjoyment.

The noise at last got to be so great that the Captain, the Count, and Procopius, came rushing in, much alarmed, and having no idea of what possibly could be the matter. Immediately separating the combatants, though not without some difficulty, the Professor's bony fingers carrying a considerable quantity of Isaac's collar,

"What in the world is the meaning of all this?" asked the Captain in perfect amazement.

The combatants being too much out of breath to speak, and Ben Zouf too much convulsed with laughter to utter an articulate sound, the question had to remain for some seconds without a reply.

It was a regular tableau. The Professor pale and trembling with excitement, his coat in tatters, his pantaloons all burst at the knees. Isaac, gasping for breath, both eyes blackened, his nose bleeding, and one side of his coat without a collar. Ben Zouf, in the highest possible spirits, and laughing so heartily that he fell off the chair.

"Ho! ho! ho!" he cried hysterically, rubbing his sides as if they were in pain. "It's too rich! I shall go off! Won't somebody put a weak straw to my back! O Captain, what a sight you missed! The jolliest row you ever set eyes on! Hang me if he is n't a regular little game-cock! Thunder and lightning, how he pitched in!"

"What's the matter, you blockhead?" asked the Captain impatiently. "Who's a regular game-cock? Who pitched in?"

"I did!" said the Professor, at last trying to speak as he nervously smoothed his clothes with one hand, and adjusted his collar with the other. "I tried to strangle the infamous scoundrel cowering there before you! And I'd do it again! His balance gave us the wrong weight! He can't deny it!"

"Is this true, Isaac?" asked the Captain.

"Signor Governor," stammered Isaac, still so much frightened as to hardly know what he said, "the bal-

ance — was so very delicate — that is to say — yes — not
quite —''

"Not satisfied with robbing you, Servadac, by selling
his goods at light weight," cried the Professor endeavoring to make another dash at the trembling Jew, "he
actually allowed me to weigh my Comet with his false
instrument!"

"Is all this true, Isaac?"

"S' help me Father Abraham, Signor Governor, I
can't tell! — but the instrument was so very delicate
that the spring might have been a *leetle* weak!"

"A little weak!" roared the Professor, squaring off
for a new rally. "That's all *he* thinks about it! But
it set the weight of my Comet all wrong! Millions
and millions of pounds too heavy! And when I took
this false weight as the basis of my new calculations,
the observations would not correspond with the results, and of course she is no longer in her proper
place!"

These terrible words threw the friends into a dreadful
state of consternation.

"Your calculations all wrong!" cried Procopius.

"Her movements unknown!" cried the Count.

"She's bound to miss the Earth!" cried the Captain.

"She!" cried the Professor, looking from one to

the other with an angry eye. "Are you all crazy? What do you mean by '*she*'?"

"Gallia!" exclaimed the friends in one breath.

"Gallia! Who spoke of Gallia?"

"You did!"

"How could I speak of Gallia, when I meant Nerina?"

"Oh, Nerina!" cried the friends, very much relieved. "We thought you meant Gallia!"

"How could I mean Gallia, you simpletons? How often have you to be told that my calculations about Gallia are infallible? There's nothing wrong about *her!* She's returning to the Earth, taking us all back — though I wish she would drop that confounded Dutch Isaac somewhere on the road!"

# CHAPTER XVI·

## TROUBLE FOR NOTHING.

THE Professor's irritation was perfectly natural. If anything can justify your anger it is to see your most laborious and persevering efforts suddenly rendered valueless for no reason in the world but some wretch's selfish dishonesty or unheeding carelessness. Isaac had been using a light weight all the time, as the reader no doubt has long since divined, though probably never suspecting to what extent.

The first thing done by the Professor after cooling off was to pick up the spring-balance and have it straightened out into its proper shape by the machinist of the *Dobryna*. Then by a careful examination, the conclusion was soon arrived at, and even confirmed by the Jew's unwilling confession, extorted through the dread of another thrashing from the terrible Professor, that for every pound Isaac had never given more than three-quarters of a pound! No wonder he had become rich! But no wonder likewise that the Professor's calculated weight of Nerina had not agreed with the reality! His joy at this discovery, however, combined with the satisfaction of having given Isaac a pretty sound drubbing, put the Professor into such good-humor, in spite of his torn clothes, that it was almost with a smile he said to the Captain as he departed:

"Good-by, Servadac! Good-by, all! Next time we meet I shall have the satisfaction of giving you the latest intelligence from my Nerina!"

Isaac would have also vanished but for the scattered coffee. Having paid his money for it, to lose it was the last of his thoughts. After the Professor's departure he crawled noiselessly out of the corner where he had been hiding, and began picking it up, almost grain by grain, and stowing it away in his pouch. The Captain and his friends, deeming the punishment he had received from the Professor quite enough for the present, were inclined to let him continue at his work without molestation. But not so Ben Zouf. He was merciless as a schoolboy.

"Ha, Pharaoh!" he would exclaim, "so you have turned champion of the *light weights*, have you? Black-leg as well as land-shark? Keep on! Nothing like progress! But I wonder you are not a little afraid. Using false weights is quite a serious matter — seven years in solitary confinement at least! And the fine! Heaven help you if you fall into the hands of one of our French judges! But I'll give you a piece of friendly advice — whoever else you may try to cheat with light weights, don't try it on the Professor any more! When riled he's very ugly, very nasty. Can't he serve out a pair of black eyes at the shortest notice! Thunder and lightning, how he rattled your old ribs!" etc., etc.

Isaac never showed by the slightest movement that he was conscious of a single word that Ben was saying. He kept quietly picking up the coffee till there was not a grain left. Then sneaking off silently, he disappeared without a word. But had he picked up anything else besides the coffee? The money too had been scattered about, and Ben after a most careful search could find no more than sixty-five francs. "The old fox has nipped us after all!" cried Ben starting in pursuit; but the Captain laughed and forbade all further proceedings in the case. It was more than two months after this that Isaac's face was seen around again.

Meantime Gallia moved on with steadily accelerating velocity. On the seventh of October she entered the zone of the telescopic planets where, as may be remembered, she had captured Nerina nineteen months ago. By the first of November half of this zone was safely got through. In the next thirty days, according to Procopius's calculation, the Comet would traverse a course of forty million leagues on her orbit, and

31

reach a point not quite eighty million leagues from the sun.

The temperature, though gradually becoming more endurable, was still a few degrees below zero, and, of course, no sign of thaw had as yet begun to appear. The surface of the sea was as glassy and steely as ever; and the two vessels, perched on the summits of their crystal pedestals, were getting higher and higher every day, and therefore more likely to topple over at any moment. But the Gallians now hardly appeared to feel the cold. They had by this time become accustomed to such extreme temperatures, and the circulation of their blood was so perfect in consequence of their regular habits of living, that they actually found the present weather rather warm and comfortable. In this, however, they only resembled the Arctic explorers, who become so hardy by constant exposure to extreme cold, that they can sleep all night on the ice with no more shelter than the ordinary sealskin day clothing.

The return of the temperate weather enabled the Captain to put in execution an idea which he had been entertaining for some time, namely, to pay a flying visit to the Englishmen in Gibraltar. Ignoring or rather forgiving the coldness with which himself and the Count had been treated on a former memorable occasion, he felt a strong desire to see the little garrison once more, to find out how they had passed the winter, and to inform them regarding their fast approaching return to the Earth, about which they were no doubt exceedingly anxious to receive some intelligence. This return, the result of a new collision, should be attended with the greatest possible danger, and such danger, to be at all diminished, should be evidently met by concerted action alone, in which all the Gallians, English as well as Terre Chaudians, should be called on to contribute their share.

The Count and Procopius approving strongly of the Captain's sentiments on the score of prudence as well as humanity, the next point, how the Rock Fortress was to be reached, did not take long to decide. Sailing was, of course, out of the question. The sea was still frozen; and, even if it were navigable, the *Dobryna* and *Hansa* were absolutely unapproachable; and to use up the scanty stock of coal still left in propelling the little steam-sloop would be to deprive the Gallians of every reasonable hope of again visiting the Isle of Gourbi. The ice-yacht was, of course, inefficient without wind, and no wind was likely to be felt in Gallia as long as the cold weather lasted. The atmosphere was still in that state of perfect tranquillity which nothing but the great heats of summer would be ever likely to disturb.

The only possible way left, therefore, to reach the Fortress was by skating. The distance, three hundred miles, though to a pedestrian a serious undertaking, to an accomplished skater did not appear more formidable than an affair of two or, at most, three days. A week could bring him back to Terre Chaude, besides allowing him time enough to get through whatever business matters he might have to transact with the Englishmen. A compass to show the way, a moderate supply of preserved meats, and a little alcohol lamp to cook his coffee, were sufficient baggage for this daring expedition, which was moreover just in harmony with the Captain's adventurous and danger-loving temperament.

The Count and Procopius proposed either taking his place or accompanying him, but he would not listen to either alternative. Their presence at Terre Chaude, he said, was absolutely indispensable; if any untoward incident should occur on the journey, what would become of their poor people? Moments were now growing more precious, and every preparation was to be made for taking all possible advantage of the approaching collision. One messenger would be quite enough to send to the Englishmen, or, if motives of prudence required two, Ben Zouf possessed every qualification for being a useful and prudent companion.

The Count and Procopius had, of course, to acquiesce, and Ben made no attempt to disguise his extreme joy at the whole arrangement.

" I 'm the happiest man living, Governor! " he cried. " Not to talk of the splendid chance it will give me to stretch my legs, I was the whole time trying to contrive some excuse to prevent you from going alone ! "

Next morning, November 2, was fixed for their departure. Everything was soon in readiness, but that night, immediately after supper, just before retiring, Ben was a little surprised at seeing the Captain quietly follow him as he left the Hall.

" Ben Zouf," said he in a low earnest whisper, " can't you find something in your stores out of which, in case anything turned up, we might manufacture a tricolor ? "

" Certainly, Governor."

" Well then, make the flag without a moment's delay ; only, you need not let everybody look at it, you understand ? "

" All right, Governor ! " answered Ben, touching his cap with a knowing look, and retiring immediately into the store-room.

" Something is in the wind ! " thought he to himself, as he began rummaging through the drawers and boxes for some red, white, and blue bunting. " What it may be is none of my business — hello ! here you are, Ben, by the great Mahomet ! Now let all outsiders keep

31 *

away for about half an hour, and the Governor will soon have as neat a tricolor as he ever laid eyes on ! But keep shady, Ben my boy ! There's something in the wind ! Something about France ! ''

There *was* something in the wind, something on which the Captain had set his heart, but of which he could not induce himself to make the slightest mention to Count Timascheff. His repugnance was founded mainly on two motives — personality and nationality.

In spite of the Count's noble and generous nature, the Captain could never forget that they had been rivals, that they had challenged each other to cross swords in deadly combat. The approaching return to Earth began to revive the old idea to some of its former intensity. Did the same sentiment animate the Count? This it was difficult to tell. The Count's demeanor was still cold, no colder, however, than it had ever been. But though a Gallian for the last twenty-two months, there was no reason to suppose that he was not still human. Was there any reason for supposing the charming image of the Honorable Mrs. Chetwode not to be still as deeply engraved upon his heart as ever? Had the Captain and the Count, with all their mutual and self-sacrificing courteousness, ever been real *friends*, in the proper acceptation of the term? In spite of himself, the Captain had always experienced a kind of shyness in his intercourse with the Count, from which he felt himself completely free when chatting, arguing, or conversing with Procopius.

But this motive of personality was only a trifling reason for keeping his project a secret from the Count in comparison with the motive of nationality.

The nature of the project sufficiently explains this. The instant Servadac had learned that Ceuta, the Spanish fortress directly south of Gibraltar, had been abandoned by its garrison, an idea had taken possession of him, which had haunted him ever since, though he had never yet seen any great likelihood of being able to put it into execution. This idea was no less than to seize and immediately occupy the southern key of the Mediterranean for the benefit of his country, and to signalize such seizure by surmounting the rocky summit with the tricolor of France !

"Who knows," he asked himself, his lively Gascon imagination in full play, "who knows but that the Ceuta rock will get back safe, if not exactly to its own place again, at least to some commanding point in the Mediterranean, where its value to the French navy would be simply immense? And our flag once there, who would dare to dispute our right to its possession ? "

This being the Captain's deeply-cherished idea, you

can easily conceive that it would never do to talk about it to the Count. At the very first hint at such a proposal, what was to prevent the Count from sending his men or even trying himself to be the first to plant his country's flag on such an important position? A port on the Mediterranean is what Russia most desires in this world; it is what she is always moving heaven and earth to obtain. The seizure of such a point for his country, therefore, would cover Count Timascheff with immortal glory and transform him in a moment into the second man in the empire. In fact, it would be an attempt that nothing short of certain death could prevent him from undertaking. No, no! The Count should not be exposed to any such terrible temptation; nor should France's advantage be compromised by the quixotic notion that there was something wrong in keeping a project secret for the divulging of which there really existed no imperious or overwhelming necessity!

These were the chief reasons why the Captain had never breathed a word to the Count regarding the contemplated conquest of Ceuta.

Leave-takings all over, the bold adventurers started in the best of spirits, but they had been half an hour on the road when the Captain broached the subject to Ben Zouf.

To say that, in spite of skates, Ben fairly danced for joy would be no exaggeration.

What! Secure territory for his dearly-beloved France! Do something that redounded at once to her honor and her advantage! Steal a march on those swaggering English! Glory unspeakable and joy forever! Ben felt as exhilarated as if he was marching to battle.

"Give us a touch of the *African Zouaves*, Ben Zouf!" cried the Captain, admiring such enthusiasm and deeply sharing it.

The hint was enough for Ben. He instantly started with a fine voice and splendid expression a song well known in the Algerian armies under the name of *A Morning March in the Little Atlas*. Like most military songs, it is untranslatable into English, but one verse may give some idea of its general spirit.

### THE AFRICAN ZOUAVES.

The rising Sun
Has just begun
With his slanting rays to blind us,
And the great effect
He must expect
Is "skulks" and "frauds" to find us.
But on, boys, on!
In the teeth of the Sun!
Is the cry of the African Zouaves!

Y

The Sun we don't mind,
*Us* he cannot blind,
Us the bully African Zouaves!
Then shout, boys, shout!
Hurra, hurra, hurra!
Shout like the African Zouaves!
And step straight out,
For *"No right about!"*
Is the ticket of the African Zouaves!

"Let me see the flag, Ben Zouf," said the Captain when Ben had got through his song.

Without a word Ben opened his knapsack and took out a pretty fair specimen of a flag, considering he had not expended more than half an hour in cutting it out from odds and ends, and putting it together without a pattern.

The Captain's emotion was so great as he unfolded his country's emblem that he kissed it reverentially, and his eyes filled with tears. Ben, pretending not to notice his master's sensibility, instantly burst again into song, this time chanting a verse of Béranger's VIEUX DRAPEAU, so beautifully translated by Father Mahoney—

"O my old flag! that liest hid
There where my sword and musket lie —
Banner, come forth! for tears unbid
Are filling fast a warrior's lid,
Which thou alone canst dry.
A soldier's grief
Shall find relief;

A veteran's heart shall be consoled —
*France shall once more*
*Her tricolor*
*Triumphantly unfold!*"

With ·plenty of songs to enliven the way, warmly clad, in splendid health and the best possible spirits, the Captain and his Orderly were not long in leaving Terre Chaude so far behind them that the next time they looked back there was not the least trace of land visible on the whole eastern horizon. They did not, however, fatigue themselves by over-exertion. Of the two, they rather spared themselves, husbanding their strength for any unforeseen difficulty that might turn up. Every three hours they stopped to rest a little and take some refreshment. But night once come, they never spent more than an hour at a time in sleep. Though the cold affected them but slightly as long as they were in motion, they were afraid that prolonged exposure would cause a fatal congelation of the blood.

The trip was effected without the occurrence of any incident worth noticing. The third morning after their departure, they came in sight of a black speck faintly glimmering in the rays of the rising sun. This the Captain after a little while pronounced to be the rocky islet of Ceuta.

Ben instantly felt like a war-horse sniffing the scent of the battle afar off. From old associations he began at once giving wild orders about "hollow squares," "echelon movements," "bayonet charges," and "form to resist cavalry!" In his eagerness he had even got several hundred feet ahead of the Captain, when he suddenly stopped with a loud shout that sounded very like a suppressed imprecation.

"What's the matter?" asked the Captain, hurrying up.

"There's something on that rock ahead of us that I don't like the looks of!" answered Ben.

"Let us push on!" cried the Captain, whose eye-sight though very keen could not be compared to his Orderly's.

Ben was soon ahead again, but in less than three minutes he had come to a dead halt.

"Captain!" he cried in a voice decidedly expressive of alarm.

"Well, Ben Zouf?"

"There's a fellow on that rock making signals, as sure as you are a living man, and pretty long arms he has too!"

"Heaven and earth!" cried the Captain. "Can we have come too late?"

In a few minutes more Ben stopped again, and this

"SOMETHING ON THAT ROCK AHEAD OF US."

time exclaimed in accents completely devoid of all hope :

"Useless going any further, Captain! That is a semaphore, and I think I see smoke too!"

"If it's a semaphore," cried the Captain, much excited, "somebody must be working it! And if there's smoke there, somebody must be lighting a fire!"

"That's what I say, Captain."

Servadac was terribly disappointed, but he would not surrender all hope.

"Look to the north, Ben Zouf, and tell me what you see!"

"A black rocky mountain, Captain!"

"Gibraltar! I see it myself. What else can you notice?"

"Something black flashing on the top! Yes! It is signalling to Ceuta!"

The Captain heaved a deep sigh.

"There can be no doubt about it," said he. "The English are beforehand with us. They have seized Ceuta, and are now signalling our arrival to their friends in Gibraltar!"

"Well, Captain, what then?"

"We must surrender all hopes of conquest, Ben Zouf, and put the best face we can on the matter!"

"But, Captain, there can't be more than five or six

32

Englishmen defending Ceuta, and, unless the English breed is much improved and the French degenerated, the match would not be so very —"

"Enough, Ben Zouf! It is they who have stolen a march on us! If words will have no effect, nothing else will avail us now!"

The disappointed conquerors started again, but very slowly and looking decidedly blue. They soon arrived at the foot of the islet, and, while peering around for an entrance, they were startled by the sudden appearance of a sentry popping up from behind a rock and exclaiming in English:

"Who goes there?"

"Friends," answered the Captain in the same language. "France!"

"England!" cried the sentry.

Four men now showed their heads over a kind of rampart a little higher up the promontory.

"What do you want?" asked one of them, still in English.

"To speak to your commander."

"The Governor of Ceuta?"

"Y-e-s, the Governor of Ceuta — since Ceuta seems to have a Governor."

"We shall inform the Governor of your arrival. Step around to the left for two or three hundred yards, and you will find the road."

Doing as they were ordered, in a few minutes they saw the Governor in full uniform coming down the ascent to meet them.

He stopped half-way, but, though considerably stouter than he had been twenty-one months ago, he was easily recognised by the Captain as no less a personage than the gallant Major Oliphant himself!

Doubt was now impossible. The Englishmen *had* forestalled him. Seizing the rock, they had hollowed out a chamber or two which they then strongly fortified. From the appearance of everything around, all this must have been done before the freezing of the Gallian Sea. Provisions and fuel were evidently in abundance. The Englishmen waddled under their fat, and the thick black smoke slowly rising in the sky showed that something quite substantial was preparing for breakfast. The little garrison could not even consider itself isolated. Gibraltar was only at an hour or two's distance. Constant communication was almost as easy by daily trips backward and forward on the ice as by the telegraphic signals.

Even the famous game of chess, now reaching a crisis, had not been interrupted. By means of an ingenious system of signals agreed upon beforehand, the players could transmit their carefully prepared moves at any moment, day or night.

"Major Oliphant, I presume?" said the Captain, advancing a few paces up the road, hat in hand.

"Major Oliphant, Governor of Ceut`a," replied the Major, also uncovering. "Whom have I the honor of addressing?"

"Captain Servadac, Governor of Terre Chaude."

"Yes," was the English officer's characteristic comment.

"Governor," began Servadac, a little nettled, "will you allow me to express my surprise at seeing you thus installed in the remains of what was once Spanish territory?"

"O yes, Captain; I have not the slightest objection."

"May I ask on what right your claim is founded?"

"Certainly; on that of first occupant."

"If the claim of first occupant be a good one, don't you think, Major, that the Spaniards entertained by us at Terre Chaude have the best right to Ceuta?"

"I think nothing of the kind, Captain Servadac."

"Won't you have the goodness to state your grounds for such an opinion, Major?"

"Certainly, Captain. Whatever claims these Spaniards may have had on Ceuta, they have formally made them over to England."

"Formally, Major?"

"Yes, Captain, by regular contract drawn up, signed,

THE GOVERNOR OF CEUTA.

sealed, and with every formality properly attended to."

"This is all news to me, Major."

"You may find it equally interesting news to you, Captain, to be told that your Spaniards have received in good English gold the full price agreed upon for this important relinquishment."

"Phew!" whistled Ben in an undertone by way of comment, "that is how Negrete and the other Spaniards came by all those English sovereigns!"

It was all perfectly clear now. The two English officers had transacted the whole business with Negrete and the other Spaniards, and unknown to Isaac on the day, as the reader may remember, of their secret visit to Ceuta.* In their desire to put England in possession of both sides of the Strait they had most unquestionably succeeded.

Further parleying being evidently useless, the Captain felt obliged to give up at once and forever all ideas of conquest; but he was so completely disconcerted by this unexpected intelligence that it took him some little time to recover from the blow.

"May I inquire to what I am indebted for the honor of this visit?" asked the Major, noting the Captain's prolonged silence.

---

* "TO THE SUN?" page 208.

32*

" Oh ! " replied the Captain readily, " I have come, Major, to offer to yourself and your companions whatever assistance you may require at the dangerous moment now so rapidly approaching."

" Now so rapidly approaching ? " repeated the Major interrogatively.

"Yes, Major.  Perhaps you are not aware of the exact state of things ?  Perhaps you have not had an opportunity of learning that some of the rocks of Gibraltar and of Ceuta are now traversing planetary space on the back of a Comet ? "

"On the back of a Comet, Captain !" said the Major, an amused smile of incredulity flitting over his cold features.  " I beg your pardon, but did you really say on the back of a Comet ? "

" Yes, Major," said the Captain, succeeding wonderfully well in keeping his temper ; " in a few words I can tell you all about it."

He then rapidly described the general state of things as well as he had understood it from the Professor. How a Comet had grazed the Earth, carrying off portions of Gibraltar, of Ceuta, of the Algerine Coast. How its orbit had carried it first around the sun and then away off into planetary space far beyond Jupiter. How, having doubled its aphelion point, ten months ago, it was now rapidly reapproaching the sun and in all probability was to meet the Earth again in about two months. How, the risks of a new collision being exceedingly threatening, and the closest union between all hands being absolutely necessary in order to insure the best precaution against a fatal result, he had come to tender every assistance in the power of his little colony in order to protect all the Gallians against the common danger.

"Therefore, Major Oliphant," he added in conclusion, "if your little garrison and that of Gibraltar would think proper to join us at Terre Chaude —"

"We are exceedingly obliged, I'm sure, Captain," interrupted the Major, in tones of the coldest reserve, "but we could never think of abandoning our post."

"May I ask why, Major?"

"In the first place, we have no orders to do so. In the second, our dispatch to Lord Fairfax has not yet been sent off."

"But, Major, you appear to forget that we are on the Earth no longer! We are on a Comet! In two months more we shall be exposed to all the dangers of a frightful collision!"

"Yes, yes, Captain, no doubt," hastily exclaimed the Major, fidgeting with impatience and evidently thinking the interview had lasted long enough. "But England, you know, attends to all that kind of thing, you know."

The Captain was puzzled. The Major evidently did not believe a word he said. Was there any use in persisting? However, he would give him one chance more.

"You decline our offer of assistance then, Major Oliphant?"

"Exactly, Captain," replied the Major, playing with his belt, "but of course, you know, we are ever so much obliged for your kindness."

"And you are determined on remaining in these two posts of Gibraltar and Ceuta, Major?"

"Most decidedly determined, Captain, commanding, as they do, the entrance to the Mediterranean."

"But suppose there is no Mediterranean, Major Oliphant?"

"Captain Servadac," replied the Major hastily and in a tone intended to cut short all further discussion, "there will always be a Mediterranean as long as the existence of a Mediterranean is necessary to England! —But excuse me, Captain," he added hurriedly, pointing at the arms of the semaphore now in rapid motion, "General Murphy has just announced his move! You will permit me? A *very* good morning!"

Hastily acknowledging the hasty salute, the Captain turned impatiently on his heel, and in a few moments found himself quietly and rapidly moving away from the rock, closely followed by his Orderly.

"Well, Ben Zouf!" said he at last, getting tired of silence.

"He did not even ask us to take off our skates!" cried Ben. "Hog of an islander!"

"That is not what I am thinking of," cried the Captain. "I am trying to reconcile myself with the result of our expedition!"

"Yes, Governor, our schemes of conquest have ended in a very pretty kettle of fish!"

"Now the watchword is *home!* Ben Zouf, as fast as ever our skates can carry us!"

"Yes, Governor, we'll —

> Step straight out,
> Though '*No right about!*'
> Is the motto of the African Zouaves!"

sang Ben, endeavoring to make as light as possible of a matter that evidently annoyed his master much more than he was willing to acknowledge.

No incident marked the home trip. In spite of Ben's efforts, it was performed in almost freezing silence, and the word *flag* was never mentioned once.

They got back on the evening of November 9 safe and sound, and their arrival was celebrated by a grand ovation, and a supper which added new laurels to Mochel's culinary fame. Even the Professor was of the party, and in unusually good spirits. He joked, laughed, made speeches, and never contradicted a soul; in a word, he was the gayest of the gay. The Captain, innocently attributing the Professor's exhilaration to the excitement of seeing an old pupil safely returned from a long and perilous journey, was deeply moved, and felt some little twinges of conscience for having caught himself doubting once or twice if such a thing as a heart ever beat in his old teacher's bosom. But he was soon undeceived. The Professor indeed *had* a heart, but it was not the joys and sorrows of ordinary humanity that excited its pulsations.

After supper, Rosette invited the Captain and his friends to accompany him to the observatory. He was still in the best possible humor, and kept on talking the whole time.

"I have overhauled completely all the calculations and conclusions," said he, "into which that confounded Isaac's false balance had plunged me. No one can imagine the horrible state of uncertainty in which I had found myself. A terrible imputation rested on Nerina's character which it was agony to think of. But the discovery of the balance gave me new hope, and I began all my investigations over again. The labor was enormous, but the hope of clearing her name from the taint of levity and capriciousness made the heaviest toil a delightful occupation. Now then, Messieurs, I am most happy to say that this day I have satisfied myself beyond all doubt that the slightest speck of uncertainty can no longer rest on my Nerina's fair fame! She is all right in all respects. She was all right all the time, though in my ignorant fury I nicknamed her, abused her, and scolded her. She is, in fact, perfectly charming, as I hope to convince you in a short time by ocular demonstration. Last night, my ephemeris told me she was to be found in a particular part of the heavens at a certain moment. At that certain moment I looked, and lo! there stood the bright and beauteous being, trembling and fluttering, within one second or the 36 hundredth part of a degree from the precise point! There's constancy for you! To-night you will find her exactly four and a half degrees west of Mira Ceti.''

With a running monologue of this kind delivered in rather an excited key the Professor entertained his companions until they reached the observatory. But they had hardly entered, when they instantly noticed that something was wrong. The Professor stopped suddenly to gaze at the sky with eyes staring, countenance horror-struck, and tongue speechless. No moon was to be seen from zenith to horizon! Gallia's faithless satellite had been captured by some of the asteroids so numerous in the zone of the telescopic planets !

The poor Professor's agony was pitiable.

"O Nerina, my beloved one!" he exclaimed in a heart-broken voice as he fell senseless on the floor.

# CHAPTER XVII.

## THE DECISION.

VERY much shocked at the sudden and painful blow experienced by his old teacher, the Captain picked him up at once, and, aided by his friends, carried him to his bed, where he lay for some hours in a state of perfect unconsciousness. All that night they watched him carefully; towards morning he began to recover his senses, till, aided a little by Procopius's restoratives, he was at last pronounced out of immediate danger. It was several days, however, before he was well enough to be left alone, and it was fully four weeks before he could move about with anything like his former activity. Even then he was by no means himself again. He was decidedly changed for the worse. He looked considerably older, was more morose than ever, avoided all intercourse with the others, and day or night hardly ever quitted his observatory. His case, in short, presented all the symptoms of a heart disappointment, but, as Procopius informed the Captain, the worst was now over, and the Professor's wound if only let alone would, like all the wounds inflicted by the little winged god, heal itself pretty soon, particularly if aided by an absorbing and active occupation.

Besides the sufferings of the lovelorn Professor, the Captain had a good many troubles of his own to be worried by. In the first place, he had a long conversation with the Count and Procopius regarding the result of his visit to the Englishmen. He told them how he had learned that Ceuta had been sold by the Spaniards — a perfect farce, the Spaniards having no right whatever to effect any such sale — and how the English, taking advantage of the opportunity, had seized and fortified the southern side of the strait. How he had invited Major Oliphant and his companions to Terre Chaude, where they might all cooperate together in making some attempt to ward off the common danger, but how, the Major having decidedly and not over courteously declined the invitation, he had returned immediately, leaving the pigheaded islanders to their fate. It is hardly necessary to say, however, that neither regarding his own little private projects nor the episode of the flag, did he breathe a single syllable. In fact, he was rather ashamed of the whole proceeding, and wished as little as possible to be either said or thought about it. In reply, his companions told him he had done what was perfectly right. He had acquitted himself of a duty. The Englishmen had been warned in good time. For anything that might hereafter befall them, they themselves were alone to blame.

In the next place, the Captain felt that the time had now come to consult and decide on the best means of counteracting the effects of the dreadful shock now rapidly approaching.

The more himself and his companions had reflected on the circumstances attending the first collision, the more they had been convinced that the little destruction of life attending it could be considered hardly less than miraculous. In fact, no living thing carried off on Gallia had suffered at all, and in all probability the Earth had been equally fortunate. But how could they expect the second shock to be equally harmless? Was it within the range of possibility, not to speak of probability, that a second encounter would take place without producing the most disastrous results especially to the smaller planet?

This was the question that the friends discussed one evening towards the middle of November, seated around a table in the little nook that served them for a sitting-room. The Captain, as chairman, opened the proceedings.

"Gentlemen," said he, "this being the 13th of November, if my old Master's calculations are right — and we have no reason to question their correctness — in forty-eight days the second and most probably the last encounter is to take place between Gallia and the Earth. The exact moment he has not given us as yet, but of the exact day there can be no doubt. Now, in anticipation of this eventuality, what precautions have we to take, in order to guard ourselves, if possible, against the terrible elementary commotions that must then ensue?"

"What precautions can we take, Captain?" asked the Count. "Are we not in the hands of Providence?"

"Most undoubtedly we are, Count," answered the chairman, "but we all know that Providence always helps those that help themselves."

"Have you any proposal to offer on the subject, Captain?" asked the Count.

"Nothing as yet, Count, I am sorry to say," was the reply. "Not that I have not racked my brains enough in my attempts to solve the problem, but so far nothing worth entertaining for a moment has suggested itself."

This made Ben Zouf open his eyes.

"How, gentlemen?" he exclaimed; "with all due

respect I must say I am greatly surprised that learned men like you cannot direct wherever you please and however you please this unfortunate Comet of ours. That an ignoramus like myself should be able to do nothing is of course only perfectly natural.''

" Ben Zouf," observed the Captain quietly, " your surprise does not show your usual good sense. In the first place, we are not learned men in the proper meaning of the word — though the Lieutenant has picked up a stock of real knowledge that many a very learned man might be proud of. In the next, were we the most learned men that ever put pen to paper, we could do no more towards directing the Comet than if we were so many omnibus horses.''

" You couldn't, Governor ! " cried Ben, more surprised than ever. " What is the good of learning at all then, if I may make so bold ? And why do people take so much pains to acquire it ? "

" The chief end of all human knowledge, Ben Zouf," said the Count with a calm smile, " is to convince us of our utter ignorance.''

This reply proving too much for Ben's powers of comprehension; Procopius put an end to the pause that ensued by observing :

" Mr. Chairman, the elementary commotions attendant on the new shock between Gallia and the Earth must

33 *

prove, as you say, fearful in the extreme, but, in order to guard ourselves against them with any prospect of success, we must first thoroughly understand the different kinds of danger to which they expose us. Suppose we examine each kind in its turn."

All listened attentively to Procopius's grave and harmonious tones, and the Chairman nodded to him to continue.

"First of all," resumed the Lieutenant, "let us ask ourselves what is to bring this new encounter about? A close examination into the cause may suggest an idea as to the remedy."

"That is the right way to view it, Procopius," said the Captain. "Well! to reply to your question. The encounter will be brought about, I should think, by the fact that two enormous bodies, rushing at enormous velocities and coming from opposite directions, will meet at the same point."

"Correctly answered, Captain," said Procopius. "Now comes the next question. Are these two bodies to meet plump, or only obliquely? The consequences of either alternative evidently must be widely different. In one case, Gallia might only graze the Earth, as she did on the first occasion, and glance off again into space, after doing comparatively little harm on either side. In this contingency, however, her orbit would be so much disordered that, even if we survived the shock, we should never have the slightest chance of meeting the Earth again."

"A prospect which might suit the Professor," muttered Ben Zouf, "but not very fascinating for us."

"Very well, Procopius," said the Count, "you have set before us the advantages and disadvantages of one variety of the encounter. Now let us take up the other. What would be the consequence of a direct, or, as you call it, a plump collision between Gallia and the Earth?"

"A mad bull's charge full tilt on a lightning train!" muttered Ben Zouf, "— rather rough on the bull!"

"Hold your tongue, Ben Zouf!" whispered the Captain impatiently.

"In examining that hypothesis, gentlemen," resumed Procopius, "we must never forget that the Earth's mass being so enormously greater than Gallia's, the Comet's impact would affect her but slightly, and the inevitable result would be that the Earth would keep on quietly revolving in her orbit, and bearing off on her surface all that was left of Gallia."

"No question whatever about that," said the Count.

"Now," continued Procopius, "to us it makes very little difference, indeed, which part of the Comet comes

first in contact with the Earth. It may be that part of
her equator where we are at present; it may be that
part of her equator which is our antipodes; or it may
be either of Gallia's poles. But the consequences
would be all the same. In the case of direct impact, not a single one of us could possibly be left
alive."

"I do not mean to contradict you, Procopius," said
the Captain, "but I should like to know on what grounds
you come to such a conclusion."

"Well," answered Procopius, "if we are on the part
of Gallia that first meets the Earth, of course we can't
help being crushed to atoms."

"We should be so flattened out," said Ben Zouf,
"that you could read the newspaper through the whole
thirty-six of us!"

"If we are at the antipodes of the part that is first
struck," continued Procopius, "we shall be crushed to
atoms just as surely. The sudden cessation of our
velocity induces a reaction of exactly the same violence
as attends the shock itself. But not only that. Even
if, through some miraculous accident, we survived the
shock itself, we should be instantly and infallibly
smothered. Not a particle of respirable air would
remain on the summit of the mountain several hundred
of miles in height that Gallia would form on the Earth's

surface. It would all rush down to mix with the Earth's atmosphere —"

"And we should be all left gasping, wriggling and floundering about like so many fishes flung forty feet out of water!" cried Ben, instantly realizing the situation.

"But, Procopius," asked the Count, "how would it be if Gallia should strike the Earth with either of her poles?"

"In addition to our other dangers, Count Timascheff," was the immediate reply, "we should be flung off with a violence that would kill us long before we should be crushed to powder by the frightful fall."

"Suppose Gallia struck the Pacific Ocean, Lieutenant?" suggested Ben Zouf.

"Gallia is so very large and solid, Ben Zouf," replied Procopius, "that even the deepest parts of the Pacific — a few leagues at the utmost — would no more antagonize the shock than — than —"

"Than a gallon of water would do for a buffer between two lightning trains," exclaimed Ben, whose ready fancy was quicker in suggesting a comparison.

"You have caught the idea admirably," said Procopius calmly, though he flushed a little at the interruption. "All the other consequences would therefore be the inevitable result of such a fall, with the certainty of being drowned in the bargain."

"Is that all that could happen us, Lieutenant?" asked Ben, so much excited that he appeared to forget that he was usurping too much of the conversation. "Flattened out like tissue-paper, smothered, crushed to powder, drowned — is that all the risk we run? Can't you think of some other pleasant adventure that the shock will be likely to favor us with?"

"Oh yes, friend Ben Zouf," answered Procopius with a slight smile; "in addition to our other 'adventures,' as you call them, sure to be the result of a shock between the two planets, we should also meet the dead certainty of being burned alive."

"Burned alive!" exclaimed his audience horror-struck.

"Infallibly," said Procopius. "It is even of all the results the most unavoidable. Gallia being suddenly brought to a stand-still by the terrific encounter, her velocity would be instantly transformed into a heat powerful enough to melt a planet of iron in a few seconds, if not to reduce it at once to a state of vapor."

The audience listened to these details without dreaming of questioning their correctness. In fact, there could be no question on the subject. Every statement of the Lieutenant's they well knew to be rigidly borne out by the principles of rigid and exact science.

There was a pause for a while. All were thinking intently. But it was the most unlearned of the party who was the first to come to a conclusion.

"There is only one thing to be done!" cried Ben Zouf.

"What is that?" asked the Captain.

"Quit the Comet before the shock!"

The Captain and the Count were silent for a moment, but Procopius trembled and shook as if he had received a sudden blow.

"How is that to be done?" asked the Captain and the Count in one breath.

"It can't be done!" said Ben in despair.

"IT CAN BE DONE!" said Procopius calmly, but with eyes and face reminding the Count of a Pythian priestess.

All looked at him with profound amazement and breathless expectation.

"Speak, Procopius!" exclaimed the Count.

The Lieutenant remained for a moment or two longer buried in the most intense thought ; then he spoke :

"Ben Zouf has suggested the only possible means of escaping our danger—quit Gallia before the shock."

"But how? How? How?" asked the others impatiently.

"*By a balloon!*" answered Procopius.

All started. A ray of hope instantly flashed through every breast.

"A balloon!" cried the Captain, in a disappointed tone, and as if hardly knowing what to say. "Balloons have, indeed, been used to make reconnoissances, to escape from beleaguered cities, to travel rapidly from one part of the earth to the other, to rise many thousands of feet in the air, but never surely to escape from earth altogether!"

"Never!" cried the Count and Ben Zouf simultaneously.

"Listen, gentlemen, for a few moments," replied Procopius, with the quiet calmness of conviction; "if we only know the exact instant when the shock is to take place, we can certainly quit Gallia's surface an hour beforehand. In her atmosphere we can assuredly float along as rapidly as Gallia herself. At the moment of impact, the two atmospheres will of course mingle together, with indescribable velocity, but the balloon may possibly glide unharmed from one to the other. In any case, being suspended in mid-air, we shall avoid the instantaneous consequence of the shock direct, and may even have some extremely remote chance of escaping with our lives."

"Procopius," said the Count with gravity approaching to solemnity, "I think we understand your ideas clearly. It may not be an infallible one, but it is certainly the only one! We shall do as you say!"

"What chances have we, Procopius?" asked the Captain.

"Nine hundred and ninety-nine chances against us to one in our favor," answered Procopius.

"Nine hundred and ninety-nine to one!"

"That at least. The instant the balloon's velocity is stopped, she too must be burned to ashes."

"The balloon!" exclaimed the Captain.

"Yes," answered Procopius, "unless — that is to say — in this mingling of the two atmospheres something may happen that's impossible just now to foresee — yes — taking everything into calculation — quitting Gallia's surface just before the shock is the only resource left us."

"Certainly!" cried the Captain; "if we had only one chance in ten hundred million we would risk it!"

"But we have no hydrogen wherewith to fill our balloon, Procopius," observed the Count.

"Hot air will answer our purpose well enough," said Procopius, "we shall not be off the land for much longer than an hour."

"All right!" said the Captain enthusiastically; "a fire-balloon! A *Montgolfier!* The first balloon ever

34

made, and the easiest of all to make! But what shall we do for a bag?"

"The bag we can easily make out of the sails of the *Dobryna*," answered Procopius; "they are strong enough and not too heavy."

"You are an extraordinary fellow, Procopius," said the Count admiringly; "you have an answer for everything."

"A good answer too," cried Ben, filled with almost as much enthusiasm as his master. "*Vive* the Lieutenant!" he added, taking off his hat and swinging it vigorously.

"Your daring plan, Procopius, is certainly worth trying," said the Captain. "From this time forward we must think of nothing else! — By the by, dear friend, how can I make myself useful? Command me."

"You can make yourself very useful indeed, Captain, by doing something which is actually so indispensable that without it no particle of success is possible. And it is no easy matter either. It is no less than to ascertain from the Professor, the exact hour, the minute, and even, if possible, the very second when the shock will take place."

"It shall be done, Procopius," said the Captain, leaving the chair and breaking up the meeting.

The very next morning saw all hands busily at work on the balloon. Procopius gave the details, and superintended the execution. It was to be large enough to bear all the Terre Chaudians, twenty-three in number. The English, having refused all assistance, were of course to be left to their fate.

The sails of the *Dobryna*, carefully taken out of the store-rooms of the Alveario, were found to be of a very close tissue. A coating or two therefore of gum varnish, plenty of which was furnished by the cargo of the *Hansa*, easily succeeded in rendering the canvas air-tight. Procopius traced carefully with a crayon the exact spindle shape of the strips, then cut them out, and soon all hands, not even excepting Nina's, were busily employed sewing them together. The Russians, quite at home at this kind of labor, readily gave the necessary instructions to the Spaniards. All worked with a will, and the balloon, though of a monstrous size, was soon so far advanced as to take a definite shape.

By the word "all" we do not, however, include the Professor or Isaac. Neither of these gentlemen ever showed his face in the great workshop. Isaac was too busy counting his money — his eyes had by this time lost all signs of discoloration — and the Professor was probably looking up some heavenly body to supply

the void left in his aching bosom by the lost Nerina.
Perhaps he was grieving over his involuntary return
to the Earth ; but anyhow he was quite inaccessible to
the Captain's persistent approaches. To no questions
would he answer a single word by way of reply. Again
and again the Captain visited him ; again and again
he withdrew, repulsed, rebuffed, chagrined. So the
month rolled away.

And yet it was absolutely necessary to ascertain with
strict accuracy the exact moment when the two planets
encountered each other with a velocity greater than sixty
miles a second. That point unknown, nothing could
be done. Procopius said so again and again. Occasionally the Captain felt himself growing impatient at
the unreasonableness, obstinacy, and moroseness of his
old teacher. But he managed to control himself, and
waited patiently every day for some chance or other
to turn up and put him in possession of the all-important secret.

In the meantime Gallia was rapidly nearing the Sun.
Every night the Gallians could easily see the large
white star, which they called the Earth, growing larger,
brighter, and more beautiful. In November the Comet
had traversed a distance of 59 million leagues, and on
the first of December she was no more than 78 million
leagues distant from the Sun. In other words, she would
soon cut the orbit of Mars.

The temperature had now so much increased that the thaw set in at last. It was a magnificent sight to see the vast ocean breaking up, dissolving, as it were, and dismembering itself into millions and millions of fragments. Even late at night in the deep caverns of the volcano the Gallians could hear now and then the mighty cry of the ice as if struggling in agony for a few hours longer existence. Down the mountain sides little threads of water now began to trickle here and there, turning, however, into torrents and even cataracts in a few days under the warm rays of the returning sun. The snowy whiteness began gradually to fade away from the landscape, and the black volcanic grisly summits soon became as sharply relieved as ever against the circumambient opal sky.

By and by mists could be seen hovering over the horizon. By degrees the clouds began to form, and to move onward, impelled by breezy zephyrs awaking up at last after their long winter's sleep. In spite of the sweet and balmy air, further atmospheric disturbances announced their near approach; but the Gallians welcomed every change with rapture. Heat, light, and life were once more returning!

Just now, however, a double disaster, though long foreseen, and every day expected, produced almost as great a sensation among the little colony as if it had taken place without a moment's warning.

The *Dobryna* and the *Hansa*, as often already stated, had been lifted, by the piles of ice accumulating beneath them, up to a height of more than a hundred and fifty feet above the level of the sea. This enormous pedestal, undermined by the warm water, furrowed and streaked by the thaw, and crushed by the weight of the super-incumbent vessels, had lately begun to bend over, and threaten a destruction that might occur at any moment.

In the middle of the night between the twelfth and thirteenth of December the catastrophe took place. Some of the Gallians, happening to be awake at the moment, even said they had heard the terrible crash. Greatly alarmed, all hastened down early in the morning, and found the shore strown with bits of the two vessels mixed together, crushed, and ground up between blocks of half-melted ice. All were profoundly affected at the sight. The Russians actually shed tears at the loss of their beautiful *Dobryna*, and even the *Hansa* came in for some expressions of genuine regret.

Old companions, from the old world, their complete destruction not only caused heartfelt grief for their loss, but was even ominous of a similar doom impending over the colony.

Every expression of grief, however, was soon cut short by the sudden appearance of Isaac. Suspecting from the commotion that something was wrong, he had come out to see what was the matter, and he was now running down the road, uttering screams more fearful than those of a young mother who has suddenly lit on the dead body of her child. He never stopped till he reached the shapeless pile of wood and iron mixed with snow and ice — all that remained of his vessel. Throwing himself on a piece of the stern where the name HANSA could still be read, he kissed it passionately, clasped it in his arms, wailed over it, and spoke to it as lovingly as if the crushed beams and twisted bars could understand him.

Was he in earnest? Judging only from what we know of his hypocritical nature, I should conclude at once that he was not, and that all this passionate expression of sorrow was merely assumed, probably to cheat the Count, or frighten the Captain out of a little money. But on second thoughts, I should consider such conclusion as too hastily formed. He certainly shed real tears ; real was the hair that he tore out in fistfuls ; the blood that discolored the snow on which he knelt came from his bleeding knees ; the language too in which he uttered his wild lamentations was Hebrew, which not one of his auditors understood. Did Dutch

Isaac really have a heart after all? Had he lavished on
the *Hansa* a love which he would not deign to bestow
on a mere human being? Be this as it may, the spectators, recognising the existence of genuine suffering,
respected it as much as they had respected the Professor's distress for the loss of the Nerina. They neither
laughed, nor mocked, nor made heedless remarks at
Isaac's wild acting, or wilder lamentations over the
remains of his beloved vessel. Of what he said, of
course, they could at first only guess the meaning, but
they could soon see that his grief was rapidly assuming
an air of anger and indignation. Instead of lifting his
voice in a loud wail, and tearing his hair wildly, he soon
began to give utterance to expressions of bitter impatience, and to close his fists with threatening gestures
of vengeance. French imprecations first began to be
heard among the torrents of Hebrew; but his language
soon became French altogether, plainly heard, and
instantly comprehended.

"The accursed race destroyed you, my beloved!"
he cried. "The merciless Governor, and his wicked
servants, envied me the happiness of possessing you!
Accursed be the day we first saw them! Could they
not have left us as we were? Why bring us to this con-
demned abode of snow, ice, cold, and darkness? And
now you're gone! But I shall be revenged on these

workers of iniquity! I shall get full satisfaction from these sons of Jezebel! They shall hear the voice of justice come out of my mouth like a sharp sword! They dragged you here in spite of me your lawful owner! Justice! Justice and satisfaction too I shall have in full, s' help me holy Father Abraham!" etc., etc.

Was Isaac still in earnest, or had his anger cunningly yielded to his avarice? We can only reply that, however that may be, his tactics did not make much off the Captain. Irritated both by his unearthly howls and his abominable injustice, Servadac at last lost his temper. Approaching Isaac with a face pale and eyes flashing with anger, he laid his left hand on his shoulder, and said in low concentrated tones :

"Isaac, if you don't hold your tongue at once — mind, at once! — I will have you instantly put in chains, and flung into the lowest dungeon of the mountain!"

Isaac fully understood the reality of the Captain's threat; he even felt the Captain's nails piercing his shoulder in their suppressed nervous earnestness; still, whether from habit or the perverse stubborness of his nature, instead of keeping silence, he actually vociferated louder than ever :

"Even the Christian Governor turned pirate! Oh! holy Father Abra——"

The sudden appearance of Ben Zouf, tearing down

the road as fast as he could in the direction of the group, interrupted Isaac in the midst of his cries. The Jew stopped instantly; he even looked wistfully, and with some alarm, into the face of the Captain.

"What's the matter?" asked Servadac, surprised at Ben's unusual haste and evident anxiety.

"Nothing worth speaking of, Governor," answered Ben, a little out of breath, "only I've just learned that Isaac here has been giving you some trouble. I'm going to stop all that, by carrying him on my shoulders right up to the Professor. He is in a dreadful state, and is actually dying to thrash somebody. The fit is on him very bad just now, and he swears Isaac's spring-balance was the whole cause of Nerina's sudden disappearance. It will console him so much to give Isaac another good choking! Come, Ishmael, no resistance!"

He turned to seize Isaac, but Isaac was already gone. The instant he heard the terrible Professor's name, he started off like a cricket-ball, and was by this time half-way back to the cavern. Ben pretended to be highly indignant, and for a while gave vigorous chase amid the cheers and loud laughter of all present. Even the grave Count himself had to wipe his eyes at the lively time made by old Isaac, as he shuffled up the mountain.

But all tomfooleries of this kind, as Procopius re-

marked, should now come to an end at once and forever. There was not a moment that could be wasted
on them. While others had been listening to the winds
roaring outside the previous night, Procopius's ears had
been attracted by very different sounds inside, apparently coming up from the very depths of the volcano.
He could not describe them more fully to the Captain
and the Count than as rumbling, mysterious, discordant,
crackling noises of a very alarming, and even frightful
character. Not a moment was to be lost! Finish the
balloon as soon as possible!

By the evening of the next day it was completely
finished. Carefully sewed, seamed, and covered with
a double coat of varnish, its strength, solidity, and
lightness were unquestioned. The net-work was made
of the fine cordage furnished by the *Dobryna;* and
the car, formed of the strong flexible wicker-work
which had separated the partitions of the *Hansa*, was
fully large enough to ·accommodate twenty-three per-
sons with tolerable comfort. Very little comfort, however, was required, the voyage not being expected to
last longer than an hour or two at most, no more time
than that being required to allow the balloon to be
transferred from the Gallian to the Terrestrial atmosphere.

Early on the following morning, every detail re-

quired by the balloon to be in instant readiness having
been attended to, nothing more remained to do than
to learn from the Professor the exact instant when the
shock was to be expected. The Captain again undertook the ungracious task, but with the same success as
before. The Professor was too sulky, too stubborn, or
perhaps too miserable to utter a single word.

Procopius now began to look seriously uneasy. Last
night also, he assured his hearers, he had heard the
same noises as before, only louder and more alarming.
The volcanic matter in Gallia's interior was in violent
commotion and would soon find a vent somewhere!

That very evening, December 15, Gallia cut the
orbit of Mars, but at a point too distant from the
planet to be in the slightest danger either of collision
or attraction. She was rapidly approaching the Earth,
which was now the brightest star in the sky and a far
more beautiful heavenly object than Venus ever appears
to a Terrestrian.

The mysterious noises alluded to by Procopius had
been heard again plainly during the day by many
others. The Captain did not know what to make of
them, but, at the Count's suggestion and to calm Procopius, he took the precaution to order his people not
to enter the mountain interior at all that night, but
to take what rest they could near the entrance to the

cavern. They readily obeyed him, conscious that something portentous was about to happen. They took supper without a word, and lay down quietly to rest, but they could not sleep. Ben's sharp eye detected even Isaac crouching in a corner. A mysterious feeling of dread from some unknown cause had dragged the miser up from his den; at last he appeared to discover that his fellow-beings were good for something else than being preyed upon and cheated mercilessly on every possible occasion.

A little after sunset, the mysterious noises were plainly heard by all, and as the night advanced they became louder and more terrible. They appeared to come altogether from the interior of the mountain. Nobody could describe them exactly. One thought they sounded like heavy chains hanging side by side and struck by a drum revolving with great rapidity; another compared them to the roar of a distant train dashing with lightning speed over a long iron bridge; another was reminded by them of sharp peals of thunder rattling among mountain echoes; while to another they conjured up the crackling, hissing, and steaming noises made by a cataract of red-hot metal plunging into a subterranean lake. The "earth" shook beneath them, like a ship hurried over hidden rocks by eddying

35

rapids. The mountain itself began to heave and rock, as if lifted from its base by some abysmal convulsion.

The Gallians, too frightened to remain lying down, had by this time all got up, and now formed a confused group standing outside the mouth of the cavern, the Count holding Nina's right hand, the Captain her left. The noises grew at last so great that no other sound could be heard. The darkness too overhead was almost intense, a slight veil of mist somewhat obscuring the glimmering stars.

All at once the noises ceased, and a pale-white light faintly illuminated every object around. A cry from the observatory turned all eyes in that direction. A form was seen hastily scrambling down the rocks with a piece of a telescope in its hand. It was the Professor, running a race of life and death!

But nobody could attend to him.

"Look! Look!" cried the Captain pointing westwardly to a meteor rising slowly in the sky like a majestic rocket. This was the meteor that had shed the pale-white light on Terre Chaude.

"What can it be, Procopius?" asked the Captain.

Procopius shook his head negatively, not able at the moment to give a better reply.

All gazed intently at the meteor as it rose higher

and higher, soon diffusing a light almost as great as that of the full moon.

By this time the Professor had reached the crowd. They respectfully made way for him, and he soon stood before the Captain.

"What is it, my dear Master?" asked the Captain, pointing at the glaring meteor. "Is it a new moon?"

"No — yes!" answered the Professor, greatly excited and panting for breath. "It is a new moon, but not a captured moon! It is a part of Gallia herself! The same catastrophe has befallen her as befell Gambart's Comet! By a sudden expansion the tremendous forces acting within her interior have rent her asunder! An enormous fragment of her surface has been suddenly launched into space!"

"Then by the great Jupiter!" cried the Captain in tones thrilling with horror and surprise, "the Englishmen are no longer in Gallia! Gibraltar and Ceuta are part of yonder meteor!"

Higher and higher it rose towards the glimmering stars. Soon it was directly over head. Soon, in consequence of Gallia's rapid revolution, it was swiftly vanishing below her eastern horizon!

# CHAPTER XVIII.

## THE START.

THE Professor's assertion, startling as it would appear at first sight, was perfectly correct. Gallia had been cleft in twain. Instead of one Comet, two were now flying back to the Earth.

"How much of her mass has Gallia lost, Professor?" asked Procopius, his senses by degrees beginning to recover from the confusion into which the late startling phenomena had thrown them.

"We can tell that in a short time, Lieutenant," answered the Professor, extremely affable and polite as long as his fright lasted. "If the sun does not rise till six, we have lost little or nothing. If it rises at three we have lost half. It is now two o'clock; let us wait a little!"

At three o'clock almost to the minute, the sun showed himself on the western horizon.

"Gallia is diminished by half!" exclaimed the Professor. "Henceforward ou: days are to be only six hours long instead of twelve — that is, every three

412

hours of light will be followed by three hours of darkness.  Of course I shall need a few observations before I am certain of all this, but I have little doubt that in the main I am quite correct.  Our pole, as you see, still points to Vega ; our rotation, as you can notice by the sun and stars, is still from east to west ; we have no reason for supposing that our velocity has been either increased or diminished by the explosion ; therefore our orbit should be still unaltered, and I can notice no further physical change in our situation but the reduction of our days to half their former length, as already adverted to.  If, however, this velocity has been retarded or advanced in the slightest degree, Messieurs, you may bid eternal adieu to all hopes of ever reaching the Earth again.  But this is a problem that I propose to solve in a few days."

He was returning towards the observatory, now that all immediate danger was over, when the Captain, finding him in such a communicative mood, again tried to take advantage of the opportunity to gain further information.

"What do you think will be the fate of the portion that Gallia has lost, my dear Master?" asked he. "Will it become her satellite?"

"No!" answered the Professor decidedly.  "You can't see it just now, nor for some little time longer, lost

35 *

as it is in the sunlight. But you must have noticed from its diminishing size that it was going further and further away from us. As soon as darkness comes, you will see it again, and find it smaller than ever."

"Has it brought off air and water enough to make it inhabitable?" asked Procopius.

"Can it ever return to the Earth?" queried the Count.

"You ask too many questions, Messieurs," was the Professor's only reply, and he resumed his walk towards the observatory.

After breakfast, the Gallians sought in a few hours' sleep the rest so necessary after a night of such bodily and mental suffering. They soon accommodated themselves to the new arrangement of light and darkness, but some days had to elapse before they could get quite accustomed to the wonderful increase of their muscular strength occasioned by the renewed diminution of gravity. Everything being now fifteen times lighter than it had been on the Earth, Ben Zouf said one day to Isaac:

"Barabbas, be more cautious than ever in riling the Professor! You were never very weighty, but you would be no more in his hands now than an eight or nine pound baby!"

Meantime the Captain, the Count, and Procopius

spent every available moment together, discussing the increased or diminished chances of reaching the Earth, as affected by the late catastrophe. Had Gallia's velocity been changed? The Captain and the Count feared it had, and said so. How could it help being changed? Procopius maintained that it had not. What was to cause the change? Neither side being able to advance a valid reason in substantiation of its views, a long argument was impossible. Both parties agreed that the Professor alone could answer the all-important question, and both parties further agreed that an answer should be got at all hazards. Moments were now too precious to be sacrificed to mere whims and silly peculiarities any longer. If he would not give a satisfactory reply of his own accord, even violence was perfectly justifiable in extorting one. Speak he *should*, as to the precise hour and minute when the collision would take place.

Days, however, passed away without affording a favorable moment for putting these bold resolves into execution. It was easy to see that, in spite of the loss of his telescope, the Professor was as busy as ever in taking observations, casting calculations, and drawing deductions. The friends could also see that both his spirits which had been remarkably lively, and his temper which had been remarkably affable, on the night of the explosion, were now rapidly deteriorating. The expression of his face was growing not only more and more snappish, but more and more melancholy. Was that a good sign or a bad one?

Procopius pronounced it the very best of all good signs. His reasoning was exceedingly simple. "If the explosion had so affected Gallia's velocity," argued he, "that her return to the Earth was endangered, the Professor's exultation would be so great that he could not possibly restrain it. He was anything, however, just now but joyful — he was decidedly dejected. What conclusion did this point at? Simply that Gallia's dismemberment had produced no effect on her velocity, and that, consequently, she would return to the Earth at the precise moment previously calculated!"

Little could be urged against this argument, but its probable correctness was not, of course, sufficient. How to get at the certainty? How to fish the pearl from its depths? How to extort the secret from the inexorable sphinx? Again and again the Captain made the attempt, but without the least success. He and his companions were at their wits' end.

Ben Zouf, passing by one day after a new failure, noticed their puzzled countenances, and instantly divined the cause.

"Gentlemen," said he, "long ago I said you were wasting time in trying to get anything out of the little

Professor by peaceful means. Whatever you want from him, must be conquered by the point of the sword. I have been thinking over a little plan, of which, with your permission, I will now inform the Governor. If it does not succeed, we must try something else."

He revealed his little plan; all approved of it highly; and Ben and the Captain instantly undertook to put it into execution.

"There he is now!" cried Ben Zouf suddenly. "He's just entering the gallery. I'll tackle on to him at once, Governor. But you must be on hand in a few minutes."

The Professor was returning to Central Hall, to detect, if possible, some error in a calculation just made regarding some late discoveries. He was in a fearful humor. He had become more and more convinced that Gallia's velocity had not undergone the slightest modification. Consequently, her return to the Earth was certain. Consequently, another trip into the depths of planetary space was impossible. Malediction!

Suddenly he heard somebody calling him by name, and, turning round, found himself face to face with Ben Zouf. He was ready to burst with irritation.

"What do you want now?" he asked with flashing eyes. "Some news about your miserable Montmartre?"

2 B

"Montmartre, Monsieur the Professor!" answered Ben insolently. "Don't be alarmed about Montmartre! Montmartre is no rotten egg burst open by its foul gases, like your miserable Comet!"

Anger and amazement struck the Professor actually speechless. Ben continued:

"Such a Comet!" he exclaimed in tones of studied impertinence and effrontery. "Ha! ha! ha! You should be ashamed to ever mention it! A heap of sand! A good squash would keep together better! Call such a concern a Comet! I call it a bladder, and a very poor bladder too!"

"Sir!"· cried the Professor, red in the face and choking with rage, "your master shall hear of this!"

"A Comet! Well, I never! Why not call a bombshell with the fuse lighted a Comet? We shall soon hear of boys calling their soap-bubbles Comets! And why not? They burst to be sure. But does that make them worse than the Professor's jigamarree that *he* calls a Comet!"

"Your language, sir, and yourself are alike beneath my contempt," said the Professor, trying to speak calmly, "but your master will soon know what an insolent ruffian he has been feeding!"

"What's the matter, my dear Professor?" cried the Captain now presenting himself on the scene. "What has made you so far forget yourself as to yield to such an unbecoming fit of temper? It must be something very serious indeed that would justify *your* resorting to such undignified language."

"How, sir, undignified!" cried the Professor, angrier than ever, as he turned on his old pupil. "Who gave you the right to address such an epithet to me? No wonder that your servant here has such an impudent tongue!"

"Professor Rosette," said the Captain with a calmness and severity too marked to be in earnest, "I am exceedingly sorry to find my old teacher in such an unbecoming condition. At first, I thought it was nothing but a momentary outbreak of his notoriously bad temper. Now I regret to find myself compelled to attribute it to his putting too much wine in his water. I must really caution the Count against being so generous with his Burgundy."

"What do you mean, sir?" shrieked the little man, hardly believing his ears. "Me to take too much wine! You can't be sober yourself to give expression to so revolting a sentiment!"

"Professor," said the Captain, with cutting sarcasm, "I would respectfully remind you of the necessity of keeping your tongue under more careful control. You seem to forget that you are addressing the Governor-General of Gallia!"

"Governor-General stuff and nonsense!" cried the peppery Professor, assuming a bold and dignified attitude. "I forget nothing, sir! But *you* must not forget that I am the owner, the lord, and the proprietor of Gallia! And that you and all the others are mere intruders here, depending solely on my will and pleasure for being allowed to remain at all!"

"Such claims are simply ridiculous, Professor Rosette," said the Captain quite loftily. "I am the Governor, and the Governor I will remain. Terrestrial laws have no force here now. Having severed our connection with the Earth forever—"

"What!"

"And being destined never to return—"

"What ignoramus says we are destined never to return?" asked the Professor in tones of the profoundest contempt.

"We *can't* return to the Earth!" cried the Captain impatiently and dogmatically. "We have split in two! Our mass has diminished enormously! Consequently our velocity has undergone considerable change! Consequently—"

"Listen to the profound savant!" interrupted the Professor with a bitter sneer. "He knows all about it!"

"Of course I know all about it!" continued the

Captain. "And so does Procopius. And so does the Count. We all know that the velocity has been modified, and that consequently Gallia can never return to the Earth!"

"Then you and Procopius and the Count into the bargain are a lot of unmitigated blockheads!" replied the Professor. "You know as much about Celestial Mechanics as this jackanapes of Montmartre —"

"Take care, little Professor!"

"Why, Dutch Isaac could give you all lessons in Elementary Physics! —"

"This flippancy, Professor —"

"Hold your tongue, sir!" cried the Professor passionately. "Don't dare to interrupt me! You never learned anything in my class —"

"Probably my teacher's fault!"

"You were a disgrace to the whole school! —"

"Professor, have a care! Such language —"

"Hold your tongue again, Sir!" cried the Professor, now blazing with rage. "You *must* listen to me — Captain, or Governor or General or whatever the demon you want to call yourself — Ha! ha! ha! Pretty savants, the whole pack! Because Gallia's mass is diminished, the oracles conclude her velocity is also diminished! As if this velocity did not depend altogether on the primary velocity, combined with the

36

solar attraction! As if movements cannot be obtained without taking the masses also into account! Does any one know the mass of the comets? No! Are their movements known? Yes! Pah! Such luminaries! Such Solomons! They're beneath contempt!"

"We are Solomons enough to know that we can never return to the Earth again!" cried the Captain stoutly and apparently with more confidence than ever.

"Of course the sages, the master minds, the shining lights know everything!" cried the Professor, now so irritated as to be thrown altogether off his guard. "But with all their wisdom they don't know that Gallia will cut the Earth's ascending node on the night of December 31 — January 1, at exactly two hours, forty-seven minutes, and thirty-six-six-tenths seconds after mid —"

He stopped suddenly. To his profound surprise he saw the Captain whip a memorandum-book out of his pocket and scribble something in it, the frowning face breaking meanwhile all over into the cheeriest and sunniest smiles. Before he could recover from his amazement, he found himself all alone, his late companions having hastily withdrawn after a hurried but most respectful salute.

Imagine if you can the feelings of the poor astronomer thus so shamefully victimized and bamboozled!

It was with saddened steps and slow that he retired to his observatory, brooding bitterly and dolefully over the too often successful attempts of ignorance, folly, and conceit to outmanœuvre knowledge, wisdom, and modest worth !

The important moment now known, the chiefs of the colony took immediate care to make the most of their knowledge. There was no time to be lost ; in two short weeks everything was to be decided one way or the other. The Gallians generally were in the highest spirits. The balloon would glide from one atmosphere to the other without the slightest danger ! In imagination they were already safely landed, and quietly making their way homewards ! But Procopius was anything but sanguine. Quite the contrary. He fully understood all the dangers to be encountered by even a balloon in the dreadful rush of the two atmospheres.

" The wildest cyclone that ever ravaged Indian seas," said he, " would be the mildest zephyr in comparison. The crash must take place at the velocity of about sixty miles per second ! What is to prevent the balloon from being instantly burned up ? Nothing short of a miracle ! "

" Might not our atmosphere, compressed into a kind of solidity by the enormous velocity," said the Captain, " possibly succeed in cleaving a way for itself through the terrestrial atmosphere, and thus serve as a kind of buffer for our balloon? To make myself clear by comparison — an ordinary river enters the ocean so slowly that the fresh and salt waters are instantly commingled; but the Mississippi rushes with such velocity into the Gulf of Mexico that a vessel fully two hundred miles from its mouth still finds herself in fresh water. May we not hope that a current of this kind, generated by the impetuous speed of the Gallian atmosphere, will maintain us at some distance from the Earth long enough to give the two atmospheres an opportunity of uniting so gradually as to do us comparatively little damage?"

"We may hope anything," said Procopius shaking his head. "'Hope springs eternal in the human breast,' as some English poet says, but I say again, as I said before, that nothing short of a miracle can save us!"

"Our life for the last two years has been little less than miraculous," observed the Count; "why despair at the last moment?"

"Certainly, Procopius!" said the Captain pleasantly. "That's the way to put it. Remember the Professor's motto, *Nil desperandum!* — and the Count's too that he gave me on the miserable day that we climbed the crystal coast of Provence:

*Orbe fracto, spes illæsa!*" *

"As for my part, gentlemen," observed Ben Zouf by way of summing up, "I must say I always did hanker after a balloon ride."

The sea being now completely free from ice, the little steam-sloop was put into requisition, and, by carefully economising the small stock of coal still left, several trips were made to Gourbi Island. Everything there was found to present pretty much the same appearance as it had done twenty months before. Rivulets fled murmuring over the green meadows. Birds sang in the leafy woods. Innumerable plants and flowers, waving in the breeze, filled the atmosphere with fragrant odors. The sun's vertical rays for an hour or two shed intense light and heat. In a word, it was an arctic winter suddenly succeeded by an equatorial summer.

Straw and dry grass were of course in the greatest abundance — a most fortunate circumstance — otherwise how obtain a sufficiency of proper fuel for the balloon? The notion of transporting the enormous machine itself to Gourbi Island was debated for a short time. But it was too cumbersome to be put in the sloop. Sending to Terre Chaude the combustible necessary for the inflation of the *Montgolfier* was soon decided on as a mode of procedure more convenient in every respect.

---

* "TO THE SUN?" page 268.

36 *

Even the short nights being now pretty warm, the Gallians required little or no fuel except for cooking, and the wrecked vessels, furnishing a sufficient supply for this purpose, were freely drawn upon. But Isaac could not endure the idea of any one making free with the broken spars of the *Hansa,* and one morning Ben Zouf found him so actively engaged in a tussle with two Russians, who were carrying a load of wood to the kitchen, that he had great difficulty in pulling off the Jew. Neither the threat of charging him fifty thousand francs for a seat in the balloon, nor even the hint of surrendering him to the tender mercies of the Professor, seemed to have much effect. It was actually only by holding him down by main force that Ben enabled the Russians to carry Mochel fuel enough to prepare dinner for the community, Isaac himself included!

All the preparations were finished on the twenty-fourth of December. Christmas Day was celebrated with pretty much the same ceremonies and solemnities as those of the preceding year, but the depth of religious sentiment was evidently more intense. Everybody seemed to feel that this was to be the last Christmas they should ever have. The Professor took a prominent part in the exercises, and even Isaac was a faithful attendant, never uttering a word above his breath the whole time that could offend the most sensitive Christian ear.

Strange as it is to say and difficult as it is to believe, now that the all important, the most dangerous and the most intensely exciting moment was fast approaching, it must be acknowledged that the Captain now found his thoughts running on every subject but that of the terrible peril to be encountered within the next few days. The last two years, he felt, were gradually fading out of his mind like the dreams of a feverish night. Approaching the Earth, it was the Earth's associations that most strangely enkindled his imagination. A sweet gentle face, long since almost obliterated, began to take sharper outlines and put on more radiant colors. A happier, warmer throb was felt in the pulsations of his heart. Old ideas, all but smothered up and forgotten, began to peep out, like violets in early spring. A dreamy languor at times came over him during which Comet, volcano, Professor, and balloon were as completely absent from his mind as if they had never existed. Old rhymes and jingles and bits of verse began once more to tingle in his ears. Why not finish those "Stanzas"? The precise nature of either their words or ideas he could not now indeed remember, but he had an impression that for him, a Frenchman, both had been pretty creditable; the verses could not of course pretend to the dignity of grand poetry, but they had a good sounding ring in them, the rhyme was faultless,

and the metre perfect. Why not start them again? A
little labor would recall them perfectly. Why stop short
when so near success? etc. etc.

These were actually the silly thoughts that, in spite of
all he could do to the contrary, kept buzzing through the
Captain's brain for the last four or five days preceding
an encounter terrific enough to appal the stoutest heart.
How was it with the Count? Was he too a prey to old
memories revived by a near approach to the Earth? This
is a difficult question to answer. Cool, courteous, and
considerate as ever, neither eye, tongue, nor countenance
ever betrayed the slightest recollections of former
troubles or the slightest anticipation of fresh ones. He
naturally desired warmly to revisit the Earth once more
and so expressed himself, but he never showed any more
anxiety on the subject than was felt by Procopius. As
for his men, they seemed to have no mind of their own
at all in the matter; *ubi ille ibi patria*, *his* presence
made everywhere their country. Even the Spaniards
showed comparatively little excitement; of course, in
their heart of hearts they must have often longed after
the green valleys, the sunny mountains and the orange
groves of Andalusia, but they were by no means tired
of Gallia, where, well fed, well housed, and treated by
all with friendship and consideration, they considered
they were living like princes. Pablo and Nina talked

more and understood less of the approaching catastrophe than any one else. Not that they troubled themselves in the least as to its probable results. Earth or Gallia made very little difference to them, provided they were always in the company of those kind good friends who loved them so dearly.

The only really unhappy mortal in Terre Chaude was the Professor. Many things indeed had conspired to make him miserable. The loss of Nerina; the rupture of Gallia; the destruction of the telescope; the certainty of another encounter with the Earth; but, as Ben Zouf expressed it, the last trick played on him by the Captain had been the straw that broke the camel's back. The balloon he detested the sight of. Catch *him* in it! He would never leave his Comet! Night and day he still prosecuted his astronomical observations. Oh! how he regretted the loss of his telescope, approaching as they now were the narrow zone of the shooting meteors! What *could* be done to increase his power of vision? In his mania for making discoveries he nearly destroyed his sight for ever by dropping a few drops of belladonna into his eyes! A giant as astronomer, as oculist he was but an infant. Knowing that this drug is used for dilating the pupil, he had jumped to the hasty conclusion that it also increased the optical powers of the eye!

No wonder that Ben Zouf, seeing him groping along

one day guiding his steps like a blind man, cried out loud enough to be heard by every one around :

" Of all the ignoramuses on earth, a *savant* is the greatest ! " (*le plus bête !*)

As the remaining days, however, slowly wore away and the decisive moment drew near, a general feverishness of feeling began to spring up, from which even the Professor was not quite exempt. As his eyes grew better, he was often noticed to quit the observatory now and then, and come down to the shore to examine the state of the balloon and the arrangements made for keeping it always in a state of easily perfected readiness.

Two masts, standing upright, with their bases embedded firmly in the strand, about forty feet apart, supported the monster between them, ready to be inflated with hot air and properly covered with its netting. The car was there too, securely attached, and roomy enough for all the passengers ; to its side some india-rubber bags, filled with air, were attached, to keep it afloat for awhile in case it fell into a part of the ocean not far from shore. There was no provision made, however, for the event of the balloon falling into a part of the ocean a considerable distance from the land. In fact, none could be made. In such a case, nothing could save the crew from being drowned, except the lucky accident of some ship passing by just in the nick of time to save them.

So the remaining days rolled slowly away, and at last December 31 dawned on all that was left of Gallia. In less than twenty-four hours more, the balloon, up-borne by its heated air and freighted with its cargo of human life, would be attempting its doubtful voyage in the Gallian atmosphere. In less than twenty-four hours the fate of that cargo was to be decided forever.

Gallia was now only about forty million leagues distant from the sun.. The Earth was near enough to look twice as large and brilliant as the full moon, and all. the preceding night she had been growing larger and more brilliant. In the morning she was no more than four or five millions of miles off. During the three hours of day, from 6 to 9 o'clock, in spite of the bright sunlight, she could be easily seen like a sharp-edged white cloud in the blue sky. During the three hours' night, from 9 to 12, she shone almost like the sun himself. From 12 to 3 she looked once more like a bright cloud, only larger than before. From 3 to 6, she took up as much room on the sky as the moon increased to five times its size.

At six o'clock precisely, all hands took their last supper on Gallia. At seven they were recommended to get what rest they could till twelve, when all were to be in perfect readiness for the final start.

At twelve o'clock midnight (terrestrial calendar) day began to break on Gallia. All were ready. The last preparations were made with the utmost tranquillity. At one o'clock, the straw in the brazier at the mouth of the balloon was enkindled; by way of precaution against accident, the canvas and cordage had been saturated in a chemical preparation that made them completely fire-proof. At two o'clock, the enormous bag, fully inflated, was tugging away with great force at the cords that still held it attached to the surface. The car was securely steadied by means of additional ropes, and its horizontal position carefully assured.

The Earth, not now quite 200 thousand miles away, was approaching the Comet at the rate of nearly 70 thousand miles an hour, while Gallia approached the Earth at more than double that fearful rate; the com bined ratio thus gave a mutual velocity of about 210 thousand miles an hour. In less than sixty minutes, therefore, the long expected contact should take place. All were in readiness.

Isaac was the first to secure a seat in the car.

He was dressed strictly as usual, but the Captain's sharp eye noticed an unusual prominence around the waist, front and back. He touched it, and found it quite hard.

"What's this, Isaac?" he asked.

"Governor," said Isaac, with the old whine, "it's only a little belt, containing my little fortune, my little all!"

"Your little fortune! What is the weight of your little fortune?"

"Only fifty or sixty pounds weight, Governor."

"What? Fifty or sixty pounds of dead weight when our balloon is hardly strong enough to lift its passengers! Off with it, Isaac, immediately!"

"Oh, Signor Governor! S' help me Father Abra—"

"Off with it! We can't encumber the car!"

"What, Signor Governor!" shrieked Isaac, falling on his knees, "all my little fortune! So hardly earned! Penny by penny!"

"Off with the belt, Isaac! No more delay! If it contained sixty pounds of diamonds, it should be left behind all the same! We *must* not have any dead weight!"

"Mercy, Signor Governor! Mercy, Father Abraham!" screamed Isaac, seizing the Captain's knees and looking into his face with an expression of intense agony.

"Hello, Bendigo!" cried Ben Zouf, now judging it high time to interfere, and seizing Isaac by the collar. "The Governor has no time to listen to this nonsense!

37                          2 C

Off with that belt, or clear out yourself! I give you five seconds to decide! No noise about it either!"

Slowly and with an expression of suppressed pain, as if he was parting with the last drops of his heart's blood, Isaac unbuckled the enormous belt, and, with an expiring effort, threw it over the side of the car. Then falling in a heap on the seat, he covered his face with his hands, and gave no further signs of life than an occasional groan dismal and heart-rending in the extreme — to any one that did not thoroughly understand Dutch Isaac!

A shrewd interpreter would have probably detected in this groan its true expression — not of grief or anything like it — but one of proud joy and triumphant success. Isaac had finely hoodwinked the Gentiles! The stuffed belt contained nothing but closely packed rags and copper money. The gold and the notes were still safe and sound to the value of probably more than four or five hundred thousand francs, sewed up carefully in his under-clothes. Except the occasional low groan, however, no sound, and, except an occasional nervous flutter, no movement, for the next quarter of an hour betrayed the form lying there to be anything better than a corpse.

It was far otherwise with the Professor. *He* made noise enough. Quit his Comet! Never! His Comet

TWO RUSSIAN SAILORS LAID HOLD OF HIM.

was his castle; by what right could any one dare to make him leave it? And what for? To take a seat in a machine that was really the most absurd of all the absurdities that ever emanated from the brain of a lunatic! In the passage from one atmosphere to the other it would go off like gun-cotton! The chances for life in remaining on the Comet would not be a millionth part so risky! And supposing the possibility of Gallia doing again as she had done before, namely, merely grazing the Earth — would he be worse off then than now? Not at all! Quite the contrary! He would once more enjoy the unspeakable opportunity of plunging into the boundless realms of space, combined with the great probability of never again coming back!

In the middle of such outcries, however, he was suddenly interrupted by two robust Russian sailors who, at the Captain's bidding, laid their heavy hands on him, and, in spite of the most rigorous resistance, made him take a seat in the car, where they kept careful guard over him till the last word was given.

To the deepest regret of all, but of Ben Zouf and Nina in particular, Zephyr, Galette, and poor Marzy had to be left behind. Not to speak of their weight, there was really no room for them in the car.

Nina and Pablo then took their places, Nina weeping, but fondling her pigeon more lovingly than ever. No one, of course, had ever thought of separating such friends — besides, who could tell? — the little creature might yet be of some use as a messenger bird between the balloonists and a portion of the Earth's surface.

The Spaniards then entered the car; then the Russians; then Procopius and the Count. The Captain and Ben Zouf alone now trod the Gallian soil.

"Come, Ben Zouf," said Servadac; "in you go!"

"After you is manners, Governor," said Ben, hesitating.

"No. As a captain is the last to leave his sinking ship, I must be the last to leave the Comet."

"Yes, Governor, but —"

"Come, Ben Zouf, jump in!"

"Enough said!" exclaimed Ben, taking his seat in the car, and busying himself in adjusting the ropes.

The Captain did not enter until he had assured himself that everything was in perfect preparation for the start.

At Procopius's signal each man knew exactly what to do — and did it.

The cords were cut simultaneously, and the balloon, inflated with hot air, rose calmly and majestically into the atmosphere to an elevation of six or seven thousand feet.

# CHAPTER XIX.

## GOOD-BY, GALLIA!

THIS was about the proper altitude in Procopius's opinion, for the balloon to maintain. The brazier, suspended in iron network, filled with straw and hay hastily dipped in oil, and near enough to be under proper control, kept the air in the vast bag warm enough to float the whole machine at that elevation.

The passengers, at first dazzled a little by the strangeness of their situation, soon recovered themselves sufficiently to be able to look around them with admiring interest.

Directly beneath them lay the Gallian Sea, resembling an enormous basin, low in the centre and high on the edges. A little speck to the north showed Gourbi Island, but, it is needless to say, no speck in the west showed Gibraltar or Ceuta. A little to the south rose the volcano, the highest point in Terre Chaude, which now revealed itself as a peninsula projecting northwards from the crystal coast enveloping the Gallian Sea. Everywhere on its surface glittered the strange substance

37 *                                              3

of metallic lustre, tellurium of gold, now more brilliant and iridescent than ever, as it sparkled like a great valley of diamonds in the full blaze of the morning sun.

All around the car, from the zenith to the circular horizon which, by a well known optical délusion, seemed to rise higher and higher as the balloon ascended, the darkish sky showed itself of an indescribable purity and serenity. Five or six degrees above the north-western horizon, however, the Gallians could still detect the floating body that they had already often noticed and which they well knew to be no planet, asteroid or satellite, but the portion of Gallia that had been detached by internal explosions. It was already dim by its distance, and gradually grew dimmer and dimmer till finally it disappeared altogether. For the last two or three days it had been invisible in the sunlight, but as soon as darkness overspread the sky it had shown itself among the stars like a fine point of blazing light.

But the all-absorbing centre of attraction was the dazzling orb of the Earth herself, floating over the balloon midway between the zenith and the horizon. The tremendous velocity at which she approached was easily shown by her rapidly increasing size. She was already too near to allow her poles to be plainly discerned, but all over her surface different spots soon began to reveal themselves with great distinctness.

The brightest reflections gradually took the well known shape of the land divisions, the oceans owing their darker colors to the greater absorption of the solar rays. Here and there, over these darker expanses of ocean, stretched long bands of very irregular and intermittent outline, sometimes white in color, sometimes gray; sometimes black as jet, sometimes reflecting every tint of sunlight like a kaleidoscope; sometimes completely hiding the terrestrial surface, sometimes shrinking and vanishing away, like our breath from a looking-glass, and leaving in full view the beautiful Earth brighter and more captivating than ever. These were of course the clouds, floating at different elevations of the atmosphere, and fortunately very thin and transparent at this particular moment, owing perhaps to the fact that our travellers were approaching the Earth's northern hemisphere in midwinter.

Rapidly, even while they were still gazing on the transcendent spectacle, the shadowy outlines began to assume distinct form and sharpness. The shapes gradually grew recognizable and consistent, the elevations became more and more defined. Mountain and plain by degrees disentangled themselves. Till the great map, flat no longer, looked like a highly finished model in perfect relief.

Suddenly, at 2.27 after midnight, when the Earth,

now fully as large as fifty moons, could not be more than seventy or eighty thousand miles distant, an abrupt sinking of the balloon together with the instantaneous sensation of a violent concussion, powerfully attracted the immediate attention of the travellers towards Gallia. Instantly looking down, they saw to their surprise and dismay that she was considerably smaller! Another explosion had rent her again in twain, projecting an immense portion of the southern continent into space!

"Gallia is breaking up!" cried the Captain.

"The less of her reaches the Earth, the less danger from the collision!" exclaimed the Count.

"I hope she will hold out long enough to take us there!" said Procopius despondingly.

"No danger of her failing," said the Professor, as if speaking to himself. "She will be there in time. I am never wrong in my calculations!"

In fact, the Earth was now approaching with indescribable velocity. At 2.37 she was only forty thousand miles away; and the great continental outlines were easily distinguished.

"Europe!" cried Procopius.

"Russia!" cried the Count.

"France!" cried the Captain.

"Hurrah for them all!" cried Ben Zouf.

THEY GAZED AT THE DIFFERENT COUNTRIES.

A wild cheer of frenzied excitement followed his words. The sensation of the travellers had now reached the highest pitch of exaltation. They felt like exiles catching sight of the loved land from which they had been separated for years. Danger? Danger was the last thing thought of! There was the home from which they had believed themselves to be cut off forever! There was the resting-place in which they firmly believed they should soon find happy repose!

It was with feelings of indescribable emotion that they now gazed on Europe stretched out there beneath them, radiant in the sunlight, as Ben Zouf said, like a great stereopticon picture shining through an immense screen!

As they gazed at the different countries, they found their imaginations just as busily engaged as their eyes. Like children looking at clouds, their fancies easily supplied whatever was wanting in coloring or outline.

There was Ireland, for instance, a broken-hearted female figure, wrapped up in disconsolate mourning-robes, her back to England, her face to the western ocean, over which she seemed to constantly peer with anxious and perhaps even hopeful gaze.

There was England, a portly dame, sweeping away in stately march towards the east, Cornwall and Wales her amply flowing skirts, and the Scottish islands the flashing diamonds of her head-dress.

There was Scandinavia, still recalling the lion of former ages that shook his mane of piny mountains and sprang with mighty roar from his ice-bound dens of the north at the throat of affrighted Europe.

There was Russia, an enormous polar bear, head on Asia, one paw grasping the Caucasus, the other grimly seizing Turkey with the grip that never lets go.

There was Austria, a large, soft-skinned and beautiful cat, curled up on herself in apparent repose, pretending to be asleep but letting nothing escape the range of those watchful half-closed eyes.

There was The Peninsula, projecting from Europe like a mighty standard, Portugal forming the field, and Spain the great waving banner.

There was Turkey, an exhausted game-cock in his last gasp, but still nervously clutching the Balkan Peninsula in one claw and Asia Minor in the other.

There was Italy, a neat leg in a tasteful boot, driving Sicily, Sardinia, and Corsica before it, like so many footballs.

There was Prussia, a formidable hatchet, deeply sunk already in the heart of Germany, its threatening edge in too close proximity to the frontiers of France.

Finally there was France herself, somewhat deformed from of old, her figure rather incomplete, but still a vigorous *torso*, Paris her thinking head and her fiery heart.

Whimsical fancies of this kind chased each other rapidly through the travellers' active brains as the fleeting moments hurried past. In the intense excitement idea followed idea with the velocity of lightning, though too hurriedly to be logical.

" Where 's Montmartre, Captain ? " asked Ben, hardly conscious of what he was saying.

For a reply the Captain silently pointed at the Professor. He was actually the personification of despair. Hanging over the side of the car, he never once thought of looking towards the Earth. All his glances and all his thoughts were for his abandoned Gallia. His face had always borne an indefinable expression of suffering, but it now looked profoundly melancholy. No wonder. Another explosion, the third, had again rent Gallia asunder. Being only about a mile and a half below them, she could still be easily seen. The third explosion had blown off the north-eastern continent, so that the Comet now consisted of little more than Gourbi Island and the surrounding sea.

"And who knows if even that will be able to resist the disorganizing forces that are fast annihilating her ? " asks the Professor of himself with a moan as melancholy as a sigh of the wind over some lonely cairn at midnight.

Procopius, chronometer in one hand, watches the

minutes and seconds; barometer in the other, he sees that the brazier is constantly replenished with a sufficiency of fuel.

Not a sound can now be heard in the balloon, except the crackling of the blazing straw.

The Captain and the Count keep their eyes immovably fixed on the Earth. Gallia — what is left of her — they notice to be a little ahead of the balloon. So far so good. The first brunt of the shock is to be borne by the Comet.

Larger and vaster now grows the Earth. She eclipses half of the heavens. But what is the matter with Gallia? Have the successive explosions somewhat deflected her course? She is now over Egypt, but, instead of approaching the Earth directly, she appears inclined to shy off a little to the right! Will she miss her landing after all?

Another tremendous explosion is shown by the convulsion of the balloon, which is evidently sinking.

"More fuel!" cries Procopius to his men. "Pile it on, and keep it well stirred!"

The fact no longer admits of doubt. One fragment of Gallia has already passed to the north-west, and another to the north-east of the Earth. The remaining portion is still in sight, but seems disposed to follow an oblique rather than a direct course. That first explosion, by blowing off her western portion containing Gibraltar and Ceuta, has certainly by reaction given her a slight inclination to the east !

The balloon ? The balloon can hardly miss the encounter ! Where will it fall ? In north-east Africa, probably in the desert south of Barca, where death by starvation is sure to await the travellers, unless they are already burned to a cinder. Or perhaps in the Gulf of Sidra, where they cannot possibly escape being drowned. Unspeakable danger yawning in every direction ! No hope ! No hope !

" Never despair, friends ! " cries the Count, solemnly taking off his hat. " We are still in our great Creator's hands ! "

His brave words restore the sinking spirits. His companions silently bow their heads and reverently submit themselves to God's will with sublime resignation.

" Forty minutes after two ! " cries Procopius.

In less than six minutes the fearful crash must take place !

It is now clear that the fragments of Gallia are following such an oblique course that some of them may escape the shock altogether. But Gallia proper, that is, Gourbi Island in the middle of a sea about two hundred miles in diameter, is plunging directly for the Earth's surface.

38

The last minutes are now come. In a few moments the earthly doom of the adventurers is to be decided forever. The balloon will probably be burned or torn in pieces; her passengers can hardly escape being reduced to ashes, crushed, or drowned; not a single human being may be left alive to tell the tale of the wondrous journey into planetary space. Is there no means of conveying to humanity some inkling of this marvellous voyage? Is every trace of it to be annihilated forever?

No! The Captain has already asked himself this question, and is now ready to answer it He takes out of his memorandum-book a leaf on which he has already written the names of the Comet, of the portions of the Earth it had whisked off, of himself and his companions, together with the date of the two encounters. This he now hurriedly signs with his name, and then he asks Nina for the little dove, which she is holding carefully cherished in her breast.

The child's eyes fill with tears, but, without a moment's hesitation, she tenderly kisses her dear pet and hands it over to the Captain.

Servadac, hastily fastening the paper around the bird's neck, drops the messenger out of the balloon. The dove at first tumbles over and over, falling rapidly; but, righting herself in a few seconds, she pauses a moment as if to take her bearings, and then heads directly for the Earth, holding herself midway between the balloon and Gourbi Island.

In two minutes more, seventy thousand miles are traversed. The heavenly bodies are rushing together at the rate of about sixty miles a second!

Are the passengers conscious of this frightful speed? Not in the least! The balloon feels as motionless as a mountain peak. It is the rapidly increasing size of objects on the Earth's surface that alone tells them they are in motion.

"Forty-six minutes after two!" whispers Procopius in a low trembling voice.

The Earth, now only four thousand miles distant, seems to yawn below them like a vast crater. Higher and higher rises the horizon, shutting out more of the sky.

"Forty-seven minutes!" murmurs Procopius, with bated breath.

An interval of thirty-five seconds yet! Ages of un-speakable anxiety! — It is come! The car jars as if dashed furiously against a wall of adamant! The shriek of a million whistles rends the ear! The rumble of a million volcanoes stuns the brain! The roar of a million cannons crushes the heart! Fainting, trem-bling, horror-struck, hardly conscious, the travellers ner-vously clutch at the sides of the car, in their last ex-piring effort towards self-preservation!

The Gallian Sea beneath them begins to smoke. Dense clouds arise, and cut off all further vision. The air all around becomes vaporous, hot, dark, steaming, stifling. The whistling, the roaring, the rumbling, still continue with all their maddening din. The balloon rushes with inconceivable swiftness through a sea of clouds, vapor, smoke, and suffocating steam. Exhausted nature gives way to the frightful strain. Consciousness fails, and the travellers feel no more!

# CHAPTER XX.

### HOME AGAIN.

THE Captain was the first to show some signs of life. He sat up, rubbed his eyes, pressed his throbbing temples, and tried to look around.

"Ben Zouf!" he cried in a half-stifled voice.

"Present!" cried Ben, poking his head from a pile of the torn shreds of the balloon.

"Where are we?" asked the Captain.

"Seems to me, Captain, we are near our old Gourbi," answered Ben, freeing himself from the straws, bits of canvas and other stuff that filled his mouth and blinded his eyes.

Both jumped up, and in a second or two were once more fully themselves. Strange was the scene all around them. The sky was still darkish, but the stars were paling in the east where a pink light proclaimed the approaching sunrise. Every one of their companions lay in the balloon-car, fainting or more probably fast asleep. Not one was missing. Not one seemed injured in the slightest degree. The Captain carefully listened to their breathing. It was perfectly calm and regular. Even little Nina appeared to be sleeping as placidly as an infant in its cradle.

"Let them rest a little longer, Ben Zouf," whispered the Captain, his eyes filling with tears as he took off his cap and bowed his head in silent gratitude for their miraculous deliverance.

Ben did the same; then, taking his master's hand, he kissed it fervently, exclaiming as tears of joy streamed down his cheeks:

"Ah, Captain, we shall see old Montmartre again!" He ran hastily into the old guard-house, but soon came out again, shaking his head doubtfully.

"Captain," said he, "for a moment I thought it was all a dream. But Zephyr and Galette are not there! It is too much of a reality!"

The sun was now rising in the eastern sky; though the first of January, the air was as pleasant and the temperature as warm as on a lovely May morning in more northern latitudes.

"Let us wake up our friends at once," said the Captain somewhat dreamily, as if even himself had not yet quite recovered his consciousness.

Isaac awoke without any difficulty. The Professor was so weak that he was not able to rise for fully ten minutes after opening his eyes. The Count and

Procopius also took some time to come to themselves. Nina and Pablo were soon able to run around, as bright and lively as ever. The Russians and Spaniards came to their senses by degrees and at different intervals, nearly all complaining of severe headache. In less than half an hour, however, all were so far recovered that they hailed the sudden appearance of the sun shining out between two streaks of clouds in the eastern sky with a loud and hearty cheer. In less than an hour they felt themselves hungrier than they had ever been before in all their lives.

But what was to be done? There was not a particle of food in the guard-house. Fish, of course, abounded in the streams, but catching them would be a slow and difficult task. Birds were flying all around, but how were they to be shot without a gun? Or where was the powder? Our travellers, though now on the Earth, were, in fact, for the moment, far more miserable than they had ever been in Gallia.

In the first place, neither the Captain nor anybody else could tell where they were. The land around was, of course, Gourbi Island, but where had Gourbi Island fallen? This nobody could tell, and it was evidently the first point to be ascertained.

That they were once more on the Earth was undoubted. There was the sun rising in the east, as of old. There was the horizon of the northern sea dim and distant, as of old. And, best proof of all, there was Negrete trying to dance as he had danced on the Comet, but, in spite of all his exertions, never rising more than two or three feet from the ground, as of old.

An exploration should be attempted at once. For this the Count and Procopius acknowledged the Captain and Ben Zouf to be by far the best qualified. They should start in a southerly direction, following it as long as the prospect was favorable. As soon as they reached a village or town, they should buy provisions, hire vehicles, and return to their companions with the least possible delay.

But here sprang up another difficulty. Buy provisions, hire vehicles — where was the money? Neither the Captain, the Count, nor Procopius had a penny left. The Spaniards had parted with their English gold long ago for Isaac's cigars and other delicacies. The Russians and the Professor were equally bare.

"And there is no use in asking Isaac to loan us a few hundred francs," said the Captain gloomily. "I am very sorry now that we did not let him keep at least a pound or two of gold about him."

"But a pound or two would not satisfy Abednego, Captain," said Ben. "That belt weighed one hundred and fifty pounds, if it weighed a grain!"

What was to be done? The situation was increasing in distress.

"Captain Servadac!" said Isaac, suddenly rising from the crouched attitude which he had steadfastly kept for the last quarter of an hour.

All instantly riveted their eyes on the Jew with fear and trembling. This their moment of anxious misery was to be rendered still more miserable by Isaac's taunts, sneers, and bitter denunciations. But to the general surprise his countenance was not now gloomy nor his voice harsh.

"Captain Servadac," said the Jew, standing erect, with no whine in his accents or grimace of any kind on his face, "in losing that belt, I did not lose all my money. I have some still left. Here is a purse containing one thousand francs in gold. You are welcome to it. Use it as you please for the common benefit. I present it to the community. It is the least return I can make for what you have all done for me."

For a second or two profound astonishment kept the audience mute; then three rousing hurrahs greeted Isaac's speech. He handed the purse to Ben Zouf. But he was very careful not to move from his place. He was afraid of attracting notice by the staggering gait which a man carrying 135 pounds of gold and

silver sewed up in his clothes cannot well avoid showing.

It was near nine o'clock that morning when the
explorers were climbing the western spur of the Dahra
mountains.  The Captain knew the place well; it was
from this spot that he had discovered the volcano on
a memorable occasion.  He was now the first to reach
the summit, and Ben saw him instantly wave his hat
with a cry of joy.

"All right, Ben Zouf!" he exclaimed.  "No difficulty now in seeing where we are!  Hurry up and
tell me if I may believe my eyes! — Tell me what
you see in the south-west!"

"I see the Lion's Mountain," said Ben, shading his
eyes as he peered over a broad expanse of heaving
waves; "it lies halfway between Oran and Arzew!"

"And directly south?"

"I see the white houses and minarets of Mostaganem
coming out of the mist!"

"What do you see nearer?"

"I see the lovely plain of the Sheliff covered with
palm-trees, fig-trees, orange-trees, crops of various kinds,
herds, flocks, and tents!"

And so indeed it was.  They were now once again in
exactly the same spot of the globe where they had

stood two years before. An astonishing piece of good luck — if anything could be called astonishing after their late experience — had restored the abducted island to its own old locality!

On their way towards the Sheliff, however, they suddenly came to a very steep precipice, running east and west, which they had never noticed before. They met with considerable trouble in descending it, succeeding only by means of broken branches, roots, rocks, and other projections that afforded momentary foothold in the difficult path. They stopped at its base awhile to look back at the slope which had given them such unexpected trouble.

"Ben Zouf," said the Captain, "I am much mistaken if that cliff does not show the line where Gourbi Island has met old Earth. We are now in Algeria."

"Let us push on to the Sheliff, Captain," was Ben's only comment.

A mile or two brought them to a point which commanded a view of the river's mouth. The Sheliff looked exactly as it had looked two years ago when they rattled over its bridge on the road to Mostaganem. On the other side, a little to the left of where they stood, they saw a village which they had no difficulty in recognizing as Ain Bou Dinar.

Mostaganem being still at least eight miles distant, the

Captain at once decided on obtaining here what relief he could for his friends. They were soon entering the village, a ferry-boat, rowed by two lusty natives, requiring no more than five minutes to cross the muddy stream. During the passage they did not exchange a word with the boatmen, the Kabyles not having yet learned French and the Frenchmen having forgotten all their Arabian.

To the Captain's great surprise, however, and Ben Zouf's undisguised disappointment, their sudden appearance in the village did not excite the slightest commotion. They found French storekeepers, who could supply them with everything necessary for their companions. They found French livery-stables keepers, who furnished them with excellent horses and carriages. But beyond a few hesitating words regarding the fare and a covert glance thrown now and then on their clothes, which had by this time come to look amazingly shabby, neither the Captain nor Ben could detect the slightest sign of curiosity or surprise produced by their appearance. Of a comet, or a meteor, or of a disturbance of any kind not the least mention caught their ears in this sleepy little town. Even in the *Mostaganem Journal* of that day, just arrived, not a word was said of any unusual appearances in the sky or of any startling phenomena on the land.

The coach-drivers, it is true, were exceedingly surprised at the sight of the precipitous cliff, which, at about a mile from the Sheliff, suddenly blocked all further northern progress; but, being Alsatian emigrants not long in the country, they never dreamed that the great wall suddenly rising before them was of recent formation, and their only trouble now seemed to be as to how they should continue their northern course.

By the Captain's advice, the ten horses were immediately unhitched and led up the cliff where the incline was easier, the carriages being left in charge of two drivers to await the party's return. Once on the summit, the Captain, Ben Zouf, and the drivers, loaded with provisions and mounting on horseback, had very little further trouble in reaching the Gourbi, where, it is needless to say, they were welcomed with the most enthusiastic cheers.

That evening the whole party arrived safe and sound at Mostaganem, and put up at the *Hotel de l' Univers.* Here a good dinner, a sleep twelve hours long, and a warm bath proved to be such excellent restoratives that the very next day the travellers felt as strong and hearty as they had ever done in all their lives, and were all in the best possible spirits.

All, that is, but the Professor. Not that he was ailing in any respect. His appetite was excellent and his color good. But he was a disappointed man. Not a word

39

was spoken anywhere about his Comet.  In the reading-room of the hotel were to be found newspapers from most parts of Europe and from several parts of Africa and America.  These he had pounced upon with the expectation of finding something to examine, to approve or, still better, to contradict.  But he could hardly believe his eyes.  To his intense disgust, neither in the Turkish, the Greek, the Italian, the Spanish, the French, the German, the Russian, the English or the American papers could a single paragraph regarding *the* COMET — his COMET — be found !   Here and there indeed some slight notice was made of a singular meteor or two which had lately attracted some attention, but so little in general was said on the subject that even total silence would be preferable.  He was in fact so painfully disappointed that under the pretence of having letters to write he retired almost immediately to his room to chew the cud of mortification in strict solitude.  But the Captain, the Count, Procopius, and Ben, though quite as much surprised as the Professor, showed far greater fortitude in bearing the disappointment.

"Ben Zouf," said the Captain after breakfast, "do the honors of the place to the Spaniards who were never here before and to the sailors who are comparative strangers.  Show them around the town a little while the Count, the Lieutenant, and myself call on some friends."

In the Café Zulma he found the Commandant of the Second Rifles and the Captain of the Eighth Artillery playing piquet, smoking cigars, and sipping Moorish coffee.

"Hey!" cried the Commandant and the Captain, jumping up at the sight of their friend. "Is that you, Servadac?"

"Myself in person," said the Captain, warmly grasping their hands. "Let me present my friends Count Timascheff and Lieutenant Procopius."

Conversation soon became exceedingly lively, though on our friends' part it was principally confined to interrogations which, though rather strange, the French officers answered with great readiness, their native politeness preventing all appearance of surprise at the singular oddity of some of the questions.

Servadac and his friends, finding that nothing whatever was known or even surmised about the Comet, soon experienced an invincible repugnance towards making it the subject of conversation. They felt, in fact, somewhat like people who, having suffered a little from temporary alienation of mind, are asked to tell some of their experiences in the lunatic asylum. Quietly conscious that, no matter what they said on the subject, they should not be believed, they wisely concluded it to be much better to say nothing at all.

The French officers naturally began to surmise that their friends had just returned from some secret expedition in the heart of the Sahara, in the pampas of South America, or, likely as not, among the Uzbecks of Turkestan.

Once during the evening the Captain could not help asking :

" By the bye, Paullin, were you not a little surprised at not finding me next morning on the ground, as had been agreed upon ? "

" Not at all, Servadac," was the reply.  " If you remember, that was the very morning after the great earthquake that almost frightened our lives out.  Though no great harm was done in our immediate neighborhood, we knew that we were in a country peculiarly liable to earthquakes.  We had often read that fourteen or fifteen hundred years ago, in the Emperor Gallian's time, the northern shores of Africa were terribly desolated by tremendous earthquakes.  Whole cities disappeared, and salt springs inundated many of the interior plains.  In all probability at that time both the Roman port of Mostaganem and a great part of the shore were swallowed up by the waves.  Knowing this, we were not much surprised to hear next day that a vast tract of land about a mile north of the Sheliff, had been submerged.  But this was all we heard.  No loss of life was mentioned. We were at first somewhat concerned on your account, but we were confident that you were well able to take good care of yourself; and we are now exceedingly happy to find that we had not miscalculated. In fact, some of us heard you had been so suddenly ordered off to give assistance in some of the submerged districts that you had no time to write."

"Well, yes, rather suddenly," said the Captain, exchanging an amused glance with his friends.

"Did you hear no noise, like that of an earthquake, the night before last?" asked Procopius.

"We hear such things so often here, Lieutenant," answered the Commandant with a smile, "that we soon forget to keep count of them. However, I will ask the landlord! Hello! Pétry, come this way," he added, beckoning to the landlord, who was standing at the door talking to some acquaintances.

Pétry came over, hat in hand, smiling and bowing.

"Anything unusual seen or heard up the country the night before last?" asked Paullin.

"Very little, Commandant, except what Picolet who has just come in from Ain-Tedles tells me. He says that, in spite of the mists and fog which have covered us up regularly every night for the last two or three weeks, he could notice a very strange bright light in the upper regions of the heavens all that evening and

39 *

night, up to later than two o'clock. Then all at once
the light was extinguished and a very decided shock of
earthquake was felt which threw down several houses,
but did little further damage."

"Is the boat from Algiers in yet?" asked the Captain.

"Ah, Monsieur," answered Pétry, "the railroad in-
terferes so much with communication by sea that we
have only one boat at present running between Mostaganem and Algiers. It left us the day before yesterday, and will not be due until the day after to-morrow.
But perhaps you would like to cast your eye over the
*Moniteur de l' Algérie* just brought in."

The Captain took the paper, glanced listlessly over
it, and was carelessly throwing it aside when something
caught his eye that made him instantly start and change
color.

"What is it, Captain?" asked the Count.

By way of reply the Captain presented him the paper,
saying :

"Read the leading paragraph of the second column,
Count.   Read it aloud."

The Count read out the following notice :

"Among the other distinguished personages leaving Algiers to-
day for New York, *via* Marseilles, we regret to record our friends
the Honorable Schumacher and his beautiful spouse, both so highly
esteemed and sought after (*recherchés*) in Algiers, where they have
been spending the last two months.   The Honorable Schumacher,

a German by birth, but a respectable citizen of the great Republic by adoption, is compelled by the imperious commands of business to return to Cincinnati, where he is the proprietor of a vast hog-slaughtering establishment. This will be sad news to the rank and fashion of Oran, where the beautiful and accomplished Madam Schumacher, well known before her late marriage. as the Honorable Mistress Chetwode, leaves scores of inconsolable friends."

The Count laid down the paper with the words :

"A hog butcher ! "

"A German parvenu ! " hissed the Captain between his teeth.

"A woman like that to kill an honorable man for ! "

"A woman like that to compose English poetry for ! "

This was the whole extent of the remarks. The French officers did not utter a word. The rivals clasped each other's hands warmly, and dropped the subject forever.

After a very pleasant afternoon and evening passed in the company of their friends and a few other military gentlemen, the Captain, the Count, and Procopius returned to their hotel, not knowing what to think of the whole matter, but fully resolved to say as little as possible regarding their astounding adventures, unless some extremely suitable occasion should occur.

In a few days the Gallian colony separated forever. The Spaniards were each presented with five hundred francs in gold by the generous Count, who also paid their passage in a steamer that soon landed them safely in Malaga.

Isaac liked Mostaganem so well that he concluded to pass the rest of his days there. To-day the leading merchant in the Jewish quarter, he has distinguished himself for his enterprise and liberality. He is one of the most active directors of the French Jew school; he contributes generously to the asylum for poor Christian and Mahometan girls in charge of the good Sisters of the Trinity; he has invested ten thousand francs for the benefit of Nina, to be presented to her on her wedding-day; in short, ever since his arrival in Mostaganem he has not only got rid of a good deal of his sordid miserliness, but also on all occasions displays as kindly a feeling towards Christianity as his nature is capable of. Still, for some cause, or other, he always manifests a most decided and ineradicable antipathy towards scientific men.

This leads us to the Professor. He spent nearly a week in Mostaganem, writing out a pretty full and complete memoir, consisting of two parts. The first contained an account of his discovery of the Comet Gallia two years before; the second, the history of his adventures in planetary space. This document, properly signed, dated, and attested by the Captain and the others, he dispatched at once to the *Bureau of Longi-*

*tudes,* Paris. Of this paper no serious notice seems to have been taken. At least in the list of Comets published a short time afterwards, none appeared bearing the name of Gallia. Imagine his indignation! But he was not made of a material to be conquered without a struggle. New communications, dashed off in dozens by his ready pen, appeared almost simultaneously in the great scientific magazines of the world, such as the *Jahrbuch* of Berlin, the *Comptes Rendus* of Paris, the *Popular Science Review* of London, the *Journal of the Franklin Institute* of Philadelphia, the *Proceedings of the Smithsonian Institute* of Washington, etc. These articles created such a stir among the learned societies that the *Bureau of Longitudes* and other Scientific Bodies found themselves compelled by public sentiment to take some notice of them, and even occasionally to condescend to a reply.

Of these replies we can give only the most condensed synopsis. Gallia? A myth; nobody had ever seen it — nothing answering its description had ever been noticed in any observatory from Washington to Sydney. Might not this, however, be accounted for by the great haziness of the atmosphere? It might — partly — but this was mere negative evidence, which of course proved nothing. But how account for the undeniable disturbance of the African coast? An earth-

quake.  The vanishing for two years of a large extent
of sea-coast?  Submergence.  Subsidence.  Happening
every day — see Santorini, Holland, Lisbon, etc.  Its
reappearance.  Upheaval — quite a usual occurrence —
look at the temple of Serapis near Pozzuoli three hundred years in the waves — look at the coast of Sicily
to-day two hundred feet higher than in former times —
look at the ruins of Ephesus, once a seaport and now
six miles distant from the shore — look at the marine
beach of Gibraltar that has actually been lifted four
hundred and fifty feet above the sea-level, etc., etc.

But this last remark brings us to what the Professor
considered his most weighty argument.  How account
for the unquestioned sudden disappearance of General
Murphy, Major Oliphant, and the other Englishmen
from Gibraltar on the very night when the collision
was alleged to have taken place?  Earthquake again.
Murphy, whilst Governor of Gibraltar, as is well known,
had taken it into his head, by way of securing perfectly
healthy quarters for the garrison in the epidemic season,
to recommend the Home Government to hew out some
additional galleries and erect some additional fortifications on the east coast of the Rock, between the
Signal Station and O'Hara's Tower a little north of the
Mediterranean Battery and south of Catalan Bay.  Here
the extremely steep face of a precipice fifteen hundred

feet high would secure a position at once safe from all malaria and impossible to be attacked. His advice was taken, though not without considerable opposition on the part of some government engineers who professed to understand the peculiarities of the place. Several hundred thousand pounds sterling were spent in fortifying impregnable cliffs which were already well known to be undermined by caverns tunnelled by the waves. The consequences might easily be divined. The earthquake that shook northern Africa extended its ravages to Spain. Murphy's expensive fortifications, a pretty little cottage just finished, the Governor himself, Major Oliphant with about fifteen or twenty others, suddenly disappeared that terrible night. But instead of being carried off on a Comet, the galleries, towers, fortifications, cannon, officers, soldiers and all were swallowed up by the Mediterranean, where they are now lying six thousand feet beneath the surface !

Of such flimsy arguments as these the Professor in vain attempted to show the utter absurdity. The learned world closed its ears to his reasoning however logical, and would not accept his proofs however convincing. On the contrary, every attack made on his statement of the case, remarkable for lucidity, consistency, and the strong testimony in its favor, was instantly and almost universally applauded in spite of the weakness, incon-

clusiveness, and assumption of his opponents. For
instance, in reply to the question, "Why was not the
Comet immediately set on fire and burned to ashes
during its course through the terrestrial atmosphere, like
every other meteor?" it was perfectly useless for the
Professor to reply: "The Comet's condition was an exceptional one, different from that of meteors in general.
Gallia was *not* burned because she *could not* be burned.
The water surrounding her, by being turned into vapor,
prevented immediate combustion. Had these learned(?)
gentlemen never heard of the resistance offered to heat
by liquids in the spheroidal state?"

This reply was, of course, a crusher, but, like all his
other arguments, statements, documents, proofs, and
testimonies, it fell on ears equally deaf to logic and
common sense. The scientists were not to be convinced,
and, as the scientists usually lead the rest of the world
by the nose, the rest of the world generally pooh-poohed
the Professor's story. Not indeed that he had no par-
tisans at all. The tale he told was too straightforward,
too circumstantial, and above all too interesting not to
find some credence among all classes and in every land.

These were few indeed in comparison with the grand
army of disbelievers, and though the earnestness of
their faith and their boldness in proclaiming it almost
compensated for the paucity of their number, still it

cannot be said that they have as yet succeeded in either convincing the world that Professor Rosette was a great astronomical discoverer or in removing the impression that he was a great astronomical monomaniac. Which of the two he really was, the fortunate reader of Gallia's adventures as given in these interesting volumes has, of course, no difficulty in determining.

To the rest of the world, however, Rosette and his discoveries will always present as insolvable a problem as the Man in the Iron Mask.

Servadac, Timascheff, and Procopius, beyond signing their names to some of the documents that appeared in the Professor's pamphlets, took no further share in the great contest. In fact, unless in a circle of very intimate friends, they preferred for a long time to make no allusion whatever to the subject.

After reporting at headquarters, where his strange story was listened to with attention if not with credence, the Captain obtained a six months' leave of absence to visit his family at their residence near Lesparre on the banks of the Garonne. At Marseilles, the Count decided to accompany his friend home, and dispatched Procopius and the men to Russia to announce his safety and early return. But his return was delayed by an unexpected incident — nothing less than his marriage with the Captain's young sister, a lady whose attrac-

40

tions, both personal and moral, made ample compensation for the loss of the English widow.

This was not to be the only tie between the Count and the Captain. During a visit to the Timascheff estates, Servadac met a charming cousin of the Count's, the lady Olga Danischeff, and, in spite of her vast riches, soon loved her well enough to marry her. He passes three months every year in Russia, but the greater portion of his time is spent in Paris, where he has a beautiful residence on the *Avenue de la Reine Hortense*, in full sight of Montmartre and all its glories. Judge if Ben Zouf is not a happy man !

Pablo, adopted by the Count, is at present pursuing his studies at Stanislas College with credit and success. He shows an extraordinary aptitude for mathematics, and is particularly distinguished for his decided taste for astronomy.

Nina, no longer a child, but a highly distinguished pupil in the Convent of the *Sacré Cœur*, takes also an extraordinary interest in astronomical studies, quite delightful to her teacher though utterly unaccountable. In spite of her great mental superiority, it is hardly necessary to say she is still the same charming little Nina, making everybody around her happy by her cheerful disposition and winning all hearts by her unselfish consideration for others.

The years fly past almost unheeded, but Servadac, now a Colonel, and the Count have so far managed to spend every other six months together. They are often visited by the Professor, who is as peppery and pugnacious as ever. But for his overbearing and domineering ways they make ready allowance, and, in spite of the scepticism of the world at large regarding the existence of Gallia, they occasionally entertain their charming wives and the younger members of the families with short glimpses at their adventures on their wonderful journey To THE SUN.

"When did these gentlemen perform that wonderful journey To THE SUN?" asked one night a young college chum of Pablo's, who had been invited to spend the Christmas holidays at the Colonel's.

"They performed it the very same year," answered Pablo, quite coolly and earnestly, "that we were all carried OFF ON A COMET!"

"What do you mean, Pablo?" asked young Bazin, much surprised. "Come tell me all about it!"

For hours and hours that night, young Bazin listened to his friend's extraordinary narrative in a delightful state of mingled astonishment, misgiving, and enchantment.

"Oh!" he exclaimed at the conclusion, "I do not know what to think of your fascinating story. I never understood it before, but the more I reflect on it the more disposed I am to believe it to be true!"

Young Bazin's enthusiastic exclamation fully explains why we have taken the trouble of laying the whole history before the reader with all its strange and wonderful details. Though an intelligent young fellow, Bazin's case is by no means an isolated one. The gracious Reader's experience may have been somewhat similar.

Merely skimming the scientific journals of the day, Bazin had never set himself seriously to acquire an exact idea regarding the precise nature of the great astronomical war at that time raging through the learned world. Like many an outsider, he had looked on the question of the Great Rosette Comet as somewhat of a nuisance and a bore — a difficult affair of endless diagrams — a matter of disputed claims involving knotty but uninteresting points in the higher mathematics. On the great Rosette too he had rather hastily and unjustly looked half in admiration, half in contempt, as one of those crazy, self-sufficient, noisy scientists so numerous in this latter half of the nineteenth century.

But Pablo's simple story, filling out and confirming the Captain's strange allusions, completely opened his eyes. Here was evidence beyond gainsay, requiring for proof no figures or perplexing calculations. The thrilling adventures, so graphically described by living eye-witnesses, bore the incontestable stamp of genuine TRUTH.

" What is truth, sir ? " he asked a few days afterwards of a young Professor somewhat noted for his love of paradox.

" My dear boy," was the reply, " *Truth is not so much what really* IS *as what* OUGHT TO BE ! "

FICTION : FIC VERNE
FIC VERNE
Verne, Jules
Off on a comet! : A journey
  through planetary space : (a sequ
Neva Lomason Memorial
31057901299878